Ella's Triple Pleasure

by

Anna Lores

Ella's Triple Pleasure

Contact Information: info@thewildrosepress.com

Cover Art by *Diana Carlile*

The Wild Rose Press, Inc.
PO Box 708
Adams Basin, NY 14410-0708

Visit us at www.thewilderroses.com

Publishing History
First Scarlet Rose Edition, 2017
Print ISBN 978-1-5092-1330-6
Digital ISBN 978-1-5092-1331-3

Published in the United States of America

One, two, or three…choices, choices.

"If I had any idea it was you, I wouldn't have brought you to the lake. I would have taken you to an exclusive retreat in the desert for pampering—clothing optional."

With her chin down, she peeked through her lashes to her hand hovering at his lips. Instead of the kiss she expected, he rested his lips on her palm and licked the smooth flesh.

"Cade," she whispered. "What are you doing?" She crossed her legs to keep the cream heating up her sex from leaking onto the thin strip of panty. She needed her granny panties because of him. Gorgeous Cade Jackson made her body come alive.

"I'm going to do everything I can think of while I have you all to myself," he whispered. He adjusted his hand under hers. "We've known each other for more than a year, and now that I know it has only been money holding you back…Ella, it's not holding you back anymore."

His tongue slid over her first knuckle and dipped into the crevice between her index and middle finger. Images of him dipping his tongue down the center folds of her pussy stirred butterflies in her belly.

"Please, don't do this to me."

"I have to."

Dedication

To Denise and Kelly.
You're my best friends, my lifelines, my cheerleaders.
Because of y'all, my life sparkles even when veiled in darkness.

Chapter One

Ella Winthrop glanced around the cowboy bar and couldn't believe she allowed her best friend to drag her here of all places. She wasn't a cowgirl. She wasn't anything close to cowgirl bar material.

"One drink," Ella's best friend Maddie said. "You're not backing out of tonight."

"Fine. One Drink." Ella pulled out a barstool and sat down next to her.

Maddie plopped her purse on top of the glossy, wooden counter. "I've watched you work your ass off for three years to keep your family together and happy while you're damn miserable."

"I'm not miserable." She looked in the mirror behind the bar. No makeup. Yuck. Her clothes… *Ugh.* At least she didn't have any sparkles of gray. She should have spent more time fixing her hair—a lot more time.

Overall, she looked ragged. She'd be in trouble if her business depended on her wardrobe. Luckily, her livelihood depended solely on her hands' ability to relax and heal. "You should be embarrassed to be seen with me in public like this."

Maddie smiled. "Nope. I've got you covered." She patted her leopard print designer purse with her perfectly manicured nails. "Come with me. Josie just walked in. We've got a little surprise for you."

Ella covered her face with her hands and sighed. “Please don’t make me look like a whore.”

Maddie took Ella’s hand and marched her from the bar straight to the ladies’ room in the back. She pushed open the cheap, barnyard door. The stench of urine and beer filled the brown tiled, three-stall bathroom.

“This place stinks. I am not staying.” Ella tugged at Maddie’s hand, but Maddie didn’t let go.

“Listen, Ella.” Maddie’s grip tightened on her. “I may have done something here you’re not going to like. But I’ve done it, and you can’t back out.”

The door squeaked as it swung in. Josie appeared and pinched her nose. “I forgot how the girls’ bathroom in bars gets just as stinky as the boys’ does.” She winced as she gave Ella a once over. “Didn’t Maddie tell you we were going out?”

Ella frowned. Cheerleader Josie who hadn’t struggled a day in her life could kiss her ass.

“Yes, but some of us have to work, and I didn’t think going to a bar meeting friends constituted getting dressed up in my Sunday best,” Ella said. “We are in a restroom that smells like piss in a shitty singles cowboy bar, if you haven’t noticed.”

Josie huffed as if Ella insulted her personal hygiene. “It’s a nice cowboy bar. And it’s not just for singles anymore. The cleaning company didn’t show up last night or today like they were supposed to. But they’ll be here before the place gets hopping tonight.”

Maddie unzipped her makeup bag. “Stop being so sensitive, Josie. Ella is just worked up because that whiney client came in for her last appointment and bitched the entire time but still made another appointment for massage a week from today.” She reached into her vanity case, pulled out the essentials, and applied foundation to Ella's face.

Josie dug into the large shopping bag resting on the floor and pulled out a knee length, jean skirt with a slit up the front, right thigh and a blue, scoop-neck sweater to match Ella's eyes. "Undress. This is what you're wearing tonight."

Ella looked at the clothes. "Those will never fit."

Josie rolled her eyes. "You wear baggy clothes that make you look fat. You're not fat. You haven't been fat for the entire time I've known you. Get a clue, and start dressing like an adult who takes some pride in herself, not some poor, homeless person."

Ella swallowed down her anger. She rarely shopped anywhere other than consignment stores for herself, and Josie and Maddie knew it. She wasn't poor or homeless, but she needed her paycheck to go further into the month. Buying groceries and paying her mortgage while spending any extra money on her kids was more important than purchasing something nice and fashionable for herself. "Yeah, I'll remember that next time I'm designer shopping with you."

Maddie tilted Ella's chin down and applied eye shadow to Ella's eyes. "Josie isn't the most tactful friend I have, but you would look a lot better if you bought clothes in your size."

Josie frowned. "I speak the hard truth, Ella. You know that about me." Josie walked around Ella and tugged down Ella's khaki pants all the way to her ankles. "I shouldn't be able to do that. I didn't even have to unzip your fly. That's wrong. And I care enough about you to tell it to your face." She tapped Ella's right leg. "This has gone on too long."

Ella lifted her right leg then the other as Josie pulled off her pants.

"Good Lord, Ella. Granny panties? Really? My worst nightmare is realized." She tugged Ella's baggy panties down her legs. "You're not wearing those. Those things should be considered a felony in all fifty states. Stores should stop carrying them. I think I may just have to start some kind of campaign against those things."

Before Ella could protest, Josie scooped up the panties and threw them in the garbage.

"There." Josie shivered with disgust. "You're lucky I came prepared." She pulled up Ella's baggy, white work tee and gasped. "Had I known I was facing this, I would have called in a team for support."

Maddie finished with a swipe of powder over Ella's face as Josie pulled the shirt back down.

"You're a bitch, Josie. How's that for honest?" Ella said. "Give me my pants back. I'm leaving."

"I don't think so," Josie said. "Lift." Josie squatted down at Ella's feet with the designer panties and jean skirt ready and waiting.

Ella lifted each foot. Josie pulled up the skirt and thong like Ella was a child and unable to do it herself. Ella wiggled uncomfortably trying to adjust the panties without touching them.

"I haven't worn a thong in years," Ella confessed.

"Dang it," Josie said. "I knew you were a two, but the saleslady talked me into a four. She said everything runs small. Not too small for you, apparently." She zipped up the side. "Those pants were eights. What were you thinking buying something so big?"

Tears threatened the balance of fluids in her eyes.

"I have three teenagers to think about. I'm not a priority right now. Buying the perfect outfit is low, really low on my list of things to do."

Josie seemed to ignore Ella's confession and the emotions behind it. Ella raised her arms as Josie won the battle of wills and lifted the white tee over her head. She plucked the matching blue bra from her bag and unsnapped Ella's bra.

"I can do that." Ella slapped Josie's hand away and removed the bra. She exchanged her bra for the pretty, new one, and Josie hooked the back together.

Maddie carefully helped Ella into the sweater, making sure she didn't mess up any makeup.

"Now that you're properly dressed…" Josie turned Ella around to face the hazy, full-length mirror desperately in need of cleaning on the back of the door. "This is the Ella Winthrop I used to know." Josie put an arm around her and squeezed. She smiled like the beauty pageant winner she used to be.

The new outfit hugged Ella's body in all the right places. The makeup made the blue in her eyes pop. She looked younger, not young, but a little younger than her thirty-seven years. She hated to admit it, but Josie was right. She looked a lot more like a confident woman, not a shy one trying to hide underneath all the baggy clothes.

Josie pulled out the elastic band holding Ella's ponytail and brushed the dark-brown hair that tumbled down. She pulled Ella's silky locks to the side and put in a star hair clip while the rest fell softly over her shoulders and down the middle of her back.

"Mark and I have been talking with Maddie and Mike about you. Be as angry as you want at us, but between the four of us, we've got your boys for the weekend. I know they're old enough to stay alone, but we're using your twin geniuses as babysitters to keep them from chaperoning you.

"And since Garrett never came back after… Well, Greg would want you to move on by now. One of the last things he ever said to me and Mark before he got so…he worried you wouldn't have a life after he was gone. He wanted you to find love again. He wanted you to find a man who would be a father to his kids, someone who would love you and them like he would have if God hadn't needed him in Heaven." Josie blinked away the tears forming in her eyes.

Maddie stepped into view. The mirror framed the three friends in a picture. "Ella, we've kind of gotten together and set you up on a weekend date with someone we think you'll love or at least like. Josie packed a bag for you and gave it to the owner of this bar. He's your mystery date. He's uncomfortable with this too but he's willing to give it a try."

"Oh, no," Ella groaned. "It's a mercy date. Please tell me you didn't tell him I'm a widow with three kids."

Maddie and Josie fidgeted uncomfortably as they glanced at each other with wide eyes.

Ella slouched. "You did. And I'm wearing brown flats in this outfit that clearly calls for boots. And yes, even I think that, so don't think the guy you set me up with won't think it." She shifted onto her heels and wiggled her toes. *This is going to be a disaster.*

Maddie cringed and shrugged. "He won't care about your shoes, Ella. He's not shallow. We've known him since high school. He's never found the right woman."

"He owns a singles bar," Ella grumbled. "That screams player. No woman in her right mind would want to settle down with a man like that."

"Thing is," Josie said. "He's not a player. He used to be, like ten years ago, but not anymore. He wants to meet someone worth settling down with, someone to warm his nights and love him when he's had a bad day."

"He's ugly," Ella said. "He's got some kind of serious ugly thing happening. A big mole on his nose with a hair growing out? Please tell me you wouldn't do that to me?"

"I wouldn't call him ugly," Josie said. "But he's no Mark."

Right. Mr. Healthy-as-a-Horse Mark. Ella sighed. "Thanks, but I'm not spending the weekend with someone I don't know."

Josie and Maddie looked at each other like they held a secret.

Just as Ella opened her mouth to demand more answers about their harebrained scheme, Josie pushed Ella out the door and into the brick chest of a towering man of pure muscle.

Thick, muscular arms wrapped around her and caught her.

"Sorry," a deep voice she recognized from somewhere sang into the air that floated to her ears.

"It's okay," Ella whispered. "I wasn't paying attention."

She looked up into brown eyes. "Cade?"

"Ella?" Cade answered. "What are you… Wow, you look beautiful with your hair down." His hands slid from her back to her arms in a heated caress. He stepped back and blatantly scanned her up and down. "What brings you here?"

She tried to answer, but her tongue tied in knots, and her mouth turned dry as the desert.

"Hey, Cade," Josie said. "This is the friend Maddie and I have been telling you about."

Cade's expression morphed from curiosity to irritation.

"Ella is your friend?" His eyes narrowed at Josie and Maddie. "Is this a joke?"

Maddie and Josie angled their heads to the side, gazing at each other, seemingly confused.

"No joke. Ella is my best friend," Maddie said. "How do you know each other?"

Ella closed her eyes and pursed her lips, trying to avoid the truth that hurt entirely too much. Her circumstances sucked.

"Ella has a strict policy of not dating her clients," Cade said. "I'm a client."

Once again, her professional life interfered with her personal life, not that she had much of a personal life. Turning gorgeous Cade down on a date a year ago because she needed the steady money more than she needed a date still bothered her. She really wanted to date him. Heck, she wanted to touch him in non-professional ways every time he walked through her spa door. She had to push all those wickedly sensual thoughts aside to do her job.

"Well, she's changing her policy this weekend," Josie said. "Mystery dates don't count."

"I don't know about that," Ella said. Cade was one of her best clients, and money was tight.

"I do." Josie handed Cade the shopping bag she brought to supplement the bag she packed for Ella. She pushed him, as Maddie pushed Ella, through the rustic cowboy bar and out to the parking lot.

Cade glanced over at Ella. "We can talk about your policy privately in the car."

Ella exhaled relief. "Okay." *At least he understands why we can't go on a date.*

Maddie reached into Cade's back pocket and took his keys. She unlocked his car, opened the passenger side door, and shoved Ella inside while Josie easily thrust Cade into the driver's seat.

"Go now." Maddie tossed the keys past Ella to Cade. "Have a great weekend and don't bring her back until Monday night. She has to work Tuesday morning at ten."

"Don't even think about backing out," Josie warned Cade. "You promised me you'd show my friend a great time even if you didn't have any sparks. Don't break a promise to me, or you'll never hear the end of it."

Cade slid the key into the ignition and started the car. Josie closed the door on Cade's side.

"Ella, you better not back out," Maddie said. "If you come home early, I'll do something even more drastic." She slammed the door closed.

Ella gazed out the side window of the car at Maddie and Josie standing under the bright, parking-lot lights, smiling and waving. Strapped into her seat, she threaded her fingers together in her lap as Cade drove out of Cowboy Corral's parking lot onto the main road for a weekend she was not prepared for and with a man she was intensely attracted to.

Chapter Two

"Sorry," Ella said. She watched the street lamps light up the dark night as Cade drove down the main road past the businesses getting ready to close for the night.

"You know we have to spend the weekend together, but it doesn't have to be a date," Cade said. "Although, Josie and Mark will have spies at the lake this weekend to make sure we're together and having fun."

"The lake?" she asked.

"It's a couple hours from here," he said. "It's the same lake where Josie and her husband take vacations with their kids during the summer."

"Oh." Ella nodded. She and Greg were never invited to Josie's lake house. She didn't even know Josie owned a lake house. "Do you hang out with them often?"

"No, not really. They're into things I'm not. They used to rent my guest house and bring their kids for a week or two before they bought their own last year." He exited onto the interstate and accelerated to keep up with the flow of traffic.

A dark cloud covered the pretty, shimmering glow radiating from the stars and clung to the lower half of the moon, dimming the natural illumination on the lazy, late-spring night. Over the years, she and Greg had spent evenings like this one outside cuddled up next to the fire pit he built in the backyard before cancer changed their world. The kids gathered their friends from the neighborhood and roasted marshmallows on wire hangers she had straightened out for summertime pit fires. She'd relished the title "Domestic Goddess" back in the day.

"Do you need to call your kids?" he asked. "You should give them my number at the lake house. There usually isn't much cell reception in the woods."

Stop being so perfect. "Yeah, um, thanks. I'll call them." She liked working on him because he told her exactly what he wanted. He talked a lot but quickly relaxed so she could get deep into his supple muscles and make all his tension dissolve under her hands. He never crossed any professional lines and never lingered after the appointment.

She glanced down at the floorboards and then over her shoulder at the back for her purse. Nothing. Damn. Maddie probably took it in the bathroom with no intention of giving it back. Now she was stuck with gorgeous Cade for the weekend, a man she didn't want to resist but had no other choice. Who was she kidding? If he made any move on her, she wouldn't be able to resist him for an hour let alone a weekend.

"Maddie has my purse. I hate to impose, but could I use your cell phone?"

He shifted his weight to the side as he drove and reached into his jeans pocket.

Ella's gaze locked onto the bulge in his jeans. She followed his hand as he tried to adjust the large mass obstructing the removal of his cell phone. With a little more effort and a slow shove of his cock to the right, he retrieved the cell phone from his front pocket.

She licked her lips. Her once-dry mouth was wet and ready to drool on the man she'd fantasized about every night since the day he walked into her massage room. One whole year of wicked fantasies of him as her lover. One painful choice to decline his offer for a dinner date and enforce her business policy turned into three hundred and sixty-five days of wishing she could tell him she'd love to go out with him. Screw the ethical and financial reasons not to.

He handed her his cell phone.

"Thanks." *Focus on the kids, not the hottest man on earth driving me to a secluded lake house for the weekend.*Her fingers fumbled over the letters on the screen as she dialed her daughter's number.

"Colleen Winthrop."

"Colleen, it's Mom." Oddly, nothing but silence came from her daughter's side. Usually Colleen was surrounded by friends, and they were all like her—loud and talkative.

"Why are you calling from Cowboy Corral?"

"It's a long story, but Maddie took my purse and phone."

"Tell her to feel free to call my cell," Cade said. "The number to the lake house is the same number, but it ends with a seven instead of a four."

"I heard that," Colleen said. "Who are you with?"

"I'm with a friend. He's a friend of Maddie and Josie's too. "

"Oh." Curiosity seemed to lace Colleen's tone. "That's different. Is it a blind date?"

"Kind of, but not really." Ella shook her head. "I just called to tell you I love you and to see how your final exams are going. Are you still coming home Friday?"

"I finished my last final this afternoon." Colleen squealed, suddenly back to her usual vibrant self. "I'll definitely be back by Friday, but I'm trying to get home earlier. I have a big surprise for you."

Colleen always came home from college with some kind of surprise she and her friends made for her and the boys. Her surprises became a tradition of sorts over the last year.

"Sounds exciting. I love your surprises. And, sweet pea, congratulations on surviving your freshman year."

"Thanks, Mom. I've got to go. I'm heading to a late dinner. Love you."

"Have fun. Love you too. " She hung up and dialed Kyle.

"Hello?" Kyle answered on the first ring.

"Hey, it's Mom."

"Why are you calling from Cowboy Corral?"

"I'm with the owner, not at the bar. I mean, I'm out with. No. I'm in the car… Maddie and Josie know him." She blew out an exhale. "It's not a date."

"We know you don't date. We're at Maddie's."

"Let me speak to her," Jason shouted in the background.

"No. So, is he nice?" Kyle asked.

"He's nice." *Ugh.*

"Give me the phone," Jason said.

"No," Kyle said.

She heard a struggle on the other end. "What's going on?"

"Nothing. We love you," Kyle said as the connection got muffled.

"Love you too?"

"Tell him, I'll kick his ass if he tries—" Jason shouted.

"—Have fun, Mom. Call us tomorrow," Kyle's voice rose. The call abruptly ended.

Ella cringed and dialed him again.

"Have fun, Mom." Kyle was breathing hard but steady.

"Maddie and Mike are in charge. No staying up past ten-thirty and—"

"—be respectful. Got it," Kyle said. "I can't speak for Jason, but I'll try and keep him in line."

She rolled her eyes. Kyle was just like his father, calm and analytical, while Jason epitomized his uncle, passionate and adventurous. "I love you. I'll call tomorrow."

"Love you too, Mom. Bye."

"Goodnight." She ended the call, thankful Jason hadn't interjected himself into the conversation again. She wasn't up for the third degree, not that she had anything to hide. She and Cade hadn't done anything. Wouldn't do anything.

"They sound like nice kids." Cade kept his gaze on the road.

"They're pretty great." *I'm so lucky to be their mom.* "I think the boys are sick of me babying them, but I can't help it. They're my boys."

"They'll miss it when they're adults and don't have you doing it all the time." He turned on the radio to the local country station. "Hope you like country."

"I do." Maybe she wasn't a total Yankee and had a little bit of cowgirl in her. She'd genuinely liked country music ever since her husband introduced her to it, and even said "y'all" on occasion.

Cade stroked the top curve of the steering wheel like he was caressing the curve of a woman's hip then tapped it three times as if he made a decision about something important.

"Ella, you know a lot about me, my medical history, all my aches and pains." He paused as if he wasn't sure he should continue.

"I am your massage therapist." She smiled. "Are you having some kind of trouble I need to know about?"

"No. Not me." He inhaled. "It's time for full disclosure for you. Do you have heart disease? Diabetes? STD's?"

Laughter rolled off her tongue like a sweet song, making her cheeks warm and her heart lighten. "Okay. Seems fair since I do know a lot about you, and you don't know too much about me. No heart disease, diabetes, STD's, cancer, or anything other than the normal aches and pains of being a single mom and working a physical job."

She loved the easy way he asked uncomfortable questions. Probably learned the skill from owning a bar. A player's bar. Quite possibly, the rowdiest singles bar in town. Her handsome, polite businessman who traveled for work had a wild side or used to. She never would have picked him for a bar owner.

"When was the last time you went out on a date?" he asked. He clenched his hands around the wheel then methodically unclenched them, one finger at a time. He seemed to be exercising a relaxation protocol where he tensed muscles from his head to his toes. He would accept the tension in order to release the contraction and breathe in the peace of true tranquility. She taught the technique to some of her clients but not him.

"The truth?" she asked.

He glanced over at her. "The massage therapist I know wouldn't tell anything but the truth."

She exhaled. She wrestled with telling the truth. The truth sounded exactly like what it was—depressing. "I know Maddie and Josie told you about my late husband. I haven't been out on a date with anyone else since the day I met him. How about you?"

He scrunched his mouth to the side and tilted his head seemingly contemplating his next explanation. "I date a few times a month. Usually ten minutes at a coffee shop is all it takes. Why endure a lengthy dinner when there's nothing to warrant a second date? Coffee is noncommittal"

Safer too. "When was your last second date?"

"Three years ago. It turned into a relationship that lasted two months before we broke it off. We didn't want the same things, and as much as I tried, I didn't love her. She remained an afterthought. I had to put her name on my daily calendar just to remember it." He dropped his shoulders and shook his head. "I sound like a jerk."

"No, I get it. Sometimes you want something so badly to be different, but, in reality, it will never be what you want it to be." She had wanted her husband to get better so desperately, she denied the fact he was getting worse until he passed on and reality without him set in. She hadn't want to give up the dream of being healthy and happy with him again, instead of dealing with the ugly reality she lived in. Her dream was gone now because he was gone. "It sucks to let go of the dream, but it's honest."

"Yeah, but do you want to hear the biggest problem I have?" He smiled and turned his head, facing her. His eyes twinkled as brightly as the stars.

"Sure." She smiled along with him.

He tapped his fingers on the steering wheel. "I have a crush on my massage therapist. I've had it for more than a year, and it shows no hope of fading. I think about making more appointments during the week just to see her."

"Cade." She sighed. "I…" Her mouth opened and closed. She couldn't bring herself to explain she couldn't afford to pay her utilities if he wasn't a client anymore. She was already behind in payments because of some not—so—good clients' checks bouncing. The electricity at her house was probably getting turned off right then. There was no guarantee she would get another client as good and reliable or who paid in cash.

"Tell me," he said. "I'm a big boy, and it's not going to affect our business relationship."

"Well, the thing is." She tugged at the hem of her skirt. "There are ethical reasons not to date clients. If you're a client, I won't date you. Period. There is also the fact that I'm a single mother of three teenagers, although one is in college, and the other two are about to graduate high school. Much to the surprise of Josie and Maddie, that's not a real benefit to potential love interests."

"So if I stopped being a client, we could date?"

"Well, yeah, but I can't lose a client in order to date one. I have a good clientele, but I can't turn away business."

"What if I found a replacement for my time slot?

Or you worked on me off the clock, under the table so to speak?"

She shook her head. "I won't work on you for money if we're dating. You should probably take me home." She sighed. "This is too complicated. I'm sorry."

"I can't take you home." He gripped the steering wheel so hard his knuckles turned white. "I've been friends with Josie, Mark, and Maddie since high school. If I take you home before Monday night, they will make my life miserable, and yours too. "

"I really like you. I would date you in a second if it weren't for the fact that I'm your massage therapist."

He relaxed his grip on the wheel. "Not anymore." He tapped his fingers three times. "You're no longer my massage therapist. I am officially firing you. I'll pay you until I find a suitable replacement for my time slot. That's settled. Let's move on. What would you like for dinner?"

"Cade, come on. I have three kids, two of whom are seventeen-year-old, identical twin boys. You'll want a bunch of kids someday, and my biological clock is running out of time." *This can't be real. He wants a date more than a massage?* "Is a weekend with me worth ending our business relationship?"

"I can't have kids," Cade said. "Got a vasectomy five-years ago while I worked on a business project in France. And no, I didn't put that on the health history form. No one except my doctor knows about the procedure, besides, of course, you now. I love kids, but I don't want children at my age."

"You're forty, not eighty. Maddie just had a baby, and she's forty."

"I'm not Maddie, and babies are a lot of work. Are you up for having more kids?"

"I don't know. If I fell in love, I might." *I always wanted a big family.*

"And if he couldn't have children?"

"Then we wouldn't have children."

"Perfect. That's settled. No babies. So, yes, I want this weekend with you over being your client. Decision on dinner? A big, juicy steak? Pulled-pork barbecue? Fish?"

Ella turned away and gazed at the night sky. *He wants to spend the weekend with me. I'm going to sleep in the same house as sexy Cade Jackson.* Her heart fluttered, and her flesh heated. Thoughts of waking up with gorgeous Cade in her bed filled her mind. Rumpled sheets. Tangled legs. His mouth on hers. His hot body gliding over hers.

Shaking her head, she rid the images of sweaty and naked Cade after an incredible round of… *Oh, no, I'm not sleeping in the same bed with him. Mr. Singles Bar owner.* Bad call to get her heart or body involved with a man like that. But damn, she wanted to rub all over his hot, sexy self. What had Maddie and Josie gotten her into?

"Steak, pork, fish." She shrugged. "Whatever you want is fine."

"You really don't care?"

"I really don't. Did you plan the weekend? Did you see what Josie packed for me?" What kind of weekend had he planned for a stranger? Sex? He probably expected sex. God, what if he made a move? A real move. She hadn't been in a sexual situation in years. Greg had been so sick for so long…

"My momma told me never to dig through a woman's purse, and her luggage was considered an extension of that rule." He glanced at her with a crooked smile then looked back at the road.

"So you looked?" She let out a tiny giggle.

He smiled. "Heck, yeah. Nice swimsuit."

"I don't even want to know what Josie bought." She covered her face with her hands and peeked at him through her fingers.

"I bought the swimsuit. Josie told me what size."

She closed her fingers, covering her burning face once again, and groaned. "You had no idea it was me?"

"None, or I would have bought a skimpier bikini." His large hand wrapped around hers and brought it to his lips. "If I had any idea it was you, I wouldn't have brought you to the lake. I would have taken you to an exclusive retreat in the desert for pampering—clothing optional."

With her chin down, she peeked through her lashes to her hand hovering at his lips. Instead of the kiss she expected, he rested his lips on her palm and licked the smooth flesh.

"Cade," she whispered. "What are you doing?" She crossed her legs to keep the cream heating up her sex from leaking onto the thin strip of panty. She needed her granny panties because of him. Gorgeous Cade Jackson made her body come alive.

"I'm going to do everything I can think of while I have you all to myself," he whispered. He adjusted his hand under hers. "We've known each other for more than a year. Now that I know it has only been money holding you back… Ella, it's not holding you back anymore."

His tongue slid over her first knuckle and dipped into the crevice between her index and middle finger. Images of him dipping his tongue down the center folds of her pussy stirred butterflies in her belly.

"Please, don't do this to me."

"I have to." His teeth grazed over her middle knuckle; then his tongue laved over it, soothing the slight sting on her skin. "You're the reason I've only had coffee dates. I've compared everyone to you."

"I have teenagers." She moaned. She had to find an excuse for him to stop before she combusted with an embarrassingly loud orgasm. "My boys are in hormonal overload. I'm part of a family package."

"I love being around teens. It keeps me young. I volunteer at church with them." He brushed his lips across the top of her hand to her wrist. "I usually help chaperone trips to the lake or the mountains for skiing. A few weeks ago we all went camping. Remember all those bruises I had on my back?" He rubbed her hand over his smooth cheek.

"Yeah." She remembered the bruises on his ass too. The man took care of his body. Not an ounce fat on him, just pure, unadulterated, delicious muscle.

"I raced a kid up a tree to win a bet I'd made with the other chaperones. But I fell and lost." He chuckled. "One of the best weekends I've ever had." He flipped his turn signal on and reduced the speed to a crawl.

So engrossed in his sensual exploration of her hand, she hadn't noticed they'd switched from the interstate to back roads. The tires rolled onto a gravel road, changing the smooth drive to a rough and bumpy slow ride heading into the woods. The bright constellations disappeared from view as they drove under a canopy of huge pine trees. The headlights of his black luxury sedan provided the only light through the heavily forested path.

Had they been on the road driving that long? Surely they hadn't talked for hours.

He placed her hand on his thigh and unbuckled his seatbelt.

"We're almost there."

The gravel path turned into a cobblestone drive, easing the rocky ride into a rhythmic thumping. The woods opened to a clearing, revealing a large, log cabin surrounded by lush, green grass. An old timer's porch with a white lover's swing and rocking chairs welcomed them.

To the right, beyond the house, the moon reflected off the dark water of the lake calling for a brisk evening skinny dip. Maybe he would lead her to the lake, and take off his clothes, and…

She swallowed down her naughty thoughts. "This is yours?"

"It is." He guided her hand closer to his cock. "There is a guest house a couple acres away to allow for privacy from the main house but close enough to walk to and visit."

He parked at the side of the house and released her hand.

Damn. So close to finally touching your cock and you stop.

"Sounds nice."

He opened his car door. She opened her door and slid out of her seat onto the cobblestone drive.

Over the years, she'd seen pictures of Josie and Maddie in their college days with the house in the background but none with Cade. He probably photographed them.

He opened the trunk, pulled out the luggage, and set everything on the ground.

Ella casually walked over and picked up the pink shopping bag Josie packed her. He did not need to see the contents before she inspected it for anything risqué. She'd almost had an orgasm from his skillful mouth on her hand. She'd really lose it if he got to one of her sorely neglected spots hidden underneath her skimpy lingerie.

"I'll take my luggage too," she said.

"I've got it." He handed over a key. "You get to open the door."

He led her to the back of the house. She opened the door to the screened-in sun porch and held it for him. Once through, she walked past wooden Adirondack chairs and ottomans over the creamy travertine-tiled floor to the handcrafted wooden door. She slid the key in, and the door clicked unlocked. A constant beeping resounded from inside the house as she opened the door.

"One, four, three, two is the code on the left wall," he said.

She punched in the code, and the beeping stopped.

"Thanks. The light switch is on the right of the security panel."

She flicked the switch, and golden light filled the room.

A chocolate-brown, leather sectional sofa with clean lines and cream chenille throws brought a family quality to the designer-styled room. She envisioned her kids hanging out and watching a movie on the large, flat-screen television. A Persian rug lay underneath the furniture, covering the same travertine tile of the sun room.

"This is really nice," she said.

"Thanks." He led her onto the soft carpet of the master suite filled with floor-to-ceiling windows looking out at the lake. The comforting aroma of wood and whiskey in the air surrounded her. A platform, king-sized bed sat waiting to be used in the middle of the room.

Her gaze stuck like glue to the big bed. It was big like him. Masculine like him.

She wanted to be in it with him.

He dropped their luggage on the cream, velvet-cushioned bench at the end of the bed and turned to her. "Are you hungry?"

She swallowed down the big-as-the-bed lump in her throat. "Yeah. I was really busy at work today and didn't have time to eat lunch. I could eat a…" *Cade Jackson* "…cow."

Brown eyes traveled along her body like a heated caress. "Dinner is at the guest house. Do you mind walking?"

Her leg had been bothering her lately with the spring storms frequently moving through the area, but a stroll in the country would get her out of his bedroom with that gigantic bed staring at her. Why would he have the same kind of bed that was in her fantasies? Maybe she was dreaming. No. They rarely talked in her dreams. Well, she rarely talked in her dreams. He talked all the time.

"Sure. Let's go."

He strode toward her, his chest rising and falling in

short, steady waves. "Great." He reached for her hand.

Closing her fingers around the side of his large palm, security, peace, and another dose of desire filled her.

"I chose steak for tonight, but we can change it." Holding her hand with the perfect amount of gentleness and strength, he gazed into her eyes.

"Whatever you want," she said. *Kiss me. Forget dinner.*

He turned on a dime and guided her out of the bedroom. They strode through the living room and straight to the beautifully crafted front wooden door. He turned the pewter door handle and paused. "Were you being polite when you said you'd eat anything?"

"I'm not a picky eater," she said. "I'll try almost anything once."

His chest expanded, and his lids dropped slightly. "That's good to know." He opened the door to the oak-stained, wooden porch with four handcrafted, rustic, wooden rocking chairs and tables, and a porch swing.

"I love your rockers." Her late husband, Greg, had worked with his hands. He built almost her entire house with his identical twin brother, Garrett. Was Cade good with his hands? In her fantasies he was incredible with his hands, lips, tongue, hips, legs, always bringing her closer and closer to ecstasy, until he thrust his—.

"Thanks." He lifted her up from her waist and swung her up as he walked down the steps, then gently set her feet on the dimly illuminated, cobblestone path leading into the woods. "It gets pretty dark at night, but it's safe."

She stepped into his personal space. She shouldn't be so close to the man driving her every depraved desire, but she couldn't stop. "Okay. We've known each other for a while. I believe you, or I wouldn't be here."

Even with his player status, she trusted her instincts. He exuded integrity. And Maddie and Josie wouldn't be friends with him, if he wasn't a good man.

"I can call and have dinner brought up here. Would you prefer that?"

"You said it wasn't too far, so let's go to dinner." She raised her gaze to his luscious lips. "The stars are out, and it's peaceful here."

She was going to be a heap of ashes if he didn't stop looking so gorgeous and smelling so good. Those darn lips were ripe to kiss, and he was probably a great kisser from owning a player's bar. He'd probably kissed thousands of woman, millions with the way he looked. She would kiss him. She would do a lot more than kiss him.

No, she teetered on her mind's seesaw back to reality. She wouldn't do more than kiss him. This wasn't one of her fantasies. It was a blind date. She would sleep alone, in the guest room. No kinky action in that super-sized, king bed.

The licking in the car was an anomaly. He hadn't touched her besides holding hands and carrying her down the stairs, since they got out of the car. Until he got too sick, Greg used to carry her down the stairs. His twin brother Garrett had too. Cade showed off his gentlemanly southern roots, nothing more.

"Yes, ma'am," he whispered. "The path leads to the guest house."

"Then show me the way." She lowered her gaze to their intertwined hands and walked into the woods with him.

****

Ready to lead his way right out of his clothes and into her, Cade slowed his pace.

What was he thinking, taking her down to the guest house for dinner? She wasn't the usual blind date where he would take her to the guest house for dinner and leave her there for the night while he walked back to the main house to sleep.

He didn't need to show her there would be no future dates or sex and avoid her like he did all the others. He needed to keep her in his bedroom and set up dinner, drinks, and dessert there. Hell, he needed to see what kind of adventures they could find together. He had a full list he'd been working on all year.

If she hadn't noticed his erection on her table every Tuesday for the past year, she was blind. He hadn't had sex in forever because he only wanted her. He almost made a mess in his pants licking her hand, dreaming it was her sweet pussy. If he let loose and kissed her, it would be all over. It would be…

"So you don't come here often?" she asked.

"No, ma'am." He needed to slow it down, or he wouldn't get the lifetime he wanted with her. He needed to follow his father's advice for a long and lasting relationship. Rule One. Keep quiet. Two. Don't brag. Three. Ask about her life. Four. Take it slow. *I don't want to take it slow. I never take things slow. But I want forever.*

"Why not?" she asked.

He exhaled. *What were we talking about? The lake house. Rule Two. Don't brag.*

"I don't know why I don't come here more." He

preferred his retreat in Nevada or his beach house in Florida. If he had a family, he'd vacation here more instead of renting it out.

A cold breeze swept over them, cooling off skin drenched with the heat of lust. No woman had ever affected him so intensely. No woman had ever refused to date him. No woman but beautiful and sweet Ella Winthrop.

She shivered.

"Are you cold?" He stopped in the darkness of the forest. He should have thought about the cool nights here and brought dinner up to the main house. He needed to be more considerate. "I can give you my shirt."

He let go of her hand and lifted his tee. He was boiling walking next to her. He was more than eager to take off his shirt or anything else he could get off for that matter. He wanted to be naked between the bed sheets, or up against a tree, or in the grass, or hell, anywhere he could get her into a compromising position. But he had rules for a lasting relationship. *Take things slow*.

"No, no." She shivered again. A pink blush filled her cheeks. "I'm not cold."

She reached for the hem of his dark T-shirt halfway up his chest, but her warm hands touched his bare abs. She told the truth. She wasn't cold. Maybe her reluctance in the car was because she wanted him as much as he wanted her.

He breathed in and slowly exhaled as her hand glided down to the waistband of his jeans. *Please, a little farther. Unbutton them. Make the first, big move. Show me you want me so I can take over.*

He tightened his abs, showing off the top and middle of his eight-pack.

She shivered again. Her breathing turned shallow. She stepped closer, and he swore she made a soft, moaning sound like she had in the car. He wanted to hear her moaning under him so badly he could barely think straight.

He sucked in his abs, wishing he had worn loose-fitting jeans, so she could slip her hand down and touch his dick. The magical hands that massaged his body every week would be on the places he fantasized about having them.

Her fingers lingered near the top button of his jeans.

He waited. His eyelids drooped. *Please, do it. Do it, Ella.*

"Ella." His voice lowered to a breathless rasp.

She quickly removed her hand and stepped back, startled.

Damn it. He talked, breaking rule number one—keep quiet. Damn it. He always talked. It's what he did, but to get her for more than a night, he needed to keep his damn mouth shut. She seemed so close, so close to opening up the door for sex. He was going to have one hell of a time getting that moment back.

"Sorry," she whispered in her sultry, Zen-massage voice. "Um." She cleared her throat. "Sorry." She licked her sumptuous lips. "You've added some definition to your abdomen. Have you been trying?"

"I've been focusing on my abs and ass." *Crap. No bragging.*

He avoided her eyes. He kept breaking his father's rules with the only woman he actually cared about. He wanted her for more than an evening. He wanted her for a lifetime. "My dad told me I was getting soft."

She laughed. Her mouth held an adorable smile on her lickable lips. "You and soft don't really go together. You're in fantastic shape."

He tucked his T-shirt into his jeans and adjusted his rock-hard cock as her gaze followed the path of his hands down the front of his pants. "Thanks. It's nice to know you noticed. You're in great shape yourself. Do you work out?" *Please don't be a die-hard exerciser.* He liked a woman to take care of herself, but not one who went overboard.

"I run, but I'm taking a little time off my morning routine to rest. Work is pretty physical."

He nodded. She worked hard during his sessions. She often perspired a little by the end of it, giving off a lovely ginger scent like the wonderful soaps she sold. He bought the ginger soaps from her shop so he could bathe in her aroma.

"We're almost to the guest house." He held out his hand, hoping she would take it again before they walked the rest of the way.

She took off at a sprint, slapping his hand as she passed him. "Beat you there."

He stood frozen for a minute, surprised she ran off down the path with only the stars and moon for light, trusting his directions to the guest house. Why the hell didn't Josie tell him her name when she set this mystery date in motion? He would have changed everything about tonight.

He gathered his thoughts and ran after her. "Game on, Ella."

Chapter Three

Ella slapped Cade's hand as she ran past him into the woods alone. She trusted the path to the guest house would be as even and clear as the way onto it.

The sounds of crickets chirping and the voices of frogs croaking didn't stop her mind from drifting to Cade and sex. *I almost unbuttoned his jeans. Cade's jeans.*

She'd had so many fantasies about doing just that, but he always said something more than her name. He encouraged her in her dreams, but here, the bunnies hunkered down in their burrows for the night talked more than him. The man was as quiet as a mouse, so unlike him.

Maybe he and Greg had more in common than she thought. Greg talked at work, but not during sex. Would real Cade be like Greg and only want sex in the missionary position? She assumed Cade would talk up a storm after all the teasing, not stay quiet and wait. She didn't need another silent man.

She didn't want Cade to be anything like Greg in bed or at home. She wanted her fantasy lover who talked a lot, ordered her around, and pushed her to explore. Maybe he enjoyed a woman who took charge? She had no idea how to take charge in bed; she wasn't sure she wanted to learn.

Maybe staying was a mistake. Maybe she wasn't

ready to move on. Maybe her reservations about Cade had more to do with her undying feelings for her late husband's brother, Garrett. God, she missed him. But the horrible fight between the brothers had pushed him away too many years ago, and he never came back. Not even for Greg's funeral.

Cowboy boots hitting the pavement and a powerful current of air alerted her to his fast approach. "Ahh." She exhaled as big hands swept her off her feet, bringing her back to the present.

He continued running as he carried her. "Didn't mean to scare you, but I can't let a little thing like you beat me to my own house. I couldn't live with the humiliation."

She wrapped her arms around his taut neck while her heart hammered at the proximity of his lips to hers. She did like him. Heck, she wanted him with every fiber of her being. She was kidding herself if she thought her feelings for Garrett had anything to do with her feelings for Cade. Cade was here. Garrett was…only God knew where.

"I did challenge you."

"You sure did," he said without any sounds of exertion.

The man took great care of himself.

"Are you going to make me cook dinner for losing?"

"No, I'm going to…" He started to say something more but didn't finish.

He slowed down to a walk as they emerged from the woods. The scent of freshly cut grass filled her nose. She gazed in the direction Cade was moving.

A large, two-story, cedar-sided cabin similar in size

to the main house stood with the glow of the half-moon as a backdrop. Overgrown bushes adorned either side of the front porch steps.

Recessed lights along the ceiling switched on one by one across the length of the portico as Cade walked up three steps to the porch. Wicker tables and chairs with overstuffed, cream cushions were organized in groups for easy conversation. The exquisite book-matched floor was perfectly pieced-together to highlight the beautiful grains of walnut. Either he spent an arm and leg on a master carpenter, or he was as skilled a craftsman as her late husband had been. Scents of cedar and fragrant flowers surrounded her.

"Are those azalea bushes?"

"Yes, ma'am. My mom and I planted them a long time ago. I didn't think they'd ever grow, but now they've overtaken the front and the back. If you want any, I'd be happy to dig some up and help you plant them."

She planned to sell her house as soon as possible, not add anything to it. It was one more gift from her husband she couldn't hold onto anymore. "I'm good for now. I bet they're beautiful in bloom."

He turned to the side and opened the front door. Layers of deer antlers, one atop another, and strung with lights made beautiful chandeliers that hung from extra-high ceilings in the foyer, living, and dining room areas. Thick curtains in rich, natural hues brought more of the lush outdoors to the luxurious interior of the hunting lodge he humbly called a cabin. He held her as he kicked off his cowboy boots and walked over the green and charcoal braided rug.

In the large, open room, a floor-to-ceiling fireplace

separated the living and dining area. Bear skin rugs in front of the living room side of the fireplace brought warmth to her cheeks. She'd dreamed about him introducing her to some very naughty things on a bear-skin rug, things she'd only dreamed of, never done.

He stepped toward the moss-colored couch and cut off the view of the dining room. Square vases filled with freshly-cut lavender and sage were displayed along the sofa table and brought the lovely scent of spring inside.

"If you change your mind about the azaleas, let me know." He brushed his lips over the top of her head. "Ready for dinner?"

"Sure, are you?" She couldn't see the dining room table without turning her torso against his broad chest and getting closer to his handsome face. She wasn't sure rubbing her breasts against any part of him would prove to be a smart move. She didn't want to set the tone of the evening. *Show me how you take control.*

He curled his hand under her and cupped her ass. A soft, approving rumble sounded from his chest as he slowly turned her front against his and slid her down his bulging body parts.

"Mmm." She exhaled as her shoes gently touched the floor. She leaned back, cradled safely in his arms, and waited for the moment he tapped his thigh and decided to kiss her or end the date and drive her home.

His hands leisurely slid up her back to her neck. He cupped her head. "Ella, I—"

"Hey, Cade," a man's voice interrupted from somewhere behind him.

Cade effortlessly tucked her into his side and adjusted her into the "friend zone" hold.

"Hey, Phil. How are you? We're starved."

A short, red-haired man with freckles wearing a white chef jacket and jeans smiled at them.

"I'm great, and you're in for a treat. I'll be back later to clean up. Dessert is in the fridge."

"Could you bring dessert to the main house on your way home?" Cade asked.

Phil nodded. "Sure." He paused for a second and raised his eyebrows, wrinkling his forehead. His mouth opened and closed a couple times. "Where would you like breakfast served?"

"We'll have the rest of our meals at the main house this weekend," Cade said. "Thanks."

Phil threw up his hand in a wave. "Have a great evening." He walked through a doorway past the dining room table and then disappeared from view.

Cade guided her to the tan-and-brown-linen covered table set for two but could easily have sat ten. "I hope this is okay. I'm sorry it's so late." He pulled out a chair for her at the end of the long table.

"I eat late most nights." She sat down in the brown-leather parson's chair.

He sat down next to her and lifted the covers off the platters.

The scents of grilled steak and garlic mashed potatoes wafted through the air. Her mouth salivated, and her stomach grumbled. "Wow."

"Yeah, Phil is a great chef. He lives locally, but on occasion I talk him into catering events for me back home." He held the platter of potatoes and offered her some.

She spooned a dollop onto her gold-ringed plate, thankful for conversation, then scooped two onto his plate. She gasped and covered her mouth. *I'm with Cade, not Kyle and Jason.* "Sorry. It's habit. I know you're capable of serving yourself."

"One more, please." He laughed. "So your boys eat a lot?"

She dropped her hand from her mouth. "You could say that." She scooped him another spoonful of potatoes.

He switched and held the platters, and she served. They worked effortlessly together.

The steak melted in her mouth. It took everything inside her not to moan and scarf it down like she hadn't eaten a good meal in her life. She hadn't eaten like this in years. Not since the money ran out.

"So how is the massage and soap business?"

"It's good." She smiled. *It would be better if clients would tell me they couldn't pay, instead of handing me bad checks. I'm getting screwed every month by all the fees and overdraft charges.*

"How long have you been selling specialty soaps? I really like them and so does my mom." He ate a bite of potatoes. "This is good. You need to try the potatoes. I can't be the only one smelling like garlic this weekend."

Her talkative Cade was back, making her body smolder in all the right places. She ate a spoonful of potatoes. "Mmm. Delicious." She placed her spoon down, picked up her napkin, and patted her mouth. "I've been selling the soaps and oils for a little over a year. They're pretty popular, but I only have two hands. Making them takes time."

"You make them by hand?" Cade narrowed his gaze and tilted his head. Curiosity flitted through the warmth of his eyes. "Like the Amish?"

She grinned. "Yes. I make them by hand, not quite like the Amish, I think. But maybe?" She shrugged. "I blend oils, soaps, and candles specifically for each client. I have a bottle of oil I use just for you with your name on it. If you want your oil, stop by Tuesday, and I'll give it to you, since you're no longer a client."

"I'll definitely be by to pick up whatever you want to give me when I stop in to pay you for my last minute cancellation."

"You fired me," she said in mock indignation.

"Yes, ma'am. I'm excited about getting free massages now that you won't accept payment for them." His grin spread from ear to ear. "I'm ready whenever you are."

"Oh, so you want a weekend with me *and* free massages?" She rolled her eyes. "Is that all?"

"No. I want much more." He paused for a moment. He slowly lowered his steamy gaze to her breasts.

She straightened her spine and pushed out her chest.

He lifted his gaze and met hers. "Some free soap too. I'll help you make a batch. It sounds like an interesting process. I thought you bought it wholesale then resold it."

He placed his firm hand on her thigh over her jean skirt. The weight of his hand on her thigh settled her, comforted her while it struck at her heart.

She wasn't ready to open her heart, not yet.

"The boys are going to help me make the soaps as soon as school is out. Kyle and Jason know how to make them, but they don't like doing it. Jason is designing some displays for me to set up in a couple boutiques in town. Kyle is setting up a website and marketing strategy for that part of my business. He's really smart. He's designing a program for my business to do things I can't comprehend."

He withdrew his hand from her thigh. "Wait, isn't he in high school?"

"Um, yeah. They both are," Ella said. *Crap. Didn't want to go there.*

"Seniors, right?"

"Yes. They both graduate in a couple weeks."

His fingers tapped on the table in a steady drumming rhythm. "Are they planning on college or something else?"

"Colleges are salivating over them." She held in a groan. *I shouldn't have said that.* Passing their history class with Mrs. Kellen seemed more improbable with each passing day, and they had to pass in order to graduate. The woman had it in for her boys.

"Are we talking scholarships?"

"Full rides for both of them wherever they want to go. Kyle is probably going to spread his wings and go off to college for mathematics. He won't go too far. I hope he doesn't go out of state. Jason is a homebody and wants to stay near me to study mathematics. He's interested in taking classes online and showing up only for the ones he has to at the university. His girlfriend is going to Memphis."

She had to stop blabbing on about her boys. She hadn't even mentioned her daughter. If he remained interested in continuing the weekend after hearing about her boys, he was worth getting to know. "Sorry. You don't want to hear about all that." She exhaled.

"So Kyle and Jason are gifted in math?"

His interest baffled her. He genuinely wanted to know more about her and her children. "Yeah." *More like math geniuses like their dad and uncle.*

"What about your daughter? She's in college?"

"Colleen isn't gifted in academics. She hasn't failed out, which is a big feat for her. She's fun, and sweet, and social. She can calculate sales tax faster than a computer and can sell you darn near anything. I keep telling her she needs to be working toward a business degree. She doesn't have a steady boyfriend, and she's not pregnant.

"So, she's successfully finished her freshman year as far as I'm concerned… Cade, stop me anytime now." Ugh. She did not want to be one of *those* mothers. She had to get out of this conversation and fast, or she'd end up ruining the evening, and making her daughter sound stupid when Colleen was no such thing.

"You should invite the boys up here," he said. "We could hang out and swim tomorrow. The pool out back is heated. It could be fun."

"Really? I don't think they're doing anything." *Do guys ask their date's teenagers to join them on a first date? Is this normal protocol? Or are you already trying to end the date?* Being so out of the loop with this stuff, she didn't know what to do.

"Ella, call them. I'd love to meet them." He reached in his pocket under the table and pulled out his phone. He handed her the phone.

She tapped the phone screen and dialed Kyle. Cade wouldn't have asked the boys over if it was an odd request on a first date. He dates a lot. He would know. She needed to stop overthinking.

"Do I need to come and get you?" Kyle asked.

“Oh, no. I’m calling to see if you and Jason want to come to my friend’s lake house tomorrow?”

“Well,” Kyle said and paused. “Jason and I have dates, and then we’re babysitting Josie and Mark’s, and Maddie and Mike’s kids tomorrow night. We’ll change our plans, if you need us. Do you need us?”

“Gosh no,” she said. “Cade asked, and I miss my boys. It’s okay.”

“Is this the same Cade you’ve been calling for in your sleep?” Kyle asked.

Ella coughed. *Crap. He heard her. They both would have heard. Oh, God.* “Uh, he used to be a client. He’s not anymore. I’ll see you Monday night.”

“Tuesday,” Kyle said. “We’re hooked up with babysitting until then. We are making some sweet cash. Maddie said you were having a great time. You are, aren’t you?”

“Yes, Kyle.” Calling them was one of the worst decisions she’d made in a while. Parents don’t invite their kids to go on a first date unless they don’t want another. What the heck had she been thinking? “Have fun this weekend, and take care of those cute little kids.”

“We will. You know Jason and I would babysit the kids for free. They’re a lot of fun. Getting the money is a bonus. Have a nice time this weekend. You deserve a break from worrying about us. I love you, Mom. Call me tomorrow.”

“I love you too. Goodnight.” She ended the call and handed Cade the phone. “They’re busy.”

“Okay. Maybe next time.”

She nodded. There might not be a next time the way things were going. One minute he was hot as fire, and the next he was backing off, inviting her kids on their date. What happened to the bold man in the car?

If the evening continued down the current boring path, she'd order the boys to visit. Jason would probably get into an argument with Cade over nothing, and Kyle would overcompensate for Jason's no-holds-barred commentary, providing an easy excuse to end the weekend.

"So, is it too soon to ask for a foot massage?" Cade sported a slight curve at the corners of his mouth. "You know how much I like my feet rubbed."

She laughed and turned to face him. He did it again. He made an uncomfortable situation comfortable and pushed away her doubts. "Cade Jackson, you're a liar. You hate your feet rubbed. You squirm like a worm while I'm working on them." She playfully squeezed his large muscular bicep. *Yum.*

He raised his hands in surrender as she let go. His shirt lifted and showed off bodybuilder abs worth drooling over. "I didn't think you noticed. You'd rub my feet for ten agonizing minutes every Tuesday. Were you trying to torture me?"

She branched out from her normal course of action and tried a move at seduction. Her first. Ever.

She leaned toward him and whispered, "I've been waiting for you to tell me you didn't like it."

"But I do like it." He placed his hands on the edge of the table. His grip wrinkled the linen tablecloth. "It hurts, but it feels *so good* afterward." He lifted a lock of her hair near her cheek and tucked it behind her ear. "Let's go back to the main house and eat dessert."

He traced the side of her neck with his fingers down to her collarbone. A soft wave of shivers rippled over her flesh. The proximity of his smoking-hot body and lips pushed her into lust hyper-drive. All he'd have to do was kiss her earlobe, and she'd have an orgasm.

"Do you want to wrap up the leftovers and bring them with us?"

"The fridge is stocked at the main house." He glided his hand over her shoulder and down her arm to her hand. "Ready?"

He curled his fingers around her hand and tugged her up.

She nodded, standing on unsteady legs.

"Um, sure?" *Am I ready for dessert with Cade?*

She swallowed.

She could do the food kind but hoped he meant a naughtier kind of ending to their meal.

Chapter Four

Lying in Cade's, big, platform bed Ella stared at the digital clock on the dresser and held the house phone to her heart. The green light marking time taunted her with a never-ending night. One o'clock shined into her eyes. *Five and a half more hours until sunrise.*

With Cade's wood and whiskey scent wrapped around her like a cozy blanket, she boiled in the sheer nightie Josie bought her. Concentrating on anything but Cade sleeping naked on the other side of the bedroom wall stood an impossible task. She couldn't fall asleep, or she might have a sexy dream. What if she called out his name in her sleep? What if he came to her wearing nothing but green-plaid boxers like he did in her fantasies? What if he didn't?

She dialed Maddie.

"Cade?" Maddie answered. "Tell me you didn't give Ella your cell, or I'll have to make sure my perfect, twin babysitters are still here and not on their way there."

"It's me," she said. "You have my cell phone and don't think you're off the hook on that one."

"What is wrong?" Maddie said.

"Everything is wrong," Ella said. "Josie packed me a sheer nightie. I didn't even know these things existed. Greg never bought me this kind of stuff. I never shopped for this kind of stuff. I slept in his T-shirts."

"It's one o'clock, Ella. Why are you calling me? I know it's not about a sheer nightie."

"Cade asked me back to the main house for dessert, and when we got back, we had dessert. Real dessert. He's acting kind of weird. He barely said two words after dinner. He's never been quiet the entire time I've known him. Is he normally the silent type?"

"Cade Jackson is not quiet. Let me call and ask what the deal is."

"No," Ella said firmly. "You are not calling him. I don't think he's into me. I'm going home as soon as the sun rises." She threw off the covers. "I can't believe I'm here acting like a fool in this stupid nightgown. Would it be too rude to ask him to take me home now?" *I'd rather be home with the power off than here with fickle Cade.*

"Wait, wait, wait. Ella O'Brien Winthrop, you are *not* going home. He's into you. I don't know what the hell he's doing, but believe me, he is totally into you."

Ella stood up and walked to the luggage case Josie bought for her. She squatted down and opened it. "You are wrong. I don't need this right now. I just lost my best client to find out he doesn't want to even kiss me."

No response came from Maddie.

"Maddie, are you still there?"

Silence.

"Maddie? Maddie?"

"Ella," Josie said. "Do not go anywhere."

"What are you doing on the phone?" Ella asked. "Josie, this is private. Why are you at Maddie's?"

"We're on conference call," Josie said.

"Sorry," Maddie said sheepishly. "But Josie knows

Cade better than anyone."

"Please don't tell me you dated Cade." *This just got freaking worse. If you even touched Cade like a lover, the weekend getaway is one hundred percent over. I'm never seeing him again. Ever.*

"Gosh, no. Gross," Josie said. "He's like my big brother. Ella, what the heck are you doing by yourself?"

She did not want to deal with Josie's blame game. So she did what she always did—told the truth. "Well, your buddy fired me as his massage therapist. Thank God for the little things, 'cause I don't want to see him after tonight's disaster. I kind of hit on him. I thought he might kiss me. Then, when we got back here…"

She picked up a damn-near transparent white bikini top from the luggage case. "He turned to ice. We had dessert. Real food dessert. Then, while I got a drink of water from the kitchen, he grabbed his things from his bedroom. I walked into the bedroom, and he practically ran into the room next door without saying a word."

"What?" Josie said, seemingly confused. "Not Cade."

"Yes, Cade." She placed the bikini top back in the case. "He barely said anything all night. One minute he stood so close, and the next he backed up or turned me around and asked me about the kids."

"Oh, I'm calling his ass," Josie said. "This will not do. What the…"

A loud crash thundered from outside her window.

"Ahh," Ella screamed, leapt up, and ran toward the bedroom door.

Cade burst into the room. "Ella, are you—"

She collided into his brick chest.

His arms swiftly wrapped around her and caught

her.

"Cade, something's outside. It's trying to get in."

Another loud boom bellowed from the backyard.

Startled again, she jumped. "Cade, do something."

"Sweetie, that noise is just some raccoon trying to get in the metal garbage bins," he said softly. "You're safe with me."

"Oh." She exhaled and stepped back. "Sorry."

She placed the phone to her ear. "I freaked out over noth…" She looked at Cade for the first time since he barreled in to save her.

She swallowed. His dark tee was on backward. His unbuttoned jeans were zipped halfway and almost ready to fall down over his hips.

"Ella." His chest heaved with exertion. "You look so beautiful."

"Hang up the phone," Maddie said.

"No," Josie said. "I want to hear how this goes down. Ella, do not hang—"

Ella tapped several buttons on the house phone as she stared at Cade's bulge. Heat flooded her system, and cream slid onto the sheer strand of fabric between her legs. She dropped the phone on the plush carpet under her feet. She needed him. She craved him.

"I'm trying to take this slow. Listen instead of talk. But damn it." He took a step toward her. "I'm a talker. You know that about me."

"Uh, huh." She inched toward him.

"I don't take things slow." His hands slid around her waist.

Mr. Cade Jackson, her fantasy lover, was finally taking charge and talking. *Please let this really be happening.*

"I'm not going to presume you want me." His lips hovered over hers. "I want to sleep with you. If you don't want to be with me, tell me now."

She raised her gaze from his lips to his brown eyes. "I… It's…" She nodded.

"Say the word, 'red', and I'll stop, but until then, I'm going. I'm going to talk." He squeezed her ass firmly. "I want you curled up next to me for the rest of the night. I want your soft, sweet, little body writhing under me. I want your warm, wet pussy tightening with an orgasm around my cock. I want to pump my cum inside you, making you mine."

The rush of blood coursing through her body thundered in her ears with anticipation and excitement. No one had ever spoken to her in such a dirty, sexy way, not even in her dreams. She liked it. A lot.

Tongue-tied, she struggled to speak and think. From the way her lips parted, and her breathing accelerated, he probably knew it. At least he couldn't hear her blood pounding in her ears, blocking all sound, as it raced through her veins.

"Ella, I want you in the worst and best way. I want." His hands slid upward from her ass and traveled the curved path of her body parts. He skimmed up her arms over the sheer fabric of her nightie. "I'm going to make you mine in every possible way. I'm going to bury my face in your creamy pussy until you beg me for my cock. I'm going to fuck you until you scream my name. I'm going to tie you up and take my time getting to know your sweet body better than you already know mine. Does that scare you?"

She shook her head. It didn't scare her. It *so* did not scare her.

"Have you ever had a man take every inch of you?" He brushed his lips across hers.

She shook her head. No. Greg epitomized vanilla sex. What Cade suggested was anything but vanilla, and she wanted it. She *needed* it.

He crushed his smooth lips against hers.

She had never experienced anything quite like the passion Cade aroused in her. Greg was sweet and gentle, while Cade was…not.

"Damn it, kiss me back," he ordered.

She parted her lips and thrust her tongue into his mouth. She stroked his tongue. She let go of a portion of her control and handed him a small piece.

His moan encouraged her to surrender more control.

Her hands glided under the fabric of his cotton T-shirt. She needed to feel the flesh of his back, his ass, any part she could get her hands on.

Their tongues danced as if they had been partners for years. Her nimble fingers unzipped his fly as if she'd done it thousands of times.

He grabbed the back of her nightie and ripped it down the center. Then, in one sweeping motion, slid it over her shoulders, letting it float like a leaf on a gentle breeze to the floor.

Fire blazed in his eyes as he scanned her almost naked body. "You're so beautiful."

He stepped out of his jeans and kicked them behind him.

She pushed his shirt up over his chest and held back the moan begging to come out at the sensual sight of masculinity in front of her. "Cade, I don't know. It's been so long."

He pulled the rest of his shirt over his head and stood in front of her in black boxers. "Don't think about how long it's been. Think about how much I want you."

She reached up and stretched her arms over his broad chest. She lifted her heels and pushed up onto her tippy toes to get the extra few inches to curl her hands around the back of his neck. With his guidance and encouragement, she'd live out one or maybe two of her fantasies. Greg's death taught her—life is fleeting. She had to take hold of moments like these and live them. The chance might never come again.

He bent his knees and lifted her up by her hips as if she were a fragile piece of priceless crystal weighing nothing. "You're so small."

"You're so big." *Everything about you is larger than life.*

She licked the curve of his neck, salty and clean like the perfect male. S*o healthy.* She sniffed his neck, wood and whiskey. *Home.*

The sensation of ice shocked her back, making her body stiffen as it pressed against the floor-to-ceiling window on the east side of the bedroom.

"Sorry, but I've got to have you. Now." He ripped the sides of her panty and tossed them on the carpet. "I'll buy more."

Her legs circled his waist for the hopefully blissful moment sure to come. His thick cock rubbed against her dripping, wet folds. "Cade," she whispered.

"I'm not going to last long." He muttered. "Normally I'd be more patient, but tonight has been torture." He pressed his bare cockhead inside her. "This isn't a one-night stand to me, or I'd wear a condom."

The hard cock entered her sex like a thick rod of

molten heat filling her empty channel. Her pussy walls contracted around him in delicious waves of pain and pleasure. He stretched her to capacity, and still she wanted…

"More." She whimpered. "Please, more."

He thrust deeper then stilled.

She raised her lids and gazed at his handsome face. The feral look in his eyes changed something inside her. She was a woman again, not just a mom, not just a widow.

"Please, don't hold back," she whispered. *Take me like a caveman. I'm ready. I want it.*

He ground his teeth together. "You shouldn't have said that."

He carried her to the bed and knelt beside it. Her butt hit the edge of the mattress. His cock inched slightly out with the bump.

She sucked in her stomach and squeezed her pussy around his cock. *Want me forever.*

He pushed her back until she lay on the soft ivory and brown comforter, never taking his heavy gaze from hers.

"Please," she begged him. "I need you."

"Tell me exactly what you need." His thick cock slid fully inside her.

"Yes." She sighed. "More."

"More what?" he whispered.

"You," she pleaded. "More of you." She needed him to move inside her and take away the ache and loneliness he threatened to ease, if only for a few minutes.

His hand glided over her belly and chest. "Do you want my cock driving in and out of your soaking wet pussy?"

A low sound of desire escaped her lips. *Yes.*

He hovered over her and whispered into her ear, "Tell me. Say the words. I need to hear it."

All embarrassment faded into thin air as she shouted, "Fuck me, Cade. Please. It's been so long."

He feverishly thrust in and out of her. Faster. Deeper. He lit up sweet spots inside her that had been long neglected and gave her exactly what she needed.

She threw her head back, closed her eyes and writhed beneath him. "Yes."

He took control and tenderly pinned her arms overhead with the perfect amount of force.

She gladly surrendered.

In and out. In and out. He thrust inside her. His cock tapped a spot that shot a jolt of pain into her belly. She gasped.

The pain quickly morphed to pleasure. "Oh, my God." She moaned. "Again. Again."

With more fervor, he thrust in and out and sent his thick cock directly to the same spot. Pain. Pleasure.

She countered his thrusts, joined him, and pulled him into a beautiful rhythm of hungry, passionate sex. She rocked her hips, ground her swollen clit against his pelvis. She needed a sexual release more than she needed food or shelter.

"Look at me." He slowed down the methodic thrust of his hips and gave her a taste of the heated desire he controlled like a master.

She opened her eyes to witness his fiery gaze locked on her. She recognized the look in his eyes. Greg had the same look when they made love, a physical hunger from deep within his spirit. The desire had sucked her into Greg's world and allowed him to consume her. Cade held the same power over her…if she gave her heart to him.

The slow rocking turned into long, deep strokes. The long, deep strokes increased in tempo gliding in, and out of her silky sheath leading into delirious, passionate thrusting. Her pussy walls clamped down around him. Sweet spots lit up inside her.

"Cade," she shouted. She rode the tide of complete bliss that she hadn't experienced in five, long years. He'd awakened her need to be intimate with a man, not just any man—him.

"Take me with you," he ordered.

The ripples of pleasure increased as she dug her feet into his ass and angled her hips for more. "Harder. Make it last." Greedily, Cade's grip tightened. He pulled out and drove into her with a force and desire that rocked her world.

In and out he hammered, faster and faster, shooting hot beads of cum deep inside her. "Ella, my Ella." He thrust one more time and held onto her, mumbling her name over and over.

Tears gathered in her eyes as her brain comprehended what she'd done. Cade was the only other man besides Greg she'd ever slept with.

"Sweetie, did I hurt you?"

"No. You didn't hurt me at all." *Far from it.*

He made her want more out of life. He made her want him for the rest of it.

She exhaled and tried not to break down in front of him. But the fluid building in her eyes leaked onto her cheeks anyway.

He wiped away her tears while his cock stayed

buried inside her.

She didn't know what to do with her hands now that it was over, and he had released his hold of her arms. Greg had never held her like a possession. He'd never talked dirty. He'd never fucked her wildly like he owned her. Greg had sweetly made love to her until he couldn't anymore. After awkwardly patting her hands on his shoulders and up and down his sides, she curled her hands comfortably behind his neck. "Sorry."

"Don't say that." He rolled over and took her with him until she lay across his chest. "I'm not sorry."

She nestled her face against his chest and hid her embarrassment. "I'm not sorry about what we just did. I'm sorry about the tears."

He wrapped her in a tight embrace. "Are you okay?" He squeezed her and loosened his hold.

"Yeah." She closed her eyes and sighed. Exhaustion took over her mind and body. "Better than okay."

His chest rose with an inhale. "Good." He exhaled. His limp cock slid from her pussy.

All the stress and insecurity from earlier vanished. For the first time in five years she'd experienced absolute sexual satisfaction. "Cade." She yawned. "I like that you're a talker."

He rolled to his side. She turned around and pushed her back against his front. He curled his body around hers and pulled the covers over them. "Sweetie, sleep. I'll talk your ear off tomorrow."

"You better," she mumbled. *Real Cade is much better than the fantasy.* She breathed in his wood and whiskey scent and hoped he'd be up for another round soon.

Chapter Five

Bright sun rays poured through the window panes into the bedroom and woke Ella from the best night's sleep she'd had in ages. Warm hands and legs tangled with hers under the covers. Deep, heavy breaths soothed her senses, and a hard, sizzling erection pressed firm and ready against her hip.

Cade…I really did have sex with Cade after I talked to Maddie…and Josie. Ugh.

She hadn't been thinking clearly. She wanted him so badly, she hadn't insisted on him wearing a condom. It never crossed her mind to even ask him about putting one on. She trusted him. Stupid. Stupid. Stupid. Vasectomies needed to be checked. Did he take the tests to make sure there wasn't any sperm still swimming? Greg didn't get a vasectomy, but she remembered Greg telling her Garrett got one or had some kind of sperm problem and got tested yearly.

Should I ask him whether he got tested? He had it overseas, so surely he got tested afterward. What should I do?

She'd only had one serious relationship in her life. She barely dated before she met and married Greg. Cade all but admitted he'd never been in a serious relationship. He was probably the king of one-night stands no matter what he'd told her yesterday. Even if he'd told her the truth, she remained at a major disadvantage.

Thirty-seven-year-old single moms with more responsibility than they could handle didn't have one-night stands. She had boys who needed her to show them how to treat women. Spending the weekend with a serial dater didn't set the right example.

She made her mind up. *I'm going home.* No more hot sex. No more living out Cade-induced, sexy fantasies. Last night she took a chance, but today she'd end whatever they were calling what they had. He was a four-alarm fire she couldn't control, and she was too responsible to stay and get burned.

"Mmm," he mumbled. His hand slid to her breast and gently squeezed.

Her nipples tightened. Her pussy immediately wept for his cock. The same hand traveled along the curves of her body until it slid between her legs. She melted under his touch and submitted to his hungry voice. *One more fantasy before I go.*

"My shy Ella." He swept his fingers across her wet folds. "Need you."

His hand slid over her hips and pushed her forward onto her belly. He glided over her back and mounted her. His fingers circled over the swelling bud of her clitoris.

So much for not getting burned, she lay submerged in blazing flames. Last night he proved he owned her like no one else ever had.

He rose to his knees and brought her hips up to the perfect angle to open her moist pussy for easy access. He thrust into her softness and groaned. "Mine." He laid his head on her back and withdrew from her pussy.

She turned her face into the mattress to silence her

whimpers. *Don't stop.*

Each thrust of his huge cock tapped a heavy need inside her to feel his orgasm. To be filled with his cum. To come apart under his careful control. He thrust again and again. His cock ran like the piston of a well-tuned engine in and out of her pussy. "You're so wet for me. You're so fucking hot. I want you under me all night long, every night."

His thumb circled and grazed over her clit, building her need until her juicy sex made delicious sucking noises around his cock with each stroke in and out. "God, I love the sounds of your body. I'm gonna come deep inside you. It's gonna feel so good."

"Cade," she cried out. She bucked her hips back and forced him farther into her slick sheath, hitting the sweetest spots previously forgotten.

"Just like that, sweetie. Take all of my cock." He thrust. Once. Twice. Her pussy walls closed in vise-like waves around him. She was primed and ready to blow apart in orgasmic bliss. *Just a little more, Cade. Please.*

One more hard thrust. He grunted with exertion sending them both over the edge of pleasure and straight to paradise. He released hot spurts of cum into the farthest recesses of her pussy.

Her incoherent shouts were muffled by the pillow.

She wanted to keep him. She wanted to make love to him again. Maybe she'd stay. Spend the weekend. Open up the possibility of a real relationship.

Maybe he would be the experimental lover she'd imagined Garrett would be. Maybe he'd have a best friend like Garrett had with Derek, one who would join them once. Or twice. Except, Cade seemed more like a one-woman guy, and Garrett was probably six-feet under.

****

Cade collapsed on top of her and exhaled a satisfied sigh. He'd had another erotic dream starring his beautiful massage therapist.

"Can't breathe," Ella squeaked.

She'd never said anything like that in his dreams.

He opened his eyes. *Shit*.

"Sorry." He pushed up onto his hands, taking his weight off her. His cock slipped free, fully sated but already getting hard for another round. The heat of embarrassment swept over his skin. He couldn't remember the last time he blushed, or got carried away with a woman. It had been years since he spent the night with anyone, and he had never slept with a woman in his bed. Ella brought out every raw emotion he held in a tight grip inside his heart.

"It's okay." She rolled onto her side.

He shifted to his side and pulled her back to his front to keep her close to him like a soft teddy bear in a sleeping child's arms. He nuzzled her ear. "Better?"

"Mmm."

He slid his hand over her warm belly as his cock hardened and rose against her thigh. "I got a little carried away." He wanted to make love to her again, but his father's words kept screaming in his ears to slow things down and take the time to show her he cared about more than sex. He did care about more than sex. His cock wanted all the sex; not that he didn't. He did. He wanted it but not at the expense of losing her.

She snuggled in closer and shifted her upper leg forward, opening up her pussy for easy access.

With a mind of its own, his hungry cock lifted right

to her entrance.

"I want you again." *Damn. I shouldn't have said that. I'm supposed to slow down. Not as much as yesterday. That was pure agony.*

"Take me," she whispered.

Hot damn.

He slid his hand between her moist thighs. "I'm going to take you every way I want."

"Yes, please." She caressed down his arm to his hand between her legs.

He circled her clit with his finger and slid his thick cock inside her. "I love your pussy." He swiveled his hips and pumped his cock in and out, eliciting a soft moan from her succulent lips.

He had her right where he always wanted her, alone in his bed for days. He planned to make love to her until they were forced to leave the bedroom in search of food and water.

The house phone buzzed on the floor and the doorbell rang.

She turned her head and gazed up at him. "Are you expecting someone?"

"No. Ignore everything." He pressed a kiss to her lips. The phone would eventually stop ringing, and whoever waited at the door would leave. The few people who knew where to find him wouldn't visit on the spur of the moment. No interruptions. He had his woman right where he wanted her.

The phone stopped ringing, then started up again. *Damn. Stop calling.*

The doorbell rang again.

Go away.

"Don't you need to get the door?" she asked.

He crawled off the bed, leaving the warmth of her body, and answered the phone.

"Hello?"

"Are you still acting like an idiot, or is she in bed with you?" Josie asked. "You better tell me I didn't make the biggest mistake of my life setting you up with the girl you're already in love with."

"Hey Josie, I'm good. How are you?" he asked. "That's how you usually start off a conversation."

"The heck it is," Josie said. "Have you told her you love her?"

No. He didn't want Ella running as far away from him as possible. She needed more time to fall in love with him. His gut, along with his father's advice, convinced him telling her too soon would be disastrous.

The doorbell rang.

"Somebody's at the door. I've got to go." He wasn't dealing with Josie-on-a-mission first thing in the morning. "Here, talk with Ella." He handed the phone to her. "I'll get rid of whoever's at the door."

Ella's gaze dropped to his hard cock. She leaned forward and kissed the head. She covered the mic on the phone. "Hurry."

The doorbell rang again.

"I'll be back in sixty seconds," he said. *The forest better be on fire.*

"Hey, Josie," Ella said. She rolled onto her back and spread her legs.

He pulled on his jeans and walked out, shutting the bedroom door closed behind him. Josie could get the scoop from Ella and then tell him everything. First, mystery visitor ringing the crap out of his doorbell had to go.

Chapter Six

Cade turned the bronze handle and opened the rustic wooden door he'd crafted with his father many years ago. Two shockingly handsome, six-feet-tall, identical-looking brothers with blond hair and blue eyes wearing matching jeans and navy T-shirts stood on his porch.

"Hi," Cade said. The boys had to be Ella's. He wondered if they looked like their father. If they did, their father was a very good-looking man.

His stomach burned like he'd eaten a bowl full of ghost peppers as jealousy consumed him. The boys should be his children. They should resemble him. He should have been the one who raised them, loved them, provided for them. What he wouldn't give to have children with Ella and a chance to be a great dad like his father.

"Dude, put a shirt on," one of boys said as he walked past Cade into the living room of the house. "I totally don't want to think about you and my mom doing it."

"Come on, Jay. That is so not cool," the other boy said.

Jason waved him off. "Whatever, Ky."

Kyle held out his hand to Cade.

Cade shook it. *Shit*. He just screwed up his only chance at a good first impression.

"Nice to meet you, Mr. Jackson. I'm Kyle Winthrop, Ella's son."

"Ky, I think he got that." Jason walked around the living room looking at everything. He stopped near the corner fireplace at the series of photos on the mantle of Cade and his father clearing the land for the house they stood in. Cade wasn't much older than the boys when he bought the land. "He invited us."

"Jay, we declined. We showed up out of the blue." Kyle followed his brother's route and stood next to him at the next grouping of photos on the ladder bookshelf beside the front windows.

"Semantics." Jason picked up the photo of Cade and his father next to the trees they crafted the doors and tables from for both houses. He carefully placed the photo back on the top shelf as if it was precious. "He invited us. We're here."

"It's nice to meet both of you," Cade said. Ella couldn't have described Jason and Kyle's personalities more perfectly. "Have you had breakfast?"

Kyle laughed. "Uh, yeah. It's noon."

Noon? He hadn't slept until noon since he was their age. He let out a lighthearted chuckle, sounding like an idiot. "Yeah, I knew that. My chef will be here soon. Did you bring swimsuits?"

Jason cocked his head back and narrowed his gaze on Cade.

"It's a little cold for swimming. Where's Mom?"

Cade's gaze flew to the bedroom door. *Fuck. What if she walked out naked? Her boys would hate me.*

"She's in the bedroom." He casually strode to the door and knocked. "Jason and Kyle are here."

"Shit," she said loud enough they could all hear

her. "I'll be out in a minute."

"Late night?" Jason's glare shot daggers at him.

"Kind of." He was under fire already and wasn't prepared for it. His first impression sucked. He'd never dealt with the almost-adult children of someone he dated. "The raccoons were making a racket outside until early this morning."

"Mom doesn't like camping or wildlife," Jason said.

"I figured as much after the raccoon incident." *Great. Ella doesn't like any aspect of camping, and I took her to my cabin in the woods. No wonder she freaked out over the raccoons. They definitely hate me. They probably want to kill me given the fury growing by the second in Jason's eyes.* He couldn't blame them. If he'd been them, he wouldn't be nearly as nice.

Jason walked over to the leather couch. "Nice TV. Do you entertain a lot?"

"I mostly rent this place out. There's a guest house through the woods with a heated pool. I have extra swimsuits if you're interested." Swimming with the boys would develop enough of a bond to stop them from taking Ella home.

Kyle walked around Cade and joined Jason on the couch. "We can't. We have plans today."

Cade sat on the edge of the ottoman across from them. "Can you stay for lunch?"

Keep things relaxed. I've already screwed up enough.

"We can stay for lunch," Kyle said.

"That's great." Cade stood up. "I'm going to grab a shirt. I'll be right back."

"Okay." Kyle slapped a tight grip onto Jason's

forearm. "We'll be here."

Maybe Kyle didn't hate him, but he couldn't be sure. Cade rounded the corner and eavesdropped on the boys as he slowed his pace as he neared the guest bedroom.

"If he hurts Mom, I'm going to kill him," Jason said. "What kind of guy answers the door without a shirt?"

"He didn't know we were coming," Kyle said. "Be nice to him."

"Mom called Maddie after midnight wanting to come home," Jason said. "Why should I be nice to him?"

Cade kept the door ajar to the bedroom and listened. He really messed up last night. He hadn't thought she was on the phone ready to bolt.

"We've been over this. You shouldn't have been eavesdropping on the conversation," Kyle said. "It's a good thing I caught you. At least we know he's not trying to… Anyway, if Mom wants to come home, we'll bring her home. If she wants to stay, then—"

"—You'll have to drag my ass out that door," Jason interrupted. "She's not staying. He should have kissed her when she made whatever move she did. Mom doesn't look twice at anybody, and she likes this asshole. He doesn't deserve her."

What the hell? What move? She made a move, and I missed it? We had one moment in the woods, but I screwed it up. It wasn't a move. It was more like a question.

"Jason, they're not sharing a room. They're not doing anything. Maybe she's been hiding all morning trying to get up the nerve to come out…"

Cade closed the door and blocked off the conversation. He'd heard enough. He had made a huge mess of things last night by not following his instincts. He loved Ella and wanted to tell her he loved her. He wanted to tell the boys he loved her. He wanted to tell the world he loved her, but he couldn't.

Keeping his feelings private and repairing the damage that forced her boys to come and check on her was top on his agenda. Making her boys comfortable enough to leave her with him for the rest of the weekend was paramount, or she would be gone no matter what he wanted.

He washed up in the sink and put on fresh clothes. He stilled the frenzied butterflies churning the anxiety in his stomach and set out to make a better second impression than the first.

Cade quietly opened the bedroom door until he could make out the hushed voices in the living room. "The power is out at the house," Kyle said.

"Could you check my business account balance on Monday?" Ella said. "I might not have the funds, if any of the checks bounced. I've hit a string of bad clients. But I'll definitely have the money Tuesday."

"What if Colleen comes home early?" Jason asked.

"Colleen never comes home early," Kyle said. "She mentioned taking summer classes a couple months ago. How are we going to pay for that?"

"I can sell the last of the jewelry to pay for her tuition," Ella said. "I need to put the house on the market. I can't afford the utilities or the small mortgage. I think, with the profits, we could move into a small fixer-upper with some land farther outside Memphis, but I don't know how much I can get for the house with the things it still needs repaired."

"I can tutor," Kyle said. "But your business is going to take off as soon as I finish the site this weekend. I called a few local retailers, and they placed orders. It will tide us over until the house sells."

"I'll help you make the soaps in the evenings," Jason chimed in. "I can get a job with Katie's dad doing construction on the weekends. He knows I can make damn near anything. Sorry. Didn't mean to cuss."

"Neither of you need to get part-time jobs. I can make ends meet until the house sells. I'm just sorry we have to sell."

Cade inched the door farther open. Did Josie know how bad Ella's finances were? Did Maddie? It didn't sound like anybody outside her two boys knew the extent of her problems, not even her daughter.

Kyle grunted. "We're not children. The house is nice, but it's just a roof over our heads."

Damn. Boys don't make noises like that. Men do.

"We're more worried about you running yourself into the ground keeping things afloat. We'll help get the place ready. I'll call our friends for help."

"We don't need help," Ella said sharply, ending the line of conversation. "I can fix the small things."

"No, you can't, but I can," Jason said. "Our friends could help with the landscaping. You can't do everything yourself, Mom. You don't have the money for the utilities. You can't afford to repair the house. None of it is your fault. So stop blaming yourself for every damn thing that's wrong."

"I paid the last of the medical bills last week. That's why we ran short this month." She released a heavy exhale. "I really will have the money for utilities

Monday barring any bounced checks."

Did she just finish paying off medical bills from her husband's cancer? Josie said Ella was rich but tight with her money. What he heard didn't sound like a wealthy person's problems. It sounded like she was struggling to make ends meet and trying to hide it by being frugal. He would talk to Maddie. She'd know the real deal. Then he'd pay Ella's utilities and take care of anything else she needed. With him as her husband, she'd never worry again.

"I think you should sell the house but not because it's a burden. You should sell it because it's time to move on," Jason said. "Money is not going to be an issue as soon as you lift your rules and let us start being men and working."

"When you turn eighteen, you can decide whether to live at home with me while you're at college or head out on your own. Until then…" Her voice hardened to stone. "…you are under my rules. And I'm going to support my children any way I can."

Damn. Her momma bear protecting her kids attitude was hot, even if it was misguided and unnecessary. *Get ready because I'm coming whether you like it or not.*

Cade strode into the living room with a plan. "Hey." He headed toward the couch.

Ella stood up and turned around wearing a sexy, little, blue-cotton dress that hit mid-thigh and an ivory, long-sleeve cardigan.

His cock rose to attention. "You look beautiful."

Her gaze dropped to the Persian rug underneath her feet. She smiled as her cheeks turned a beautiful shade of pink. "Thanks. Phil is in the kitchen."

"Oh, great. I'll check on lunch," he said.

"Hey, Cade," Phil said. "Lunch is ready. I've got to head out, but I'll be back to cook dinner."

Cade turned around and grinned at the red-haired man. "Thanks, Phil. I'll see you later."

"Bye, Cade." Phil waved and walked out through the back door.

He turned around. All three Winthrops stood on the other side of the couch. He imagined himself in the mix, standing beside Ella in the middle of the two boys as if they were his. *One day they will be mine. My family.*

"Who's hungry?" he asked. His mother insisted good food could buffer the most uncomfortable of circumstances. He had to get the boys on his side by the time lunch ended so they would tell him about Ella's troubles. Then he could help Ella get out from under her financial stresses. If there was one thing he was good at it, it was making money. With a few phone calls her side business would thrive. With her boys in his corner, he could make her fall in love with him.

"Dude can't cook?" Jason leaned closer to Ella. "Not too impressed with this one."

"Jason," she grumbled. Her eyes widened, and her mouth dropped to a thin line. "Be respectful. I didn't raise you to be rude."

"I can cook," Cade said. The boisterous teen wanted to see what kind of man he was? He would show Jason he was worthy of his mother's interest and affection. "The area is economically depressed this time of year. I try to help the local economy, and Phil is an exceptional chef."

"I'm ready to eat." Kyle's lips curved into a tight

smile. “Jason is too.”

“I’m ready,” Ella said.

Cade held out his hand to her, and she placed her small hand in his.

Jason and Kyle walked on either side of her around the edge of the couch to him. Jason didn’t seem too happy about his mom dating. Or maybe the hostility radiating like a nuclear fallout from Jason was about Cade coming to the door without a shirt. Or it could be the boy didn’t like what Ella said over the phone last night. Whatever the reason, Cade needed a do-over, and he hoped lunch would give him one.

Chapter Seven

Ella placed her hand in Cade's over the back of the couch and walked around the corner of the leather sectional like a queen going to the king's Ball.

She glanced down at Jason's clenched fists, and her stomach tied up in baseball-sized knots. Her son made no effort to hide the fact he could punch Cade in the face with only the slightest provocation. She prodded Jason to talk to her, but he wouldn't say a peep about his unreasonable resentment toward Cade. They'd never met before. There was no reason for his behavior.

She stood in unchartered territory with no clue how to fix or make the situation better for everyone. She liked Cade. She could even fall in love with him, if…

"Nice table." Jason skimmed his hand over the natural dips and crevasses along the side. "Did you make it?"

"My father and I made it," Cade replied. "I wanted to keep as much of the natural beauty of the wood as possible." He pulled out a chair for Ella, and the boys positioned themselves on either side of her.

Play nice, please.

"My dad built most of our house." Jason gazed at Ella and tapped the top of her chair like his father used to when he wanted her to sit.

She nodded and sat down. "Garrett helped."

Jason pulled out his chair and sat. "You helped

too."

"A little." She gazed at Cade. *They blocked you out from being near me. I never should have called them yesterday.*

"Dad and Uncle Garrett made all my bedroom furniture," Jason said. "Did you build this place?"

"Yes, and no." Cade walked to the other side of the large table. "I contracted out all the basic construction. I'm not that great of a carpenter."

I bet you're a wonderful carpenter, maybe not as good as Greg was, but close.

"The place is beautiful, Cade," she said.

He sat down directly across from her. "Thanks. But I can't take too much of the credit."

"Didn't think so," Jason mumbled.

"My father sounds more like your dad," Cade said. "Pappy, my father, can build or make anything. I'm more of a lifetime apprentice. He supervises and signs off on my final work so it's not a hazard to anyone."

She half-laughed, but it came out more like an awkward giggle. *I'm so bad at this.*

He smiled. For every ounce of angry energy Jason emitted, Cade seemed to counter with happiness and light. He picked up his napkin from the table and set it on his lap. "Do you like carpentry work, Jason?"

Jason picked up his napkin and shadowed Cade's movements. Maybe lunch wouldn't be so bad after all. Cade seemed to know how to handle Jason's protectiveness and calm his hostility. They could find common ground in carpentry. Cade was probably a better carpenter than he let on. The man seemed quite capable of doing anything with his hands and mouth and legs. *Mmm.*

"Yeah," Jason said. "I like working with my hands, but Mom is afraid I'll hurt myself. She won't let me near the tools without a responsible party to supervise."

Kyle raised his hand. "That would be me." He put his hand down on his lap and cracked a smile.

Jason reached around Ella's back.

"Jason," Ella warned. "Don't." *I will never date again. You're in so much trouble.*

Jason hugged her. "I love you, Mom." He squeezed her shoulder then slapped Kyle on the back of the head.

Kyle's head jerked forward from the sudden, playful hit. He laughed.

"Jason, quit it," she warned. *You're embarrassing me.*

"You have to meet Pappy." Cade rubbed his mouth and partially covered his grin as he shifted his gaze from the table to Jason. "He's got a few projects in the works and needs an apprentice. I'll introduce him to you. He pays well." He fidgeted for a second and lifted his cell phone to the table.

Jason leaned forward a few inches toward Cade. "Are you serious about an apprenticeship job?"

"Yeah." Cade nodded. "Absolutely. Pappy will have to talk to you about pay and time, but he has three bedroom suites to fill with furniture and has the wood picked out already. He needs someone to teach, or he's not a happy builder." He tapped the screen of his phone. "I'll see if the position is still open."

"Does your father live close by?" She couldn't believe he would recommend Jason for anything, let alone a job after the reception he received. Maybe Cade liked a kid who spoke his mind. If things didn't work into a relationship between her and Cade would Jason lose the job?

"He's about an hour outside of Memphis," Cade said. "Pappy will pay for gas for the truck, and Jason will have to use the company vehicle to pick up supplies. It's a real job with potential. It won't be easy, but he'll learn a lot." He uncovered the silver platters in the middle of the table.

Starved from the morning activities, Ella salivated as the wonderful aroma of grilled steak surrounded her. *I could eat every piece of deliciousness on those platters and then go for another evening fulfilling fantasies with Cade.* Her pussy quivered. *Stop thinking about Mr. Sex. Ugh. Jason and Kyle are here.*

"Wow," Kyle mumbled. "I'm glad we came for lunch."

Cade's phone rang. He lifted his phone to his ear.

"Hey, Pappy. Yes, sir… Okay… Good. Thanks." He placed his phone face down on the table. "Jason, Pappy wants to meet you tonight at Maddie's to talk business. He looks like me, but he's an inch or so taller, and a couple inches broader. He's huge, and he's a hugger. So take a deep breath when he comes at you, hold it until he lets you go, and you'll have a good chance at survival."

Half of Jason's mouth turned up into a smile, a twinkle of amusement carried over into his blue eyes. "You're serious?"

"Dead." Cade handed Jason the platter of steaks. "It's some kind of test. If you don't cry or faint, you pass. Although, I've seen a couple men cry and get hired. But he never hired one who fainted and several have."

"That's interesting," Kyle mumbled.

"Everything looks delicious." She attempted to change the subject. Cade in a psychological testing discussion with Kyle equated to a whole other special level of misery. Her super mathematician had his own tests, and so far, it seemed Cade was passing.

Cade handed the bowl of salad to her and she served the boys. Then he passed Ella his salad plate, and she filled it without thinking. She slouched. She'd served him like he was her child, not her date.

Cade seemed to suppress a grin like a kid trying to keep a funny secret. "A little more, please."

She straightened her spine. Her cheeks heated as she added more salad to his plate. *Thank you for being so easy-going.*

Jason leaned over to her and whispered loud enough for Cade and Kyle to hear. "He can't serve himself? Not too impressed."

She sighed, ready to choke Jason. Her protective son leaned back against his chair, seemingly pleased with himself, and waited, like always, for her response.

Whatever Cade did before she got out of the bedroom didn't make a friend in her boy. The job with Cade's father probably wouldn't work out if Jason didn't start lightening up on Cade.

Cade said a short blessing over lunch. They ate mostly in silence, with intermittent polite conversation thrown in which consisted mostly of carpentry work.

Kyle finished the last forkful of steak on his plate and set the napkin on the table. "What's on the menu for dinner?"

"Whatever your mom would like," Cade said.

"Do you have kids?" Jason asked Cade.

"Jason, stop." She'd be in the car and on her way

home in minutes with Jason's obnoxious inquisition.

"No, sir." Cade bypassed her objection. "I've never been married. I don't have any children."

Jason nodded and stacked Ella's plate onto his. "Mom, you didn't eat much."

"I ate plenty. I'm not a growing boy, remember?"

"Yeah, but—"

"—No buts, Jason." She placed her hand on his arm, trying to calm him. "I'm fine. If I ate as much as you, I'd be as wide as you are tall."

Jason's lips pressed into a tight line. "Did you bring your vitamins?"

"No," she whispered. He worried too much that something bad was going to happen to her like it had his dad. "I thought I was meeting Maddie and Josie after work, not going to a lake house with a friend for the weekend."

Kyle huddled close to his mother. "Does Cade take vitamins? Everyone should take them."

"I don't know. We haven't exchanged dietary information, and I really don't plan on it." She wanted the boys to like Cade. She wanted more than one night with the man who brought out the woman in her. Passing her boys' tests or performing well enough on them for her to stay with Cade for the rest of the weekend seemed unlikely. Without some kind of miraculous intervention, Jason would insist she go home, and Kyle would back him up.

I never should have called them. Cade never should have invited them to visit.

"I take a multivitamin every day," Cade said. "Ella can take some of mine, if she wants."

She turned and gazed at him, having forgotten he

was in the room.

"I can hear you." Cade nodded. "I'm right here."

"Uh… I'm sorry." She had to do something. After the nutrition discussion ended, the boys would turn to exercise routines. They had to stop trying to manage her health. There would be no more talking about health and fitness. Not with the dull ache in her leg, from an old injury, bothering her.

There would be no physical challenges. No races she would have to participate in to prove her leg was okay. The weather changes made her leg hurt, not anything else. No evaluation of Cade's physical health. No more of Jason's control games. She needed some acetaminophen, not a conversation about taking better care of herself.

Cade stood up and gathered the rest of the plates. "I'll be back in a few minutes." He carried the dishes out of the dining room.

Jason immediately scooted closer to her. "What is going on with you and him? He seems too comfortable."

Ella's mouth dropped open. "I… Well… We're on a first date."

"Mom, the guy shows up at the door wearing jeans and nothing else. It's noon, and you're just getting up? I don't think I've ever seen you sleep past six unless you were sick." Jason paused. "Are you sick?"

"No. I'm fine. You know how I don't like wild animals. Late last night, raccoons were outside trying to get into the garbage. I didn't sleep well."

The blue of Jason's eyes darkened like his father's used to when he wasn't sure he was getting the whole truth. A rush of happiness filled her heart. She suppressed a smile, keeping her expression stoic. Her little Jason was a man. He and Kyle were all grown up. Her babies were ready to spread their wings.

"Is he pressuring you?" Jason raised his brows and lowered his chin. "I kind of like him, but I'll kick his ass. Screw the job with his dad. I can find something else to help out until we can sell the house."

"Listen." Heat crawled up her neck as embarrassment seeped in. "Cade was a client until yesterday. There isn't anything serious between us. He is not—and I repeat not—pressuring me to do anything."

"Yeah, we know." Kyle shrugged. "We wanted to make sure he didn't start up today. We were worried when you called Maddie last night. Jason eavesdropped some."

"What?" Ella shouted. Her eyes widened to popping out proportions, and her jaw dropped open. She covered her mouth. *What did they hear? They must not have heard everything, or they would have shown up last night.*

Her heartbeat tripled in time and not in a good way. "Oh, my goodness. Jason Gregory Winthrop." She couldn't form any other words, not knowing for the life of her what to say, utterly dumbstruck from the revelation.

"We know you like him," Kyle said. "I'm sorry he acted like a jerk during dessert and the noise scared you."

Blood rushed from her extremities to her cheeks. *They heard me talk about dessert and kissing. Did they hear about the nightie? I am going to die.*

"Hey, does anyone want any dessert? There are

leftovers from last night," Cade said as if cued for that perfect awkward moment. "It's delicious."

Ella turned her head toward Cade and again wanted to die. He stood in the entryway into the kitchen holding a silver tray with chocolate-covered strawberries and whipped cream in martini glasses. Delectable on all sorts of levels. Her face burned with desire and embarrassment.

"Yeah, dude. Hook me up," Jason said.

Ella lowered her gaze and clasped her hands in her lap. "None for me."

Her belly burned along with her cheeks. What she had hoped to do last night with him and that dessert flashed through her mind. Renewed disappointment fell heavy on her heart from the memories of the previous evening when he didn't touch or talk to her while they ate the strawberries made for naughty fantasies. Her embarrassment stayed, but the warmth in her body faded to cold. Would he play uninterested now that he'd met her boys?

"I'll have some, Mr. Jackson," Kyle said. "Thanks."

Ella pushed back her chair and stood up as Cade set the tray of dessert on the table. "I'll be right back." She practically ran to the bedroom, ignoring the ache in her leg. She didn't want to end her weekend with Cade, but she wanted to leave immediately. She didn't want to chat with anyone, but she wanted desperately to talk to someone. She closed the door to the bedroom and slumped down to the lush carpet.

Since Greg died, life hadn't been terribly complicated. One night with Cade, and she was an emotional mess.

Chapter Eight

Ella's dress lifted, showing off more of her lean legs as she sped to the bedroom like a bat out of hell. The trail of wind from her racing exit sent her sweet ginger perfume up into the air. Cade breathed her in, and his cock rose to attention.

The door slammed shut. His erection died.

He lowered his chin and raised his brow as he gazed down at the boys. *What did you do?*

"Is everything okay?" Everything couldn't be okay with her reaction to dessert, but he would do whatever it took to convince her to stay.

Kyle took a dessert glass and spoon off the tray, seemingly unaffected by his mother's sudden departure. "Mr. Jackson, what do you think?"

He dipped his spoon into the dessert and lifted whipped cream and sliced strawberries to his lips. He opened his mouth, placed the spoonful inside, and closed his lips. His intelligent blue gaze focused on Cade. He removed the spoon from his mouth and held it in contemplation like a university professor.

Jason folded his arms over his chest and leaned back in his chair like a father sizing up his daughter's boyfriend. "I'm very interested in finding out your thoughts on what just transpired."

"I'm thinking she's not okay. What happened?" Cade sat down. "I'm kind of in the dark here." *Should I barge into the bedroom and find out what is wrong, or wait to see what information the boys surrendered before barreling in and talking to her?*

Kyle placed the spoon down on the table. "I'm in the dark too. What do you want from my mom? We know what happened last night."

Cade cleared his throat. *Crap.* Was that why Ella ran out of the room? How would they know about last night when they didn't know anything earlier? Did they get a text? Did Ella say something? Maddie and Josie wouldn't say anything. Maybe Maddie sent the boys to pick Ella up this morning because of the phone call last night? What if Ella told Josie he sucked in bed and had Josie text the boys a few minutes ago to bring her home after lunch? No. Josie would have called and bitched him out first.

"Last night wasn't what either of us planned. Not that we planned anything."

"What are your intentions toward my mom?" Jason asked.

Cade's heart raced a mile a minute under their scrutiny. He needed to calm down. They were Ella's boys, not her father. Why did he feel like a guilty child? They didn't know about the sex or Jason would be throwing punches, not talking to him about his intentions. *I'm the adult in the room, not them.* The pressure of their approval was killing him.

Her boys were formidable, but so was he. He had a lot more experience in hostile situations in personal and business matters. He stared Jason straight in the eye.

"I really like your mom. I'd like permission from you and your brother to date her. I'd like to take her out alone. I'd like to hang out with all of you, get to know you better, and you get to know me."

He thought he saw a glimmer of acceptance in Jason's eyes, so he turned his attention to Kyle. "Your mom is smart and funny. She's straightforward and honest. She's an incredible massage therapist and business woman. I respect her immensely. She's a great listener which comes in handy because I like to talk."

Jason laughed. "Mom is a good listener, but Mom talks too. Actually, she talks a lot."

Kyle smirked as if he kept a secret from him. "She discusses things."

"She discusses everything." Jason rolled his eyes. "Do you know what it's like to have your mother talk with you about guy things she shouldn't know about, let alone explain?"

"Are you talking about the birds and the bees?" Cade asked. That would be awkward for a teen.

"That is exactly what I'm talking about. If it's embarrassing, she wants to talk about it at length," Kyle said. "If she thinks it's going to impact our lives, especially our *childhood*, we're in for an hour-long discussion."

"Doesn't she get embarrassed?" The person they described didn't sound quite like his shy Ella. But he could see her pushing through difficult conversations because it was the right thing to do.

"Dude, it so doesn't matter whether she is embarrassed or not." Jason shook his head. "Mom is not like other moms."

Cade waited for him to elaborate, but he didn't.

"What do you say about giving me permission to date your mom?" He glanced from one to the other.

"Depends on what you're going to do now," Kyle

said. "Go with your gut or your head?" He crossed his arms over his chest, mirroring Jason.

The two cornered him like seasoned businessmen. Kyle hid his intelligence well, but no teen spoke to him like Kyle had. No normal teen would have asked him what drove his decisions in a simple question. "Gut and head, Kyle. Never make a decision without both agreeing." He pushed away from the table and went after Ella.

"Interesting," Kyle mumbled. He didn't seem too pleased with Cade's answer by the change in the tone of his voice.

"You've got our permission," Jason added.

The boys shifted in their acceptance of him. Now he had to win over Kyle, not Jason.

Cade knocked on the door. "Ella?"

"Yes?"

He opened the door and walked into the bedroom.

Her luggage lay on the flawlessly made bed. She zipped up her suitcase and faced him.

He closed the door behind him and strode right to her. "Ella, please don't leave."

She turned away as he wrapped his arms around her.

"Please stay," he whispered.

"Cade, I—"

He turned her around and kissed her sweet lips. She tasted too good, too delicious, too perfect.

She hesitated.

He parted her lips and delved into her mouth. He needed her. He needed to make her see what they could have together.

She slipped her hands under his tee. Her hot touch

dipped down under the waistband of his loose-fitting jeans and made his sudden erection throb to be let out.

Her tongue dipped into his mouth and slowly stroked his.

She pushed away from his chest and left his lips. "This is complicated. Cade, I can't do—"

"—Stay," he whispered. He cradled her head and brushed his lips against hers. "Please stay with me."

"This is too complicated. You've just met my boys, and it's already a disaster."

He drew her closer and pressed his body against hers. "I like your boys. They're protective as they should be. They love you. You love them. That isn't complicated."

She curled her hands around his neck. "But this thing between us—"

"—Doesn't have to be complicated." He kissed her. "Give me a chance. Stay. I'll drive you home later, if you really want to go."

He dropped his left hand to the small of her back. Her boys worried about her for a good reason. She took care of everyone else before herself.

"If you'd rather not stay here, we can go to my house in Memphis." Her warm breath on his lips sparked more than desire. It reached into the center of his soul, making him work harder to win her. *Let me take care of you the way I want to.*

"I should probably go home with my boys."

He held her tighter as she relaxed into him. "Stay. When your boys leave, we'll be back in bed. I'm thirty seconds from ripping off your—"

"Mom?" Kyle interrupted.

Cade glanced over his shoulder. *Shit.*

Kyle and Jason stood at the open bedroom door staring at them like two deer caught in the headlights.

"Get your hands off my mom, or I'm gonna toast your balls on a stick over a barbecue pit." Jason lunged toward him. "I'm gonna…"

Kyle pulled Jason away from the threshold.

"We'll call you later tonight," Kyle shouted over Jason's growing epithets. Slapping and grappling sounds echoed from the living room into the bedroom. "Have a nice afternoon," Kyle said. "We do *not* need to talk about this. *Ever*. We didn't see anything. You didn't see anything. Thanks for lunch, Mr. Jackson. We'll talk to you later."

The front door slammed, leaving the cabin silent.

The two obstacles in his way were gone. She hadn't moved from his arms. Unless he read her wrong and he was a total idiot, she wanted him.

Ella sighed. "I do not want to deal with that when I get home."

"Then don't go home." He rubbed his bulge against her belly. "Tell me you want to stay with me."

She closed her eyes. "I want to, but—"

He crushed his lips to hers, shutting off any excuses.

Rip. Rip.

Her panties dropped to the carpet.

The suitcase landed on the floor with a loud thud.

Like a tornado, he lifted her, strode forward, and dropped down on the bed with her underneath him. "This weekend is not over. We're at the beginning."

She pushed down his jeans and boxers. Her fingers traveled over the head of his cock and caressed the slit. Precum slipped out the top.

He rolled his hips and slid his cock along the length of her hands. *I can't come, yet. I've got to make you orgasm so fucking hard you'll want to move in with me.*

Then we'll get married.

Her hands closed around his shaft. "I want you inside me," she whispered.

Hot damn. Yes.

"As much as I want to come inside you—and I will—I want something else too." He rocked his hips back and her hands slipped from his cock. He had to show her he wanted all of her. He crawled backward to the foot of the bed and dipped his head between her legs. "I've been dreaming about licking your luscious juices. In my fantasy, I look into your blue eyes as I dip my tongue into your pussy and lap up all your cream. You taste so sweet in my dreams. Do you want me to lick you?"

A rush of juices slid from her sex.

Yeah, you want me. But I need you to want more than my body. I've got to keep working on those rules to convince you to marry me. He had to ask her more questions. Find out more about her. Sex questions counted, didn't they?

"Tell me you want me to lick you." *Okay, maybe not questions.* Sexual demands counted as part of the rules. She likes sex but what about oral sex? Fuck. What if she hated it? He couldn't live without licking her pussy.

Her breathing turned into panting.

"Open your legs wider if you want me to lick you," he whispered. "I won't quit until you come on my tongue."

"Oh God." She widened her legs and lifted her hands over her head.

"I want to hear your voice," he whispered. "I like encouragement." He loved hearing her moans with his every touch. If she didn't want to talk, he was good with that too.

She shuddered. "I…uh…I."

He gently rolled her onto her belly. "Oh, my shy, little Ella is a secret screamer. I know you are." He lifted her hips. She drew in her knees and arched her back. Her pussy glistened with juices. He kissed the center and licked his lips. "You taste like sweet honeysuckle."

Her legs trembled as she inched her knees wider and lifted her ass a little higher.

"Has anyone ever feasted on you?" Her reactions weren't like a woman that had this done before, but she'd been married for a long time. Surely, they had a lot of oral sex. With a woman like Ella, he couldn't fathom her lover not taking advantage of every opportunity to explore her body.

She shook her head.

"No?" She had three kids. Maybe her husband tried oral with her but she didn't like it? Maybe her husband didn't? Cade loved going down on a woman. He couldn't give that up for the rest of his life. He had to master her body and make her come fast and hard, so she'd want him to do it often.

She shook her head. She wiggled her ass and showed off her pretty pussy. Her breasts rubbed against the sheets.

You have no idea how sexy you are. God, I love you. He dipped his head down and breathed in the honey scent.

"So sweet." He kissed her folds. "So wet." He dug his fingers into her hips and lifted them higher, holding her in position. He had to make this so good she'd beg for him to do it again. "So beautiful." He lapped in small sections from her clit to her perineum.

She buried her head partly under the pillow and muffled her moans.

"Oh hell." He flipped her over and grabbed her knees. "I need to watch you." He lifted her legs over his shoulders and opened her delicate folds with his fingers. "You're so damn gorgeous." He licked the length of her pussy. "Tell me you want this." He swirled his tongue around her clit.

She moaned.

He grazed his teeth gently over her sensitive clit.

She jerked her hips up.

Yes, so sensitive. "Tell me you want this, or I'll stop, and I don't want to stop."

"I want it," she shouted. "Cade, I want it."

He covered her swollen clit with his lips and sucked.

"Oh. My. God." She ground her pussy into his face. "It feels so good. I'm gonna come."

He released her clit and thrust his tongue into her center. *Honey sweet. Delicious.*

Already in love with her, he was in the danger zone of revealing his feelings. He slid the tips of his teeth across her clit. He dipped his tongue in and out. *I love you.* "Come for me."

She wrapped her legs around his head and bucked her hips.

The gratifying taste of orgasmic cream gushed onto

his tongue. He couldn't slow down. He needed to make her his in body, mind, and soul.

He lapped up her blissful juices. "Was that good?" He kissed a trail from her center to her clit, over her mound and up her belly.

"I…" She paused. Her blue eyes held the beautiful gaze of satisfaction.

"Ella, would you consider…" He kissed between her breasts. He should hold back from asking, but he'd slow down after he came inside her. He would take his father's advice for a long and lasting relationship, but right then, he needed her.

"What?" she whispered.

He gazed into her blue eyes. He should have watched her when he feasted on her. But he got lost in her taste, her pleasure. He wouldn't get lost in her this time. He would bask in every—.

"Would I consider what?" Her voice sounded steady and strong.

"Staying over at my place?" *Sleeping in my bed every night for the rest of your life.* He inched his cock into her wet sex.

The heavenly sound of pleasure left her lips. She nodded.

"Maybe move in with me once the boys graduate?" *I love you.* He slowly pumped more of his cock inside her.

"I don't know," she whispered.

He covered her breast with his mouth and sucked. Her eyelids lowered, but she held his gaze. He rocked his hips, gliding his cock in and out of her warm, slick sex. *I've been waiting for this feeling for my entire life. You're my home, Ella.*

He raised his head. "Think about it." He slid his hand under her and cradled her head. "It's up to you." *I'm going to do everything in my power to make it happen.*

She tilted her head up, her gaze weighted with lust. "Mmm." She reached up and softly guided his face closer to her red lips. She closed her eyes.

"I want you to stay over at my place." *Move in and marry me.*

He thrust and retreated faster and faster. Her pussy squeezed him tighter and tighter. *I want you exclusively. Tell me you want me too.* He kissed her luscious lips.

"I…" He stopped from saying the words that wanted to come out so easily for the first time in his life. He wanted her to know the softer side of him. How he ached to be near her all the time. How he worried about her working late at night without any security. How he wanted to care for and protect her. How much he loved her.

Her channel clamped down on his cock. *Yes. Hug my cock and never let me go.*

"Cade," she cried out.

His heart soared hearing her call his name. He erupted like a volcano inside her. "Mine."

"Mmm." She sighed.

"My Ella," he whispered, coming down off the orgasmic high. He intended to have more than a weekend with her. He would spend the rest of his life making love to her in every conceivable way. If he hadn't gotten that damn vasectomy from that crackpot doctor years ago, he would have had babies with her. He loved kids, but had given up the dream of having them. For the first time in his life, he regretted having it done.

He’d settle for being a stepdad to her kids. He could do that. Their kids wouldn’t carry his genes, but he'd have them and Ella for the rest of his life.

Chapter Nine

Ella's car rolled into a parking space a few feet from the back entrance of The Cowboy Corral. Smoke rose from the edges of the hood. The glow of the headlights interrupted a couple in a passionate kiss. A loud, whistling crack rattled the car. Ella gripped the steering wheel with all the strength she had left. The lights died. The engine shook, sputtered, and took its last breath. She moved her foot to the brake, but the wheels stopped spinning. The car had found a place to rest. Shifting the gear to Park seemed fruitless, but she did it anyway.

Ella climbed out of the car and stared at the vehicle that should have lasted another four years. The damn thing seemed to laugh at her. One more "fuck you" in a day chock-full of them. She turned away from the car and everything it symbolized. *Two drinks with the girls and then I'll deal with the car.*

Dinner plans developed into after-dinner drinks that turned into an attempt to make it there before they gave up on her and left. Maddie and Josie insisted they weren't leaving until she arrived. There was a slim chance Maddie and Josie had stayed even though she arrived hours late.

She walked with an acid-filled gut of insecurity into Cade's bar. If she hadn't promised Maddie she'd be there, she wouldn't have come, not after the shitty day she had, not after the week from hell.

She had cried on the phone to more customer relations people at the utility company than she could count before they agreed to turn her power on in her house today. She and the boys had been living without utilities for a week. After paying late fees, and penalties, she still owed more than she thought she'd ever be able to repay without taking out a personal loan or selling her house. Out of options, she had to put the house on the market and sell it quickly.

She couldn't get a damn break, but her neighbor in the house next door could. Out of nowhere, they won some kind of random gift of one year of free utilities earlier that week. She needed a freaking random gift of free utilities, not her wealthy neighbors.

She weaved through the dense crowd of couples to the bathroom. She was ready to let down her hair, and reapply the makeup she cried off in the car on the way here. She wanted a drink of whiskey for the first time in a long time, and tonight of all nights she deserved to indulge in one or two.

A tall blonde swung open the door and headed straight for the bathroom stall.

"Thank God it doesn't smell bad in here anymore."

"Yeah," Ella said. "I heard they had some issues with the cleaning service."

She turned on the cold water and splashed her face. *Yep, I'm having a drink tonight.* She had enough cash for two drinks and a decent tip for the bartender. She hadn't seen her friends at any of the tables, but they were probably on the dance floor having fun with the way the place was hopping. The girls wouldn't have left her tonight when they insisted she come out. At least she hoped not.

"Have you seen the owner?" the woman asked.

"Nope." She hadn't spoken to Cade since he dropped her off at Maddie's Tuesday morning, not that she had time to talk with work keeping her busy. Hearing his voice while he was out of town would have been nice instead of the few sterile texts she received. Texts that clearly stated he only wanted her in the friend category which screwed her in more ways than her heart. She never should have got sucked into that weekend with him.

She grabbed two paper towels from the dispenser and patted her face dry. She opened up her black leather purse, pulled out some essentials, and began applying makeup.

The toilet flushed and the blonde walked out as Ella finished putting on mascara.

"Mrs. Kellen?" Ella asked.

The woman tilted her head and took a closer look at Ella.

"Mrs. Winthrop?"

"Yes," she said. "You can call me Ella. How are you?"

She didn't want to talk, but she didn't want to be impolite to Kyle and Jason's high school social studies teacher. Her boys had been rude enough to her the first day of school and were still paying for it.

Mrs. Kellen sighed.

"Ella, I heard Kyle has been accepted into a few colleges, but he's failing my class. If he doesn't pass my class, he won't graduate. College will be lost to him."

Ella tucked the mascara into her purse.

"He's been studying for finals." Not that it mattered. The woman had it in for her boys.

"He needs to have a serious turnaround for the final, or I'll call and tell the colleges that accepted him about his attitude. Both your boys don't respect me. I know they're smart, but they're never going to get a job, or be successful if they keep treating everyone as if they're stupid. They are barely passing with D's, and they think they're more intelligent than everyone else."

The woman turned on the water and washed her beautiful, French manicured hands.

"I would hate to have to do something so drastic as to fail both of them, but they need to find a more appropriate way to treat their superiors, or life will be a challenge for them. Better they learn now…"

Ella clenched her jaw and politely listened. She seethed as Mrs. Kellen babbled on and on about the boys' lack of social and writing skills. Her boys had aced all the dual credit courses available to them. Mrs. Kellen's class meant nothing to their ability to get into the college of their choice.

The woman was an idiot. Kyle and Jason could study for an hour and get an A on the final exam, if the damn things were graded without bias. Her boys *were* smarter than everyone else. But Mrs. Kellen was right about one thing. In an academic setting, they treated everyone else around them as if they were dumber than dirt, probably because, compared to them, they were.

"I'm sorry to interrupt, Mrs. Kellen, but—"

"—I know it must be hard to hear your sons have problems that will stop them from being successful in life." Mrs. Kellen reached across the counter, shoving her large, diamond engagement and wedding rings in

Ella's face on the way to grabbing a paper towel from the dispenser. "It must be hard to hear your sons might not graduate because they aren't smart enough to pass my class."

She turned from Ella, dismissing her. "Jason is putting forth a hair more effort, but he's got a borderline D in my class too." She flipped her hair and turned her head back to Ella with a big smile on her face.

"If I think for one minute Kyle and Jason are cheating, they'll both be expelled. The only job they'll be able to get is as a massage therapist." She opened the door and held it.

Ella squared her shoulders. She crossed the threshold with her head held high and wished she wore something nicer than a blue-cotton T-shirt and baggy, work khakis.

Why did Cade have to rip off her clothes last weekend and ruin everything Josie bought her? It was pretty great being wanted like that, but she'd have enjoyed wearing an entire outfit that fit for this encounter. Mrs. Kellen and her cute little pink-and-silver-threaded western shirt, knee-length jeans skirt, and cowboy boots, trampled on Ella's last nerve talking bullshit about Kyle and Jason. Then, the crack about massage therapy being a lesser occupation. *Bitch.* There was nothing *less* about being a massage therapist. She healed people.

"My boys don't cheat. They're honest." She walked out into the hallway toward the crowd, standing as tall as her sneakers would allow her. Damn, Mrs. Kellen was tall. She should have thrown some freaking heels into her car this morning. Screw the leg pain. She wanted to glare at the blonde bitch, but she had to be polite. She didn't want to make any more waves at the school. With a miracle, Mrs. Kellen would pass her boys, and the woman would be a distant memory.

"Have a nice evening, *Ella*." Mrs. Kellen sashayed over to a table near the dance floor where a good-looking man waited for her. A beautiful couple. *Ugh.*

"You too," Ella mumbled.

Mr. Kellen kissed Mrs. Kellen on the lips and pulled her onto the dance floor to the sounds of an old-time, country ballad.

Ella's chest constricted around her heart. Being around people in love today sucked. She barely kept it together as it was. Why did Josie make plans for them to meet at Cade's bar on couples' night? What was the perky, ex-cheerleader thinking?

She surveyed the crowd for her friends. They hadn't waited for her. They hadn't called or texted to tell her they left. Tonight was a mistake, and she hadn't even had a drink. She never should have walked through those rustic, bar doors.

Instead of calling for a ride home, she strutted straight to the bar for the two drinks she shouldn't have. She shoved her way between two overweight men in western shirts and jeans and called out to the busy bartender for a shot of Irish whiskey. Two drinks—one for her, and one for Greg—and she would go home.

The handsome, mocha skinned bartender placed a shot of whiskey in front of her while the man to her right paid for it.

Ella slid onto the vacant bar stool between two men. "Thanks"

She downed the whiskey and exhaled. Smooth.

Warm. Numbing. Just what she needed. She raised her hand and caught the eye of the bartender. She pointed to her glass and dug through her purse for cash.

"I've got it." The man to her right in the blue-and-white-striped western shirt added it to his tab.

The bartender needed help but handled the rowdy crowd well. He took his time getting back to her side of the bar, but she had nowhere else to be. She'd call someone to pick her up after another drink or two. The odds of her car starting again was slim, very slim.

The bartender easily hustled from one patron to another, reminding her of the days she used to bartend at her father's Irish pub before she married Greg. She'd been underage, but her drunken father hadn't cared and neither had anyone else in her small town. Working as a bartender, she'd found a taste for whiskey—good whiskey. Her husband had enjoyed whiskey too. Cade always smelled like whiskey, although it had to be something in his cologne, because he kept the scent all weekend, yet only drank water.

Finally, the bartender served her side of the bar and poured whiskey into her shot glass and the man's beside her.

"Thanks." She looked up at the handsome bartender without a name tag. "Is it always this busy?"

He genuinely grinned for the first time since she sat down. "Yes, but normally two of us are behind the bar. Tonight, I'm on my own."

She nodded. "You're doing a great job."

"Thanks." He picked up a shaker and filled the next order.

She raised her glass. *This one's for you, Greg. I'll always love you.*

The whiskey caressed her tongue as it slid down her throat, leaving her with the taste and feel of days long ago. *Greg*. And a weekend not so long ago. *Cade*.

She exhaled. She liked Cade more than she should. After their weekend, she wanted things she hadn't wanted since Greg and everything good in her life seemed to die. She called out for one more drink as another country ballad blasted over the speaker system.

She glanced around. Couples her age held each other on the dance floor and swayed to the rhythm of the music. If Greg hadn't died, she would be one of those women hanging onto their husbands with a promise of a memorable evening at home. She wanted her heart to go numb for a little while so the pangs of missing him wouldn't hurt so much. So she wouldn't miss Cade, either. But she could still feel, and she didn't have enough money to stop her heart from aching. Damn Cade for awakening her heart.

The bartender set down the shot and looked her in the eyes. "You okay?"

"Yeah." She raised her gaze to his seemingly concerned hazel eyes. *No, I'm not. I miss my husband.*

Greg would have taken care of Kyle's bitchy history teacher with one look. She just took whatever someone threw at her. She had children and a job to protect. She couldn't make any waves in any social circle, or she might end up losing her spa. Her business was the only thing keeping things afloat.

When she eventually made it home, she had plenty to do before her head hit the pillow. Make more specialty blends for the large order that came in over the website Kyle set up. Develop more scents for her oils. Laundry. Dishes. The list never ended. She had to suck up her heartache and get back to reality. She raised the shot glass in her hand to her lips. Last one.

"Greg, I tried," she whispered, then gulped the top-shelf whiskey down.

The house is all I have left of you, and I have no other choice but to sell.

She was drowning in debt. She'd finished paying off the final medical payment from Greg's cancer, but her clients started bouncing checks left and right. The mortgage on the house was small, but the taxes were too high. The second mortgage was coming due. Her car was on the fritz. She had to sell her house but that could take months.

Maybe she'd have another drink after all. She hadn't spent any of her money. She didn't want to go home and deal with reality quite yet. One more drink. No more. Just a little relief from the pain.

"Another for the lady," the man on the right said, making the decision to stay easy.

The bartender nodded in acknowledgement but worked the opposite side of the counter, mixing drinks and entertaining as the crowd thinned.

One boot-scooting song after another bled into the background as one last drink turned into four. The deejay transitioned the music to the old, heartbreaking, country ballads Greg had introduced her to. The songs they had danced to in the backyard after the kids were tucked in bed.

She looked over her shoulder at the couples on the dance floor and sought out the blonde bitch of a teacher. Mrs. Kellen clung to her husband, happily in love, without a care in the world.

I used to dance like that with Greg. I'd get lost in

his world, in his love. Her heart seemed to stop working. A thick lump formed in her throat. Moisture filled her eyes.

She wanted to be in the safety of his arms again. She wanted him to be alive, and healthy, and the last seven years to be one bad nightmare, not her life.

The dance floor emptied as the tone of the music changed from sweet, love songs to rocking country. She held out her shot glass for another refill. The bartender poured amber liquid into her glass.

The couples on the dance floor left for the night. She needed to leave with them. She couldn't remember how many drinks she had, but it hadn't been enough because her heart still bled for the man she'd lost. She downed the shot her new friend paid for and held her glass out to the bartender. Being numb would give her some peace. She wouldn't get sloppy drunk, just drunk enough for a reprieve from the memories.

One more drink and she might finally be free from the void, the loneliness haunting her heart and soul.

"This is it, darlin'," the bartender said. "Hand over your keys and see me for a cab later."

"I've got a friend picking me up." She exchanged her keys for another shot. After the night ended she wouldn't drink like this again for another year or two.

With no money for a cab and her needing-an-overhaul car—she would never cry over the damn thing again—calling Maddie for a ride became her only option. Maybe she'd get Kyle and Jason a manual and parts to repair it. Jiggling wires and praying for it to start wasn't the answer long-term. It got her here. She might not have wanted the company she had, but it was better than being alone.

"What time is it?"

"Midnight," the bartender said. "Your man didn't show?"

"My friends probably left a while ago. I was late."

Fate was against her. Cade wasn't here, either. His flight was supposed to be in this evening. She'd texted him her plans to meet Maddie and Josie at his bar. He probably came and left too unwilling to wait for her. Or he wasn't interested in seeing her. He probably forgot all about her. Or he had planned on meeting her here for the "friend talk," not that he owed her anything after their weekend. They hadn't made any promises. They had talked about seeing each other when he got back, but those lame texts didn't mention getting together this weekend or anything resembling concrete plans for a future date.

She sipped the comforting whiskey. Warmth bloomed inside her belly, unraveling the knots of stress from the miserable day. She would call Maddie for a ride after one more drink.

"Did you just get a divorce?" the man to the right asked.

"No." She made quick eye contact with the bartender. She pointed to her shot glass and hoped for another refill before he truly cut her off.

The bartender nodded.

"Are you a regular?" the man who bought most of her drinks asked.

She reached into her purse and pulled out her cell. "No." She dialed Maddie and searched for cash to pay the bartender. She placed the bills on the counter, but the man next to her handed back the money.

"I've got it," he said. "Have another one with me."

"Thanks, but this is my—"

"Ella, where are you?" Maddie asked.

"I'm at the bar you're supposed to be at." She boldly drank the last shot of the night.

"You're drunk," Maddie said. "What happened?"

"I'm not drunk, yet. I'm selling my house, Maddie. My realtor thinks it will go quickly. She's checking on comps, and I need a ride home. I need someone to tow my car home too. It's acting up."

"Mike is hanging with Mark at Josie's. I'll call him," Maddie said. "Stay put. How much have you had to drink?"

"Not as much as I'd like." She looked at her filled glass and smiled. *So much for not having another.* "I haven't been here long." Long enough to get her keys taken away, not that she would even consider driving home after having more than one drink. She wouldn't.

The man next to her lifted his vodka shot, tapped her glass, and they drank together.

She listened as Maddie called Josie with her home phone and got back on the cell phone with her.

"The guys had a little too much tonight too. Crap, Ella, why were you so late?"

"I took two evening walk-in appointments, car trouble, utilities, the list goes on and on. Did I tell you my neighbor won some kind of contest and got free utilities for a year? Apparently she came home, and a note was posted to her door Monday afternoon from a CDJ Enterprises telling her all her utilities were prepaid for a full year. Do you believe that? I have the shittiest luck."

"Wait, who got a year's worth of utilities prepaid?" Maddie asked.

"My neighbors. You know the yuppies from Chicago." Ella turned and winked at her drinking buddy. He didn't look half bad.

She stared more intently at the man. *I have to be at the apex of drunk, if my drinking partner is suddenly semi-appealing.* She really needed to stop drinking and find a ride home. With her glass magically filled again, she paused from talking with Maddie and downed another shot.

"They're great neighbors as long as you don't have to talk to them. I've got to go, Maddie. I'll call somebody else. I'm fine. Feeling good for a change. Sorry about tonight."

"Call Cade. He'll come and get you."

"No." She swiveled around in her stool. She had entirely too much to drink, which only led to crying after the numbness wore off. If Cade had wanted to see her, he would have been here. Anyway, she didn't want her crappy circumstances touching him.

She caught the side view of a handsome blond walking through the door. "Well, I really must be drunk because I'm seeing Greg's ghost again." She laughed languidly. "It's the healthy ghost, Maddie."

"Are you really at Cowboy Corral. Or are you at Maggie's Pub?" Maddie asked. "I'll come get you."

"No, Maddie. I'm good." She hopped off the barstool and traveled through the dwindling maze of people toward him. She hadn't been to Maggie's Irish Pub and Grill, the last place she overindulged, for three years. She and Greg went there every Friday night until he got too sick to go. The last place she would step into today was that place. It hurt too much to think about the day of his funeral, and she didn't want to hurt or think anymore.

"I wish you were here. The similarity…" The closer she moved to him, the more he resembled Greg.

"Maddie, I'll be fine. I've got to be hallucinating, but I don't want to wake up. Not after the day I've had. I'll call Kyle and Jason after the ghost leaves. Don't worry. He always leaves when I touch him." She hung up and dropped the phone into her purse.

"Ella," Greg's ghost said.

"I've missed you," she said. "Are you really here?"

"I'm here," he said.

"Kiss me," she whispered. "Kiss me like you never left. Kiss me like you've missed me as much as I've missed you." She closed her eyes and waited for all of it to end like it always did when they touched.

His solid lips met hers. Electricity crackled between them. He pulled her against him and guided her out the door to a waiting black limousine.

He opened the back of the car and helped her inside.

"I've missed you so much," she whispered. "Are you really here?"

"I'm here." He grinned. "I'm here, and I'm never leaving again."

"Make love to me," she murmured.

"Are you sure?" The strong and controlling hands holding hers were exactly like her dreams, but this dream seemed more real. With any luck, she wasn't having a one-night stand with the semi-cute man buying her drinks who kept looking better and better as the night wore on. That wouldn't work.

The man she held couldn't be her drinking partner. He was dark-haired and overweight, not blond and athletic with muscles upon muscles.

"I'm sure," she said breathlessly.

Her dream ghost gently and carefully lifted her shirt and kissed each nipple over the last surviving bra Josie bought her. He unsnapped the front clasp and pushed the delicate lace cups to the side.

"I've wanted this for so long," he whispered.

His lips circled her breast agonizingly slow.

She kicked off her sneakers and tried to undress as quickly as possible to get an orgasm before he vanished, and she awoke alone again.

"Please hurry." She pushed up his black tee as he pulled down her pants and panties in one quick tug. *Why am I still wearing baggy pants? I should be wearing something sexy. One of his white dress shirts and nothing else.*

She unbuttoned his jeans as he took over. He lifted his shirt over his head showing off his perfectly developed symmetrical chest and abs.

"I love you," she said.

"I love you, Ella. I always have," he whispered into her ear.

She spread her legs. "Now. Please, now. I need you so much. I need to feel you inside me." She needed to be taken care of, and Greg had always done that for her, in real life and in her dreams. She didn't have to think about money or having enough groceries or hocking the last of the jewelry he bought for her. She could trust he would take care of her financially, and he had until he…

He pulled her legs up around his waist and produced a condom. He ripped it open and slid it on. She had safe-sex-Greg in her dreams tonight? Strange.

But she liked the safe-sex-Greg ghost.

"I love you, Ella. I love you." Slow and steady, he made vanilla love to her like he had their entire marriage.

She moved naturally against him. His familiar body rose and fell in all the right ways to make her orgasm. He fit her better than she remembered.

He drew out her juices, coating her inner thighs with liquid desire, in every masterful retreat.

The scent of fresh, summer lemon groves seemed to surround her, taking her back to the days in Florida when he was healthy. She licked his neck and tasted him—salty man with no metallic chemicals burning her tongue. She was in a heavenly dream because he wasn't there no matter how real he felt making love to her. He'd died three years ago that day.

Chapter Ten

The rich spicy scent of Ella's favorite Irish whiskey spread across his senses with each word she spoke. Almost twenty years Garrett had waited for her, for another taste of her mouth, her lips, her tongue. The sensual kiss they shared on her eighteenth birthday had started their journey of love. The kiss she welcomed him with at the Cowboy Corral kept the intensity of its original fire. *You were never Greg's. You were mine. Always mine.*

His lips met hers as the limo hit a pothole and bounced them with the perfect amount of force to bring them closer together. Electricity skittered over his skin as he controlled every movement and relished each moment of their bodies and souls coming together as one.

I'm never letting you go.

"I'm so close," she whispered in a lazy, sexy rasp.

Garrett groaned as he buried his cock deep into her pussy. "Come for me."

Making love to her all night long until they passed out from exhaustion wouldn't sate the decades of desire he'd held back from acting on because she married the wrong brother.

"I love you." She came apart around him. Her pussy clamped down in strong, pulsing waves around his cock.

"I love you." He'd never loved vanilla sex, but this was different. This was a beginning. This held a promise of forever. He shuddered. His heart opened up a new place for her, a place he'd kept closed until now.

He would show her his kinky side soon. He would help her discover her true sexuality, the one she suppressed to be with Greg. The one she should have enjoyed all these years.

"Don't leave me again." A relaxed sigh came from her mouth as she fell asleep under him.

He wasn't leaving ever again. He was in her life to stay for good. She wasn't married to his twin anymore. No one stood in his way. No competition. No promises to anyone else. Nothing holding them back from being together. And, she missed him, nearly attacked him when they saw each other. He'd never had a better homecoming in his life.

He held onto the base of the condom as he withdrew from her. He knotted the top and dropped it into a small plastic bag on the floor. Once his test results were posted in his patient portal—hopefully tonight—condoms would be a thing of the past.

With a smile on his face, he pulled another condom from the box under the seat, in case she woke up hungry for him. He'd waited to have her for years. Now she was his.

A phone rang from inside her purse. He dug through her purse and looked at the screen. *Cade Jackson. Huh?* He'd have to check the guy out. Clients shouldn't call after midnight.

"Hello?" He answered her phone.

"Is Ella there?" the man asked.

"She's not available. Who are you?"

"I'm her boyfriend," the man said. "Who are you?"

What the fuck? When did she get a boyfriend? Colleen hadn't mentioned any men in her life. "You're no longer her boyfriend. She's mine." He nearly hissed at the man. He waited too long for her, and now this guy thought he could take her away.

He gazed down at his beautiful Ella. No one was taking her from him. He kissed her dreamy lips. "Delete her number."

"Who are you, and where is Ella?" The man had the nerve to demand answers.

"I'm Garrett. Ella is sleeping with my cock buried in her pussy." *That will end the conversation and her relationship with this guy. Mission accomplished.*

"Grr." She slurred loudly enough for the asshole to hear. "Make luuuv to meee."

"She's drunk, Garrett. She's very, very drunk. I got a call to pick her up. I am at the bar holding her keys, and she's gone with some blond guy with blue eyes. Is that you?"

"She's with me, and she knows exactly what she's doing. If you were her boyfriend, you would have been with her, not letting her get drunk alone at a bar while she sat unprotected surrounded by other men." *Why am I explaining myself to this guy? I don't have to explain shit. Ella wouldn't choose anyone over me, especially some idiot who hadn't cared enough to go out with her.*

"I'm sorry," she mumbled. "I tried to hold onto everything, but it's all falling apart."

"Ella," the man shouted. "Get out of—"

Garrett hung up. He'd find out exactly who the man was, and what kind of relationship she had with him later. He turned her phone off. *No more interruptions.*

"Ella? How many drinks have you had?" The Ella he knew could drink him under the table which was no small feat.

Her eyelids lifted a little, just enough to see the glassy sheen of drunkenness in her beautiful blue eyes. "L-luuuvvv y-you."

Her lids slid closed. Soft, steady inhales and exhales left her lips.

Shit, she was drunk. Really drunk, but she wasn't before they made love. She was coherent and all over him. Whatever she had must have started with whiskey and evolved into shots of something just as potent, and a lot of them in a short period of time. "Derek, take us to her place, and park in the garage," Garrett said to his best friend and life partner. "Make sure we're not followed."

"Yes, sir," Derek said.

Garrett lifted her up and sat down on the seat with her head on his lap. "I want pictures of us together when she sobers up, if she is willing."

She moaned as she shifted and faced his rising cock.

"I've got it covered," Derek said. "No one is following us, and the latest intel on the boys states that they are asleep in bed."

"Thanks," Garrett said. "I'm not letting her go this time."

He outlined the curves of her breast, licked his fingers, and drew spirals down to her navel. He always loved her belly. Even pregnant her belly was beautiful. He'd wanted her to pierce her navel, but Greg didn't like body piercings. Greg was boring. No threesomes.

No piercings. No tattoos. No ropes or handcuffs. No toys. They all could have been so happy together if Greg hadn't kept her all to himself. Greg didn't share. Ever.

She nuzzled his erection and mumbled something while she lay half-asleep and half-awake. "Make love to me again."

"Hang on, baby. We're home."

The limo stopped.

Garrett shifted her around and into his arms. He stealthily walked into the house he'd helped build with his brother and headed straight to her bedroom.

With a professional digital camera and tripod, Derek entered the pastel-yellow bedroom a few minutes later. He turned on the lamp on the maple dresser Garrett and Greg made to match the rest of the bedroom furniture, most of which was missing.

"Test results are all clear, as usual," Derek said. "Helps that we practice safe sex. Give me a minute, and I'll set up."

"Ella, babe? Can Derek take some sexy pictures of us?" He would ask her again when she sobered up. He needed to make sure she wanted the intimacy of naked pictures with him.

He placed her on the metal bed and settled next to her on the white lace sheets. *Cheap sheets on a cheaper bed? Why? The one Greg made you was beautiful and cost a fortune…son of a bitch… You sold it…*

"I'll do anything with you, Garrett," she mumbled.

Garrett slid her onto his chest until she straddled him. "We'll get the pictures later. Right now, sleep." He gently rubbed her back and lulled her into dreamland.

He gazed over at Derek extending the legs on the tripod. "I can't believe she's passed out. She can handle more liquor than either Greg or I ever could. How much do you think she had?"

"I don't know. I've never seen her drunk, have you?" Derek asked.

The evening when the twins turned three, she'd had a little too much to drink and confessed wishing Greg was more experimental sexually. She had been far from drunk, but her lips loosened up and spilled some of her naughty fantasies the night before he went back to his military unit.

He confessed to asking his brother to let him join them in bed, to be a third in an alternative relationship. He wanted Ella so badly, he had suggested every possible alternative scenario to share Ella to Greg, but his brother wouldn't even consider it. His brother was convinced she would be appalled at the suggestion of a ménage or a foursome partnership that included Derek. Garrett knew different. Ella had the spirit of an adventurer. Greg stifled her need to explore anything outside of his conservative world.

"Not like tonight. I tried getting her drunk one night when Greg was out of town, but she won all the drinking games and tucked *me* into bed. I never lost a drinking game to anyone before, and she beat me straight up."

"Something must have happened. This isn't like her." Derek tightened his camera onto the tripod and walked to the side of the bed.

Ella mumbled something and reached out to him. She hooked her fingers into his waistband. Derek stepped forward and her hand grazed his cock as it fell limp to the mattress.

"She was always adventurous." Derek waggled his brows and winked at him. "Remember the nudes I took of her when she was pregnant with the twins?"

He remembered. "They were beautiful." He was furious when his brother threw a fit over them and burned the portraits she hung up in the master bedroom as a birthday present. Greg was too traditional for her. Now she could spread her wings and fly. She would explore sex with him and Derek, and document their journey along the way.

Garrett caressed along the curves of her back and gazed at the ceiling. "The chandelier I bought her is gone."

"Yeah." Derek covered Garrett's hand at Ella's back. "She's walked a tough road, but she has us now."

Garrett nodded. "Do you think my parents took it, or did she have to sell it?"

Ella sighed and snuggled against him.

"Either way it's gone." Derek squeezed his hand. "We'll take care of her. Once Colleen tells Ella her secret, Ella will need us even more than she does now."

Garrett nodded. *I hope you're right.*

Chapter Eleven

Ella's brain pounded against its skull reminding her why she didn't drink. Her tongue scraped like sandpaper against the inside of her dry mouth. Whiskey was never the answer. Although, seeing, and making love to Greg in her dreams was a worthy side effect. The way his body gently and carefully glided against hers contrasted with Cade's rough and tumble bedroom acrobatics.

Cade, her one-weekend stand she thought might be more, talked dirty and took charge. Her Greg didn't speak much, but made love to her with tenderness even when they were in a hurry.

Hot lips kissed the back of her neck. "Are you awake?"

She rolled over and looked into the deep blue eyes of her healthy dream husband.

"No, and I don't want to be." She didn't care about her dry mouth and whiskey morning breath. She kissed his smooth lips. "Make love to me, then I'll wake up." Her head hurt, but she wanted another happy dream with her husband. He stayed solid and healthy. It had been so long since she'd dreamed of him strong and powerful. *I don't want to let you go.*

He groaned as she slid her leg over the fine blond hair of his thigh.

She was bold in her dreams when she made love

with Greg. And even bolder when she dreamed of making love to kinky Garrett. But Cade made her orgasm without even touching her in her fantasies.

She closed her palms over Greg's cock and stroked. He thrust into her hand and pumped up and down. Beads of cum dripped over the top. Her fingers dipped into the sticky liquid. "I want you inside me. I want this." She lifted her fingers to her mouth and licked. *Salty man. Mmm.*

"Yes," he whispered. "Put me inside you."

She guided his cock to her wet center. *I want to remember this forever. Please don't vanish.* She rolled her hips, rubbed the head of his cock up and down her slit, and nearly orgasmed as she thought of making a baby with him. She swiveled her hips as his cock touched her clit.

His lids fell over the beautiful blue in his eyes.

She reached between them and grew more confident. She curled her fingers around his cock, and with her other hand she spread her folds apart with her fingers. "Feels so good."

Round and round she moved her hips as she held his cock in place. Her clit throbbed and swelled. "Oh, God. Oh, God."

"Yeah, Ella. Do it. Come."

Her clit swelled and buzzed with electricity. *I'm going to come.*

She arched her spine, dropped her head back, and closed her eyes. Her legs shook as her pussy contracted around a void. She needed him inside her, coming with her. *God, I need you to stay.*

She bit her bottom lip, moved his cock to her center, and gasped as he thrust up. He grabbed her leg and held her as he flipped them over.

"I've needed this for so long, and now I've got you forever." On top of her, he pulled out and dove back inside her pussy and filled her up with his incredible length. In and out. He ground against her clit.

Over and over, he built her up until her entire body thrummed with need.

"Come, now." He grunted as he powered into her. Hot cum spurted inside her.

"Yes," she screamed as she came apart in his arms. Memories of making their children rushed forward into her aching mind. So many years of love. "Please don't go." She clung to him, tears of love fell from her eyes knowing at any moment he would be gone. Reality would come crashing back. The dream would end.

"Babe." He dried her tears. "I'm not going anywhere. I'm here for good."

Her heart stopped beating. Greg never called her babe. The only one who ever called her by that endearment was…

"Oh my God." She wiggled to get out from under his body. *Not a dream. Not a dream.* "Oh, my God. Oh, my God."

He held her tight. "Babe, it's me. I'm here. Everything is going to be okay."

She gasped and continued to squirm. "You're real. Oh, my God. You're Garrett. You're Garrett."

"Shhh," he said softly like he was calming a wild animal.

She felt like a wild animal, cornered and freaked out.

"It's me, babe. Everything is going to be fine now that we're together."

"Oh, my God." They were in her bedroom naked under her favorite sheets. "This isn't happening. We had sex. Oh, my God."

They had a lot of sex. They'd had so much sex she was sore, and she kept asking for more. Shit. Derek took pictures of them having sex.

"Derek. Derek is here." Derek always traveled with Garrett when he visited but last night… Last night was a dream. She'd gotten crazy with Garrett. She talked dirty to Derek. She talked about fucking both of them. It was supposed to be a dream. "This is not happening." *You're supposed to be Greg's ghost. I damn near attacked you at the bar. The bar.*

She sucked in a breath. *It was all real. Fuck.* "I've got to get up. I've got to go to work. I need some aspirin. I need a coke, and, oh, hell, I need my car and office keys. I need a shower. Crap. You don't look like you. You look…" *like Greg.*

"Where the heck is your goatee? Where are your war scars? I don't remember seeing them last night." She didn't remember every detail, but the orgasms—she couldn't get those out of her head. The way they fit so perfectly together. So familiar. So right.

She stopped wiggling under him. The pulsing cock shoved deep inside her hardened.

"I haven't worn a goatee in seven years, and the scars are there, Ella. You licked over each and every one of them last night," he said with a smug grin. "I loved it."

She swallowed hard. The scar on his inner thigh. She had licked the full length of it as she traveled to his balls. He'd ordered her to suck, and she had. She followed every sexy command.

"You knew it was me. You called me by my name. You damn near tackled me at the bar. It was the best homecoming I've ever had. The way your hands…" He continued recounting one of the more recent moments they'd had together.

She shuddered but gathered herself together. He'd been gone. She thought he might even be dead, assumed he was. "Where have you been all these years?" *Didn't have time to make it to your only brother's funeral? Didn't have time to leave any contact information? Let me know you weren't dead?*

She pushed at him, so angry with herself at getting so darn drunk. How could she be so stupid? So irresponsible? She should have thought it could be him, but it had been a lifetime since she'd seen him. Seven. Long. Years. With. No. Word.

"Get off me." She didn't want to like the way he felt on top of her. "I have a full schedule today. I don't have time for this. You're not showing up out of nowhere and shocking the shit out of my boys." *Like you did me.*

He rolled off her, but kept his body glued to her side.

"I found out about Greg very recently, and I immediately asked for a transfer to Memphis. There were some issues. I retired and partnered with a company here. My personal belongings should arrive today. I planned on talking last night, but you had other plans for the evening. Great plans."

She scrambled off the bed. "Get out, Garrett. He's been dead three years, and you're telling me you didn't know?"

He had to have known. His parents must have told

him how they screwed her as soon as Greg told them he was dying. The lengths they went to change Greg's will, change the names on every legal document, every vacation home, all the bank accounts… The things she learned about what she thought had been an insignificant word "or" in Greg or Ella. One of them could sell a house without the other's signature. One of them could empty the bank accounts without the other's signature. One of them could transfer, sell, give away… No legal recourse.

She glanced up at the empty space on the ceiling where the chandelier Garrett bought her for her thirtieth birthday used to hang. His greedy parents stole the precious gift while she drank away her sorrows at Maggie's Pub after Greg's funeral. They manipulated Greg out of almost all the money he'd saved. Screwing her kids from a worry-free future, acting like loving grandparents while Greg lay dying was bad enough, but sending a team of movers to strip the interior of the house while her life bottomed out… If Maddie and Josie hadn't stopped by to check on her, the house would have been emptied.

She covered her chest with her hands and ran around the bed to the bathroom, glaring at him. He looked good too good. Everything last night and this morning had been her idea. Damn. It all originated from her. Double damn.

He followed on her heels. He moved too fast, held too much confidence. And his touch proved too irresistible. "Babe, I didn't know about Greg."

She turned on the shower and took a quick look at the clock above the French doors to her bedroom. *Five a.m.*

"You have to leave now. The boys can't see you like this. They'll be up soon." The loud spray of the water didn't help the drum solo pounding her brain into a new kind of hell. She needed caffeine, and aspirin pronto. "Colleen is coming home this week."

She turned and faced him. Staring straight into his summer-blue eyes, she attempted to hide her embarrassment, desire, and anger. She opened her mouth and then shut it.

Garrett Winthrop, the man she'd been in love with for her entire marriage, stood in her house acting like her husband. She made love to him but couldn't remember all the details. She swore if he ever came back for her, she would memorize every kiss, every glance, every caress, but she didn't. She only recalled the highlights. The moment in the bar when they kissed and electricity shot through her, rocketing her desire for him into outer space…

"I want to see the boys. I'm going to see my nephews."

"Not right now. You have no idea the hell we went through. Look at yourself. You look exactly like Greg. You look so much like him I had sex with you."

"You called me by name. So, babe, don't try and act all angry like you didn't know it was me." Garrett's lips tightened into a suppressed grin, seemingly amused.

Part of her knew she made love to him. He was too solid to be a dream. Greg never would have made love to her in a limo, but Garrett would. Garrett did.

"I need to prepare the boys and Colleen before you show up. It's shocking to see you." She paused, debating on how to proceed. She crossed her hands over her chest. She had to appear livid and strong while remaining calm, or he wouldn't listen to her. He'd do whatever he wanted like he always had.

"Listen, you can't walk back into our lives acting as if you never left and everything is perfect. Jeez, Garrett, wait a few days, and grow a beard or something. Let your hair grow out. Just don't screw up my kids' heads showing up here looking exactly like their father."

She had buried Garrett's memory along with Greg's body three years ago. She hadn't been prepared for his sudden resurrection. Her children... *God, how will they react?*

"They'll be fine. They know we look alike. Identical twins look exactly alike. Your boys *understand* that, being a set of *identical* twins themselves. They'll make sense of why I left, after I talk to them. You will too."

He followed her into the shower. He closed the glass door behind him and blocked her exit. "I never thought in a million years Greg would die before me. It never crossed my mind he could. He had you and the kids. He had a safe career while I didn't." He ran his hands through his thick, blond hair just like Greg used to. "When I found out he was gone, my first thought was of getting to you and the kids."

She turned into the spray of water and let it fall over her head. Wet layers of her brown hair covered her face allowing her to hide from his very real presence.

"Please, Garrett," she said softly. "If you care anything about the kids, leave. Let me prepare them. Don't come over until ten tonight. I need to go to work, and I have a full day. I'll decide what I'm going to say to them later. You figure out what kind of bullshit tale you're going to spin about why you came back."

Was it bullshit? Could she trust him like she used to? He did leave under the worst of circumstances. She had contemplated taking the kids and running away with Garrett. But Greg needed her. It wasn't Greg's fault for acting on impulses he'd never had before.

The tumor that ate away at his brain had taken his logical mind and scrambled it. Paranoia, rage, memory loss, jealousy, and hallucinations became more prevalent as his illness progressed. But Garrett didn't know about any of it. He left without hearing her out. He probably thought he'd heard her excuses for staying a thousand times, but the incident which led him to disappear had been different. Greg had never been violent before that day.

Once Garrett was gone, Greg's manic episodes increased. The doctors. Nurses. Medications. The money. All the wealth Greg accumulated to support her and the kids trickled out the door. Greg's parents took advantage and siphoned money from his accounts. The only things remaining were his wedding gift of the house to her and the jewelry he had showered her with over the years. Now the jewelry was almost gone. After she sold the house, there would be nothing left of his gifts of love except the memories.

Garrett's strong arms wrapped around her. His warmth and love tugged at her heart. "I came back for *you* and the kids." His words were clipped and biting in stark contrast to the soft way he held her. "You were always supposed to be mine. Greg got you to the Justice of the Peace before me. We both know you married the wrong brother."

She melted a little against him at the familiarity of his body. Greg had lied to her and pretended to be Garrett when he picked her up. She had thought they were going to buy rings for the ceremony they planned for the next day, but he'd taken her to the wedding chapel.

The wedding had been such a rush, she signed the papers without asking questions and didn't speak up when the preacher called him Greg instead of Garrett. She assumed Garrett was his middle name, not realizing the brothers were *identical* twins. The excitement of love at first sight and a future far away from her parents broke down all rational behavior.

After the ceremony when their lips met for the first time and a slow sizzle worked through her system instead of the out-of-control blaze she'd experienced, Greg confessed his deception. *"We've already signed the papers and made vows to each other,"* Greg had said. *"Give me a chance. I have a stable life, a solid business, and land to build a home for a big family. My brother can't have children, and he's gone for months at a time. If you want a divorce, I'll give you one, but one way or another you'll end up married to me. There is nothing in this world I want more than to be your husband until I take my last breath."*

She had asked for a divorce. Greg drove her to the bar to explain to her parents they were married but would be divorcing within a few days. He never got the chance to explain. Her drunk father saw the plain wedding bands on their fingers and spewed the words she'd heard a million times over the years. *Disrespectful whore. Not worth a damn. Dumb as a box of rocks...*

Greg's gaze had held a softness, an understanding as if he lived her life. His blue eyes opened a portal to his soul and in that split second, they connected.

She tried to speak, but her words fell on deaf ears. Her parents remained like they had for most of her life too drunk, too stubborn, and too lost in their own misery to care about anyone or anything else.

Greg guided her outside and away from the drama. She sat motionless in his car in the parking lot. Her options closed around her. Stay in town and continue riding on the rollercoaster of her parents' alcoholism until she could afford to leave on her own. Take a chance on a future with a man whose eyes spoke to her soul.

As if he stood beside her, his voice from all those years ago whispered in her ears… *"You're none of those things. The instant we met, I knew you were the only one for me.."* He kissed her forehead. *"...You're beautiful, intelligent, loving, and..."* He chuckled. *"Impulsive. I'm not spontaneous at all. Only this one time with you. Whatever happens, stay married or choose to divorce me, you will never step foot in this town or be spoken to in that manner again. I will take care of you whether you want me to or not."* Love grew from his heart's words.

The forgiveness she usually offered her parents, she presented as a wedding gift to him. She had only seen him shed tears twice in her life—that fateful day and the last night they made love. She hadn't intended to marry Greg, but she had, and she didn't regret it. She may have always dreamed of being with Garrett, but Greg had given her three wonderful children and a family. She had Garrett in her life too. The best uncle to her children, a best friend to her and her husband. Even with the jealousy and competition that hung in the air whenever Garrett stayed with them, she had a great life back then.

"I didn't marry the wrong brother. I loved Greg. I loved him more than you'll ever know." The sting of Greg's death filtered through her soul again and manifested a wound she thought healed years ago.

He kissed the back of her head. "I know you loved him," he whispered. "I loved him too." He exhaled a long sigh. "I'll go, but I'm not leaving you again. You're going to marry me, Ella." He pulled her out of the spray of water. Tenderly, he turned her face to his, traced her lips with his thumb, and kissed her chastely. "You need me. The kids need me. I need my family back."

"Go." She withered inside. Their relationship remained too complicated for her to deal with him in the shower first thing in the morning. Not with a hangover and guilt riding her emotions. "Please, just go."

He kissed her again and stepped out of the shower.

She washed off the evidence of the evening as she berated herself for last night's wanton stupidity. She watched him dry off outside the shower door. His old war scars were there along with a few new ones. She must have been beyond drunk not to notice them. Had she called him Greg when she first saw him? She couldn't remember. But she did remember spending part of the night making love to Garrett or dreaming about it. She definitely called out his name in her dreams and apparently while awake.

She turned off the shower and stepped out. *What's*

done is done. Focus on the present.

She picked up the white towel off the hook next to her and dried off as Garrett strode back into the bathroom fully dressed in black from his tee to his boots.

"Some guy named Cade called last night. I told him to get lost."

All the blood quickly drained from her face.

He kissed her cheek.

"I'll be here this evening." His blue eyes seemed to see deeper into her soul than ever before. "You're mine, not his." He kissed her lips and walked out of the room exactly like Greg used to, head held high, shoulders back, with a gait that screamed total confidence.

She couldn't fall apart. The possibility of a relationship with Cade was over, like so much in her life, but Garrett wasn't going to take control. Not anymore. She wasn't the same girl. She didn't want someone to run every aspect of her life like Greg had, like Garrett wanted to. She had been in a sad and weakened place yesterday, but she wasn't weak anymore. She was getting her shit together, and moving forward. She wanted someone to care of her, not rule her.

Time to wake the boys up and get my butt to work. She would figure out a way to get the car from Cade's bar. She'd deal with the fallout from having sex with Garrett later. Her sheets were getting thrown away or maybe burned. The things they did in those sheets while Derek took pictures and watched and talked about joining them.

Mmm. No. I need acetaminophen.

She opened her dresser drawer. *No undies. Damn.*

The last clean, white-cotton discount bra sat alone in her drawer. Whatever cash tips she received, she planned to spend it on a bra and panties, something soft and feminine that actually fit her. It would be a far cry from the designer bra and panties Josie bought her, but a hundred steps up from the utilitarian undergarments she usually chose.

She put on the simple and ugly bra Josie would picket the store over, slipped on a white tee, and threw on an old pair of loose, but not falling-down-her-legs-without-a-belt faded blue jeans.

She woke up the boys, stripped the bed, and popped some acetaminophen. She met the boys at the front door and walked outside to their old red Jeep.

"Look at that." Jason pointed at their neighbor's driveway next door. "They got two top of the line Jeep Wranglers wrapped with big, white, satin bows. How freaking sweet?"

"They arrived yesterday afternoon," Kyle grunted. "I wonder what kind of sweepstakes they're entering."

"Good for them." Ella stared at the vehicles. A chunk of her heart tried to break off into the abyss of failure but she held it together as determination to thrive won out. "In a couple years, I'll buy you any car you want with all the profits I'll be making from the handmade soaps and oils my brilliant sons are helping me sell."

Kyle put his arm around her. "No, Mom. We'll be buying you new cars, and clothes, and taking you on trips with all the money we'll be making in our high-power jobs. Between me and Jay, you'll be set for life."

Jason opened the door to the Jeep their father used to drive to work. "Cade is coming over tonight and bringing pizza."

Ella breathed in.

"When did he mention that?" She would have to call him and apologize for last night and whatever Garrett said. Her chance with Cade was over. No man in their right mind would want to deal with a man like Garrett in her life.

"I talked to him on the phone yesterday while I was at Pappy's. He's been out of town at a conference," Jason said.

"Well, I don't think he's coming over." She climbed into the back seat. "I had a little too much to drink last night, and I think it's over between us."

"I thought you went out with Maddie and Josie, not Cade," Jason said.

"Maddie and Josie were gone by the time I got there. I didn't see Cade last night."

Kyle backed out of the driveway. He slowed in front of the neighbor's house with the shiny blue cars. Lawn workers mulched their already-beautiful flower beds.

"We've got to work on the lawn and flowers," Kyle said. "Colleen mentioned spending most of her time with Sammy Granger down the street. I didn't even know he was back in town. She said that he's out of the military and took a job here with some kind of private-sector, military-defense company."

"I get paid today." Jason changed the subject. "I'll buy the mulch. And Momma Louise bought more flowers than she needed, a lot more. She's been trying to get me to bring them home, so I'll accept if you're okay with that. Pappy told me no matter what happens with you and Cade, he's not giving me up."

Ella exhaled relief a little too loudly. Whatever Garrett had told Cade had to be a relationship breaker. Garrett had a way with words that cut straight to the quick. She didn't want anything to come between Cade's father and Jason. Her drunken mistake shouldn't cost her son his job.

"What happened last night?" Kyle asked.

"Guys, I had a really bad day and evening. I planned on two drinks with Maddie and Josie, but I showed up late. The person next to me bought. I ended up having more than two." She breathed in. *I have to tell them before he shows up acting like no time had passed.*

"Your Uncle Garrett is coming over tonight." She trembled and beat herself up again over what she did with him. "I thought I was hallucinating, or dreaming, or…" She stopped talking and swallowed down the mixed emotions bubbling up from inside. "I…it… I…"

She clasped her hands together, trying to get them to stop shaking. The real shock of his return hit her in the gut. Garrett was back in town and planning on moving in with her. She didn't think she wanted him anymore. She wanted Cade, but wonderful Cade had to hate her now. And if he didn't, he sure would as soon as he met Garrett face-to-face.

Jeez, seeing Cade would be miserable. Cade probably didn't want her anyway. Texting never equated to anything real. Only calls mattered. Jason called his girlfriend a bunch, but Kyle only texted. Jason was in love while Kyle was in lust.

"Garrett looks just like your father," she blurted out. "The healthy one. The nice one. The one who loved and knew us. Not the sick one."

"I don't want to see him," Kyle said. "He damn near killed Dad. Then he took off. We needed him back then, and he vanished into thin air. I'm sorry, Mom, but fuck him. He's playing some kind of head game with you, and I'm not going to allow it."

"He's moving here permanently," she said.

Her boys both turned back and glared at her.

"He's not moving in." She lifted her hands up in surrender. *Please don't move in while I'm at work today.* "So don't look at me like that."

Kyle turned his focus back to driving and left Jason with the job of giving guilt producing stares.

"He'd better not," Kyle growled.

"He isn't moving in. Hopefully the house will sell quickly." She inhaled deeply and rubbed her clammy palms on her jeans.

"It will be sold before he gets his first bag from wherever he lived last," Kyle said.

"I hope so," she mumbled. *I need to start over.*

Chapter Twelve

Pacing the white-onyx floor in his father's home office, Cade's blood pressure rose. His hands clenched into fists as he fumed over his father's assistant's screw up.

"The wrong house got the free utilities. The wrong house got the gift cards for a week's worth of meals. The Jeeps for the boys got delivered to the wrong fucking house."

He picked up two, large, stress balls from the big glass bowl filled to the brim with a wide variety of them on the top of his father's mahogany desk. He tossed them up in the air, caught them and then squeezed them over and over.

My Ella got so drunk she screwed her brother-in-law because I wasn't there to take care of her. I had to go to that stupid conference when I finally had the woman of my dreams in my grasp. Dumb ass decision.

He strode forward along the path he'd worn to the door then pivoted for the millionth time to do it all over again. "Who gets an address wrong when the right one is in the fucking email I sent you? It's cut and paste." *I should have handled it myself.* He threw the fourth set of stress balls in the last ten minutes against the light-blue wall across from him. They bounced off the wall and dropped to the floor next to the others.

I should have listened to my gut and stayed to work

on our relationship. Garrett fucking Winthrop never would have gotten his hands on her. Why the hell is he back in town? The guy hadn't been home for seven years. He didn't show for his own brother's funeral.

Pappy stopped going through the stack of invoices on the top of his desk and leaned back in the chair. "Calm down. We'll fix this."

"How the hell does this get fixed?" Cade shouted. "I leave something so simple in Nikki's hands, and she screws it up. It's not like I can take the gifts back and say, 'Oh, hey, Ella. These went to the wrong house. I meant them for you.' It was supposed to be anonymous but give enough clues she could figure out it was me."

He had to stop yelling, or he'd never calm down. He grabbed another set of stress balls hoping they would actually lower his stress level at some point. He dropped his voice a few decibels. "If Kyle and Jason figured out my company gave away the gift cards, cars, and utilities, they're going to think I'm not only an asshole, but I'm stupid too. I bet they've already nicknamed me 'dickhead'."

"Excuse me," Nikki peeked into the room.

Pappy sighed. "Yes, Nikki?"

"What did you screw up now?" Cade asked in a strained, yet quiet voice, squeezing the new balls in his hand at an unprecedented speed. His Ella thought he didn't care because of Nikki's mistakes.

"I, um," Nikki mumbled.

"Cade, stop being an ass, or I'll take you out behind the shop and tan your hide," Pappy said. "She made a mistake. Everyone makes them, and this can be rectified." He stood up and walked around the front of his desk. "Nikki, what is it, honey?"

“Um, Jason is here with his brother,” she whispered.

“Send them in.” Pappy placed his hand on Cade’s back. “Son, you’ve got to take it slow. Show her you’re looking for the rest of your life. Show her boys you want them as your family. She’ll choose you because you’re the best man.”

Jason walked past Nikki with his head hung low. “Hey, Pappy.” He hugged Pappy and held onto him.

Pappy let go of Cade and wrapped his arms around Jason. Kyle hesitated at the doorway, but he stepped into the room and walked toward them.

“Come here, Kyle,” Cade said. “What happened?” *Have you been crying?*

Kyle walked over to Cade and shook his hand.

“Mr. Jackson, we’ve never skipped school before. Could you call the office so they don’t call Mom? We’re not missing anything…” His voice cracked. “…Important.”

Cade grabbed Kyle’s shoulders and pulled him into a hug. His boys were hurting. It had been less than a week, and he already thought of them as his kids.

“Everything is going to be okay. What happened? Is your mom okay?” Cade asked.

Kyle and Jason both shook their heads but didn’t say anything. They stood silent except for the slightest sound of sniffling hiccups muffled by Pappy and Cade’s broad chests.

Cade held Kyle while he picked up his cell from his father’s desk. He called the school and explained the boys’ absence.

“Dad died three years ago yesterday,” Jason said. “We knew it was a bad idea for her to go out last night.

We didn't think she'd actually go, but when Maddie said she was going to your bar—"

Kyle picked up the sentence. "—we thought she would be safe, because you were coming home, and could take care of her. But—"

Jason continued, "—your flight got delayed, and she was late, and we didn't know. She's so strong, but every year she falls apart. We screwed up. We should have made plans with her."

"I didn't know." Cade squeezed Kyle tighter. He dropped the stress balls to the floor at his feet. The boys had each other to grieve with, but his Ella grieved her late husband alone while he was out of town. "While I waited at the airport for my luggage, Maddie called me to pick her up. By the time I arrived, your mom had vanished."

He should have called her this week instead of texted her. He should have left voicemails. If Nikki hadn't screwed things up, Ella would have known he cared for her more than it seemed. His woman had been vulnerable and turned to another man. That wasn't happening ever again.

"She trembled during the entire ride to the spa this morning." Kyle gazed up at him. The poor kid looked as though a dam broke loose inside. Tears filled his eyes. "She tried to act like nothing was wrong." His breath hitched as he sucked in air.

"Uncle Garrett is in town, and something serious happened between them last night. She said it was over between you two, but I know she doesn't want it to be. The way she talks about you is different than… My uncle is selfish."

Cade rubbed Kyle's back and wanted to cry along

with him. Their asshole uncle took advantage of their mother's vulnerability. His anger resurfaced, and his face heated as he remembered Garrett's comments along with her pleas to make love. *I never should have left for that damn conference*.

In a small, insecure voice, Jason whispered, "Uncle Garrett and Dad are, were, geniuses. They excelled at everything. They… When Dad got sick he changed. They got in a big fight and nearly killed each other. Mom pushed Garrett away as Dad swung; Dad hit Mom near the stairs. She fell. It was bad. Uncle Garrett knocked Dad out. Then, he drove Mom and us to the hospital. When Mom woke up, she and Uncle Garrett argued. He hugged us then left. We were ten. He never came back."

"Dad's rages got worse as the disease progressed," Kyle added. "I emailed and called Uncle Garrett to come and help Mom, but his numbers and emails had all changed. He disappeared."

Pappy kissed the top of Jason's head like he'd done to Cade as a boy. "You've got a strong Momma."

"Yeah," Jason whispered.

"Please don't break up with her," Kyle said. "You're good for Mom, and she really likes you."

The door to the office opened.

"Cade?" Nikki stepped halfway into the room. "You've got a call."

"Take a message," Cade said.

"Um, he says it is important." Nikki cringed as if she were in pain. "It's Garrett Winthrop. It's the fifth time he's called."

"Get his number. I'm busy."

"Yes, sir." Nikki closed the door.

Cade patted Kyle on the back. "I'm not breaking up with your mom. I'm crazy in love with her. I know she's not in love with me yet, but I'll be damned if your uncle waltzes back into town and takes her from me." Now that his feelings were out of the bag, he hoped he hadn't made a mistake.

Jason and Kyle exhaled.

"See, Ky." Jason nudged Kyle in the side. "I told you he loves her."

"Boys, we have some shopping to do," Cade said, unable to stop the smile curving his lips. Jason actually liked him after only one week of conversations. Kyle was in his corner too. He wasn't doing too badly with her boys after all. Getting rid of Garrett as competition for Ella would prove difficult, but true love trumped a long history.

She hadn't made him any promises. He hadn't made her any promises either, but he wanted to. He stepped over the line last night by claiming boyfriend status to Garrett. He and Ella hadn't set rules about their relationship or defined it, but they would. Tonight, they would.

Jason breathed in and stepped out of Pappy's embrace as Kyle did the same with Cade. They lifted the bottom of their shirts up to their eyes and wiped them, mirroring each other's actions.

"We need help with the flower beds in the front of our house," Jason said, taking the lead. "I wouldn't normally ask, but Momma Louise mentioned getting rid of some extra flowers she ordered. May I have some of the extras?"

"We'll load them into my truck," Cade said. "Pappy, thanks for listening earlier. Jason won't be at work. I've got him all day."

Pappy walked behind his desk and picked up an envelope with Jason's name on it from a large stack. He handed it to Jason. "Here's your check. Let me know if you need anything."

Jason slipped the envelope into his jeans back pocket and thanked him. "We're putting our house on the market, so I may need to take tomorrow off to finish up some repairs before the realtor comes."

"You're moving?" Pappy asked. "Not far, right?"

"Not far," Jason said. "Mom talked about buying out this way."

Pappy walked around his desk and hugged Jason again. "I'd really like for you to be closer to me. It might be a far drive for your mom to get to work, but it would be relaxing once she was out of the city."

"If we can get her specialty soaps and candle production streamlined, she might not be working as much at the spa," Kyle said. "We're looking for a small house on some land with possible space to build a warehouse."

"That's a great idea," Pappy said, taking the words right out of Cade's mouth. "There are several farms close enough to drive into the city but far enough away to get a good price. We could build her a warehouse for next to nothing."

Cade wanted to thank his father for being so supportive of the boys. Hopefully within the year they would be the newest editions to the Jackson family.

"Thanks, we might take you up on that," Jason said.

"Where are you planning to go to college, Kyle?" Pappy asked. "We have a great community college ten minutes down the road. Jason said you might want to stay close by too."

Kyle looked at Jason and something unspoken moved between them.

"I'm not sure, yet," Kyle said. "Jason is staying with Mom, but I think I'm going to my dad's alma mater, if Mrs. Kellen doesn't screw it up for me."

Cade gazed at his father, searching for guidance, but the blank look in his father's brown eyes showed no signs of help. "What's going on with Mrs. Kellen, and what does she teach?"

"She teaches social studies. We've had some issues," Kyle hedged.

"What issues?" Cade gave them a don't-bullshit-me glare.

A sheen of perspiration broke out over Kyle's forehead as he explained the situation with his teacher. "We're not the only ones to complain."

"Mom complained," Jason added. "The principal won't listen."

"We have a habit of correcting her in class, and we probably wouldn't be in this situation if we had played along. But she's wrong, and I'm not going to write down a wrong answer to please her when I know the correct one." Kyle straightened up, gaining his composure once again. "So, we're on the borderline of flunking her class."

"What happens if you don't pass her class?" Cade asked.

"We don't graduate from high school or—" Kyle abruptly stopped and cleared his throat. "But it doesn't affect the scholarships we have. Mom called a couple of the colleges we're, um, interested in, and talked to them about the situation after the first parent—teacher conference at the beginning of the year. Mrs. Kellen has a reputation for flunking those with a higher IQ than hers." Jason's eyes widened, and he cleared his throat. "Well. We. Sorry. I. Dad told us not to talk about it."

"What Jason so ineloquently is trying to say is we haven't had problems with any teacher or class until Mrs. Kellen. She has the administration backing her." Kyle rolled his blue eyes like he'd seen Ella do many times over the year he'd known her. "College isn't an issue for either of us. We can go wherever we chose for free."

"But we can't go anywhere until we graduate high school. We need a passing grade in history, and Mrs. Kellen knows it," Jason picked up the conversation. "She did the same thing last year to two kids. She kept the grade at barely passing all year, then failed them."

Kyle added. "Her tests are all essays. Every one of our answers is irrefutably correct, yet we receive failing or barely passing grades."

"Do you have the tests?" Cade asked.

"No, sir," Jason said. "She keeps them. She could give us any test she wanted, even the final in front of anyone she wanted, and we'd ace it."

I can fix this. "Do you need any preparation for the final?"

"No, sir," Kyle said. "Why?"

"I'm taking you to the principal. We'll get this taken care of. Then, we'll head to the house and fix whatever needs fixing. Let's go," Cade said.

"But what about our other classes?" Jason asked.

Kyle's gaze dropped to the floor as a grin spread across his face.

Cade patted Kyle on the back. "I have a strong suspicion today is the last day you will be attending high school." If the boys were half as intelligent as he presumed, his father would finally have a business partner in Jason, and Kyle would spread his wings and fly toward a future he seemed ready to conquer.

"Jason, I need you here tomorrow, or I'll have to call on Cade. I love my son, but he isn't worth a damn as a carpenter." Pappy winked at him.

Cade laughed. "Thanks, Dad. Nice to know how you really feel."

Pappy swung his arm around Jason. "Don't even think Cade doesn't know his weaknesses. The man is a machine in what he's good at, but carpentry isn't one of them. Not like us." They walked out of the office together.

"Looks like you've been replaced," Kyle said.

Cade picked up his cell phone from the desk and strode to the door. "Nope. Jason has been adopted. You have too. Come on. We have a full day ahead of us." He walked through the open door as Kyle followed.

"A full landscaping crew will be at the correct address by the time you get there." Nikki stood up behind her desk. "Felicity is having lunch delivered at noon to Ella's office. I've taken care of the first oversight you asked me to fix. Felicity sent flowers to her office this morning along with a card stating when you'll pick her up. Josie is out shopping for an outfit which will be delivered at three with more flowers. I called ahead to the dealership and told them to have new vehicles delivered to the correct address."

"Thank you, Nikki," Cade said. "Sorry about earlier."

“I’m really sorry about the mistakes. I’m not sure how it happened, but I’ll find out.” She held out a piece of paper. “Here is the message and his number.”

“Just trash it,” Cade said.

Nikki stood up with the paper in her hand. “Um, I think you should read it.”

Cade took the paper from her hand.

Ella is mine. She always has been. You have no chance with her. None. Call me, and I’ll explain why you need to let her go.

Nikki gulped. “The number is on the back.”

Cade turned the note over. Ella’s cell phone number leapt out at him. Garrett still had her phone from last night. He crumpled the piece of paper and handed it to her. “Throw this away, please. If he calls again, tell him I got the note. Come on Kyle, we’ve got work to do.”

Chapter Thirteen

Derek stood in the laundry room of his new condo and folded the last of the white towels embroidered with Ella's name in pink. He placed them on top of the stack in the pink basket he picked out just for her. *She should be here, not at work.*

He carried the basket through the house into the bedroom he shared with Garrett. Their bed had arrived, and Garrett spent the afternoon carefully assembling it.

Garrett gazed up at him, worry etched deep in his eyes. "What do you think?"

"She's going to love it." Derek walked past the open French doors into the bathroom. He placed the basket in the empty space between two other pink baskets on the bottom, built-in shelf between the shower and the extra-large bathtub. He imagined her naked on her hands and knees searching for her washcloths. *You're going to bend over to get your towel and show me your pretty pussy.* He cupped his cock and squeezed. *You're going to love my plans for the three of us.*

"Do you love it with the canopy attached?" Garrett asked.

"I do." He ran his fingers over the embroidered "E" on the front of each basket "We're finally going to have her." He held his raging cock as he walked into the bedroom.

Garrett sat naked at the edge of the bed, silent, his gorgeous body a picture of perfection. Every thick grouping of muscle, beautifully developed to allow for explosive movement. The military's ultimate warrior—physical dominance, superior intelligence, and an iron will.

"You're not dressed?" *You should be on your way to get Ella before Cade shows up.*

"Remember when you used to write the names of the muscles on me to help you memorize them?" Garrett asked.

"Yes." Derek said. "I told Ella about it while she was in massage school. She wrote on you and me and Greg as we took turns quizzing her. We had so much fun. Do you want to play later? I can pick up some body markers after work. Ella will be into it." He strode toward him.

Garrett held out his arms, and Derek walked straight into them.

"Not tonight," Garrett whispered. "Cade is a guy's guy. He's a beast at the gym. He is as affluent as Greg had been." Garrett rested his head against Derek's neck. "I think she found a combination of me and Greg in him."

"There is no one like you," Derek said. "You're wealthy. Between your investments and the trust fund my parents set you up with, you are pretty damn close to Cade Jackson rich."

"I looked at his finances. Mine, yours, and your parents' combined wealth is like looking at the cash in his wallet. I can't compete with him. I'm going to lose her again."

"Hey." Derek exhaled. "She doesn't care about

how much money you have. You're not going to lose her. She loves you."

"I've got the worst fucking timing with her. She looked like a ghost when I told her it was over with him. I think she loves the guy." Garrett hooked his feet around Derek's legs.

Derek cradled the back of his head and forced his head up. He gazed into the soul of the man he loved more than life. "Listen to me. She *loves* you. She doesn't know how much she loves me yet, but she will." He kissed Garrett's lips and let go. Garrett snuggled his face against Derek's neck. "She'll understand after you explain what happened. She will understand why we both left. You made mistakes. I made mistakes. She made mistakes. I should have figured out Greg's illness. I should have connected his dramatic change in behavior to some kind of brain cancer.

"Instead, I assumed it was an outward manifestation of something your parents said or did…narcissistic assholes. The way they doted on him after they found out about us… It had to have screwed him up somehow." Derek draped his arms around Garrett's shoulders.

Garrett inched to the edge of the bed and closer to Derek. "He hated it. He apologized a thousand times to me for their behavior. The more Mother and Father tried to rip us apart, the closer we got. What they did with Greg and me—they kept him and threw me away like trash—was just like when they made the ultimatum to me about you—either end my relationship with you, or they would cut me out of their lives completely."

It had been years since they talked about his

parents and longer since he opened up about the past.

"Greg stood by you like you stood by me." Derek kissed the side of his forehead. His cock grew harder. *You've shown me you've loved me over and over throughout our lives. I'm going to make sure Ella takes us as her husbands. I want it for you and selfishly, for me too.*

Garrett's hands slid under the waistband of Derek's scrubs. "The way you and your parents stood by me all these years."

"Like that was hard." *You are so easy to love.*

"My own parents didn't want me. I'm difficult and controlling and competitive when I shouldn't be."

"That was Greg, not you. If Greg hadn't been so controlling of Ella and jealous of you… I should have forced him into my office for tests, physical and psychological." *The four of us could have had everything we ever wanted.*

Garrett pushed down the waistband of Derek's scrubs to the crack of his ass. "Hindsight is twenty-twenty."

"I should have checked up on them more thoroughly. If I hadn't believed Greg's lies, Ella would be married to me with a herd of your kids. Now, she can't have kids, she's involved with a great guy, and she doesn't trust me as far as she can throw me."

"Stop that." He caressed down Garrett's back. Greg had been so jealous of Garrett, he scheduled seven years' worth of fucking monthly updates to come to Garrett's inbox. If Sammy hadn't been transferred to Garrett's unit, they would have no idea Greg died until the updates ended in four more years. *God, your bastard parents didn't even call.* "The more we hear about what happened, the more I'm sure your parents manipulated the crap out of Greg early on in his illness."

His blood pressure rose as the memories of the calls he made after he found out Greg had passed away to Mr. and Mrs. Winthrop came rushing forward. The initial denials. The glee in their voices when they revealed Greg gave them the savings and investments he'd worked his entire life to give to Ella and the kids.

I fucking hate your parents. Ella had fought them all by herself. She'd lost big but she managed to make things work and raise her kids like a pro. Derek ached for her to have his children. Maybe she would consider reversing the tubal ligation, or agree to get a surrogate.

"What if she chooses Cade like she chose to stay with Greg?" Garrett mumbled. "I've got to do something."

"The last time was my fault." He had made Garrett promise to call him if he found the right woman for them to marry. While Garrett waited on Derek to show up for the quick wedding, Greg had gone to check out Ella's family. Ella had been waiting outside for Garrett. Greg fell head-over-heels for her exactly like Garrett had, and Ella mistook him for Garrett. Greg didn't have to wait on anyone. He married Ella as Derek's plane touched down on the tarmac.

"It wasn't your fault."

"If it weren't for your promise to me, she would have been your wife, not Greg's. Greg impersonated *you.* She wanted *you* as her husband back then. She wants *you* as her husband now. If she and Cade were serious, they would already be married. Cade is a non-issue. So, get your shit together, and get *our* girl." He stepped one foot back. *Cade isn't our hurdle. Ella's reliance on me is. She has to want more than me and you. She has to want to make love to me without you too.*

Garrett raised his chin. The determined gaze Derek loved so much locked onto his.

"I'm getting *our* girl. There is no way Cade can compete with us as a team."

"Yeah, and the way she rode your big cock all night, she's going to need more than one man to keep her satisfied."

Garrett slid off the edge of the bed and stood up. He wrapped his arms around Derek and pressed his lips to Derek's ear. "I love you."

Hugging Garrett, Derek's heart rate slowed and evened out to a natural rhythm.

"I love you too." He rubbed along Garrett's back. "Stay honest with her about us. She comes first. We come second. She's our priority. She marries you, so her last name stays the same, but she belongs to me too. "

"We'll gently guide her into our lifestyle, Derek. She's not going to be into it right away. We can't let Cade shame her into—"

"—Stop. Cade is not your brother or your parents. He did all kinds of crazy shit in his youth. He's not casting any stones at either of us or her. Remember, you're the one she loves. You. Not him."

Garrett's warm lips pressed against Derek's neck. "Two big cocks are better than one."

Derek laughed and slapped his ass. "Yes, they are."

Garrett nuzzled under Derek's ear. "Are you going to show her you're the dominant one in our relationship?" He nipped at Derek's lobe.

"I told you to stop worrying," he said. "She's the real submissive for both of us. She won't care that I'm the one who calls the shots when I'm in the room. She's used to me in that role." *I'm going to fuck the fear out of you tonight.*

"But she's not used to me giving up any control." Garrett curled his tongue around Derek's earlobe and sucked. He pushed Derek's scrubs down over his cock and rubbed the length with his cock.

Heat flooded Derek's groin, chest, and cheeks. "I'm going to punish you." *We don't have time for the kind of fucking I want from you. Hell, there's not time for a quickie.* He caressed over Garrett's ass and pressed his fingers against his dark hole. Hard plastic met his touch. "Getting ready for me?" *After all these years, are you ready to give me your virgin ass?*

"Right now, I'm getting ready to suck your dick," Garrett whispered.

"I decide when you lick, suck, swallow or get fucked," Derek said.

"Yes, sir."

Precum trickled from Derek's cock. *You're ready. It's all because of Ella. Our girl brings out the best in both of us.* "No time to take the edge off. Pull up my pants."

Garrett swept his finger over the tip of Derek's cock and adjusted his scrubs. "Yes, sir." He sucked his finger and sighed.

"You're lucky I have more important things on my agenda. I didn't say you could take a taste." He swatted Garrett's ass. "Get dressed, and go get our girl. Talk to her."

"Damn, you're harsh." Garrett picked up his clothes from the bed and dressed. "Any advice on how to handle the boys? They're not going to believe me."

"Show them the emails. They know how Greg operated. They will believe you. My parents will back us up. Sammy will too. Once the truth is out, everything will fall into place."

Garrett sat down on the bed and tied up his boots. "I'm bringing everything out in the open. No more secrets. No more lies. No more assumptions." Determination seemed to fill his every step to the door. "Cade is not getting what is mine. If he wants to fight for her, I'm bringing a war."

Derek cupped his cock and squeezed. *You kept the plug in.* He rushed over to the bathroom drawer where they kept all their toys. He slipped his hand into his pants and ran his hand over the top. He drew the precum down over his shaft and pumped up and down. *You opened the biggest one. You promised once we agreed on a woman to marry, you'd give me every inch of you.*

"Clean up my toy," Garrett shouted. "It's in the laundry room washtub."

Derek fisted his cock and held it. *Ella, we're coming for you. Everything you ever needed, we're going to give you. All I need is for you to love me a fraction of how much I love you.*

Chapter Fourteen

Ella stripped the cream-colored bamboo sheets off the massage table, carried them into the back of the spa, and deposited them in the washer. She started the machine and pulled out the warm sheets from the dryer into a basket. The more she tried to focus on the simple, closing routine, the more she agonized over the choices she'd made that day.

I need the security guards to come around more often. If she weren't behind on her lease payments, she would demand the owner follow through with the contract's clause providing security patrols during the day. There hadn't been any patrols in more than a year.

Unnerved from a few clients she'd worked on earlier in the day, Ella's hands trembled as she folded a flat sheet. Felicity had been nice during the session, but afterward she strutted to the display in the waiting room, picked up a ginger soap, and sniffed it. Out of nowhere she went berserk, flailing her arms, trying to destroy the new display… *Crazy bitch threw one of my ginger soap bars at me.*

If my next client hadn't come in, I would have had to call the police. I should have called the police.

One strange occurrence after another. Thank God she had a full day with people coming and going one right after the other. Repairing the display made her run late, but it was the client who wouldn't take no for an answer around noon that really frightened her. If she hadn't gotten a surprise lunch delivery, she might have been in trouble.

She shivered as if she were trapped in an ice bath. *I need to hire another therapist. I need some safety procedures. I need that damn street light fixed in the back of the building. I need the security guards to patrol the area like they used to.*

She shook her head, banishing all thoughts of the strange clients. She racked her brain for a massage therapist to hire, someone she could trust to increase her profit margin and add a little security. Clients like the ones today made her work harder to get her skin product business profitable. She loved massage, but it was demanding and exhausting work. When the rare uncomfortable moments came, they seemed to come with a vengeance. Unstable women. Men who tried to stretch or break down her rigid boundaries.

She inhaled deeply. *Think of the good, not the bad. Power is on at the house. The boys are graduating and turning eighteen soon. Colleen is coming home. Everyone is healthy. My leg doesn't hurt as much today. Thank you, acetaminophen.*

The chime from the front door, indicating a visitor, pulled her away from her thoughts. She put up the clean sheets and headed to the entrance to the waiting room.

Ella's heart skipped a beat at the sight of Garrett in black cargo pants and an army-green athletic tee looking more like himself and less like Greg. Why did her body automatically react so strongly to him? She was over him, wasn't she?

"Hey, babe. All done?" He swiftly and stealthily strode to her.

"I'm—"

He cupped her cheeks and tenderly kissed her like she was his to protect and love. He leisurely dragged his lips and chin, lightly scratching her cheek with the stubble in the form of a rough goatee, over to her ear. "Do you need help? I can set up your rooms or do laundry."

"I, uh." Her hands automatically glided up his muscular chest to his strong neck. She wrapped him up in a lover's embrace.

He licked her earlobe as his hands slid around her back. "We could make love in the back. I bet Greg never did that when you worked at that spa before the kids were born. I bet you always wished he had." He pulled her against him. "I'm not like Greg. I'm adventurous. Some might say I'm a little alternative." He guided her back a step toward her office. "I locked the door. Let's make love. Let's get married tonight."

"No, Garrett. We're not having sex or getting married. I'm not eighteen, illegally bartending in my father's pub. I have responsibilities that do *not* include running away with you."

She had a life and business rooted to this city. Colleen was technically an adult, and her boys were less than a week away from turning eighteen, but they still needed her.

She leaned against his familiar body. She should have stepped back, put distance between them, but her body disagreed.

"Marry me. I never stopped loving you, and I know you still love me."

She couldn't help but rest her head against his athletic chest. He hadn't listened to anything she said.

He never had. Greg rarely had either, but Greg loved her in a way that made up for it.

"There was a time I would have jumped at the chance to marry you, but you cut all ties with us. When Greg needed you, when the kids needed you, when I needed you… You vanished. I couldn't find you, and I tried." She inhaled and steeled her nerves for his excuses. She wasn't upset anymore. Dealing with work and clients put life in perspective.

She raised her chin and gazed into his eyes. "I survived without your help, and I'm better because of it." She stepped back and gently pushed him away. "Last night was a mistake, Garrett. I wasn't thinking clearly. *Obviously,* I was drunk. I'm not angry about it."

"It wasn't a mistake. We would have ended up in bed regardless of your sobriety. Don't kid yourself." His arms encircled her waist.

She curled her arms around him again and pressed her breasts against his chest. They fit together so perfectly. "You're right. We probably would have, but it's not happening again." Her nipples beaded. She gave into the need to rub against him.

"I want to be inside you." He pushed his leg between hers. "I want to play with you, explore you, and expand your horizons. I want to give you everything my brother wouldn't."

His hand squeezed her bottom as moisture slid from her folds onto her jeans.

She had always wanted to explore with Garrett. She used to fantasize about Garrett joining her and Greg in bed, both of them taking her, focusing totally on her pleasure. She never put words to her desires, afraid of the consequences of Greg's jealousy. Those erotic cravings played out in her dreams over the years and shifted to Garrett and Derek. The dreams faded as her heart closed when she stopped believing Garrett would come back for her.

Last year, fantasies of Cade took over in the midnight hours and strengthened every week. Suddenly a new fantasy formed—Garrett and Cade. She shuddered. *Yes. My talkative Cade would call out orders while quiet Garrett joined in, giving his own silent commands*. If Derek joined them, her fantasies would be complete.

"Please forgive me for leaving," he whispered. "I loved my brother. I love you, have always loved you. I couldn't stay, or I would have killed him for what he did to you. As jealous as he was of our connection, I was twice as jealous of him in your bed. Protecting you became… If you hadn't stepped between—"

"Stop." She remembered that night like it was yesterday. Colleen had been away visiting her grandparents. Garrett had been helping her put away laundry in the boys' room. Greg walked in on the edge of a manic episode. He looked back and forth between the two of them and then at Jason's unmade bed. He'd jumped to all the wrong conclusions.

God, he'd lost it. He had screamed so many accusations. So many she'd never forget. He grabbed her, flung her like a rag doll on the bed, ripping her shirt. Greg had never laid an angry finger on her before then. And she'd never seen Garrett truly fight until that day. He rushed toward Greg, screaming right back at him.

Greg had his hands around her throat, choking her. Garrett threw Greg off her then picked her up like she weighed little more than a baby bird, and shoved her behind him.

It had all happened so quickly. One minute they had been laughing in the boys' room, the next Greg flew into the first violent rage of their married life. Garrett protected her and forced Greg back into the hallway. Garrett screamed at her to get the boys, and get in the limo with Derek, but she couldn't leave.

She wouldn't abandon Greg when the tumor was driving his rage. The cancer was to blame, not him. The doctors warned her of the possibilities of rages. She had planned to explain everything to Garrett, but fate had different plans.

Garrett had turned and pleaded with her to leave with him immediately. Out of the corner of her eye, she saw Greg pick up a lamp from the top of the hallway table. She didn't know how she did it, but she pushed Garrett to the side and took the brunt of Greg's swung. She remembered the initial impact then falling, tumbling down the beautiful staircase… Garrett's and the boys' wails along with the lack of sound from Greg before she lost consciousness still haunted her dreams.

"I went back to the house. I spoke to Greg. He begged me to leave. He promised if I left and never came back, you would be safe. He promised to get help. I got updates. They were all fake. I didn't know." He sucked in a deep breath. "I never should have left. Had I known about the tumor causing his strange outbursts all those years, I would have stayed. I would have helped him through it. I would have been there for the kids, for you. I would have retired from the military."

She melted into his warm embrace, tears she vowed never to shed threatened her eyes. For so many years she'd longed to hear those words from his lips, but now, hearing them hurt. Not knowing whether he would have stayed through the worst of Greg's illness made her ache. Garrett had always been a trooper with physical pain but not so much with the emotional kind. *I want to trust you.* "It's all in the past."

"I wanted you to know," he whispered. "I didn't leave without giving him ways to get in touch with me in an emergency. He never told you, and I'm sorry."

Greg's mind had already been too far gone by then. She'd never know how he interpreted the conversation or what he did with it. He had relied more and more on technology as his illness progressed. The way Greg's mind worked, he could have set up fake updates for Garrett within the time it would take for him to forget the information or remember doing it. From the look in Garrett's eyes and the truth of his words, she believed him. He would have come home for Greg's funeral at the very least.

"I forgive you." She had. It was such a difficult time. Surviving remained the top priority back then. She still searched for ways to survive and keep her children protected and healthy. "I really need you to wait another day or two before you see the boys. You look more like yourself but not enough."

"They'll be fine. They know what I look like. You're worrying about nothing."

No, she wasn't worrying about nothing. Garrett didn't know what she and the boys went through. He didn't know how they suffered. He didn't know how the last seven years had forced her boys to grow up.

How the boys stayed in their rooms most of the time to avoid any kind of outburst from their father.

How they'd all shielded Colleen from the ugly side of the cancer. How they made deals with Greg's parents to keep her for the summers because Greg hadn't wanted his baby girl to see him go through the worst of the treatments to extend his life.

Ella had been naïve to think his parents' motives to help out were from genuine love. She found out how wrong she'd been when she took over paying the medical bills and the money was gone. His parents had convinced Greg to transfer almost all the money out of his business and personal accounts to theirs. Greg's will had changed too. He'd fired his attorney and hired his father's lawyer.

At the end of Greg's life, his parents had stripped them of everything that was solely in Greg's name and most of what was in both hers and his. She had no clue how much nastiness Greg had shielded her from with his parents until the perfect grandparent smiles turned to sneers, the comforting hugs changed to handshakes, the gifts of beautiful flowers switched to bills for babysitting Colleen.

Maybe paying all that money to them had been worth her daughter missing the worse of the rages doled out to Ella and, on rare occasions, the boys. Maybe they all would have been better had Colleen stayed with them. Maybe Greg wouldn't have been so paranoid.

She stiffened in his arms.

"What?" He loosened his hold.

She dropped her hands from him and stepped backward. "Please, don't do this tonight." She loved him, but she backed up a few more steps toward the door, ready to usher him out of it. She didn't need the painful reminders and neither did her boys. *Not today.*

Top on her things-to-do list was to get the house ready for the realtor and Colleen's return home. Talking to Cade and apologizing had top billing too. It didn't matter whether the big man had planned to give her the "friend" talk or not. They had known each other for more than a year. He deserved an explanation from her.

The door chimed behind them.

"Ella, are you ready?" Cade's deep voice filled the room.

She looked toward the door. Cade strode into the waiting room wearing a dark-brown business suit and stopped two feet away from her.

What are you doing here? How did you get in? Her mouth gaped as she checked him out more thoroughly from head to toe.

Drop-dead gorgeous Mr. Cade Jackson stood in her waiting area like he owned the place. A rush of desire hit her like a tidal wave. Every inch of flesh heated as she met his sexy gaze. *Dang.* Why couldn't he be ugly? She had to tell him about Garrett and didn't want to be drooling, ready to combust, while she did.

"You must be Garrett." Cade switched on his easy southern charm and made Ella's pussy quiver for attention. "Nice to meet you."

Garrett pivoted around, pulling and twirling Ella in his arms, to face Cade head-on.

"You must be Cade Daniel Jackson." Garrett extended his hand, and Cade shook it. "Dropping off her keys?"

Cade held his open palm out to Ella.

She focused on all his hunky-sexuality filling his suit. *Damn.*

"Did you get the lunch I sent over?" Cade asked.

"I wondered who that was from." No note accompanied the lunch. Assumptions were Garrett's modus operandi, not Cade's. Her giant didn't seem the sneaky type. No, not hers. Why would he send her anything? Had Garrett lied about talking to him? No. They each seemed to know about the other.

She placed her hand in his only to be swallowed up within, but kept her head lowered to avoid his eyes. "Eggplant parmesan is my favorite."

"I know," Cade said. "Did you get my note?"

"Um. No." She crumbled a little in Garrett's arms. The gift had to be the "it's-me-not-you" note placing her in the friend category. He was bold and upfront about his intentions like he had been as her client. "Was it supposed to come with lunch?"

"Yes, ma'am," he grumbled. "Did you get the flowers?"

Garrett snickered. She elbowed him in the side, but the solid man didn't seem to notice.

"You sent me flowers?" She raised her gaze to Cade's. *Are you still interested in me?* The sadness in his eyes propelled her forward into the warmth and safety of his arms.

"I did." He held her hand in his as he pinned her wrist to the small of her back. A soft rumble filled her ear as he brushed his lips over her cheek in a soft kiss. "Did you get any of the presents I sent, besides lunch?"

She wanted to please him, wanted to tell him she had, but she hadn't. She wouldn't lie to the man who gave her one of the best weekends of her life. She'd never lie to him.

"I'm sorry, but no, sir." She had no idea why she added 'sir' to the end of her sentence, but he seemed to like it.

Another low rumble moved through him, but this one wasn't the sexy kind. The undertone managed a jagged edge. Could he be angry? Why? Why send her presents? Surely his interest in dating her ended with Garrett's return. But he had her in his arms in a compromising position, the same position he'd held her in against the tree outside the lake house when he dropped to his knees and…

"*I'm* sorry. I wanted to call this week, but I didn't want to interfere with your work. I hated being away from you." He nibbled the very edge of her earlobe. "We'll talk at dinner."

"Ella, come on," Garrett interrupted her melting session with Cade. "We need to close up and get the boys." He walked with an easy stride toward her and stopped at her side. His gaze drifted up and down her body.

Cade skimmed his lips up and over her forehead. "Do you need my help closing up?"

Her tongue nearly fell out of her mouth at his sensual tone. He knew when to ask, when to demand, and when to rip her panties off and fuck her.

"Enough of this, Cade," Garrett said. "You want her. I want her. We'll both date her and see who she chooses."

"No," Cade said. "She's mine." He held her hands behind her as he pressed his pelvis forward and pushed his hard bulge against her belly.

She bit her bottom lip to stop from whimpering. *I'm yours.*

Garrett maneuvered around her back, removed Cade's grip on her wrist, and introduced his own. "I'll endure you in her life for six weeks. You'll realize she's mine and always has been. Then you'll walk away."

Cade bellowed with laughter. "You're funny, Garrett." He stared into her eyes and stopped laughing. "Three weeks or less. She'll have you out of her system by then. Won't you, sweetie?"

She opened her mouth to speak, but Garrett's voice filled the space around her. "It won't take her long to experience your business schedule, and you'll be reminded why you've never had more than a dozen dates with the same girl. Ella will have no regrets kicking you to the curb."

"Stop. This is stupid," she said, confused. *They're fighting over me?*

"I get her three weekends out of every month, along with Monday, Tuesday, and Wednesday nights," Cade said.

"Wait. Are you serious?" *They both want dates and sleepovers? Sleepovers. Sex. Really?*

"Yes, we're serious," Garrett said.

Her mouth gaped. "You can't decide my dating schedule."

"We're negotiating," Cade said. "You can change the dates and times or cancel. You have choices, but Garrett and I will work out our demands with each other."

Garrett countered and counter-offered as they negotiated her evening schedule between the two of them without asking her opinion. They decided times for pick up and drop off, and where they would be sleeping, her house or Cade's house or Garrett's condo.

When did Garrett get a condo?

"Hey, maybe I don't want to date two men." The heat in her cheeks had to tell them volumes. She couldn't deny her attraction to both men, but dating them might not be a good idea. In fact, it would be a horrible idea.

When Garrett acted like the take-control-and-make-all-the-decisions Garrett she loved, she couldn't resist him. She definitely couldn't resist Cade. There was no way, no matter what kind of naughty fantasies she had with both of them, she could handle the kind of sexual activity they would expect while dating.

Garrett had few sexual boundaries from what he'd told her, but she had plenty. She suspected Garrett and Derek had something going on. What if Derek showed up for some action while they were in bed? Sweet shudders washed over her.

Derek's knowledge of her body rivaled Greg's. Fantasies of him fingering her, licking her pussy while she sucked Garrett's cock heated her belly. She'd swallow all of Garrett's cum. Derek would push Garrett away as he crawled up her body. He'd shove his big cock into her pussy. He'd order her to come, and she would obey him, the way she obeyed him as his patient. He'd spurt his cum inside her and smile with satisfaction.

She exhaled as her pussy clenched. The attraction she had for Derek could make things weird. She was pretty sure it was one-sided. Being a third in a relationship didn't work for her. She needed to be loved the way Greg had loved her. Sharing was for fun, not long-term. Anyway, she liked monogamy. Being with one man gave her stability, someone to count on.

She didn't want one-man vanilla sex, but Cade

rocked her world the previous weekend, and maybe his just-off-the-beaten-path kind of adventure would be plenty. She didn't necessarily want Garrett's kind of kink all the time. Although it would be worth trying if Derek became attracted to her. But she'd only fantasized about making love to two men.

As she found out with other aspects of her life, the fantasy proved wonderful, but reality? Similar to massage, everything would go smoothly and the world of healing she imagined would be as lovely as ever until a client started acting weird. Then they'd ask for sex or try to touch her inappropriately.

Ugh. Exhaustion would take over, and—overrun with bills—financially, the spa became a loser. *I'm an injury away from bankruptcy, clients are bouncing checks, and days like today happen. Asking the lunch delivery guy to escort a client out when "no" wasn't enough to make him leave. Thank you, Joey, for showing up at the perfect time.*

"You want to date both of us. Admit it," Garrett said.

"I'm not sure I do. Maybe?" *I can't believe I'm considering going along with this.*

"You like it when I take care of you," Garrett whispered. He pressed his body flush to her back, his erection hard and ready.

I do. Sandwiched securely between the two formidable men, the day's events disappeared. A deeper heat pummeled her insides. She couldn't move, and all the reasons she shouldn't give into the fantasy of surrendering to two men seemed to vanish.

"I bet I could give you the ultimate ménage fantasy. We could have Derek join us, but only after you choose me as your husband."

"She's mine," Cade said. "You had her yesterday—"

"I sure did," Garrett said. "I had her this morning too. Her sweet pussy sucked every last drop of cum from my balls before we got out of her bed."

All heat drained from her and ice filled her veins.

"Garrett Winthrop, you are the biggest damn jerk in the world." She wiggled out from between them. "Get out of my office. Now." She poked his chest, but he didn't move.

He stood unaffected like a brick wall.

"Let's go, Ella." Garrett winked at her as he held out his hand. "Family business awaits."

"No. You are not going to see my boys tonight. We are not dating, having sex, or anything else which requires you to touch me. Got it?"

She slapped his hand away. His grin widened as he took a step forward toward her. *I'm going to slap that grin off your face. How could you say something so...* "I hate you right now."

"You love me, but I love you more," Garrett said like he'd said a thousand times when he and Greg did something to upset her.

"Ella." Cade pulled her behind him and obstructed her line of sight. He was so big…everywhere. "Go finish closing up. Garrett and I need to have a private conversation."

She didn't think about it. She followed his order and walked into the laundry room.

Chapter Fifteen

Cade stared at the forty-something face that resembled Ella's teenaged sons. Garrett was the most attractive man Cade had ever seen. A true guy's guy. The guy everyone wanted to hang out with and every woman wanted to fuck and have babies with. One of those guys that if Cade were gay, he'd go after. A guy who was real competition. *Damn it.*

He had an uphill climb to win her away from the man Josie told him too much about. Why the hell did the guy have to show up when he finally had started setting a foundation with Ella? "I know you had sex with her. She loves you. You have a long history with her."

"Exactly," Garrett said. "She *loves* me. She *likes* you. You're a nice guy, rich, stable, available, and in love with her. If I hadn't found out about Greg…" a sadness crept into the eyes of the man before him. The emotion seemed genuine, and a part of Cade felt sorry for him.

"I never would have come back. I love her, have always loved her, and I couldn't stand watching my brother." Garrett paused and inhaled. "She needs me. I wasn't there when I should have been. I'm never leaving her again. I will do absolutely *anything* to be with her."

Cade kept a poker face, but elation filled him.

Garrett admitted there was a chance to win her. The beautiful brunette held his heart and soul. He was fairly certain he had a piece of her heart, but not all of it, not yet.

"It's ultimately Ella's decision, not yours or mine. Although, because of your family relationship, I will always accept you in her life as a friend when I marry her." Ella came as a package deal, and Garrett was now a part of it. Her strong reactions to the man emphasized the depths of love she held for him.

"You'll be gone within six weeks. You're not a monogamous guy, and no matter what kind of kinky fantasies Ella has with multiple men, she won't tolerate you cheating on her. She'll choose the one man she can count on for the rest of her life as her anchor. That man is me."

Ella has kinky fantasies? I'm going to have to find out exactly what kind and give her every single one.

Garrett turned toward the door. "Enjoy dinner with her. It won't last long, and I'll pick up the pieces when you fuck up tonight."

"I'm not going to fuck up." *I'm going to fuck my Ella until she forgets you.*

Garrett opened the door and sauntered outside with a spring in his step and his arms swinging like the world was his for the taking.

Damn, the man has confidence.

Cade needed more of that kind of confidence with Ella. When his clothes were off and he held her in his arms, nothing stood in his way, but dressed with Garrett in the mix? He worried. Garrett carried a lifetime of history with her while he only tallied up a couple weeks' worth with their weekend and the hour massage sessions. Building a solid foundation took time. He needed more time.

He ran his hands through his unruly hair. He needed a cut to tame it.

"Is he really gone?" Ella's sweet voice whispered from behind him.

He pivoted around and smiled.

"Yes, ma'am. It's you and me."

Her shoulders dropped an inch.

He searched her face for a sign, any sign she could love him more than Garrett. "Are you ready for a…"

Her gaze swept up to his. She stiffened again. "Cade, thanks for coming over, but now you know what Garrett is like—"

"I can deal with him."

"But—"

He laughed. "No buts, Ella. I'm a big boy. I can take care of him."

"He's not going to stop," she insisted. "You don't know him. He's relentless." She squeezed her eyes closed. "I'm sorry. It's been…" She stopped speaking, shook her head, and lowered her gaze.

He strode forward, taking her into his arms.

"I can only imagine." He caressed along her back over her soft white T-shirt. "Let's talk over dinner. You've got to be hungry, and I'm starving."

Dinner alone would take him one step closer to making her fall for him as deeply as he already had fallen for her. *One obstacle at a time.*

Chapter Sixteen

On edge from the silent ride to the restaurant, she sat still as a stone while he seemed to contemplate whatever he and Garrett talked about. His fingers hadn't stopped moving since he'd gotten in the car. He tapped the seat, his leg, the dash of the car, the radio, and the steering wheel. He tapped his thigh as they waited for the hostess to take them to their table. He tapped the goblet before the waitress filled it with water. He tapped the white linen covered table. His mouth didn't move, but his hands were in constant action.

Tap. Tap. Tap.

Stop. Stop. Stop. Talk to me. Talk, Cade. Tell me what you're thinking. She placed her hand over his and ended the incessant finger movement. "Maybe dinner is a bad idea."

"Sorry," he said. "I haven't eaten since breakfast, and I get jumpy when I'm hungry."

She exhaled, the tension from the silence easing. She had to give him an easy out, even with the brewing chemistry between them. She removed her hand from his and clasped her hands together on top of the table. "We spent a weekend together. Go find someone less complicated. You don't owe me anything."

Cade covered her hands with his own. "Our weekend changed my life. I don't care that your life is complicated. My life is complicated sometimes. Wait until you come to a Jackson Family Intervention. You don't know complicated until you've experienced one." His smile flashed all the way to his eyes.

She laughed. Cade in any kind of intervention seemed ridiculous. The man was too perfect. "A Jackson Family Intervention?"

"I don't want to scare you off, so I'm not going to elaborate. But we typically have one or two a year, and I'm hosting the next one unless I'm the one who is getting the intervention. We typically rotate homes."

"Who are you, Cade Jackson?" He had barely texted her while he was gone. Now, they were having dinner like they were a long-term couple after he challenged Garrett for her hand like she was a prize. Well, she kind of liked the way that made her feel. Really, every part of her liked it. He was going to fight for her, but for how long? Garrett wasn't a give-up kind of guy. He'd often told her he would "never fail, never give up, never back down," but he'd done all those things. Would Cade stick around through tough times? Surviving Garrett's challenge would be enough of a test to find out.

"What do you mean?" His face softened to a cute bemused smile.

He embodied honesty, determination, security, loyalty, and humility—all the things she'd come to know him as over the past year. She didn't want to give up being with him, but she wasn't ready for a commitment, either. She had a house to sell and a substantial amount of debt to get out from under before she could even think about making some kind of promise. Even then, she wasn't sure marriage was in her future.

"Mr. Jackson," a man's voice said from behind Ella.

Cade looked up.

"Yes, sir?" His eyebrow shot up, seemingly irritated at the interruption.

"Could my wife and I have our picture taken with you?" he asked. "We're both big fans and saw you speak on Tuesday at the conference in California."

"I'm in the middle of dinner." Cade tilted his head to the side and shook his head. His fingers tapped the table near his water goblet.

Ella laughed. *Cade has fans?* She glanced over her shoulder.

"Oh, Kenneth." She jerked her head back.

The short, mousy man with dyed blond hair and a spray tan who stood behind her wearing a designer suit had worked for Greg. Her husband fired him because money disappeared.

Last she'd heard, Kenneth had opened his own financial consulting business and was doing very well—probably cheating his clients out of their retirement.

A beautiful, slender redhead in her early thirties wearing a green designer dress posed like a model beside him. She held her cell phone out to Ella.

"I'm sorry about Greg," Kenneth said politely.

The man didn't have a genuine bone in his body. He leaned over. The scent of a heavy musk fell from him. She arched to the side to get away from the stench. The man took his time looking her up and down like she was a commodity he considered buying.

"Thanks." She pulled the hem of her shirt down to

straighten the sweat-wrinkles, suddenly aware of how underdressed she was compared to everyone else in the restaurant. "Congratulations on your new marriage."

"Thanks. I didn't realize I was interrupting business."

"She doesn't mind taking the picture, Kenneth," the snobby redhead interjected, and gave Ella the same thorough once over. "She obviously works for him. She can think of it as part of her job." The redhead swung her hips, flaring the skirt of the dress out to show off her lean legs, as she walked around the back of the black leather booth to Cade's side. An aroma of chemically-derived rose petals smacked Ella in the face and smothered the musk of Kenneth's scent. The redhead bent over, shoved her ass up next to Cade, and reached across the table in a grand gesture of offering her phone to Ella.

What a bitch. I should cut her out of all the pictures. Heck, maybe I'll make them all blurry. She accepted the phone from the woman. *One pic and they'll be gone.*

****

Cade gripped his knees so he didn't push the woman with her ass near his face to the ground and stomp on her damn phone. He had no idea who the couple was, but his Ella certainly did. Her entire demeanor changed as soon as the tiny man named Kenneth appeared.

She stiffened as the redhead pointed to the oil stain on Ella's shirt.

"You should change from your dirty uniform before entering this establishment." The bitch spoke as if Ella was nastier than moldy garbage instead of his girlfriend.

Ella's beautiful, summer-blue eyes dulled to a rainy-gray. She sat up straight with the phone in her hand and held an expressionless smile, so unlike his genuine and easy going woman.

"You don't mind, do you, *Ella*?" Kenneth's condescending tone pushed at Cade's patience. Fury surged as his blood pumped adrenaline in preparation to fight to the death for his woman. Words didn't come. His mind froze at the audacity of the couple's actions. *Are they fucked in the head?*

Kenneth's gaze dipped to Ella's chest and lingered.

The asshole wants my Ella. No chance you prick.

Kenneth joined his wife at Cade's side, standing as close as they could to him.

"I don't mind." Ella tapped the screen and lifted the phone.

"I mind." Cade squeezed imaginary stress balls in his hands. "I stayed for hours answering questions and taking pictures all week. I recently arrived home and want a private dinner with my *girlfriend*. Catch me another time and a quick picture won't be a problem, but right now, I'm busy."

He stretched his fingers and reached across the table. He gently removed the cell phone from Ella's hand. Kenneth could kiss his ass for looking at his girl. *No one treats my future wife like she's a piece of meat.* He handed the cell phone back to the redhead.

The redhead huffed. "It's just a picture."

"Then get it another time at one of my public events." *Bitch. How dare you talk to me or my Ella like...*

Ella grabbed the phone from the redhead.

"Just smile for the camera," Ella said. "It's not a big deal." She stood up and tapped the screen. She winked at him, and the pretty blue returned to her eyes. She stayed glued to his gaze. "Smile."

He frowned as the phone flashed. He didn't want the rat and his flirtatious wife to have a picture worth displaying.

Ella tapped a few times on the phone. "Cade, smile this time." She seemed tickled with his defiance. "Come on, honey. Smile for *me*."

He smiled and showed off his pearly whites for his Ella, not the interlopers.

"Perfect." She handed the phone back to the unnamed redhead.

"Thank you," the redhead said. "Who are you again?"

"Ella Winthrop."

"Oh." The woman's face paled. "Related to Gregory Winthrop?"

Ella nodded. "My late husband." Ella's eyes sparkled like stars in the midnight sky on a clear night. The love and longing in her gaze reminded him of the way his mother looked at his father, even now, after forty-eight years of marriage. Whatever problems she and Greg had before he died, she loved him as much as Josie had said. From his conversation with Garrett earlier, Greg loved her more than he loved anyone else in the world. Could she love like that again?

"Oh." The redhead froze in place.

Interesting her late husband's name would instill that kind of reaction three years after his passing. Had Greg threatened the couple?

"Did you know him?" Cade asked the redhead.

She nodded. He was dying to know why she was so affected by Greg's name. He needed to find out more about Ella's late husband. He'd learned a little from the boys, but not about the man's business acumen, not about life outside being a family man.

Kenneth put his arm around his wife and nodded to Cade. "Have a nice evening, Mr. Jackson." He smirked at Ella. "Found another big fish I see."

"I haven't found anything, Kenneth." The vibrant blue of her irises seemed to fade to a distant gray again.

Whatever that comment meant, it pained her. She'd been hurt enough. He wasn't going to put up with some idiot upsetting her.

"Cade, I'm ready to go." Ella slid out of the booth. Without looking back or hesitating, she walked, favoring her right leg, past the obnoxious couple toward the exit and out of sight.

Cade stood up. "Give me your phone." He held out his hand to the redhead.

She handed him her phone.

He deleted the picture of them. "You just pissed off the wrong person." He tossed cash on the table and walked out of the exclusive steakhouse hoping Ella waited outside. He questioned if she would be there, a feeling he wasn't used to having, and one he didn't want to experience again.

He rounded the corner of the restaurant. Ella stood alone by his car, looking beautiful in her little, white T-shirt and loose khakis. Her long, brown hair pulled into a ponytail showed off her smooth, clear skin and delicate features. She had no idea how naturally stunning she was. Every man in the restaurant had watched her with desire in their eyes as she walked in and out of the building.

"Hey," he said. "Sorry about that."

"It's okay. Can you take me home?"

He opened the passenger door, and she climbed in without looking at him. He walked around the front of the SUV and got in the driver's seat. He didn't want to take her home without having dinner first. She looked like she'd lost some weight since he last saw her, and she couldn't afford to lose anymore.

"Are we okay?" He started the engine and drove out of the parking lot toward her house.

"Why does Kenneth Kraus think you're a celebrity?" Ella gazed out the side window.

"Haven't you heard of me?" *Surely you checked me out on Google.*

"No, should I have?" Her tone held an undercurrent of hostility. She crossed her arms over her chest.

You didn't? I've been a client for more than a year, and you never Googled me? "Most people know me. Cade Daniel Jackson Enterprises ring any bells?"

"Nope. I guess I should see what I can find about you, Mr. Jackson."

"I'm not that big of a deal." Out of the corner of his eye, he saw her head turn.

She gazed at him with a smug smile on her sexy lips. "Glad to hear that. I was starting to think you suddenly turned into an egomaniac."

Maybe she wasn't angry at him. Maybe something else bothered her. "No, sweetie. No ego here. My girlfriend keeps me grounded."

"Am I your girlfriend? What if I go out with Garrett?"

He rubbed his lips together. *Yes, you're my*

girlfriend. "Do you want to go out with Garrett?"

"I don't know." She squeezed her arms together under her breasts, accentuating their fullness. Her lips flattened to a straight line. "Am I your girlfriend?"

"Do you want to be?" He planned to solidify his title as boyfriend and turn it into husband as soon as possible.

He took a left onto Poplar Avenue and headed east to her house.

"My life is complicated."

His hands tightened around the wheel. "We've established I can deal with complicated." He needed to relax, or he'd lose her. Pappy said she would set up roadblocks to any real commitment out of fear. *Keep to Pappy's rules. Listen to her. Show her unconditional love.*

"Garrett is difficult." She paused. "Please, don't be angry with me."

"I'm not angry with you." *I'm angry with me. I keep making the same mistakes with you.* "I know Garrett is the one you were waiting for before I came along. I think you need to make sure you're over him. I'm good with that."

"You're good with that?" Her cheeks blushed a pretty pink. "How good with that? So good you can share me?"

Where did sharing you come from? Is that one of the fantasies Garrett referred to? Do you want to have a real ménage? Me and Garrett?

His dick twitched. *If she wanted me and Garrett to fuck her together, I'd try...but damn. I don't know.* Ella brought out the caveman in him. Cavemen didn't share. He contracted the muscles in his hands around the steering wheel and relaxed them.

"I understand why you're hesitant to commit to me now that he's in the picture. Make no mistake, Ella, I do not want to share you. I'm *not* good with sharing you forever." *Unless there is no other way to have you.* "Because of the circumstances, I'll tolerate us not being exclusive for a short period of time."

She turned the rest of her body toward him and leaned against the door. "Why would you tolerate it? There are lots of women who would love to be with only you."

"Garrett was right. I've never been faithful to one woman, not that I've been unfaithful. Until you, I've never wanted to be exclusive with one woman, never said I'd be exclusive to a woman. Ella, I want you. Only you. You need to figure out that you want only me." His hands relaxed as she exhaled. The tension between them lessened with each breath she took.

"I don't know what I'm doing. My life is not my own right now. My boys need me. My daughter, as independent as she is, needs me too. "

"Your kids are your top priority as they should be, but your kids aren't kids anymore. Kyle and Jason are days from turning eighteen. They're eager to start their lives with all the difficulties that go along with adulthood. You can trust me to walk the road ahead with you. I'll be by your side the entire way. Just…" He exhaled. "…Trust me." *Your boys trusted me enough to confide about the problems with their history teacher. Can't you believe in me too?*

"Can I trust you? Can I *really* trust you?"

"Yes, you can."

"Can I trust you not to tell anyone something really

private?" she asked.

"I won't tell anyone anything you don't want me to. You *can* believe in me." *Please talk about the messy financial situation you're in. Confide in me about the last few years with Greg. Your leg injury. I want to take care of you.*

"I'm selling my house," she said.

Not quite the non-secret I hoped for, but I'll take it.

"What do you need me to do?" *Take it slow, and show you I love you—the woman inside, not just the hot, little, shy, sexy woman I made love to last weekend. Damn. I could pull over, and we could relive the crazy fuck we had in the car on the way to Maddie's. Start by unzipping my pants and licking my cock. Then open your mouth and suck the head. Suck it and swallow...*

"I need a favor."

He cleared his throat and tamped down his desire.

"Sure. Anything."

"Could you..." She closed her eyes as if she wasn't sure he would do what she was about to ask.

I will do anything you want.

"...Um, could you help me and Jason fix a few things around the house? My realtor thinks it will sell quickly, but I'm not so sure without some touch ups here and there. I have the tools and paint, but Jason might need some help with the carpentry work. I'm not great with power tools. I can't risk injuring my hands."

He made a right onto her street. "Absolutely." He would finish anything left over from earlier. Helping his future wife wasn't a favor, it was a privilege. He relaxed into his seat and felt good about the future. He pulled into her driveway, and watched her face beam with joy as she gazed on the newly manicured lawn and sculpted flower beds. His heart skipped a beat as the tension she'd held onto since he walked into her spa fell from her face. He had made that happen.

She swung open the car door in a hurry and jumped out of the SUV. "Oh crap." She landed awkwardly and fell down. "Shit."

Cade ran to her as she forced her body up. He picked her up and cradled her like a baby in his arms.

"What happened?" *Did you reinjure your leg?*

"I was stupid. That's what happened. It's an old injury. The weather is screwing with it. I'm fine. I can walk," she insisted, but didn't even give a half-hearted struggle to get out of his arms.

"Okay." *You don't have to ask me to take care of you, I'm just going to do it.* He carried her into the house.

"We're home," he shouted. He expected the boys to rush to the foyer, and tell her all the things they worked on in the house and then point out the new ivory leather sectional in the living room he'd bought her.

"We're in the kitchen," Garrett's voice rang through the house.

"Mom, I'm home early. I've got a big surprise I want to share." *Must be Colleen.*

Ella wiggled in Cade's arms. He hesitantly helped her down.

"It sounds like Colleen has already adjusted," she mumbled. Her small hand trembled as it slid into his. She looked down at the wood floor. "He wasn't supposed to see the boys without me. Please stay."

"I'll stay for as long as you want me." *Hopefully forever.*

Chapter Seventeen

The new stainless steel appliances shined, bringing new life to the gourmet kitchen Greg and Garrett designed and built for Ella years ago. A soft breeze blew a hint of new paint into the room, drawing her eyes to the open window over the extra-large double sinks in the Mediterranean styled, L-shaped kitchen. Lovely burnt-orange walls covered the old, boring ivory, giving the room a warmth it hadn't possessed since Greg's passing.

Maybe it is Cade's presence warming the space? Or Garrett's? Could it be from both of them?

"Wow, who did all this?" she asked. *Jason and Kyle couldn't have managed everything themselves. They didn't have the time or money.* She gazed up at Cade. His grin widened as they made eye contact. *Was it you? Why? How would you know when I just told you in the car?* She glanced at Garrett. *You?* He probably checked out the house before he left this morning.

Wearing a dark-blue tailored suit, Garrett opened a pizza box on the black granite countertop island in the middle of the kitchen and offered her a slice. He gave her his trademark knowing smile.

Must be you. He could have done all the changes today without anyone knowing. He had the means and the time.

Kyle and Jason stood like ghosts, seemingly shell

shocked, in dirty jeans and sweaty tees on either side of Garrett. Had Garrett already talked to them before he showed up at her work? *No. He wouldn't. He hadn't been here long, or Jason and Kyle wouldn't look so pale.*

"Mom, I'm getting married," Colleen squealed, shifting Ella's attention to her and Sammy Granger on the opposite side of the island.

Blinking back tears and smiling but feeling sick inside, Ella let go of Cade's hand and hurried over to Colleen. "Congratulations." Ella hugged and kissed her. "How exciting." *You're only nineteen. Damn it. This wouldn't be happening if Greg was alive. Where did I go wrong? Didn't you learn anything from me? From Greg's passing? Everyone needs a profession to fall back on if life takes a bad turn.*

Maybe she could talk Colleen into a long engagement. Maybe they'd wait to get married until after Colleen graduated college or decided on a trade school.

Colleen stuck her left hand out, wiggled her ring finger, and showed off a golf-ball size, princess-cut diamond.

"It's beautiful." Ella hugged Sammy. "Sammy Granger, I can't believe you're standing in my kitchen." *And you didn't ask me permission to marry Colleen like a nice, respectful, southern boy would.* She hadn't known her daughter was dating him. Suddenly they're getting married? She retreated back to Cade's safe space and held his hand.

"I already told Kyle and Jason. Uncle Garrett's known for a while." Colleen's smile beamed like pure sunshine. "Sammy asked Uncle Garrett's permission because he's the head of the family now. Isn't that so sweet?"

Garrett isn't the head of the family. I am. Sammy should have asked me. Damn it, Colleen. What the hell are you thinking? Thanks for the fucking ambush.

A serious talk was in the cards for her little girl about growing up and being an adult because the girl was acting like a toddler.

"Sammy's a good man." Garrett smiled at Colleen.

Ella squeezed Cade's hand, confident he could take her strong grip. The man stood like a mountain of muscle beside her. She was ready to rip Garrett's head off. Rip. It. Off.

Colleen ran her hand over her belly.

Ella's gaze wandered to Colleen's undeniable baby bump under the tight-fitting, summer-yellow, silk dress. *Oh, my God. No. No. No. No. No.*

Sammy adjusted his feet shoulder width apart behind her. He rubbed her belly like a proud father. How long had they been together? Colleen hadn't been home since… She tallied the months up in her head. Four months. With the size of her belly bump, she could be five months. Maybe six? Surely not.

"I guess you're not attending college this fall?" Ella tried not to sound bitter. She wanted Colleen to have something she never had—a college degree. She should have forced Colleen to take cosmetology in high school. It would have given her a solid profession to fall back on. She wanted Colleen to have some security before marriage and motherhood consumed her.

"I'm done with school," Colleen said. "Sammy has a house down the street. He just moved back, so we'll be close."

Of course he had a house on this street. His parents probably bought it for him. Silver-spoon Samuel Granger, the man who screwed her daughter out of finishing college.

"Have you decided on a date for the wedding?" She kept her voice steady and forced a big smile on her face. She wasn't going to be like her parents when she told them she'd married Greg after only meeting him that day. She'd be supportive no matter how much it hurt. No matter how angry it made her. No matter what she thought of her soon-to-be-son-in-law.

"Well, Sammy's parents think a July wedding at the country club would be perfect. They're going to book The Peabody for the rehearsal dinner," Colleen said. "They're so excited for us." She gazed at Sammy and innocently leaned back against his chest.

"Have you thought about, um?" *Should I mention the baby elephant in the room? They're not hiding it, but they're not announcing it either.* "What about the baby on the way?"

Sammy grinned and kissed Colleen's cheek. "Coll, I told you your mom would know."

"I didn't think anyone would notice." Colleen stared like a lovesick puppy up at him. "I'm only four months. Your mom didn't think anyone would know."

"Colleen," Ella said. "Anyone who looks at you will know you're pregnant. Are you sure you want to wait until July?" She couldn't afford an expensive wedding. She couldn't afford a cheap wedding. She would have to sell all the jewelry she had in order to pay for Colleen's wedding to Samuel Granger.

She'd have to work every day until the wedding, and she still might not have enough. If they went to the local chapel and kept the guests to a minimum, she might be able to swing it. It wouldn't be the wedding of Colleen's dreams, but it would be intimate and cozy, something real and beautiful.

"But the Magnolia Room at the Country Club isn't available until July," Colleen pouted.

What was her little girl thinking? Had she raised a child that shallow? Had she hidden her financial problems too well? Was Colleen blind to the struggles? Hadn't her only daughter noticed the missing wedding and engagement rings from Ella's hand? The void of jewelry in the once-filled-to-the-brim boxes? She wanted to scream, but she kept up appearances. She kept up the charade. She kept the secret of her terrible finances.

"Is it more important to get married in the Magnolia Room? Or is starting your marriage on the right track more important?" Ella asked.

"Ella." Garrett barked her name like a command to stop. "We'll talk about it later."

"We can talk about it over dinner," Colleen said. "Uncle Garrett, you didn't cancel dinner plans yet, did you?"

Garrett shook his head. "I pushed them back a little."

"I don't know how you knew she'd be back so soon," Colleen said.

"I have a little idea," Cade mumbled. He squeezed Ella's hand softly and gazed down at her. "Are the boys going?"

She didn't know when Cade ended up behind her, holding her steady, but she was glad he was there, supporting her. So overwhelmed, her stomach clenched tightly around all the knots it formed as each second ticked by waiting for Colleen's answer.

"No, sir," Colleen said. "It's adults only. No little brothers allowed."

"Then I'll take the boys with me," Cade said. "Y'all good with that?"

"Yeah," Jason said.

Kyle nodded.

Although seemingly relieved, her boys' lack of color in their faces made them look as sick as she felt.

"Sweetie." Cade lightly hugged her. "Are you okay with it?"

"I am. Thank you." She backed up closer to him. He radiated heat, warming the chill in her bones. She wished Cade had been invited to the dinner or that she stayed at dinner with him instead of running off. She felt so inadequate in her own kitchen with her daughter gushing over rich Samuel Granger and Garrett as if they were the only two who mattered in the world.

Why was I the last to know? Why would the Grangers know about the pregnancy and not me? Why the hell is my life so damn miserable right now? Why isn't Cade running for the door after seeing this debacle first hand?

"Mom, you need to change into a pretty dress," Colleen said. "Put on some makeup too. Gosh, you need to think about your image. You are a Winthrop, and you need to start dressing like one again. Thrift store fashion isn't in."

Oh. My. God. You didn't just say that. "Colleen Winthrop—"

"—Get over yourself," Jason interrupted Ella and glared at Colleen. His face flushed red. "Mom looks great. Sammy's not gonna want to marry a disrespectful bitch." He paused. His glare softened slightly. "He thinks you can take care of a baby? You can't even take care of yourself. Has he seen your room once you've been in it for like five minutes? You're a slob. You make Kyle look like a neat freak." He knocked his big sister off her royal pedestal.

"Ha-ha, Jay," Colleen said. She slipped into the regular sibling banter. "I'm not a slob and neither is Kyle. You are. For your information, little brother, Sammy has seen me—"

"—Stop." Garrett strode as fast as a leopard around the center island straight to Ella. "That is enough."

Ella froze. Her mind flashed with memories of Greg's sudden rages. She closed her eyes, and forced her thoughts to a happier place. *The beach house on the Gulf at sunset with healthy Greg. Cade's floor-to-ceiling windows in his bedroom at the lake house.*

"Mom," Colleen said, in a softer apologetic tone. "I didn't mean it like it sounded. I love you, but you've let yourself go the last few years. I know how beautiful you can look. You need to make yourself a priority now that I have Sammy to take care of me. The boys are kind of adults and can take care of themselves. You've got Uncle Garrett too now that he's home where he belongs."

Ella blinked, uncertain of the right response, and unable to make her mouth move to speak even if she could think of something to say. Her little girl didn't need her? Since when? Just last month Colleen called, crying after receiving a failing grade on a test. Now, she was inconsequential in her daughter's life.

"Sammy," Garrett said, sounding too much like

Greg. “Ella and I will meet you at the restaurant.”

“I thought I was the one invited, not Garrett.” Ella lifted her heels and balanced on the balls of her feet. She leaned to the side to see her daughter behind Garrett. *Shit. I can’t afford an expensive dinner, and the Grangers would choose the most lavish restaurant for appearances sake. My luck sucks.*

“It’s for the six of us,” Colleen said. “Uncle Garrett is always invited to anything having to do with the family. He’s walking me down the aisle and dancing with me at the wedding.”

Ella’s mouth gaped. She’d assumed Jason and Kyle would walk Colleen down the aisle. She’d imagined Kyle and Jason dancing with her, not Garrett. Garrett abandoned them. Garrett didn’t deserve a spot of honor. Kyle and Jason did. She did. She closed her mouth and gained some composure. How long had Colleen been talking to Garrett? How long had they been secretly planning the wedding? Since when had Garrett become a father figure to Colleen? When had they become such great pals?

I hate you, Garrett. How dare you?

“Cade, the boys are hungry,” Garrett said. He took over the head of the household role in the family dynamic while Ella stayed tongue-tied.

“The boys are always hungry. Tell me something I don’t know,” Cade said with an edge of irritation in his tone. He unbuttoned his jacket and slipped it off. He kept one hand on Ella the entire time as if she’d crumble under the pressure if he let go.

She might have.

Sammy followed Garrett’s order, and swept Colleen off her feet and into his arms. Her beautiful, blonde hair fell in soft waves over her shoulders He carried her off while she squealed like a little girl in total delight and utterly oblivious to the tense mood in the room.

"Now that they're gone," Cade said. "Garrett, why are you here?" He smoothly moved Ella from in front of him to behind him and became a barrier from Garrett's hungry hands.

"I wanted to see my niece and nephews," Garrett said.

"Give that bullshit to someone else," Cade said. "You can't waltz in here and walk all over Ella and her children." He stood a good four or five inches taller than Garrett. He didn't back down. Everyone backed down to Garrett. Everyone but Greg and now Cade.

"But you can?" Garrett argued. "Buying her new furniture, appliances, and the boys cars?"

"And taking care of her lawn with the boys help. Don't forget the paint in the kitchen, and fixing a few things around the house," Cade said. "I can buy Ella and the boys anything I want. She needed a few things, and I wanted to get them for her. End of story. I'm not emotionally fu-messing with them. You seem to be."

The boys hurried around Cade's back to her and hid behind the huge, protective man who wasn't afraid to get involved, and stand up to the most intimidating man, besides her late husband, she'd ever known. They seemed to time travel back to when Greg was sick and the boys huddled together behind her hoping he wouldn't become violent. Only this time, they had a formidable a protector—Cade—to save them.

But Garrett wasn't a threat. He hadn't and wouldn't hurt them. He only looked like the man who lost his mind from cancer.

"I needed to explain to the boys why I left. I wanted to do it without Ella worrying about their reaction." Garrett kept his feet planted and didn't give Cade an inch of space.

He cocked his head, studied the boys, and seemed confused by their reaction.

"They're fine, like I knew they would be." The normally strong and steady cadence of his voice faltered. His voice lowered as the lilt shifted to a soft questioning tone like he wasn't so sure they were all right. "They're Winthrops, and we're strong in mind, body, and spirit. They're my family, not yours."

"They are." Cade nodded. "They sure are." He turned around and faced Ella and the boys. He gathered them inside his expansive frame. He mouthed to them, *"Are you okay?"*

Kyle seemed reluctant as he nodded.

Cade's lips pressed together and his eyebrows scrunched up. He gently placed his hand on Kyle's shoulder. "You two worked hard today. I'm really proud of you. We have some more work to do before your mom and uncle get back from dinner, don't we?" He winked at them.

A big smile filled Jason and Kyle's mouths. A little color filled their cheeks.

"We sure do." Kyle straightened up and snapped out of the place his mind went.

"Go get changed, and we'll get to it," Cade said.

The tender, yet firm way Cade spoke made her want to follow him. She liked the way he talked with such authority. Whatever had happened over this mess of a week endeared her boys to the giant man, and it wasn't because of the cars he'd bought them. They'd have to give those back. It was the man.

Kyle and Jason hugged her.

"Mom, we're going to show you everything we did to the house later," Jason said.

"Thanks for working so hard. The place looks incredible." She kissed Jason's cheek and held both boys close. "I told Cade about selling the house," she whispered. "I don't want Colleen or Garrett knowing about it until it's sold." *They might try to stop me.*

"I love you." Jason nodded.

"Try not to strangle Colleen tonight," Kyle whispered.

She smiled. "I think Garrett's the one you need to be worried about."

"Do you mind if I talk to your mom for a minute?" Cade asked the boys.

"That's our cue," Kyle said to Jason. They left the emotionally charged kitchen to get ready for whatever Cade had planned for the night.

"Do you want to go out with me and the boys? I'll buy you a dress for tonight?" Cade lowered his voice to a whisper, "I owe you about twenty outfits." He curled his arm around her and drew her inside the safety of his embrace. "I really want to buy more clothes to rip off you."

Shivers ran through her. "I'd—"

"I bought you a dress. It's in your bedroom," Garrett said from behind Cade.

Ugh. Nothing got past Garrett. "Oh, okay," she said. "Thanks."

"Ella, we really do need to go," Garrett said. "The Grangers are a pain in the ass, but they're pretty happy about Colleen and the pregnancy. She hasn't said it, but Colleen's been on edge about giving you the news about the baby. She remembers when you lost the—"

"—that was a lifetime ago." She hugged her waist. So many things changed the day Garrett walked away from all of them. That day started her on the hardest road she'd ever traveled and the end to the easy love she shared with her husband. She leaned her head against Cade's chest. "I need a drink."

"Sweetie, I'm sorry," Cade whispered. "You don't have to go tonight. Reschedule it."

"Tonight. Tomorrow." She shrugged. "Putting it off won't make it any easier."

She wanted Cade to take her to dinner to be a buffer with the Grangers. She didn't know what to expect with Garrett anymore. One minute he was sweet and loving, the next he was someone she didn't recognize. She breathed in Cade's whiskey scent. "I really want a drink…" *of you.*

"We'll get one at dinner." Garrett picked up where she wanted to go with Cade. "Ella, go on and get dressed."

She reached up and curled her arms around Cade's neck as he bent toward her. She lifted up onto her tippy toes and kissed his smoothly shaven cheek. "My life is a train wreck. Be smart, and run away from me."

"I can't. I need you," he whispered.

She pressed her lips just below his ear. "I'm not strong enough to push you away. You need to walk away on your own."

"I'm not walking away." Cade turned and kissed her so sweetly it tore at her heart. "I'm going to make you fall in love with me."

She drew her arms down from his neck and over his broad chest. “That’s what I’m afraid of.” She pivoted away from him toward the hallway, left the two men she didn’t know what to do with in the kitchen, and hoped they could find some common ground.

Chapter Eighteen

Sitting at the upscale steakhouse at a table across from the booth she and Cade had been in two hours earlier, Ella kept the forced smile on her lips through the entire patronizing dinner. She nibbled on her salad, choked down a small portion of her steak, and handed her dessert to Colleen. Her daughter was sixteen weeks pregnant and had supposedly told the Grangers about it twelve weeks ago. Although something didn't ring true about Matilda Granger, Sammy's mother's confession.

"Oh, Ella," Matilda cooed across from her. "I couldn't help myself from buying the house. It's so perfect for a growing family."

The portly woman reached over the white linen table cloth, past the empty dessert plate, and patted Ella's hand like a grandmother would a child. She inhaled and dramatically slapped her other hand to her chest and held it as she nodded. A puff of baby powder spiraled through the air and dusted the woman's neck and plates. Her eyes filled with tears for the hundredth time. "We're going to be grandmothers."

"Colleen is so lucky to be getting you as a mother-in-law," Ella said. Maybe Colleen will appreciate the family she has after getting to know the obnoxious in-laws. "The generous engagement gift is spectacular. It will be wonderful to be so close." *At least until I sell the house I can't afford.* She held up her water goblet for the waiter to fill. "I think it would be best if she and Sammy marry sooner than July."

"But she's so small." Matilda removed her pudgy hand from Ella's and placed it on Colleen's.

"Which is why she needs to get a dress and get married immediately." Ella scooted forward in her chair. Her hands clenched to fists "Soon she'll have to wear a maternity wedding gown." *She might need one now.* "Colleen, what do you think?"

"I'm barely showing. A couple months won't make a difference, will they Mrs. Granger?" Colleen asked.

"I didn't show until my sixth month." Matilda beamed at her husband Nathaniel.

"I noticed my pants were tighter at seven weeks with Colleen and five weeks with the boys." Ella's cheek twitched. Her fake smile faltered. "It's up to Colleen and Sammy whether they marry now or in July. They need to decide whether being married matters more to them than the venue where the ceremony happens." *You've got so much to learn, Colleen. Marriage is hard work, not playtime.*

Colleen's gaze fell to the third empty dessert plate in front of her. She blushed a bright pink.

Garrett gently patted Ella's back and kissed her cheek. His lips lingered near her ear. "Let it go."

"She could stand to gain a few pounds." Matilda patted Colleen's hand.

"She's perfect the way she is." Ella straightened up in her seat. With the week she'd had, she was ready to explode on the woman. Colleen wasn't perfect. Right then, Colleen was high on her shit list from all the deceiving she'd been doing for months, but damn it… Colleen was her child, not Matilda's. She'd be damned if Matilda said anything negative about her daughter, ever.

Garrett slipped his arm around her and squeezed her tightly against his side. “Drop. It. Now.”

“She is perfect.” Sammy pulled Colleen onto his lap. He wrapped his arms around her and kissed her cheek. “She couldn’t be more perfect.”

“Aw.” Ella sighed. *Maybe Sammy isn’t so bad. She needs a strong protector.*

His hands slid to Colleen’s belly.

Shit. She hadn’t signed up for a pregnancy rider for her medical insurance. None of Colleen’s appointments would be covered. They needed to get married now. Tonight. Colleen needed Sammy’s insurance to cover all the pregnancy and baby expenses.

“We could always get married in Vegas this weekend with just our families,” Sammy said.

Now we’re talking. Get married as soon as possible. Don’t wait.

Colleen gazed up at Sammy. “We could do it here in a couple weeks with family and friends.”

“Sounds great.” Garrett held up his hand for the check, and the waitress hurried over. He handed her his credit card.

“We’ll have close to one hundred guests on our side wherever they get married,” Nathaniel Granger said. “We expect a picture-worthy wedding and reception.”

The Nathaniel Granger Ella knew finally reared his ugly head. He had been surprisingly reserved the entire evening, allowing Matilda to talk incessantly about how Colleen was the daughter she never had while making left-handed compliments about Colleen’s weight, hair, and clothes. All she needed was Mrs. Kellen to stop by for an impromptu visit about how Jason and Kyle would never graduate high school. Then her day would be complete.

Colleen bit her bottom lip and glanced at Ella like she always did when she worried.

"Colleen and Sammy are a gorgeous couple. They are picture-worthy in their pajamas. As for you and your guests, I can't speak to your photogenic qualities," Ella said. Her heart softened as Colleen's back straightened up. Maybe Colleen had seen all the sacrifices. Maybe she was scared like every first-time mother.

"I expect perfection, Ella," Nathanial snorted. "Not some red-plastic-cup wedding and reception in your backyard."

"Dad," Sammy grunted. "Jeez, stop it. The wedding doesn't matter. I love Colleen, and I don't care about anything but marrying my girl."

Nathanial frowned. "Let's get real. She hooked you with a pregnancy. You never looked twice at her the entire time she lived down the street."

"She was twelve," Sammy said. "That would have been sick. But you know what? She was nice. She was always a nice girl with a sweet attitude and a confidence that drew people in. She's still that way. If you want to get real, let's let it all out. *I* got her pregnant. *I* roped her in. *I* wanted her so badly I did damned near everything I could think of to get her…"

Sammy stood up, holding Colleen in his arms. "…So, if you don't want to come to the red-plastic-cup wedding in Mrs. Winthrop's backyard, then don't. We'll have a great time with our friends, and we'll have the best photos ever made because they'll be real. They'll be honest. And they won't be staged."

Colleen closed her eyes and buried her face against the collar of Sammy's white dress shirt.

"Mrs. Winthrop, I'm taking Colleen home to our house. Thank you for enduring tonight. I love your daughter, and I genuinely hope my parents' poor behavior doesn't sour you on me. I know the wedding and reception will be perfect, just like my Colleen, with or without plastic cups." Sammy took a step toward the exit.

"Oh, and we could have plastic cups in our favorite colors—blue and yellow and pink would be perfect." He winked at her and grinned. "In fact, if we get married in your backyard, Garrett and I could make a pavilion and stage for the ceremony. We could grill out and make the reception fun and casual. Maybe get a fire in the fire pit and roast marshmallows once it got dark like you used to when we were all kids? That would be my kind of party."

Ella grinned. Sammy Granger was all right. "Colleen and I will talk about it," she said. "We'll work something out." *And it won't break the bank.*

"And Mrs. Winthrop, I'd appreciate your blessing on me marrying your daughter. I would have asked sooner, but I've been working up the courage. I know I'm older than Colleen, but I promise, I'll take care of her for the rest of my life."

Warmth filled Ella's heart. It might have come late, but he cared enough to stand up and ask her approval even after his parents insulted her and Colleen.

"You have my blessing, Sammy." She'd have a discussion with him about Colleen's future after they got to know each other better. One way or another, Colleen would be trained in a career outside the house too.

"Thank you, Mrs. Winthrop." Sammy turned toward his parents. "Mom, Dad, if you can't be nice, I don't want you around me and my fiancée. We have a baby on the way, and we don't need the extra stress. *My Colleen* doesn't need the extra stress. I'm sure Mrs. Winthrop doesn't need it either. Your bullshit about knowing about the baby before today was just that—bullshit. The only person who knew about it prior to now was Garrett because Colleen was nervous about telling her mother."

Sammy pivoted away and strode out of the restaurant with her daughter like the knight in shining armor he was.

Ready to jump up and down with joy for the smack down Sammy gave his parents, Ella held in her glee. Her daughter'd found a strong man who loved her. There were worse things in life than not finishing a college degree immediately after high school.

And she wasn't too far out of the loop in her daughter's life after all. She might not have to take out a loan for the wedding and reception, depending on what Colleen really wanted. Her evening was turning around.

"We hope you're happy," Nathanial said. "Our only son is marrying a girl whose only aspiration is to be a loser like her mother."

"Nathanial, that was rude," Matilda said. "Let's go. Maybe we'll talk him into adopting the child instead of marrying such a young girl."

"You two better not say another word against my

niece or Ella," Garrett said in his no-nonsense military voice. "You will not like the consequences, if you do."

Nathaniel sputtered, "W-well, I'm not sure I know what you mean."

Garrett raised his eyebrows and tilted his chin down at Nathaniel. "I think you do."

Ella shivered as Garrett glared at the man. Garrett didn't threaten unless he meant it. Greg had been the same way. Garrett could make people disappear, not that he would do that to the Grangers, but he might make life difficult or scare the shit out of them. Greg would have ruined them financially. It wasn't beyond Garrett's abilities to do the same.

The waitress came back with the receipt and saved them from more awkwardness. Garrett signed the receipt and stood up.

"Matilda, Nathaniel." He nodded at them and grinned as if he hadn't just threatened Nathaniel with a scary unknown. "We hope to see you at the wedding, whenever and wherever they choose to have one." He pulled Ella's chair out and held out his hand.

Ella delicately placed her hand in his and joined him at his side like she would have Greg. Her leg ached with the effort, but she refused to show any weakness. "Thank you."

"Thank you for dinner, Garrett." Matilda stayed frozen in her seat.

"You're welcome." Garrett led Ella to the front of the steakhouse and held open the door. "What happened to your leg?"

A black stretch limo pulled up to the side of the curb in front of them.

"It's nothing," She said. A couple painkillers

would make her forget about it.

The driver stepped out of the car and opened the back door as Garrett guided her to the limo. The man looked down at the sidewalk away from Garrett's gaze. "Mr. Winthrop."

"We're ready to go. No interruptions," Garrett ordered. He gently coaxed Ella into the backseat and climbed in after her. The car door closed. They sat next to each other in a soundproof box with a tinted window divider between the driver and the back.

"Why don't you have a regular car?" she asked. She rubbed her hands back and forth nervously on the black leather seat beside her. She had never asked him why he always had a driver when he visited. Usually Derek drove, but he wasn't in the limo tonight.

"This one is safer for me and I've been doing it forever. It's habit."

"Why does Derek usually drive you everywhere?"

"Honestly, he's a control freak. He has to be the one in the driver seat in everything he does. People think I pay him, but I don't and never have. I don't care one way or the other who drives, but I prefer this arrangement when I'm with you."

She slid to the opposite end of the back seat away from Garrett and stared out her side window at the darkness of the clouds covering the moon and stars. Maybe her leg hurt worse this evening because of the storm system moving in or because she reinjured it falling out of Cade's car.

Garrett moved over and lifted her right leg onto his lap. "How long has it hurt?"

"It's been a while." *I'm not sure I can handle your touch tonight. You were so good at dinner. So strong.*

"It's probably the weather."

He tested her range of motion and pressed the exact spot of the injury. She jerked away.

"I don't think it's broken," he said. "It may be bruised or sprained. Your ankle looks swollen. Baby, did you fall?"

"I fell earlier. Sometimes I'm a little clumsy when the weather changes," she said. "I'm fine."

"Your ankle needs to be wrapped." He slipped her heel off and rubbed her foot. "Sneakers for the rest of the week. If you want a second opinion I can get Derek to give you an x-ray. He's working tonight."

His familiar hands rubbed at the knots in the arch and heel of her foot. It had been too long since she'd been able to afford a massage. She gave but rarely received anymore. Once she sold the house, she would get a massage. "Mm. You're good at that." She adjusted her body to get more comfortable. She wouldn't get an x-ray, at least not one tied to Garrett. He'd take over her life if she let him.

"I learned from a master," he said.

"I am a good teacher."

"Are you still mad at me?"

She closed her eyes and sighed. "Yes."

"Marry me," Garrett whispered.

She shook her head. He hadn't changed at all. He always strove to get what he wanted. "No."

He lifted her foot and kissed her ankle and then massaged her foot again. "Get rid of Cade."

"Don't kiss my foot," she said. "And no. I like Cade. We're dating."

"You understand why I left, right?"

She nodded. "I understand you thought you gave

Greg what he wanted. But he didn't want you gone."

His explanation of leaving hadn't minimized the hurt. The shock of his return had lessened some of the pain from his abandonment. In her heart, she hoped he would never leave again, but her trust was shattered. It would take more than one night to glue the pieces back together. "It doesn't matter. I'm not the same anymore."

"You are the same in all the ways that count." He caressed over her calf, up her thigh, under the hem of the chocolate-brown silk dress he bought her, and up to her hip.

She placed her hand over his but didn't stop his exploration as it focused over her panties along her pubic bone. She wanted to be angry with him for manipulating her, but she couldn't bring herself to hold onto the grudge. She loved him. She shifted her hips and gave his long fingers more room to wander. "How do you do it?

He slid his fingers back and forth along the edge of her panty at the crease of her leg and hip. "How do I do what?"

She removed his hand and sat up. "Make me forgive you so easily." *Just like Greg*. They always found it easier to ask forgiveness than permission, something she never understood.

He settled his hand on her foot again. "You love me. I love you. We're free to be together. There's no guilt being in the same room alone anymore. You can touch me without Greg screaming bullshit infidelity. We can dance, hold hands, kiss, and make love." He released her injured leg and pulled her other leg onto his lap. He began massaging her other foot. "The kids are grown. We can indulge in each other without any worry of interruptions or complications."

He shifted and spread her legs open. He slipped out of his jacket and tossed it to the seat across from them.

"Garrett, we're not having sex." She couldn't make love to two different men. She couldn't date two men. She needed to walk away from both of them. It would be the right thing to do.

"Why not?"

"Because we're not." He would walk away from her now that he couldn't get into her panties.

He unknotted his yellow and blue diagonally stripped tie, slipped it off, and threw it onto his jacket. He continued stripping off his shirt and undershirt as she watched in rapt attention. The scars over his abdomen gave the pretty boy a sexy edge. Greg always reminded her of a male-fitness model, ripped muscles over flawless skin, while Garrett was more of a warrior, a masculine machine, scarred yet powerful and tough, and sculpted from years of training and combat. "If we're not making love…"

"Get dressed," she whispered.

He flexed his muscles as he steadily seduced her. He pulled her legs around his waist and gently pushed her down on the backseat. God, help her, he knew her body like he knew his own.

Juices dripped from her sex, dampening her panties.

She wanted to make love to him knowing it was him. But she couldn't do it with Cade in the mix—even with Cade's permission. Could she? Was it possible to get Garrett out of her system without having sex with him again? Not with years of desire brewing inside them. One night wouldn't be enough. But, would a month? *I need to stop this line of thought.*

She sat up. He sat up too and took control.

"Anyone can see inside." She needed to get distance from him. He was too tempting. She was too vulnerable too confused with all the changes in her life.

"Tinted windows," Garrett murmured. He pulled her against his chiseled torso.

Her chest heaved with anticipation at his next touch. Was he really adventurous? Or had he been teasing her earlier? He'd been mostly vanilla and missionary last night. But that was her Greg ghost. She had been wild with Garrett. Did she touch Derek? *Derek hadn't touched me. He took all the pictures.*

"I can feel your heat," Garrett whispered a hairsbreadth from her lips. "You want me as badly as I want you." Desire rolled off him like steam from an overheated engine. She parted her lips for a kiss. He pressed his smooth lips to hers.

His fingers slid between them as his tongue stroked and explored her mouth. He adjusted his hips as his fingers pushed her drenched panties aside. The tip of his hot length pressed against her pussy. She slowly inched down onto him as he guided her. His thick cock filled her, stretched her.

She groaned. *So good.*

He rocked her back and forth as she dropped down his shaft all the way to the hilt. Her heart hammered inside her chest. She shouldn't be doing this, but she couldn't stop. She needed this. Needed him. Needed to remember every kiss, every caress, every thrust, and every orgasm.

She hadn't felt the limo stop with the motion they

had going, but the car door opened.

Garrett shifted his hold, and slid out, carrying her with his cock buried inside her pussy. Her dress covered their joining as he strode past the driver, through the garage, and into his home.

They weren't supposed to be at his place.

Garrett stopped kissing her and held her against the smoke-colored wall in the hall next to a closed door. "No barriers. No boundaries. We can get as kinky as you want."

The door swung open, and he carried her inside an undecorated bedroom with a king sized, poster bed she remembered him designing. She'd forgotten how talented he was as a carpenter. Hand carved into the wooden headboard framed with mirrors were large figures of the Greek gods in all their nude magnificence.

Her back hit the soft mattress. Gazing upward, she saw her own lusty smile reflected in the hidden mirror embedded inside the canopy.

"Wait until you see my cock sliding into your pussy. I built this for us. I built it so I wouldn't miss seeing every inch of your incredible body."

She had no words as his back flexed and rippled with muscles honed through a lifetime of military training. He pushed his pants down, uncovering the firm ass and powerful legs that would make sure nothing was vanilla about their coupling. He carefully lifted her silk dress over her head.

"I'll get the size right next time," he said. "No bra?"

"No." *Nothing clean. No time for shopping at lunch or after work.* She shifted her focus to his blue eyes instead of the mirror and his back. She traced the edge of his stubbly cheek. "Thank you for dinner."

"You're welcome. I'd do anything for you. Anything, except leave. I'm never leaving again. Don't ever ask that of me. I won't do it." His hands dropped to her breasts, but his gaze stayed focused on hers.

"I won't ask you to leave." She wouldn't. She loved him. She and the boys would adjust to and process his return over time. They'd find a way to let go of the fear Greg instilled in them at his quick approach and remember it was Garrett, not Greg, coming for them. The goatee would help. The rough outline of shadow on his face distinguished him from her late husband.

He inhaled slowly and drew circles around her nipples. "Every Thursday and Friday night you're going to sleep over here." He continued teasing her nipples, squeezing, circling, as he told her the schedule he and Cade had made for her.

"I don't think so." She wasn't allowing him to dictate her life. "I'm not staying the night. I have children." She wiggled to break their physical connection, but his hard cock grew harder inside her, and his hands shot like bullets to her wrists. He pinned her arms down to her sides.

"We're going to hash this out now. The boys were uncomfortable around me. It's been a long time since they've seen me. It seemed like their hesitation wasn't about me, but something else they wouldn't talk about. I wasn't sure if it had to do with Colleen and Sammy, or with you and Cade walking in on our conversation. Do you know what spooked them?"

"I don't want to be in your bed with your cock in

me while we discuss my boys. It seems wrong, really wrong." A sudden rush of guilt clouded her mind. *I'm in bed with my brother-in-law.* "I can't do this. Please get off me."

"Ella," he whispered as he shifted off her. He rolled to the side and pulled her back against his chest. "It's me. We're not doing anything wrong."

"It feels wrong." She loved him, but she couldn't shake the guilt. Why couldn't he have just continued seducing her until they were sweaty and satisfied? She'd feel guilty enough for having sex with him when she had been determined she would only make love with Cade. Now she had to deal with the memory of Greg too. "I don't want to date you and Cade."

"Great. Let's call him, and tell him it is over. You've made your decision, and it's me." He kissed the back of her head and got up from the bed.

She took the break and righted her uncomfortably wet panty. Ugh. She grabbed her dress and pulled it over her head and down, covering the rest of her, before climbing off the bed.

Garrett stood with his cell phone to his ear. "Hey, Cade. Ella has made her decision… Yes, you can talk to her. Putting you on speaker."

"Ella," Cade's deep voice vibrated from the phone.

"Hi," she said. She walked over to Garrett and checked out the detailed scenes of demi-gods in multiple sexual acts with men and women, men and men, and women and women on his nightstand, dresser, and the mirror above his dresser.

"We need to talk before you make any decisions," Cade said.

"I'm not going to date either of you." *I want to.*

God, I want to do so many of the things Garrett carved into his furniture with you and him. "You guys make me feel like I'm a child dealing with a divorce, being shuttled from one parent to the other with the way you two are dividing up my week."

Garrett's blue eyes grew as wide as an owl's. "What?"

"I'm not doing this. I thought maybe I could, but I can't."

"What about hanging out?" Cade asked. "Pizza at the house with the boys? Watching a movie on the couch kind of stuff?"

"That's fine but no sex. No demands. No seduction. No sleepovers. At ten o'clock y'all go home."

"What about hanging out with Maddie and Mike, and Josie and Mark?" Cade asked.

Garrett stayed surprisingly quiet as his pale face returned to a normal healthy glow.

"That's fine. We're not going to be alone together." She'd keep it platonic with both of them. The only way to keep from jumping either of them would be to make sure other people were present.

"Great. Tomorrow we're meeting…" He continued talking. He explained the week he'd planned with her and his family along with all the construction plans for Colleen's backyard wedding. "The ceremony will be three weeks from tonight, right?"

"I don't know. I hope so. I can't let your parents do all that for free."

"Don't insult them. Mom is giving the flowers and food as a wedding gift which means it will be over-the-top, and the most beautiful arrangements you will ever see. The men in the family will build all kinds of arches and platforms. The vases for the ceremony are taken care of, and Mom promised the reception flowers around Sammy's man cake will be masculine. He wants the cake to be a football. Did you know he got a scholarship for football but turned it down to go into the military?"

"I didn't know that. You got all that information since dinner ended?" Wow, he was good at getting information. Not only could the man talk, but he was a master listener.

"Well, yeah, sweetie. Colleen said dinner didn't go so well. Sammy said it sucked. The boys and I were having dinner with my parents, so we put them on speaker, and talked as we finished dessert. They're great kids, well, young adults. Are you home?"

"No." Garrett broke his silence. "I'll help you design and build the backyard structures for the ceremony. Greg and I designed the house and landscaping, so I can help with placement of the structures."

Really? She mouthed to Garrett.

He winked at her and nodded.

"All right, I'll have Pappy send out group emails with the information. We'll meet at Ella's within the next couple days and go from there." Cade rattled off his father's email, and Garrett typed it into his phone. They exchanged more information and once again scheduled her nights around platonic get-togethers which sounded more like chaperoned dates.

How did I end up with two men controlling my days and nights again?

Garrett ended the call. He stood naked with a red,

throbbing erection against his eight pack abs. "A platonic relationship will not work with us, not when you're available and so am I."

She burned to have him, to love him, to feel him inside her again, but this time there would be no games, no questions as to his ghost status. She knew exactly who he was and what she was doing. "I'm making an exception to my 'no sex' rule for tonight."

After she got the initial need out of her system, she would put him back in the "friend" category and take the time to figure out her feelings for him and Cade.

A bead of precum gathered at the top of his cock.

He closed the space between them. In less than five seconds, she lay nude in the middle of his bed. "We both want this for forever, Ella."

Her chest heaved with anticipation at his next touch. She didn't want him to affect her so much. She didn't want to want him so badly. Part of her didn't want to find out if his talk about being adventurous and sharing her with Derek was just talk, but as soon as he touched her, the other part that did, really did.

She closed her eyes, gave in, and took a chance. "Just tonight, Garrett. Only once."

"This is a sample. We'll be doing this plenty more than once."

She shook her head. "Once. Then we're back to friendship only."

"Neither of us want *only* friendship." His lips met hers, planting a tender kiss. "I'm going to give you a fantasy tonight."

Soft, cotton linens caressed her back as his chiseled body hovered over her. He nudged her knees apart and settled his pelvis against hers. It was so familiar, yet different.

"What fantasy?" *Is Cade coming over? Is Derek joining us?*

"Open your eyes," he said softly.

She opened her lids. The minute her gaze found his, he rocked forward and drove deep inside her pussy. She whimpered as he kissed her lips. His tongue delved into her mouth, bringing with it the burning desire she'd held in her soul. Her hips undulated against the familiarity of his body, rocking her to the core.

He wasn't Greg, but his body matched his in every way, and she automatically reacted to him as if he was her husband. She opened her body and heart to him.

She wrapped her legs around his hips, stretched her arms straight over her head, and pressed her hands against the Greek gods in the headboard for counter pressure to his thrusts. Her fingers fit perfectly inside little grooves, allowing her to curl her fingers, and grip it tightly.

"That's it, baby. I made it for you, for your hands." He rocked back and thrust forward.

She moaned as his hot cock slid in and out. In and out.

He grunted. His rod jerked and hit the perfect sweet spot. All of her inhibitions vanished.

Her body sizzled and begged for more. Pieces of the previous night came together. The positions. The photos. Derek's gaze always on them. Her pussy contracted around him.

"Hold on tight, baby." His fingers curled into the ridges and valleys in the headboard over her hands.

She had no idea how he could have constructed something so complex. *Genius. Always seeing things no one else does.*

He scooted forward and drove his cock deeper. Her hunger for more increased and pushed her closer to ecstasy.

He lifted his chest and lowered his head. His gaze met hers. "I—"

"Garrett, you're going to be late for work," Derek shouted.

She stiffened. *Shit.* "Is this Derek's place?"

"Yes. I couldn't get transferred to a base nearby, so I retired from the military. That is what took me so long to get here. I yanked every chain I could and called in every favor to get out. I thought they'd never let me go. But they did."

"How long has Derek been here? Isn't he in the military?" She swallowed hard. He suckered her in again. When had he truly arrived in town? Had he been watching her? The boys?

"Derek was honorably discharged from the military about five years ago. He has been in Memphis for a month. He's the chief of surgery at a private sector defense company of which I am now a partner. The corporate headquarters is here in Memphis. It's as close to a normal job as I'll probably ever have. Field missions will be rare—maybe twice a year."

"Please don't tell me you have to leave tomorrow." She inhaled as her heart sank to her stomach. "Please, Garrett, don't make love to me and leave. Don't tell us you're staying and be gone the next day." *You need to make up with us. You need to prove we can trust you again.*

"I'm not leaving. The next assignment isn't for a few weeks. My schedule is all over the place, but it's only because I'm heading up some training. I'm here for the rest of my life."

"Oh," Derek said. "Good reason to be late." She turned her head toward his voice.

The gorgeous doctor in all his naked glory strode toward the bed. His erection bobbed against his abs.

"Beautiful sight," Derek said. He climbed on the bed and kissed her lips.

"So glad you're here with us." He cupped the back of Garrett's neck and kissed his mouth. "Dinner went well?"

Her eyes widened. *I thought you guys had something going on, but you're a couple?* "Are you two fucking each other? Are you in love?"

"We—" Derek started.

"I haven't had anal sex," Garrett said.

Derek frowned. "We've been best friends for more than thirty years. We've been sleeping together, sucking each other's dicks, and sharing women for decades. Last night scratched the very surface of our sexual interests. The photos are a part of our journey. The way you spread your pussy lips showed me you are open for trying new things."

She nodded. *I did do that. I must have rubbed your cock too.*

"Are you ready for a real adventure? One you'll want to continue for the rest of your life?" Derek asked.

"Um." *If you only knew about the dreams I've had about you and Garrett and me. Fantasies of me making love to Garrett and Greg and having you join us. I'm up for an adventure.* Would he want her too? Would he want to make love to only her, sometimes? She'd fantasized about having sex with only him too.

Garrett shifted forward. Her hips curled farther upward. His cock tunneled deeper inside her. "You weren't sure I was serious about my sex life," Garrett said.

"I believed you." *Your cock is in me and Derek is here*. She should have been embarrassed but she wasn't. "Why does this feel so—"

"—much like home?" Derek said.

Home. Comfortable. Right. She gazed at Derek and nodded.

"Because it is." Derek kissed her lips. "Ready to experience a real adventure?"

A lopsided grin took over Garrett's mouth. "You are."

"She is," Derek added. "Her nipples are hard, and she's blushing. She wants a taste of two men."

She opened her mouth to say something. To deny their claims. Nothing came out. They were right. All her intentions to get rid of anything too complicated flew out the window. *I want to experience something new. One time and never again. I could never keep up with two men.* "If we did do something, it would have to be confidential. No one talks to anyone else outside these walls."

"I'm not ashamed of Derek in our bed, but it wouldn't be wise to broadcast it around in our circle or yours," Garrett said.

"When you're ready, we're going to make it so fucking good, you'll want to do it every day for the rest of your life," Derek said. "We get you Sunday, so we'll prep you tonight." He climbed off the bed and strode toward the door. He glanced back. "I'll grab the supplies she'll need while you're getting alone time with her. I'll be back soon to drive her home and you to work." He walked out of the bedroom and left the door wide open.

"I could call him back." Garrett wiggled his eyebrows.

"This is about us, Garrett. I thought you wanted to marry me?"

"I do. We can go to the chapel now."

"Um. No. I'm trying to figure out what all this means? Are you gay?"

"I'm attracted to Derek. I love him. He's the only guy I've ever wanted and done anything with. I love women. I love you. I want to marry you."

"But you want Derek to join us?"

"Yes. We would be in a permanent relationship. The three of us."

"That is more than adventurous. That is… I don't know." *It's sexy, and why am I so turned on by it?*

"Wait until he sticks his cock in your ass while mine is in your pussy." He swiveled his pelvis and rubbed circles over her beaded clit. He stimulated a sweet spot the tip of his cock pressed against. "You're going to love it."

Her legs trembled with pleasure. The words she'd kept to herself for years fell out. "I want to know what that feels like."

"I know you do, baby." He rocked back and thrust forward. "We're going to give it to you."

She slid toward the headboard with his powerful thrust, but she locked elbows stopping her head from making contact with the carvings. Her hips lifted off the bed as his cock tunneled into her depths and lit up her pussy with an electrical charge she'd only felt with

Cade. "Oh, my God. Yes."

"Like that?" He groaned. "Look up, and watch me fuck you."

She spread her thighs and planted her feet flat on the bed as her gaze drifted to the mirror above her.

He adjusted his legs and positioned her so she could see their joining. Slowly, he pulled out. Her pussy juices glistened on the smooth flesh of his cock.

She needed to install ceiling mirrors in her new house so when she made love to Cade, she could see every glorious inch of him. Her pussy contracted and more juices trickled from her slit. Cade would be all over her, taking her hard, not waiting. He'd tell her exactly what he was doing as he was doing it. He'd make her talk. Except, he wasn't there.

"You want my cock?" He lowered his pelvis, tapped her entrance, and lifted up again, not giving her the orgasm she wanted, teasing her.

"Yes, sir." She whimpered. *Just do it. Fuck me. I need to know I can walk away from this, from you, from the possibilities of wanting two men for more than an evening.*

She lifted her hips and tried to get closer to his beautiful cock. Precum dripped from the head onto her clit.

"Derek is watching us," he whispered. "He wants to taste your pussy, but you're mine. Your pussy is mine. Your ass is mine. Your mouth is mine. Your breasts, your neck, your back, every inch of you is mine. All mine."

"Fuck her, Garrett," Derek ordered. His gorgeous, athletic body came into view from the side mirrors around the top of the canopy. His hand wrapped around his thick cock and pumped up and down. Pearls of cum covered the huge head. He skimmed over the top, drew the liquid down, and lubricated the shaft. "I'm going to be deep inside you."

Derek's abs contracted. Ripples of muscle formed an eight pack as his hips thrust up into his hand. He'd always been in shape, but damn, he was as cut as Cade and Garrett.

She scanned him more thoroughly than before. Gorgeous, smooth, tanned skin all the way to a low speedo swim line. His cock stood firm, thick, and long with clean-shaven, heavy balls drawn up against his shaft.

Garrett drove into her, awakened her G-spot, and roughly rubbed against her breasts with his chest. Energy crackled in the room. Her breathing grew shallow as her pussy contracted in waves.

"She wants us." Derek's voice sounded gravelly and deep. He stepped closer toward the bed. He reached out with his other hand and caressed along Garrett's firm ass while he glided up and down his own length with the other.

Garrett moaned loudly. In and out, Garrett thrust. Harder. Faster. Deeper. "Watch my cock take your sweet pussy."

"Pull out and let me see her pussy juices all over your big dick," Derek demanded.

Garrett's legs shook as he lifted his hips. The mirrors around the top edge gave her a crystal clear, three-sided view. Her wet pussy spread open and waited for his return.

Her juices dripped from his cock. Her slick, pussy cream glistened along her inner thighs.

The bed dipped as Derek crawled between their legs.

"I need a taste," Derek said like an order. Like Cade.

"Oh, my God," she muttered.

Derek's tongue dipped into her pussy. He lifted his head and licked the head of Garrett's cock.

"Oh fuck," Garrett said.

Derek licked Garrett's balls and sucked on them as Garrett inched into her again.

"Mmm." Derek's voice vibrated into her sex. Painfully slow, Garrett retreated from her center. Derek's mouth took over. He licked her pussy, sucked her clit and then deep-throated Garrett's cock.

Her heart pounded out of her chest. Her legs shook as hard as Garrett's. Her clit throbbed. Her pussy contracted. She was going to explode.

"Derek," Garrett moaned. "Yes. Oh, shit. Yes."

Derek's tongue lapped at her center. His teeth tenderly raked over her sensitive, swollen clit. His lips brushed along her labia. He opened his mouth and traveled from her to Garrett's cock. He sucked down Garrett's shaft then dropped back to her entrance and dipped his tongue inside her.

She lifted her legs, needing more of his tongue's caresses.

His finger entered her as his hot mouth covered her clit.

"Yes," she whispered. "Yes."

Derek moved from between their legs.

She whimpered. "Please?"

"Garrett, fuck her," Derek demanded.

Garrett moved in a blink of an eye. He slammed his

cock into her pussy. In and out. In and out.

Derek crawled behind Garrett. “Let’s give all of us a real adventure.” His hands caressed Garrett’s sides and down along his abs to where his cock joined her pussy. Derek whispered, “I’m going to make this so much better.” His fingers slide back and forth over her sensitive clit.

“Please,” she begged. Her body trembled with the oncoming orgasm. She was so close. So damn close.

In the mirror, Derek’s cock slid against Garrett’s ass cheeks. His mouth pressed against Garrett’s neck.

“I love you,” Derek whispered.

Garrett’s lids closed and his lips parted. He thrust down into her.

“Need this. Need you. Oh fuck. Feels so good.” He rocked back.

“Push against me.” Derek groaned. He pinched Ella’s clit and held it as Garrett drove into her.

“Yes,” she cried out. Her pussy clenched around Garrett’s cock.

“Yes,” Garrett grunted. “Fuck. Yes.”

Derek’s fingers let go of her clit. Blood flooded to the hard bead and sent her careening into orbit.

“Watch me take Garrett’s ass like I’m going to take yours,” Derek said.

Garrett rocked back as Derek’s length disappeared into Garrett’s dark channel.

“Yes.” They both grunted.

Derek’s right hand caressed along Garrett’s side as they all held still, panting.

“You’re so tight and sexy.” His hand moved upward, sliding between them over her breast. “Ella, we’re going to worship you.” He pinched her clit and let go.

Her hips jerked up and trembled. *Again.* "Please, more."

Derek's hand glided up over her arm and to the headboard, taking hold of an area beside Garrett's firm grip. He thrust forward, propelling Garrett forward, both cocks disappearing once again.

Garrett's cock seemed bigger, longer as he withdrew and reentered her.

"That's it." Derek found her beaded clit and squeezed harder than before. "Fuck her. We need to fuck her."

She bucked. "It's like you're both inside me." *I want you both inside me. I want both your cocks in my pussy. I want your cum dripping down my thighs.* "I'm going to come again. I'm going to…"

Garrett grunted. He rocked back and forth, faster and faster.

Garrett's mouth covered hers as his incredible cock vibrated against all her sweet spots, and Derek's fingers gave her the edge of pain she'd learned she loved.

"This is how it will be from now on," Derek said.

"I've had so many fantasies of doing this," she whispered. She held strong as their bodies glided, rocked, and pounded into her. Slow, then fast. Slow. Fast.

Derek lifted her legs up and changed the angle of Garrett's entrance into her, pushing him in deeper.

She let go of the headboard, and curled her arms around Garrett's strong neck. His mouth crashed onto hers. Her tongue stroked his and begged for more.

He silently demanded control. His tongue stroked and guided her toward the next orgasm.

Derek's hand let go from the headboard. She sucked in an audible gasp as her clit and pussy throbbed in unison. Derek glided up over her mons between Garrett's and her flesh. Garrett sucked in his belly and gave Derek's fingers room to explore.

Garrett retreated, but his tongue danced in a frenzied pace with each solid thrust. Derek's fingers slid to her throbbing clit. He tapped it and brought her to the very edge of climax.

Needing more, she writhed under the two men as the three moved as a unit. In and out. In and out. Garrett's cock seemed to grow. Derek's hand at her pussy reached up to the headboard.

Electricity shot through her, causing an orgasmic earthquake.

"Come," Derek commanded.

Her partners joined in the shaking of the world inside her and scorched her as a bigger orgasm hit her system.

The men shouted something, but nothing made sense. She shuddered and trembled as absolute bliss held her captive, and her body came apart beneath them.

The two men collapsed on top of her, moaning and panting.

"I love you, Ella," Garrett whispered in her ear. "Once will never be enough."

She let go of the headboard and let her arms fall to the mattress as all the tension from his unexpected return left her. "Wow."

"We can do that again." His cock stirred inside her.

"We can't." Her pussy embraced his cock like she would never let go and gave her real desire away. She wanted more, so much more.

"Not tonight," Derek sighed. "Garrett has to work." He kissed Garrett's neck. "That was better than it's ever been. Thank you."

A smiled grew on Garrett's lips as he pressed them against Ella's ear. "You've just had the best sex of your life. Admit it."

It tied with Cade.

"The best? I've had just as good."

He puffed out a laugh. "Did you hear that, Derek?"

"Damn. Yeah, I heard her. We've got to up our game. One guy can't outdo us."

She gazed up at the mirror. Derek withdrew his cock from Garrett and spread his ass cheeks. Cum dripped from the passage. A stroke of jealousy hit her. *I want him to look at me like that. I want to please him too.*

Garrett moaned.

"God, you're gorgeous." Derek kissed the base of Garrett's spine. "Stay here, and I'll be back to clean you up."

He crawled off the bed and walked to the master bathroom.

"Was it the first time you've done that with him?" she asked.

"Yes." He nuzzled her ear. "We've played with toys but never actually fucked."

"Oh." She bit her bottom lip. "Did you like it?"

"Mmm." He rolled his hips and moved his cock back and forth inside her. "Did you?"

"Um…" She rolled her hips and joined in on his gentle glide, keeping the sensual connection. *I did, but something was missing. More like someone.*

"You won't get in trouble for liking it, Ella. I'm not my brother."

"I liked it. I'm not sure it's for me long-term." *I love Cade too. I don't love Derek. I like him. But he's not into me. Not like he's into you.*

"We're dating to figure it out," Garrett said.

Derek returned with a tray of wet and dry washcloths along with bowls of soapy and clean water, reminding her of all the times she'd bathed her husband once he couldn't clean himself. Years of the most basic care, the kind she'd done for her children.

"I'm going to hop in the shower while you two clean up." She wiggled out from under Garrett. His semi-hard cock slipped from her center. She needed to get away before the memories of Greg consumed her. "I'll be back in a couple minutes."

She hurried off the bed as Garrett followed.

"Let her have a few minutes," Derek said. "She'll be fine. It's been an emotional day."

Garrett's footsteps behind her stopped as she entered the bathroom. She turned on the shower and stepped in. Under the spray of warm water, the memories of her husband, the guilt for giving in to her desires for Garrett, and the love she had for Garrett and Cade overwhelmed her. Silently, she let it all out under the cleansing flow of water where no one would hear, no one would know.

She missed her husband.

Chapter Nineteen

The street showed no sign of life. Empty driveways, no streetlights, nothing but front porch lights shined in the darkness. Powerful gusts of thick, hot air rocked Cade's SUV parked in Ella's driveway. Black clouds rolled in signaling a dangerous change in temperature.

Droplets of rain splattered on Cade's head as he picked up the clothes hanging on the hooks from the back of his car. "We've got to get this inside before the bottom falls out of the sky."

Jason gathered an armful of shopping bags. "Come inside and visit. Mom said she'd be home by midnight. It's still early."

"She might not want company." Would she want to see him tonight? She had a challenging day. No doubt it had been a rough night with Garrett. Did she like company when she was upset? Would she rather be alone?

Kyle grabbed the last bags of clothes out of the back and closed it. "When she gets home, if she's worn out, you can go. If not, we can hang out." Kyle followed Cade and Jason to the front door and out from under the light rain.

Jason jostled the bags and pushed his key into the door. "It's unlocked. Did we lock the front door when we left?"

"Yes," Kyle said.

"Stand back." Cade stepped forward and Jason moved aside. "I'll check the house."

Cade peeked through the window. The lights in the living room that he'd turned off before they left, were on.

"Stay here. If you hear anything strange, call the police." He opened the front door and slipped inside the house. He considered calling Jimmy, his head of security, to come over as backup. Instead, he carefully made his way to the living room. He hadn't been on security detail in ten years, but the process was so ingrained he automatically followed normal procedure.

A new sense of urgency consumed him. An armed criminal could be inside. He slowly breathed in and found the calm he needed to thoroughly check the house and keep his family—his Ella and boys—safe.

He set the wardrobe bags on the couch. Only the slightest crinkling sound came from the plastic.

Footsteps from the kitchen area grew louder.

Shit. He quickly moved into the shadows and pressed his back against the wall. A soft scraping of something against fabric caught his attention.

Burglars? Fuck.

Someone was coming right toward him. He inhaled. He should have called Jimmy for backup. He had one chance for a surprise.

Closer. Closer. Closer.

He stepped out, ready to knock the person out, and…

"Ahh," Ella screamed.

"Fuck." Cade changed his punch into a grab and hauled her into his arms. "You scared the crap out of me." Relief washed over him. *You're safe. You're safe.* "I thought someone broke into your house. Thank God, you're all right." He squeezed her tightly against his chest. "What are you doing with your door unlocked?"

"Cade," she mumbled against his chest. "Can't breathe."

"Shit. Sorry." He loosened his hold on her.

"You scared me." She panted against him. "Don't ever do that again."

He held her shoulders, leaned back, and scanned her sweet, sexy body. Her beautiful brown hair billowed down her back. The dark-blue T-shirt made her look like a college student. A college student without a bra. *Mmm. Are you wearing panties?*

His entire body jerked to attention. He was ready to find out.

"Are you listening to me?" Ella glared at him.

He tried to stifle his amusement but failed. She was adorable angry. He liked her fierce glare. He liked it a lot. A lesser man would be terrified of her. "Every word," he said. "You're tough." *Except when dealing with wildlife.*

She tilted her head and bit her bottom lip, seemingly bemused. "Where are my boys?"

"Jason. Kyle," he shouted. "It's all clear. It was your mother." He couldn't keep his eyes off her. "Gosh, you're beautiful."

She gazed down. Crimson filled her neck and cheeks.

Are you blushing on your belly? Your pussy?

"Cade," she whispered. "Being friends isn't going to work."

"What? Why?" *I can't make you fall in love with*

me unless we spend time together.

"I'm going to date Garrett."

Shit. "Then date me too. "

Her chin stayed down but her gaze lifted. "I'd like that. I know it's different, and we've talked—"

Jason and Kyle ran into the living room, dropped the shopping bags on the floor, and swooped in on Ella with a big hug. "Mom, we thought someone found the extra key and broke in. We're so glad you're safe," Jason said.

"What are you doing home so early?" Kyle asked.

"I've been home for a half hour," she said. "I was doing laundry."

They all looked behind Ella. A white laundry basket was on its side with the once folded clothes scattered on the floor near it.

"Sorry," Cade said. He hadn't heard it fall, he'd been so focused on keeping the boys safe. He left Ella to her boys and walked over to the basket. He sucked at folding clothes. He turned the basket right side up and tried to salvage the folded pieces as he gathered them from the floor. "Where do you want this?"

"My, um, bedroom," Ella said. "Don't worry about folding anything."

He carried the basket over to the couch and placed the wardrobe bags over it as he blocked her view. "I'll take care of this."

"Thanks, Cade," she said.

"My pleasure."

"Mom, are you up for seeing what we did today?" Kyle asked. "Cade, meet us in the living room."

Cade looked over his shoulder. "I'll fix the lock in her bedroom and wait for y'all on the couch." He resumed his trek into her bedroom, a place he hadn't been inside but the boys had pointed out.

He pushed open the door and stepped into the pastel-yellow bedroom. There wasn't much in the large space. A white, metal queen-size bed with a green comforter and sheets stood out as the only truly feminine pieces in the house. It didn't belong with the beautifully crafted wooden dresser and armoire in the room. *Did you change the bed to start over?*

A platinum-framed photo of Ella and Greg at the beach sat on the dresser. He put the laundry basket on the bed and picked up the frame. Engraved in some kind of Celtic calligraphy was a note for Ella at the bottom.

"To my lover, my wife, the mother of my children, the most beautiful woman in the world—Always think of me like this when I'm gone."

He set the frame down. Greg understood what he had with Ella. No matter what her feelings were for Garrett, they wouldn't be anything close to how she loved her husband.

He picked up the frame again and looked at the picture in more detail. She had a carefree glint in her eyes, like she did in the woods when she ran off to the guest cabin alone. He hadn't seen it since. He wanted to see that expression on her face all the time for the rest of his life.

Greg's eyes in the photo were more of a gray than a true blue like hers and the boys. There was a happy but calculating look to them. Kyle had that same look when he talked about his mother or mathematics. He'd researched Greg online during dinner. The man was a genius on multiple subjects, not just one. Kyle had understated his father's intelligence. The boys took after their father but held their mother's heart and determination.

Maddie told him about the last few years of Greg's illness. All the money he'd accumulated, millions from the banking industry, had been "given away" but really stolen by his parents and by those who knew about the man's diminished mental capacity. Ella was left with tons of medical bills, the house, and nothing else. She had a small account in her name that funded the startup costs for her business, but almost all her profits, which have been substantial, were taken away to pay for the medical bills.

He set the frame down again and walked back into the living room to retrieve the rest of the clothes he bought her.

By the time he finished fixing her lock and putting her clothes and shoes away, he had a knot the size of Texas in his stomach. His Ella had a bare closet, empty dresser, and a jewelry case marked "for emergencies" that was darn near void. She didn't have enough money to give her daughter a backyard wedding let alone the extravagant one Colleen had been lobbying the boys for.

Ella didn't have enough money to buy herself a decent wardrobe, and he had ruined every nice thing Josie bought her. No more ripping clothes off her until they were married. She needed every piece of clothing he had bought her tonight and more.

The windows rattled. Low rumbles of thunder sounded in the distance. He trudged into the living room and sat down on the couch. Buying her a few clothes and items for the house wasn't enough. She needed real help. Everything from food to utilities to finding her the best land for her business. He was on it.

"Hey," Ella whispered behind him.

"Hey," he said. "How are you doing?"

She walked around the leather couch and sat down next to him.

"Thanks for helping the boys with the house. I really appreciate it. I'll give you back the furniture when I sell the place, and I'll pay you back for the appliances then too."

"I don't want anything back. Keep it all."

"I can't. No matter how much the boys love the Jeeps, they can't keep them. It's too much."

He faced her. His blood boiled. *I'm taking care of you whether you like it or not.* "They are gifts. I gave them because I wanted to. I don't expect anything in return. Kyle and Jason are great kids, and they deserve a break. I make plenty of money. Everything was freely given, Ella. Don't mention it again."

She rose to her feet and glared down at him. Her red face and pursed, pink lips turned him on. She was so sexy when she was worked up. "It is too much. I'm not being beholden to anyone and the gifts are extravagant. A gift is a free pizza or a movie, maybe a game. Cars are not on that list. You're taking this stuff back, and that's the end of it."

Cade stood up. "The hell I am." He cupped the back of her neck and kissed her. He hadn't planned to kiss her, but it had been too long since they touched. Too long since they made love.

Her lips parted on a gasp. He thrust his tongue between her teeth and tasted her, danced with her, devoured her mouth. He slid his free hand around her back and pulled her against his chest. "You're not giving anything back to me. You're accepting it all." He crushed his lips to her. Damn, she tasted of minty goodness.

She curled her arms around his neck as she returned his kiss. Hands, lips, bodies pressed together. "Bedroom," she whispered.

His feet and heartbeat raced to see how quickly they could get into the bedroom. He had to slow down and follow Pappy's rules. "Ella."

"I don't want the kids to hear me scream at the top of my lungs at you," she whispered between kisses. She ran her right leg up and down his outer thigh.

Were they going to argue or make love? Either way he'd enjoy it. He slid his hands to her ass and lifted her up. She wrapped her lean legs around his waist.

"Hurry, please," she whispered.

He strode to her bedroom and locked the door. "Ella, damn it. I want to take things slow with you." No, he didn't but he needed to follow his father's advice. Love shouldn't be this much hard work, but his father often said loving someone was the best kind of work. Getting through tough times made the easy times that much sweeter.

Her sexy mood shifted. Her eyes shot icicle daggers at him.

"Listen up, Cade." She unwound her legs from his waist.

He helped her down but firmly held her hand. *You're not running away from me.* "I'm listening." He proudly stopped a smile from forming on his lips. *Damn, you're sexy.*

"I am not accepting your gifts. None of them. Well,

the painting, and the landscaping I will, but only because I think the boys helped. But nothing else. You don't know me. With Garrett here, I don't have time for any games."

"I do know you, and I'm not playing games. I've done that with other women. I don't want a relationship with someone I have to dance around. The gifts are just that—gifts. Don't worry about them. Don't think you owe me. You don't."

She huffed.

"Yes, I give better gifts than most, but I can afford them. I'll say it again—I don't expect anything in return." He tugged her into his arms. "I know you had a hard day. Let me hold you. You don't have to be strong all the time. Let me help you get your house sold. Let me help you and the boys get through the move. You don't have to do it on your own."

"I can't accept the gifts," she said. "I can't deal with owing another person anything."

"Sweetie, if you didn't want to see me again, I still wouldn't want anything back. It's all yours." *Along with my heart and soul and body, especially my body.*

"Why didn't you call me this week?" she mumbled.

"I should have. The conference schedule made it near impossible to call you at a decent hour. This week was not one of my best." *Understatement of the year.*

Nikki double checked the companies who messed up the deliveries to Ella. The vendors had the correct addresses and account numbers, but somewhere between the order and the deliveries, the addresses got changed. A royal screw up. Even today had a screw up with the dress Josie picked out and sent to Ella's work but never arrived.

"You can call me anytime," she whispered. Her sweet, lithe body leaned into him.

"I'll take you up on that." He glided his hands up and down her back. No bra. No panties. None were in her drawers until he filled them with his purchases from the mall. "I missed you."

"Did you?"

"I did."

Her hands slid around his waist and pulled his dress shirt from his pants.

"Slow down. I'll attack you, if you get to my skin," he said. Her fingers met the heat of his flesh. He fought the desire to get into her and tried to follow his father's sage advice. Attempting to stop his instincts wasn't working. He wanted what he wanted, and he wanted her.

"I thought you didn't take things slow," she said in her husky, Zen voice.

"I don't. But I'm trying to."

"Maybe I want fast." She tilted her chin up and locked onto his gaze as she slid her hands down his suit pants and squeezed his ass.

His hips jerked forward.

"El-la," he warned.

She removed her hands and backed out of his embrace. "Fine." She turned around. "You know where the exit is."

"Oh, screw it." He wasn't replaying the first night at the cabin. She needed him, and he needed her. They had more than sex to keep them glued to each other. He unbuttoned his cuffs and pulled his shirt and undershirt off. "You want my cock inside you?" His voice lowered.

With her back to him, she barely nodded in an affirmative motion.

He emptied his pants pockets and set everything on top of the armoire. Garrett made love to her in this room.

"Did you have sex with Garrett this evening?" He unbuttoned his suit pants.

She straightened her back into a stiff rod.

"It's okay." He unzipped his pants. "You're not going to want him soon enough." He stepped out of his shoes and pants. "You're mine, not his."

Her breath hitched, and her arms wrapped around her ribs.

He placed his hand at her waist.

"Drop your arms." He was going to make certain she knew who owned her body, and it sure as hell wasn't Garrett Winthrop. He was going to blow her mind tonight. He was good at a lot of things, and sex was probably number one on the list. Maybe it was a tie between business and sex. He gently guided her around until she faced him, and her butt hit the edge of the bed.

With her gaze downcast and a pink flush to her cheeks, she dropped her hands to her side, obeying him.

"Um. Cade?" Her succulent lips taunted him.

Those sexy lips were his tonight.

"Ella, do you really want this?"

She nodded and gazed up at him through watery eyes.

"I need this. I need…" she hesitated. "…You."

She paused again.

She seemed to want to say more, but what? His confidence waned.

"If I start, I won't be gentle," he said.

"I don't want gentle. Tonight with Garrett." She closed her eyes. "I missed Greg. I missed you. I kept thinking of you. How you make me feel…" She exhaled. "…Alive."

A deep, gratifying rumble started in his chest and filtered out his mouth. He'd never made a sound of that nature before. The confidence he lost after meeting Garrett came roaring back to life. His skin tingled with electricity. He skimmed his fingers down her delicate cheek to her mouth. "I can do that." He traced the seam of her supple lips.

She parted them on a moan.

"We're sleeping in tomorrow," he said.

She opened her dreamy eyes. "We can't. The kids."

"We can." He dragged his fingers from her lips down her neck over her breast. "The boys invited me to stay." *Kind of.*

"Jason will go ballistic if he suspects." She arched her back and pressed her breast into his hand.

She didn't say he couldn't stay, or she didn't want him to. "Jason will never know."

"Cade, please."

Was she begging for him to make love to her? To kiss her? To say he'd leave? He lowered to his knees.

"Take off your T-shirt."

She panted softly as she revealed porcelain skin shaved free of hair. He offered up a silent prayer of thanks as she dropped the T-shirt to the area rug. Her sweet, ginger scent filled his nose. He knelt on one knee, curled his hands around her calves, and slid them up the back of her thighs. *So lean and strong.*

She moaned.

"You want me to lick your pussy?" He brushed his lips against her belly.

Silence.

"My shy Ella," he cooed. "Touch me if you want me to lick you."

She reached down, weaved her hands through his hair, and widened her stance.

"Did Garrett do this to you?" He had to know. It was killing him to know details.

"I…um. I don't remember if he did," she rasped.

He smiled. "You remember me doing this."

She swallowed. "Yes."

"And you want more." He pressed a soft kiss to her navel.

"Yes."

He lifted her right leg over his shoulder. "Sweetie, I have three hundred and sixty-one more fantasies all starring you." He dipped his head and licked between her legs. Her honey cream flowed onto his tongue. A silent orgasm wouldn't do. He needed to hear her orgasms.

Her legs trembled. He slid one hand up her back and the other pulled her left leg over his shoulder.

"Cade," she gasped.

He leisurely lapped the cream between her thighs and set the stage to dip in and take the spotlight at the main event.

"De-li-cious." He tapped her clit with the tip of his tongue between each syllable.

She gripped the back of his hair and pulled.

He jerked his head back. "No, ma'am. I'm choosing when you come."

Her pelvis froze. "Yes, sir."

He kissed the top slit. “That’s good, sweetie.” He dragged his lips up and down along her fold. A rush of cream slipped from her pussy. “Ready for my cock?” He circled her clit over and over with his tongue.

She whimpered.

He shifted into a squat and lifted her. He sucked on her clit as he guided her onto the bed, but kept her ass off the edge.

Luscious juices flowed from her pussy onto his tongue. His cock ached to get inside her. To feel her orgasm squeeze him. To cum inside her.

She trembled and gripped his hair. “I can’t stop.”

“Come for me,” he whispered against her plump clit.

She curled her legs around his head, blocked his peripheral view, and ground against his face.

His heart soared with joy. *I made you come. I made you lose control. With some work, you’re going to fall in love with me. I’ll have your body, heart, and soul for the rest of my life.*

“Cade,” she cried out, shuddering in his hold.

Her scent increased his desire. He rubbed his face in her pussy, feasted on her as her clit throbbed, and her pussy walls closed in on his tongue.

“Need a minute to breathe.” She panted. “It’s too much.”

“No.” He had a plan in place to make her fall in love with him, and multiple orgasms were paramount to making it happen.

He got back to the real business of making memories. Every time she walked into her room, she would remember him feasting on her. If Garrett even tried to do this, her mind would go to him instead, and stay there. "I need more," he murmured against her clit. "Knees up. Arms overhead."

She followed his orders and lifted her knees to the sides of her chest. Her pussy opened.

He dipped the tip of his tongue into her sex, pulled down his boxers, and freed his aching cock.

"It's sensitive. I can't…"

In and out he dipped the tip of his tongue. He mercilessly teased her overstimulated clit with the light graze of his teeth. A ripple of pleasure from her channel flowed around his tongue with a burst of pure, heated pussy cream—the precursor to a monster orgasm for her. This one would be around his cock.

He cupped the junction at her inner thighs and held her hips down as he rose to his full height. His cock aligned with her pussy. Every basic instinct in his bones screamed at him to fuck her and make her his wife.

Beads of cum that should have been inside her dripped from the tip of his cock. He rotated his hips and her wet pussy squeezed around his rod as it disappeared into her center. In and out. In and out. He thrust and retreated from her tight pussy. He ground against her swollen clit. "Mine. Mine." *You're going to forget loving anyone but me.*

Her blue eyes opened, and her chest bowed up. Her lips parted. "I'm coming."

The tremors of another pussy orgasm rippled around his cock, a bigger one. The explosion was seconds away. Her walls clamped down around him in hard, breaking waves.

He plunged into her pussy and slid her to the opposite edge of the mattress as he climbed onto the bed. Her legs splayed with his as he dropped into a wide legged push-up.

Lightning flashed. Thunder roared and shook the house. The lamp lights flickered. Her hips bucked and drove his cock deeper. He dipped his lips to her clavicle and licked upward to her ear while her pussy rippling channel squeezed his throbbing rod. Over and over, he repeated the dipping pushup. His climax rose. She felt too good around him. Close to losing it, he squeezed his lids shut and continued to suppress his desire to come. Determined to bring her to the space where she flew apart, lost her mind, screamed, writhed, and gave him her pleasure, he pressed on.

A sheen of sweat covered his chest and back. He dipped down into his pushup, nipped at her neck and earlobe. He glided over her big breasts.

"Oh shit. I'm… Yeeeess!" She writhed underneath him and screamed his name over and over.

His balls clenched so tightly he was sure they were going to burst. Then it came. His ecstasy rushed out in pure triumph. *Mine.*

She bit down on his neck, not too hard, but it muffled her wild cries of bliss.

He loved it. Loved her. Loved making love to her. Loved the way he lost control. Loved the way she did too.

She released his shoulder, and dropped her head to the bed. She panted for air. "Wow doesn't really describe how incredible that was."

"Yeah," he said. *If I weren't sterile we would have made a baby or two.* He dropped down to his elbows and kissed her lips. *There is no one else for me, but you.*

"Mmm," she mumbled in a sweet satisfied voice. "Hold me."

He shifted to his side and pulled her into his chest. "Tired?"

"Yeah." She snuggled closer to him.

"Rest, sweetie."

"I missed you," she mumbled as her breathing slowed into the steady rhythm of sleep.

The first real sleepover at her house, and he wasn't prepared. No clothes. No toothbrush. Remedying the situation, he slipped out of bed and called the head of his security team Jimmy.

Jimmy answered on the second ring.

"Hey, it's Cade."

"What do you need?"

"Clothes, sneakers and a toothbrush brought to Ella's house." *I'm claiming a drawer and leaving a toothbrush.*

"Got it. When do you need it?"

"Half-hour. Any more information from Nikki about the delivery mistakes?"

"Not yet, but we're looking into it. I'm checking into Felicity's part. Nikki says she's capable of simple tasks, but I think your assistant is an idiot."

"She's not the sharpest tool in the shed, but she tries." He never should have hired her, even with her stellar recommendations. He slipped into his suit pants.

"I'm heading over now," Jimmy said. "Did you know Jerry Wynn is in town?"

"Since when?"

"Since last night. His mom died. The funeral is Monday."

"Damn. Mae Wynn was a good woman. What happened?"

"Murdered," Jimmy said. "They found her this

morning. No one is talking."

"I guess I'll go and see him Monday." Cade unlocked the bedroom door and quietly strode through the dark house to the front door. He looked out the window for Jimmy.

The storm had passed, but leaves were scattered across the lawn. The flowers they planted had taken a beating, but looked like they would survive.

"Cut the lights when you get here. I don't want to wake the boys."

"Never thought I'd see the day," Jimmy said. "Cade Daniel Jackson is in love."

"Shut up, and get over here, old man." He hung up. Garrett Winthrop. Jerry Wynn. Strange deliveries, and even stranger non-deliveries.

The black SUV driving down the street cut the headlights and pulled up into the driveway. Jimmy hopped out of the car and jogged to the door.

Cade opened the door and Jimmy handed him a black backpack.

"Thanks. I think I'd like Jason and Kyle to get the company's advanced bodyguard training. It would be a good skill for them." Maybe they wouldn't have been so nervous tonight if they had a protocol to follow.

"You know their uncle trained them when they were kids," Jimmy said.

They played him earlier when they acted nervous or had they? The way they huddled with Ella behind him when Garrett had strode quickly toward him hadn't seemed fake. The blank looks seemed more like they'd been in shock or possibly fear, not for themselves as much as for their mom. "I didn't know that. I'd still like them trained in our system. Did you pull Kyle and

Jason's SAT's?"

"Perfect scores from both of them when they took it in the *third* grade.

"Damn. I shouldn't worry so much about them taking the final for Mrs. Kellen on Wednesday.

Jimmy chuckled. "Yeah. They could have skipped high school. I asked Josie why the boys didn't get transferred out of Mrs. Kellen's class. Josie said Ella tried and brought other parents along with her for backup. It got ugly. So ugly Josie wouldn't elaborate."

"That doesn't sound like Josie." *I had no problem scheduling the boys to take the final in front of me and the principal. I'll take pictures of their answers in case there are problems.*

"I know. You should talk to her."

"I will. Thanks," Cade whispered. "I'll touch base tomorrow."

Jimmy nodded and headed back to his car.

Cade locked the door and walked back into the bedroom. Ella's boys were two geniuses like their father and uncle, but they had a lot of growing up to do. He'd help them navigate the waters of life like Pappy did for him.

In the bedroom, the light from the lamp shined enough light to see her eyes flutter open. He set his bag down on the floor near the armoire. "It's just me."

"Come back to bed." She closed her eyes again. "I want you to stay."

He took off his pants and climbed into bed.

She cuddled up against him exactly where he wanted her to be.

Home.

Chapter Twenty

A long, muscular leg lay between hers. *Cade*. She glanced at the time. *Crap*. She'd slept in. They slept in.

"Good morning," he whispered. His strong hands traveled down her belly to the junction between her thighs. He licked the lobe of her ear and sent sparks of fire straight to her core.

"I have to work today." Her first client was new and booked online. She couldn't be late.

"What time?"

"Eleven."

"We have time." His hot breath teased her flesh with promises he was more than capable of fulfilling.

"Are the boys okay?"

"No punches were thrown at breakfast." He chuckled. "They're running with Derek."

At least Derek isn't in the house waiting outside the bedroom door. Maybe Cade will scare him off. She wouldn't hold her breath. She turned around and faced him. He struggled as he shifted from the edge of the bed closer to the middle. *My big guy needs a larger bed to be comfortable.* She traced the masculine line of his brows.

"So handsome, Mr. Jackson."

He blushed.

"I guess you hear that a lot," she said. The epitome of giant masculinity lay in her bed.

"You're the only one I want to hear that from."

Yep. You hear it all the time.

"When should I pick you up from work?" he asked.

She traced the line of his nose down to his lips. "I don't know, later." *Hopefully much later. I have bills to pay.*

"I have dinner plans with the most beautiful woman in the world, and I need to know when to pick her up from work."

Ignoring his compliment, she slipped her finger into the skillful mouth that wore her out. "Mmm."

He rolled on top of her, gently biting down on her finger.

A promise maybe? She tangled her legs around his. "Make love to me like you did last night." The way he dipped, and dragged, and thrust at once…

His bulge pressed against her wet sex. She was so ready for him to take her.

"How about a variation on last night?" he asked.

Oh, yes, oh, yes, oh, yes. She gazed into his intense brown eyes.

"It's going to be fast. Really fast."

"Oh," she exhaled. "I love your fast."

His breathing grew ragged. "Tonight, we'll take it slow. But right now, I need to make you come." He slid one hand under her chest and the other outside her shoulder.

In some kind of strength move he untangled his legs from hers and straddled her. His cock pressed hard against her pussy.

"Move your legs closer." He grunted as his cock inched into her sex. He was huge, and long, and hot, and so, so hard.

She inched her legs together.

"Yes," he hissed. "Right there." He dipped his head to her breast and licked up to her neck.

Electricity whipped through her and crackled into her pussy. Her belly buzzed with energy. His mouth latched on her neck. With every dip, he twisted her body one way and then the other. Her senses scattered. He alternated licking and sucking and nipping her breasts and neck. She didn't know what to do with her hands other than hang onto the sex god and enjoy the ride.

"You're mine," He grunted. His cock ground into her.

Do it again.

He thrust and brought her closer and closer to combustion. His muscles bunched and stretched with each passing glide. Her skin tingled and burned with so much stimulation. "It's too much," she cried out. "Cade, it's too much."

He growled. "Feel it all and let go. I'll put you back together."

Her pussy and clit throbbed for him to take her there. In and out. In and out. Up and down and up and down. Back and forth, inside and outside. Hovering. Caressing. Nipping. Sucking. Keeping her on the edge of bliss. He pressed into her, and swiftly moved his hand out from under her. He grabbed her wrists, and pinned them over her head.

"Give me everything. Now." He glared into her eyes and silently ordered her surrender. He shifted again, pushed her legs apart with his own. "I'm going to fuck you until you give me all your control, all your worries."

He slammed into her so fast and furious she almost found ecstasy, but her body was so over stimulated it wouldn't let go. She couldn't or wouldn't release control to him.

He grunted. His mouth formed a crooked smile, and his eyes shone with happiness. He leaned over as he continued his wild assault. With the softest, deepest voice, he growled into her ear. "You're mine, Ella O'Brien. Only mine."

She gasped. Hearing him use her maiden name took her to a new place. She flew apart and scattered into space in the most intense orgasm of her life. The second he took over, she connected to the part of her she gave away to Greg so long ago. She became Ella O'Brien again, the fighter, the young woman, the lover, the conqueror of all things. This wonderful man brought those parts back to her.

He dropped to his elbows and rested his head above hers. "Damn."

She raised her lids and gazed at his beaming smile. "You look very pleased with yourself."

His smile fell a little then brightened again. "Shouldn't I be?"

"Why, yes, you should be. In fact, you can pick me up from work at five for dinner," she said, trying to sound casual.

"How about you stay over my house tonight, and I'll take you to work tomorrow too?"

Jason and Kyle have school. Colleen's wedding. Jewelry hocking. Calling in favors. Work. Finding another therapist to work at the spa to help with rent.

"Monday is going to be a busy day."

"What if I stay here tonight and leave at six in the

morning?"

"Five-thirty?" *We could shower together... Mmm. The shower at the cabin...your soapy hands on my—*

"Deal." He interrupted her salacious thoughts. "Now let's get you to work on time. If I look at you like this much longer, we'll never get out of this tiny bed."

"My bed is not tiny. You, sir, are a giant."

She climbed out of bed. Her body ached in all the right places. Her leg and ankle didn't hurt nearly as badly as they had the day before. She added a little swing in her hips as she sashayed past him.

"I'm not a giant." He followed her into the bathroom. "You, ma'am, are tiny."

"I'm not that tiny," she said.

His clothes sat neatly folded on the vanity stool.

"Do you fold everything?" She stepped over the threshold into the walk-through shower and turned on the water.

"No. I really don't fold," he said. "Takes me forever. I hate it. I don't iron, either." He joined her in the shower. "You're great at it all, aren't you?"

She glanced over her shoulder at him. "I do all right."

"More than all right. There doesn't seem to be anything you can't do well."

"Thanks." *You make me feel as though I can conquer the world.*

Chapter Twenty-One

The ride in Cade's SUV took forever. He didn't seem to want to drop her off, so he drove the speed limit, or just under, and hit every red light possible until they finally arrived in the front parking lot of the small brick-and-glass strip mall housing her independent spa.

"Pick you up at five?" Cade seemed to force a smile.

"How about I call you when I'm finished here?" Ella answered. "I don't want you waiting."

"Like Derek?"

She sighed. Derek barely spoke to her, but kept his eyes on her every move and had the time to glare heat-seeking missiles at Cade when they left the bedroom. The talk about respecting her choice to date Cade and all that it meant that she'd planned to have with him had turned into a loud lecture from him about eating at regular intervals. He added another segment on how "real" boyfriends made sure their girlfriends had food in the house. As much as she disliked the situation, she enjoyed the surprise of a fridge stocked full of food thanks to Garrett and Derek.

"Is he still behind us?"

"Just pulled up." She glanced at the car clock and sighed again. "Thanks for driving me. I'd like to have my car back tonight. I don't like being stuck here, dependent on someone else to drive me home."

"It didn't work when I tried to drive it. I had it towed to my mechanic yesterday. Might be Monday before I know what is wrong. In the meantime, if you need anything…" His nostrils flared as he inhaled. "…Derek is available. Have a good day, and I'll be waiting for your call." He leaned over and kissed her. "I wish you didn't have to work today."

"Well, I do." She unbuckled her seatbelt and opened the door. *I need a profitable day.* "My first client will be here any minute. I'll call you later." She stepped out of the car onto the paved parking lot and walked to the spa entrance. Cade and Derek's cars reflected in the tempered glass as she unlocked the door. *They should be gone.* She turned around and threw up her hand in a Josie-style pageant wave at the two men idling in their cars. A black, luxury car drove into a space in front of her.

A gorgeous, redheaded man around her age emerged from the car and walked toward her.

"Oh. My. Goodness," Ella shouted, recognizing him immediately. "Carter O'Donnell." She ran and launched into his arms.

He grunted with the impact. "Long time, Ellie."

"What the heck are you doing here?"

"Hopefully getting a massage," he said with a wry smile.

"I can't believe it's you." *You're not on my schedule, but I'll fit you in.* "Dang, it's great to see you." She kissed his cheek. "You look great. Come on in."

She heard two men clearing their throats behind her on the left.

Carter let her down, but she held onto his hand.

"I think we have company." He kissed her cheek, and his smile grew bigger as he turned to the two men to his right. "Mr. Jackson." He narrowed his eyes and nodded at Cade and then acknowledged Derek with a slight rise to his chin.

"Hey, Jerry," Cade said. "I heard about your mom. I'm sorry."

"What happened to Jackie? Jerry?" Ella asked. *Should I call him Jerry now? He never used his first name when they were kids.*

"Wrong, Mom," Carter whispered. "It was Aunt Mae."

She didn't know much about his life after he left town other than Aunt Mae came up and took him and his mother out of town one night after his father went missing. The authorities found Mr. O'Donnell a week later in the woods, dead from an "overdose" but the man was heavily burned all over his body, and his neck was broken. Everyone suspected Aunt Mae's son of killing him, but no one had ever voiced the rumor to the authorities.

"Oh, is she here?" Ella asked, confused. When he left her small town, he'd moved to a farm in Oklahoma. They wrote for a while and then lost contact. She tugged him inside and away from the two men.

Derek and Cade followed them inside.

"I'll wait in your office." Cade attempted to walk into the back.

"Um, Cade, sorry, but no. Derek, go find something to do for the rest of the day." She grabbed Cade's arm and tugged gently. "I've known Car—um, Jerry forever and a day. Go. I don't need a stinking babysitter."

"But I—"

"—No buts. I'll see you later," she said. Cade didn't move from the spot beside her. "Don't screw up my energy. Go."

Derek knew the drill, but he seemed a bit off with his goofy smile and hesitancy to leave. "I'll be in my car."

"Go to the Chinese restaurant across the street. It's awesome. Tell them I sent you." She glared at him. "You're not sitting in my waiting room all day. Not happening."

Carter laughed. "Little Ella, always fighting the bully."

She smirked at him. "Neither Derek nor Cade is Ryan Fitzgerald."

Carter laughed harder. "That's a good thing, or we'd be in real trouble."

She gently elbowed him in the ribs. "You stop that, or it'll be you I give the black eye to."

Carter backed away, and held up his hands in surrender. "You've got the meanest right hook I've ever seen. I'm not challenging you."

She playfully slapped his rock-solid bicep over the long-sleeved, black tee. *Dang, he's strong; not the scrawny redheaded kid I used to protect in elementary and middle school.*

Derek walked out the front door and held it open. "Come on, Cade."

Cade slid his hand around her back and the other around her neck, pulled her into his arms, and kissed her…really kissed her, eliciting a soft purr from her lips. *Wow. What was that about?*

He released her and walked to the door. "Sweetie,

call me when you're ready for dinner."

"Um." He threw her off her game.

"Jerry, I'll see you later." Cade sauntered past Derek.

The door swung closed.

Derek walked across the parking lot while Cade climbed into his car.

"Possessive?" Carter asked.

"Honestly, I have no idea what that was about," she said. "Now, do I call you Carter or Jerry?"

"Jerry. Jerry Wynn."

"Oh." *You're my first client. Cool.*

"Aunt Mae adopted me after my mom died when I was fifteen. I took her last name. We moved here. Long story. Aunt Mae passed on, and that's why I'm back in Memphis."

"I'm sorry." Aunt Mae was old as dirt when they were kids; at least sixteen years older than Jerry's mom, and she wasn't a spring chicken. "How old was she?"

"Ninety-two," Jerry said. "Someone robbed her house and beat her up. Looks like it was a mistake. The neighbors skipped town last night. They were rumored to owe a shitload of money to a local drug dealer. The police are searching for them. They found the two guys who…" He breathed in slowly and deeply. He swallowed. "…Aunt Mae was dying of heart failure. I came back to take care of her for the little time she had left. I was a day too late."

"That's awful. I'm so sorry."

A frown formed on his mouth, and he shrugged. "Do you remember my cousin Highland?"

"Highland was older, right?" She welcomed the change of subject. "How is he?"

“He died five years ago. Car accident. Drunken driver hit him.”

“Damn, Jerry. I’m sorry.”

He shrugged again. “Thanks. He was like a dad to me. He taught me how to fight.” He winked and gave her a crooked grin. “You know, since you weren’t around.”

She nodded. *He’d lost his entire family.* “Right.” She gazed at him like a client instead of a friend. His hair was buzzed pretty short, but his thick, red hair still flamed like a bonfire on his scalp. His eyes sparkled green but held a sadness she knew all too well—deep, heartbreaking loss. A few wrinkles around his eyes added a layer of wisdom to his baby face. He didn’t appear anywhere near his thirty-eight years. His nose had to have been broken a time or two but not as much as a seasoned boxer. He either hadn’t been fighting long, or he was significantly better than everyone else. “I’ve got to turn on the lights and see what’s going on with the alarm. It should be beeping like crazy by now. Do you mind waiting here for a few minutes?”

“It’s all good. Do what you have to. I was early. Do you mind if I look around?”

“Go ahead. I’ll be right back.” She walked to her office and checked out the alarm. *No power. Huh?* She jotted down a note to call the building owner and then powered up her computer.

She came out and closed the door behind her. Jerry stood at the display of her handmade products. She scanned his left hand. No wedding ring.

“You can customize these?” He ran his fingers over a bar of soap.

“Yeah. If you’re looking for something special, I

can probably make it." Was he divorced? Did he have kids? A girlfriend? He hid his feelings well when they were young, and it seemed he still did. She did too except with Cade. Cade and that kiss. Her belly warmed deliciously at the memory.

"I like the ginger. Do you make soaps and oils for guys? These seem girlie."

She laughed. "Kyle and Jason say the same thing. I guess I need to change the packaging for my male clients."

He looked at her bewildered.

"Kyle and Jason?"

"My sons. They would love to meet someone from my past. You are coming over Monday night for dinner. I won't accept "no" for an answer. My daughter may or may not be there. She's engaged, and well…" She rolled her eyes. "She's too young and too in love to be bothered."

"Three kids. Wow. Who was the guy with Cade?"

"That's Dr. Derek McGregor. He works with my late husband's brother, Garrett Winthrop."

"I know Garrett Winthrop. Seems we've come full circle, huh?"

"Yeah," she said. *Full circle without asshole fathers around to add to the misery.*

She stood silently staring at him for a few minutes. She soaked in the subtle, and not so subtle changes. It should have been awkward, but it wasn't.

She breathed in. "Come into my massage room, and tell me what's going on with your shoulder." She showed him into her room and clicked the music remote. Soothing sounds of rainfall filled the room.

As kids, they used to hide from their drunken

fathers in his barn when it rained. Did he remember those times in the barn talking? They were so young and tainted with a difficult life. It seemed they both found their way out of it, and got sucked back into a different kind of mess as adults.

He took off his shirt, and she worked on his upper body for the session. "Take a few minutes to rest on the table while I wash my hands. Don't immediately get up," she said. *I don't need you fainting on me.*

"I don't think I can get up," he mumbled. "I've never had a massage quite like that."

"I combine multiple modalities. It works, but it's different than most." She turned the handle on the door with her elbow. "Take your time, and come out whenever you're ready."

She walked out and closed the door with her foot. She washed her hands in the bathroom and checked her messages. Two people booked appointments online for later that day.

"Ella?" Jerry called softly.

She walked out of her office and smiled. His shoulders were lower than when he'd walked in, and he seemed to feel better. *This is why I love my job.* "How are you doing?"

"Surprisingly great," he said. "Haven't felt this good physically in a while."

"Good." She handed him three different soaps and a sample bottle of jojoba oil with arnica. "Try these out and see what you like."

"Can I get another massage on Tuesday and also on Thursday?" he asked. "Is that too soon?"

"It's not too soon. Let's get you fixed up." They hashed out times and dates for the next two months.

"Don't forget dinner tomorrow at six." She handed him one of her business cards with her address written on the back.

"The funeral is tomorrow afternoon. I might not make it for dinner if it runs late."

"Come over anyway. Do you want me to go to the funeral?" she asked. "Do you have someone to sit with?" She didn't know what she would've done if she hadn't had her kids with her at Greg's funeral.

"I don't know who is going to show up tomorrow. If you're not busy, it would be nice to have a friend with me."

"I'm not too busy. Friends forever, right?"

He nodded. "Aunt Mae liked you a lot. Said you were a friend for life, the kind time doesn't take from you. The kind..." He swallowed hard. "...that's got your back no matter what."

"You know it. Always." She inhaled and held her emotions in check. They'd been through enough in their childhood to solidify a friendship nothing would ever break.

He walked toward the door. "It's casual tomorrow. Aunt Mae requested me wear black jeans and a green T-shirt with a four leaf clover on the front. So." He looked down at his feet and avoided all eye contact like he did when his father came home late from the bar roaring drunk.

"I have some black jeans and a green shirt," she said. *Thank you, Cade.* "We'll match."

"Thanks." He was out the door in a flash.

She blinked, ridding the watery emotions from her eyes. *Jerry Carter Wynn.* He'd always been good luck for her. Maybe with him around, she'd figure out how to uncomplicate her life. One thing was certain, he'd have her back if Cade or Garrett pissed her off.

She cleaned up the room and waited for her next client to arrive.

Chapter Twenty-Two

Ella sat in her office and dialed Cade while Derek folded sheets in the laundry room of the spa.

"Ella?" Cade answered.

"It's me," she said. "I'm closing up. I had a great day." One new client after another came in for a massage. *Thank you, Jerry, for the fantastic referrals.*

She sold out of her citrus and lavender soaps and oils, along with all the salt scrubs she recently added to her product line. It was the most profitable day she'd had in months.

"Derek there?"

"Folding sheets as we speak," she said. "He's a neat freak, so he reorganized my laundry room, cleaned my bathrooms, and put up the wall cabinets I had sitting in boxes in the laundry room."

"I could have done that…not the folding," he mumbled.

"It has kept him out of sight for most of the day," she said. "Are we still on for dinner? I know it's late."

"Yes, but what about the boys?"

"They won't be home until eleven."

"So, I have you all night?"

"Dinner. Garrett and Derek want to talk about the boys."

"I'm done with the sheets," Derek shouted. "Are you ready to go?"

"You haven't told him you're going out with me?" Cade asked.

"I haven't, but I will. I'll see you when you get here." She recognized the hurt in his tone, but she'd been busy and hadn't spoken much to Derek; although he helped ring people up, and even consulted on an injury for a new client. Having him around had turned into a good thing.

Derek slid his hand around her waist. He had always been affectionate when Greg wasn't around, but it was different this time. Her feelings for him intensified as the day progressed. His touch warmed her in places she wanted to keep cool until Cade came to get her.

"I'm on my way," Cade said, and ended the call.

She placed her phone in her purse and gazed up at him. *What would you do if I kissed you?* She licked her lips. "Thank you for helping out today."

"My pleasure," he said. He stepped to the side and faced her. His hands drifted to her hips. "I had fun."

"I enjoyed you being here." She caressed up his arms and wrapped them around his neck. She leaned her head against his chest. *I could fall so hard in love with you.*

"We need to talk about setting you up for a physical. It won't cost you a dime. And I won't tell Garrett anything, as always doctor-patient confidentiality is in effect." He slid his hands to the small of her back. "I missed you. I missed—miss Greg too. I'm sorry. I would have come back sooner too. My parents would have come, but they didn't know either."

"Thanks." She backed out of his embrace. *Mistake thinking you might be interested in me and not just*

Garrett. "What is in the past is over. I understand what happened." She turned to the door. "I don't need a physical. I'm going out to dinner with Cade. You can go home."

"Not your call." He walked to the door. "When would be a good time for a physical?"

She pulled her office keys from her jeans pocket. "No physical. I'm good." *I've got insurance, and you're not my doctor.*

"I'm taking you to my office for a checkup. It's been more than five years since you had one. I checked with Kyle and Jason." He opened the door, and she followed him out.

"Cade is picking me up. And, Derek?" She squared her shoulders and gave him her best stern look. "You don't tell me what to do. You have to ask my permission to give me a checkup, *and* I have to give it to you. I am not giving you permission. I'll decide when I'm ready for an appointment with you, and I'll pay for it with my insurance. I also want to see the pictures you took the other night. I want anything too revealing deleted." *Which is every freaking photo.*

He pressed his lips into a thin line. "Sorry, but you'll have to talk to Garrett about those pictures when he's home. He got called in to work for an emergency."

She turned her back on him. *Dang it. I'm never getting rid of him. Now Cade is going to be even more upset.* She locked the door. "Could you tell Garrett I'd like to talk to him about the photos?"

"I could, but I want you to promise you will come to my office and get a checkup within the month. I won't wait any longer for you to start taking care of yourself."

He probably had his orders from Garrett to make sure she wasn't deficient in some vitamin or mineral, and that all her vitals were in working order for whatever strenuous exercise regimen he had planned for her.

She turned around and faced Derek's cold hazel eyes. "Okay, but go home. Cade will be here any minute. We'll talk tomorrow."

Derek's gaze drifted to her mouth and the flat line of his lips turned into a sexy curved smile. "I can't go home. I'm worried about you." He gently placed his hand on the small of her back and nudged her forward toward his black limo. "I added Colleen's appointments with me to your calendar. I know you'll want to be there, and she wants you to be with her. I can add an appointment for you after hers if you'd prefer. You'll already be there."

"I'll be there for Colleen, but I don't need an appointment." *I could use a checkup, but I need to get through Colleen's wedding first.*

He led her a few steps before she realized what she was doing. With Derek around, her day settled into an easy routine. Her tendency to rely on a strong man pulled at her nature to please. Derek embodied strength in body and mind. Like Garrett. Like Cade. She couldn't let her guard down for an instant with any of them, or she'd end up doing whatever they wanted, whenever they wanted, however they wanted.

Stay vigilant. I have plans with Cade for dinner. "I'm not getting in the car. Cade is picking me up."

"Get in the car, and we'll wait for him. I'll drive you to the next destination."

"No." She gazed into his eyes, and her insides

melted into a sugary sweet mess. *Yep, I could fall hard for you.* "Cade will drive me. You are going home."

"We've been over this. I'm here whether you like it or not. Get in the car."

"No. I'll wait out here." She shooed him away. "Go spy on me so I don't see you. Spend some money at the Chinese restaurant."

"The food is great, but the place needs renovating. The owner sat down and talked you up. She likes you."

"She's pretty great. Tell everyone you know about the place so they can afford renovations." She rocked on her feet from side to side. *Cade, where are you?*

"Are most of your clientele men?" He relaxed his stance, but his shoulders seemed to rise.

Why all the tension? You need an appointment with me more than I need one with you. "No, it's split down the middle. On occasion I even work on dogs."

He laughed. "What about cats? My mom has got a tabby cat that needs to relax."

A forest-green luxury SUV pulled in next to the limo. Cade hopped out of it, smiling from ear to ear. "Ready?"

She hurried over to him. "Hey."

He bent down and hugged her. "Hey, beautiful. Good day?"

"Yes, sir," she whispered. "Nice car." She had an SUV just like it before Greg got sick. She had loved that car.

He handed her the keys.

"Here. You drive."

Without a second thought, she took the keys and brushed against his hard body, igniting a flame deep in her belly. She stopped, pressed tight between him and the car.

He reached around her, and opened the door enough to accommodate her size as he whispered, "Get in the car, Ella."

The flame turned to burning need down in her groin. Shit. She wanted him to get crazy with her, rip her clothes off, and lick her clit. She swallowed down the onslaught of desire surging through her veins, and crawled into the driver's seat.

Cade closed the door. He strode to the other side, past Derek, and climbed into the passenger's seat.

She started the car and backed out of the space as Derek casually slid into the back of the limo. *Why isn't Derek driving?*

"Take a right and head toward your house. I'm just around the corner from you," he said.

"Derek is going to sit outside your house," she said.

"Sweetie, he's going to be hanging out with my security guys who won't let him anywhere near the house."

"You have security?"

"Yes, ma'am," he said. "Some people think I'm a bigger deal than I am."

Greg was well known and rich but never needed security. Garrett needed it because of his job. But Cade?

"Have you had trouble in the past?"

"Nothing I couldn't handle, but having a full-time security team at the house stops most stalkers from walking over that invisible boundary. It's a precaution, nothing else."

"I see." She didn't understand, but she also didn't

have a clue where he lived. His address sat in his client file on her computer, but she never looked him up, never thought to. She sent a thank-you note when he first came to her, but that was so long ago. Would she be in danger dating him? "You don't have a bodyguard, do you?"

"I do, but only when I'm going to something really big locally or elsewhere. Around town, I can take care of myself, and you, just fine."

She kept her eyes on the road. An ounce of paranoia set in. With Garrett and Derek around again, she questioned every miniscule action, every minute thought. Garrett was screwing with her head. *He wants me to cling to him for safety, but I'm not counting on anybody ever again, not after Greg.*

"Turn left on the next road," Cade said.

She turned left.

"Slow down, lead foot," he said. "The entrance is on the left."

"Where?" Nothing but huge magnolia, pecan, and sycamore trees lined road.

"Slow down. It's on the left. Slower, honey. You passed it. Turn around."

"I didn't see it." She clenched her jaw. Crawling down the side street, not driving fast by anyone's standards, she searched for entrance.

"It's right between the trees." He pointed to a grouping of sycamores. "There."

Giving up, she pulled to the side of the road.

"You drive." With no one around to watch her frustrated failure, she climbed out and switched places with him. "Amaze me by finding a road that doesn't exist."

Without bothering with the seatbelt, he made a slow U-turn and drove between a set of pecan trees in the midst of the sycamores onto what looked like a dirt road but wasn't. *What on earth is that made of?*

The hidden, dirt road changed into a stone-and-pebble concrete path through dense woods. She glanced out the back, and sure enough, Derek's vehicle dutifully followed them.

"So, you need security in this place?"

"A couple times a year someone unwanted wanders onto the property." He tapped on the steering wheel. "I run a few security firms that cater to high-profile clients."

"Besides the bar?"

"Yes, ma'am. I'm in construction too. I love the bar. The others are strictly for future building."

She turned all her attention on the man driving her to his place. Cade wasn't dangerous like Garrett, was he? He never gave her a dangerous vibe before and wasn't now. He seemed a tad nervous? *Jeez, I've got to stop analyzing everything.* She closed her eyes and breathed. *In with the good. Out with the bad. In with the good. Out with the bad.* She repeated the mantra until she found a sense of peace then opened her eyes.

The woods opened to a beautiful, cream-brick house twice the size of hers with a large, black-iron gate in front of it.

"Wow. Is that your house?" she asked.

"Um, no." He blushed a heavy pink. "It's the security building."

"Oh," she mumbled. *Dang. If your security building is a mansion, what is your home?*

"My house is out of view at the moment."

The gate opened. He drove down the stone-and-pebble pavement to the side of the house and stopped the car.

An older man probably in his fifties or sixties with a shaved head wearing a white polo shirt, khaki cargo pants, and beige, military-style boots stood waiting for them.

Cade's window lowered. "Jimmy." He greeted the man. "This is Ella O'Brien Winthrop, my girlfriend. She can come and go as she pleases whether I'm here or not."

Jimmy nodded. "Mrs. Winthrop, if you need anything, please ask for me."

"We'll be here for the night," Cade said.

"Um, no." She had work and a funeral to go to tomorrow. The discussion earlier involved dinner plans, not sleepovers. "I'm not staying the night."

Cade turned toward her. His brows crinkled together. "Can we talk about it privately?" An edge of frustration lined his question which seemed more like a command.

She sat back and crossed her arms over her chest and glared at him. *I'm not a child to be ordered, but you're right. We should talk in private, not in front of anyone.*

"Yes. Sorry." *Not sorry.* She swiveled in her seat and gazed at the mixture of beautiful lush landscaping around the building and the unkempt wild brush and trees lurking on the edges of the property.

He placed his hand on her thigh as he rolled up the window. "Hey, sorry. I had a stressful day."

Yeah, like I didn't? Whatever. "I think I'd like to pick up my car and head home."

"Come on," he said. "I didn't want to argue in front of my head of security. You're the only non-family female I've ever brought here. I've never introduced him to anyone I've dated, and I didn't want the first introduction to include us arguing in front of him."

"Just dinner, Cade."

He nodded and headed straight for the trees. The road underneath them changed to green and blended into the surrounding landscape while staying firm beneath.

She sucked in her breath as he skillfully drove between two trees which magically seemed to move before her eyes, accommodating the width of the vehicle.

Oh, my gosh. Fake trees.

Cade easily navigated the winding path she struggled to remember while the trees in their way swayed to the side in an imaginary breeze and returned as the bumper cleared the invisible mark, hiding the entrance.

"Where are you taking me?"

"My house," he said. "I think the boys liked it yesterday. I hope they did. Sometimes they are hard to read, like you."

"Hasn't Josie been here?"

"No. Only family and house staff. I like my privacy."

She held her gasp as a glass-and-white-brick mansion appeared through the break in the trees. The security building couldn't hold a candle to the place Cade called home.

He drove out of the strange woods to a fuller view of the front of the home. Flowers bloomed all around the house with sculpted trees and bushes resembling woodland animals.

"Why the squirrel trees?"

He cleared his throat. "My nieces and nephews talked the gardener into making those." His face blushed a darker red as he swallowed. "Most of my nieces and nephews are young. I was relieved they didn't want pink princesses and white knights anymore…"

Dumbstruck at the extravagance, she stared in silence. As they neared, she saw magnificent dining and music rooms through large, arching windows. The place resembled a modern twist on a *castle*? She struggled to categorize it properly. She'd never seen anything quite like it. The building embodied a striking feminine beauty entwined with extreme masculinity at every layer.

He tapped a button on the dash as they rounded the next corner. Double doors opened to a garage. "…I've thought about having a party for friends here, but it never felt quite right. I designed the house with my sister-in-law. She used to be an architect. What do you think?" He parked in an empty space between two antique sports cars.

She unbuckled, spun in her seat, and faced him. Somehow her mouth worked, and she blurted out exactly what she thought before she could rein it in. "It looks just like you, masculine, attractive, striking, beautiful, strong, confident, open, fearless, gigantic for a giant, but for one person? Does one person need all that? This house is for a family or three. How long have you had it? Why haven't you invited Josie and Mark over? Are all these cars yours?"

His brown eyes widened in surprise? Confusion? While her mouth moved in direct conflict with her brain, she avoided his gaze. Maybe not avoided eye contact as much as not paid attention.

"You like it?" he asked.

"I…" She shook her head in confusion. "I don't know. Yes. I like it. It's so you." *It's you with a huge family, not you alone.*

He grinned. "I'll have Josie and Mark over for dinner sometime. We can invite Maddie and Mike too."

"Okay," she mumbled.

"Good." His voice lowered, and his hand on her thigh inched up closer to her groin.

She tamped down the sudden awareness of his body closing in on her. His hand reached the vulnerable spot between her legs.

"Cade."

"Come here," he said with an undercurrent of a growl. He cupped her sex, reached around to the nape of her neck, and lifted her onto his lap. In one swift move, he strode from the car, and carried her through the vast garage jam-packed with all kinds of cars.

He plastered her to his muscled body.

She wove her fingers into his silky hair. Her lips pressed against his strong neck. Her legs cinched around his narrow waist.

His hand slid to her bottom, and rocked her back and forth over his growing bulge with each stride. His breathing accelerated along with hers. His strides lengthened until he raced through the house at top speed, bumping and grinding her pussy against his full erection.

Her tongue flicked out and licked the heated curve

of his neck. *Mmm. So clean and male.*

"I'm going to fuck you so fucking hard, you'll have to stay the night."

A door slammed behind them, and her back hit a soft comforter. His lips found hers. She moaned as their tongues danced. His hands. Her hands. Shirts flew off. He grabbed the front of her jeans as if he was going to rip them, but stopped. His hands fumbled unbuttoning, and pulling down the zipper, so unlike him. The wild frenzy slowed.

She kicked off her sneakers as he tugged off her jeans. She sat up, and unzipped his jeans. She pushed them down. *Plaid boxers. Yes.* Placing her hand on the band of his undies, she traced the outline of his bulge. How that thing fit inside her was nothing short of miraculous. But it did. What he could do with it was truly amazing.

He backed away.

"No," she whispered. *No teasing. No going slow. Please.*

He dropped his boxers. "No one has ever made me so…" He slid her farther up the bed, pressed his hand on her chest and gently pushed her down onto the soft mattress. He skimmed his hands down her chest, over her belly and, agonizingly slow, drew her panty down her legs.

"I have never wanted a woman like I want you."

She couldn't think or speak, so her body took over. She splayed open her legs and gazed up at him. *Take me. Fuck me. Make me forget about Garrett and Derek and all their promises of adventures. Make my decision to be with only you effortless.*

He dipped down and licked the creases of her

thighs. “Tell me you’ll stay. I need you tonight.” His hot breath blew against her sex with each soft spoken word.

“I can’t.” She lifted her hips and begged him to commit to what he started, but he moved with her, not closer or farther away.

“Tell me you’ll stay,” he whispered. He flicked his tongue over her bare mons, teasing her.

She closed her eyes. “I can’t. I don’t have any clothes here.”

“Whatever you need I can have for you by morning.” His hands glided over her belly, and up to her breasts. “Say you will.”

She trembled with adrenaline filled desire. Perspiration dotted her flesh. She was about to combust, and he wouldn’t have her at all if she turned to ash. The man was a force of sexual nature. What was she doing getting deeper involved with him? She needed to simplify her life, not further complicate it.

Her pussy shouted at her to give in, to surrender, but the responsible adult in her took over. She swung her leg over his head and rolled to the edge of the bed. She sat up and pushed her hands against her belly. *No sex for years, and I’m making up for it all within a week? Shit. I’ve got to stop.* “I need my car. I need to go home.”

The warmth of his body pressed against her back. His powerful arms embraced her. He nuzzled under her ear. “Whether you decide to go home or stay the night, you are mine, not Garrett’s. Deep down, you know you are only mine.”

Not up for delving into her emotions, she stayed silent. *I can’t have sex with all of them.* Moving from sex with Garrett and Derek immediately to Cade or vice versa was wrong. Although she already had, but she wouldn't do it again.

She closed her eyes as images of her wrists tied to Garrett's headboard while Garrett and Derek fucked her, lazily played in her mind. *I can't be that girl, can I? Am I?*

"Talk to me." He circled her right nipple, and drew a curved line around the outside of her breast and up the middle to her other nipple.

"I have to replenish my display and make more product. I can't stay. I really can't." She stared at the masculine dresser. "I like you. No matter how much I may want to, I can't stay over. I have boys, and I'm their example. I'm ready to go home."

"Your boys are more mature than a lot of thirty-year olds I know. They love you. You're a wonderful mother. You have and do set a great example for them."

She shook her head. "I don't feel like a good mom. My boys know you slept over last night. They know Garrett slept over the night before. I…" She exhaled and shook her head. "…I don't know what I'm doing. Everything is so out of control."

He kissed behind her ear. "Are you hungry?"

"A little." She seesawed between reveling in the way he wanted to take care of her and frustration at wanting to be independent. So much had happened in such a short time. She had to stand strong and avoid depending on him. No matter where things headed, she couldn't let go of her work, her home, her life.

Do you want to have dinner with me?"

She shook her head. "I'll just end up spending the night, and I really can't."

He crossed his arms around her and squeezed. "I understand. Really. I do. I don't like it, but I can compromise and even deal with not getting what I want."

She cuddled into his embrace. "That's very big of you, Mr. Jackson."

He chuckled. "Is there anything I can do before I drive you home?"

She blew out a long exhale and mumbled, "Pay off my utilities."

"What was that?" he asked.

"Nothing." She shook her head. "I was joking."

She still needed to pay off the utilities before anyone could buy the house. She was eight months from having the funds and no bank would give her a loan. Maddie didn't have the extra money. God, Maddie cried when she found out how much she owed. She couldn't ask Garrett. The explanations. She didn't want to relive it all. Leaving her only other possible option—Cade. She didn't have the heart to ask him. He'd do it, and she'd be stuck with an inordinate amount of guilt until the house found a buyer.

"Is this about the amount you owed on your utilities?"

"I got in a bind. I have to pay it off before I close on my house. I'll find a way to handle it."

"I handled it. Did someone call you asking for a payment?" He let her go and climbed off the bed. "I will call them right now and that harassment will stop. I will raise hell if they contact you again about that." He mumbled as he pulled out a drawer from the dresser and grabbed clothes. "You don't owe them a dime. I told them if a problem arose to call me. You don't need that shit right now. Son of a bitch. They overcharged the fuck out of you. You overpaid those sons of bitches. Your roof is covered in solar panels. Your water bill should have been more than your utilities." He dressed and turned, facing her. "Did you get a name? What time did they call?"

She pinched her arm. *Ouch. I'm awake. This isn't possible.*

He held his phone and stared at her. "All I need is a name."

"No one called today."

"Tell me who called. I will make sure they are dealt with."

Her chin crinkled and trembled. "You really took care of it?"

"Yes, of course I did. Maddie and the boys told me what happened, and I got to the bottom of it. It's what I do."

A rush of relief washed over her. A weight fell from her shoulders. "I owed thousands."

"That was bullshit. You overpaid them. You'll be receiving a check with an apology and two months' free utilities. If you want, we can sue them."

She swallowed the lump of emotions lodged in her throat and shook her head. Fluid filled her eyes. She'd prayed for help for so long. So long. She slipped off the bed and dressed. Breathing proved difficult as she held back the tears. *I love you. I love you.* "I don't want to sue anyone. Thank you. Thank you so much."

He took her hand in his. "I love you. I've loved you since the day we met. I would do absolutely anything for you. I'm going to drive you home, but I want you to know I'm not in a competition with Garrett. Not really.

I can't stop you from loving him. I don't want to. I do want your love. Tonight didn't start out right. The way this dating thing began was all wrong. Heck, it's crazy."

"It is crazy." *Tell me you love me again.*

"I got overzealous, but Garrett and I are working together on the wedding. My parents are behind us, supporting us and him. I am listening to you. My life makes sense now that I have you in it."

Chapter Twenty-Three

Effleurage. Knead. Cross-friction. Drain. Stretch.

"Can you do that skin rolling thing over my back?" Troy asked.

"Sure." Ella used her soft, Zen-massage voice. *Don't ask me anything else. And please. Don't. Moan.*

She gently pulled the skin at Troy's shoulder between her fingers and rolled it in short waves down his back.

"That feels so good." He moaned. "You're amazing."

She ignored his comment, blocked out his voice, and worked the motion in reverse to his shoulder.

"That's all the time we have today." Instead of slowly gliding her hands over his back one more time, feeling for any last minute issues she would normally take an extra few minutes on, she quickly glided down his back and pulled the sheet up. One, swift brushing over the sheet to his feet, and she let go.

"I don't want it to be over," Troy sighed. "A few more minutes?"

"I'm sorry, Troy. That's all the time I have today. I'll see you in the waiting area. Remember to go through two breathing cycles before getting off the table." *Getting up too quickly could make you faint. I don't need you fainting on me all naked.*

She pumped hand sanitizer into her palm and

walked to the door. She finished rubbing it into her hands, then turned the door handle.

"Ella, when is your next client?"

She opened the door. "You're my last one." *I've got to get you out and get ready for Derek.*

"Oh."

She heard the sliding of skin and sheet. *Shit.* She hustled out and closed the door behind her. He got bolder with each appointment. Ignoring his interest wasn't working. Making him read her massage policy every time he came in wasn't working. If he didn't always pay in cash, she would have refused to work on him. The saving grace was that he hadn't crossed the line and touched her or asked her to do anything extra except massage techniques she offered on her modality list. Her gut screamed at her to cut him off. She couldn't do it without a concrete reason, and so far, he hadn't given her one.

Troy strode out of the room and joined her next to the product display. "I saw you with Cade Jackson the other day. Are you two dating?"

Phew. "Um. Yes. We're dating."

"He comes here for a massage?"

She cleared her throat. "He's no longer a client."

He slipped his hands into his suit pants pockets. "That's a violation of your policies."

Shit. "We got set up on a blind date. It was awkward, but we ended our business relationship before the date got started."

"I wonder if the Massage Board would consider your relationship with him an ethics violation." He tilted his head, scrunched his brows together, and pursed his lips together.

"Are you threatening me?" *Oh shit. Fucking shit. I haven't done anything wrong.*

"No, Ella." He rubbed his lips together, straightened up, relaxed his brows, and scanned her from her face to her feet. "Would you'd have lunch with me tomorrow to talk business. I like your soaps and oils. I'd like to offer your line to my customers. Could you develop special oils and lubricants for couples?" He adjusted the bulge in his pants.

"What are you implying?" she asked. *I don't do sexual favors.*

"I'm not implying anything. I'm asking. I know you're dating Derek McGregor too. He frequents my stores, and I am aware of the kind of fun he enjoys. I'm going to be blunt."

Her eyes had to have bugged out at him.

He laughed. "I'm interested in sexual oils safe for licking off. Sweet, sour, bitter, salty. This is confidential. I want to do some blind tests for a party I'm hosting next month. I'm not asking to fuck you. Although if you offered, I would be happy to oblige."

She swallowed.

"It's three hours of your time," he said. "I'll make it financially worth your while. We'll talk details tomorrow. Let's meet at the restaurant across the street for lunch." He turned and strode to the door.

Derek appeared at the entrance. Troy glanced back at her and smiled. "Sexy Vixen is the party theme. Doctor Derek McGregor will be there."

Derek opened the door. "Hey, Troy. What did you think?"

"Ella is the best massage therapist in the area." Troy shook Derek's hand. "She is going to work the party I'm having. We're partnering in a product line exclusively for my stores."

"That's great," Derek said.

The two men switched places, Derek inside and Troy outside. "I'm taking her to lunch tomorrow to go over details," Troy said. "You'd use her oils, right?"

"I do use her soaps and oils. They're high quality. I'll even give a written endorsement of them."

"That's what I thought." Troy smiled.

Her stomach clenched. *Sleazy man.*

Troy walked to the red luxury SUV parked in clear view of the entrance.

****

Derek closed the door and gazed at his beautiful Ella highlighted against the lavender walls. "Troy is a good guy."

She rolled her mesmerizing blue eyes. "I don't know about that."

"He is. He's always on the prowl, but he doesn't step over any boundaries. His toes will be on the edge, but he *never* crosses without absolute consent." *Did Troy do something?*

"Tell him to stop moaning on my table. It creeps me out." She stomped to her massage room like an angry toddler.

He followed her. "I moan."

"You're different. I've always liked you, and you don't do that sexual moan on the table. You give more of a damn-that-hurts moan. I don't want to hurt you, so I try to avoid those."

A hundred-dollar bill lay on top of the hot pink sheets.

"He tips well. What's with the sheets?"

She smirked and lowered her chin.

"He loves pink," Derek said. "He's a dominant with some interesting tendencies, but he loves sleeping and fucking on pink sheets."

She frowned as she plucked the bill from the sheet and put it in her pocket. "Great."

"He didn't do anything, did he?" *Troy likes smart brunettes, but he wouldn't make a move on her. I told him she was mine and Garrett's.*

"No. He moans. I had to tell two clients to leave. I hate these kind of days…"

"Is there a problem I need to take care of?" The neighborhood was safe, and the restaurant owner across the street kept an eye out for her. He'd hear about it if she needed him at the spa all the time.

She handed him a container of cleaning wipes and removed the sheets from the table. "Should I have lunch with Troy? Is he serious about selling my products at his stores, and what stores does he actually own?"

He wiped down the table and placed the wipes in the basket on the counter near the corner sink. "He owns fifty upscale, adult bookstores across the country. You'd be smart to do business with him. If he likes the oils, you'll have to expand your business. Hire a few people…" Derek continued telling her about Troy and his business as they cleaned and finished closing procedures.

All he needed her to do was talk business with Troy. The man needed a motivated partner who accepted his life and didn't want to get intimate. Ella desired financial independence, and he would make sure she had it. Joining the two in business made sense.

"Ready?" he asked.

She nodded. "Did you talk to Cade?"

"Yes, ma'am. He's running late and going to try and meet us at the funeral home."

"Garrett?" She'd invited Garrett, but he was on an emergency mission and couldn't commit.

"I'm not sure he'll be debriefed in time. But if anyone could make it happen, it would be him. He'll be back for movie night at our house."

"Jerry is coming over for dinner. Movie night might not happen."

"You told me that five times. Are you avoiding me?" He placed his hand on her mid-back. *You're underweight. I'm going to change that.*

"Uh. No."

He guided her out of the spa and into the back of the black limo. He tapped his finger to the tinted glass separating the driver from the back.

The vehicle rolled forward. He patted his lap. "Come here."

She shifted and faced him.

He steered her until she straddled his lap. "We're close?"

She nodded.

"I'm going to be honest." He leaned forward and kissed her nose. "I'm upset with you."

"You are?"

He nodded. "I am." He gently cupped the back of her neck. *How far will you let me go?* His cock ached to have her, to mark her as his woman. "I've known you for close to twenty years, and you never told me you knew Highland and Jerry Wynn. You know I'm a huge cage-fighter fan."

She laughed. "Are you serious?"

He nodded and spread his legs, widening hers. He flattened his hand over her ass and pulled her against his ready-to-fuck cock. "Garrett met Highland at a coffee shop in Vegas, and asked him to send me a signed photo. Highland actually did, and…" He grinned like a man who just won the lottery. *You're friends with Jerry, and you're following all my physical cues.* "…he sent one of Jerry too. Said his brother was going to be unstoppable, and he has been. He's never lost a fight. Garrett won't officially introduce me. He has forbidden me to go any closer than ten yards from him. He thinks I'm going to go all crazed fangirl like, but I promise I won't."

"Oh, my God. You want me to introduce you to him?"

He nodded. His eyes widened. "Please?"

"Why don't you join us for dinner?"

"I'd love to. Thank you." He leaned closer until his mouth hovered millimeters from hers. "Really, thank you."

"Anytime." The pulse at her neck throbbed.

He leaned back against the seat and closed his eyes. *You want to fuck me. Should I make you wait? Yes. I think I will keep you guessing about my intentions.* "After dinner, I've got to run to the hospital, but I'll call you."

"Sounds good." She stayed in his lap but averted her gaze to the window.

The limo slowed. The warmth of the ride hit a cold patch. *Should I show you how much I love you?*

The car stopped too soon.

"I've got to check on a patient. I'll be back soon," he said.

She climbed off his lap. “I’ll be with Jerry until it’s over.”

****

She stepped out of the limo and strode toward the entrance to the brown, brick funeral home. *I made an ass out of myself. Derek is not into me at all. He’s only into Garrett.* Jerry stretched his shoulders beside a white pillar near the side entrance. His green shirt with a white clover on the front and Wynn in white letters on the back clung tightly to his muscular chest and biceps. She semi-matched him with her green shirt, black jeans. She hurried forward, her black sneakers barely making a sound.

Jerry shook out his shoulders and arms and sauntered down the green carpet of the portico. His gaze remained cast down and his face marred with the unnatural paleness of anguish.

“Jerry.”

He spotted her and visibly relaxed. “Ellie.”

“I’m sorry I’m late. What can I do?” She hugged him and stepped back.

“I have a shirt for you,” he said. “Can you say something, or read something, or something? The director has options for you, but he wanted an open casket, and when I saw her again… I told him to close it. I can’t…”

He pulled her in and hugged her. “I forgot how horrible this was. It’s been years since I had to bury anyone. I always had Aunt Mae beside me, holding me up.” His voice cracked. He sounded like a little boy, not the strong, resilient man holding her. His breath hitched. Moisture from his eyes fell softly against her cheek.

"It's going to be okay," she whispered. "I'm here, and you can lean on me." *Some things between friends never change.* "I've got your back."

"Thanks." He held her tightly as if she were keeping his head above water. She supposed she was. "Now, take a deep breath in with me." She inhaled, catching a scent of ginger from his skin. *You used my soap.*

He mimicked her breathing.

"Jerry, it's time to straighten up, and find the director. Miss Mae deserves to be honored, and you have the privilege of making it happen."

He released her from his embrace and ran his hands over his face, wiping the tears away. He stood up straight. "I'm good."

She cupped his cheeks like she had her boys at Greg's funeral to give them the encouragement to get through it. "You represent the Wynn name. She gave that name to you because she loved you."

He nodded and lightly bounced on the balls of his feet as if he were getting ready for a fight. "She did. Hell, yeah." A small smile formed on his lips. "Thanks, Ellie."

She mimicked his nod. "I'll change into this tee, and we'll be twins for the rest of the day."

"Okay." He straightened his spine and once again stood strong and confident.

She wiped the last bit of moisture under his eyes away. "There's that handsome Wynn boy I knew growing up."

He slid his hand to the small of her back and guided her to a private room for her to change. Once changed, he led her into the director's office. Cinnamon candles burning on the table behind his desk couldn't mask the stale smell of ash inside. The funeral director sat at a clutter free mahogany desk wearing the classic black suit of death.

"Mrs. Winthrop will say a few words about Mrs. Wynn," the director spouted off as soon as they crossed the threshold of his inner sanctum. "Then she will say the Twenty-Third Psalm as Mrs. Wynn requested in the will. Mr. Wynn, you will…" The director continued with the instructions and answered questions. Then he walked to the door and shooed them out.

"That was weird," she whispered.

"I beat his son in a high school wrestling match. Kid started a fight afterward. I finished it. It happened more than twenty years ago, and they're not over it." He shook his head. "Some people."

Jerry took Ella's hand and strode to the empty main entrance. She should have had Kyle and Jason come to be pallbearers, but she assumed he'd have friends to help him. She should text Derek and have him help. Maybe she had time to text the boys too.

He stopped at the doors to the main room and closed his eyes. "I'm sorry for bringing you into this, but I trust you. You never sold me out, and you could have so many times over the years. I looked for you when Highland died, but couldn't find you. I even talked to your father, but all I got out of him was you moved south, and he hadn't seen you since. Thank you for being here. I owe you."

She stared at him bewildered. *What? Sold you out? You looked for me? Why?*

He squared his shoulders and inhaled, keeping her from asking what he meant.

She straightened up next to him, remembering their tradition before entering school. Nothing could harm them if they steeled themselves from insults, didn't get involved, didn't fall into the trap of caring. They achieved their childhood goal of leaving town and never going back but not in the way either had expected.

He pushed the double doors open, and walked inside with her at his side to a standing-room-only crowd of celebrity types. Healthy, athletic men in designer suits stood next to pretty, perfectly proportioned, plastic-doll looking women wearing slinky black dresses on one side of the room, while on the other side, local men and women of all ages and sizes stood in their Sunday best.

Jerry gripped her hand tightly as he strode down the aisle without stopping until he reached the front row. They sat down together. He draped his arm around the back of her chair while they waited for the funeral director to appear.

The man in the black suit entered from the side, said a few sterile words, and called Ella to the front. She carefully walked forward and turned toward the crowd. Her stomach clenched as nerves hit her. The last time she spoke in front of a crowd was at Greg's funeral, and that had been a blur.

"Thanks for coming and remembering Mrs. Mae Wynn." She inhaled. *Shit. I don't know the Twenty-third Psalm by heart.* She didn't know any bible verses by heart, and the director hadn't handed her a Bible, so she decided to go in a different direction.

"I hope Jerry doesn't mind, but my story about Miss Mae involves him."

"Tell it," a few deep voices shouted.

She glanced at Jerry who nodded. Taking that as affirmation to continue, she gazed back at the crowd. "Well, those of you who know Miss Mae know she was a no-nonsense kind of woman. The best kind of woman."

"Yes, ma'am," she heard someone say like an "amen" in church.

"So," she looked at Jerry for validation. He didn't give her any indication it was okay or not okay to talk. She headed into no man's land and proceeded. "So, Jerry and I were maybe eight or nine playing at recess in school."

Jerry smiled in approval.

She turned to the crowd, confident. "Well, playing was probably not the right word. Jerry was getting his butt kicked by Ryan Fitzgerald, who was the biggest and meanest kid in elementary school. I missed a good deal of the fight…" She cocked her head to the side, and stifled a smile.

"…if you can call it a fight. Jerry lay on the ground with a bloody lip and scraped up face. I ran over to him from where I played on the swing set, where he was *supposed* to be—not in the dirt fighting with Ryan." She rolled her eyes. "But, that's Jerry. He never knows when to quit."

"You know it," Jerry said with a half-smile, and a wink.

She laughed. "Right. So, there I stood, angry with him for not playing on the swings with me and choosing *instead* to get in a fight with Ryan. But all that shifted when Ryan said something derogatory—which I will not repeat. I got right up in Ryan's face, drew back my arm, and threw a right hook, connecting with his jaw in pure, never-would-happen-again-in-a-million-years perfection. Ryan dropped to the ground."

Mouths gaped in the crowd.

"I know what you're thinking. Me?" She nodded her head. "Yes, me. I got some serious street cred from it. And so, I became Jerry's enforcer." She lifted her hand in a flourish and bowed.

Giggles and hearty laughs filled the solemn space.

"That's not the whole story," Jerry said.

"Right." Ella winked at him. "It just so happened Highland, Jerry's brother, and Miss Mae were standing behind me, probably giving Ryan dirty looks causing him to stay on the ground, and act dead—"

"—But she's not dwelling on that right now," Jerry added.

"Hush now, I'm telling the story."

A few chuckles moved through both sides of the aisle.

"Highland, of course, said to me, 'Ellie, you'll break your thumb if you don't make a proper fist.' And Miss Mae said, 'Ellie O'Brien, you should have fiery red hair with the last name of Wynn to match your determination. You darn near scared me something fierce, and nothing scares me, child.' "

Jerry laughed. Amusement flowed through his emerald eyes.

She pressed her lips together. She hadn't thought about that time in forever. "Miss Mae was the most fearless woman I have ever had the pleasure to know. Jerry gets that from her."

The director slipped her a Bible opened to the Twenty-third Psalm. She opened her mouth to read when Jerry joined her.

"Can we read it together?" Jerry whispered. He covered her hand with his and intertwined their fingers.

"You start," she said. They read the psalm together. He hadn't needed the Bible but she had.

She closed the book when they were finished and stepped forward, ready to get out of the spotlight. He clutched her hand and stopped her from leaving.

"Stay," he whispered.

She squeezed his hand and stood by his side as he addressed the audience.

"Thank you for coming..." He acknowledged person after person. She had no idea who they were, but they all had famous-sounding nicknames. Derek mentioned cage fighting. Did that mean fists and kicks fighting? She really needed to up her social media game, use a search engine, get out of her small massage circle.

Three of the largest men in the crowd joined them at the front. Bagpipes and drums began playing outside. Jerry and the three men lifted the casket and led the trek to the gravesite.

She walked beside Jerry and worried about his shoulder, hoping he wouldn't reinjure it. None of the men acted as though the weight of the casket was taxing, but she knew differently.

They walked steadily and smoothly over the uneven ground. Once there, they set it down on cords next to the grave in the way everyone in Ella's hometown had done for hundreds of years. Then, they lifted the ropes with the casket balanced on them and lowered it down into the ground. They dropped the cords over the casket.

The music stopped. Jerry picked up a fistful of dirt and let it fall through his fingers over the open grave. Ella did the same and then held his hand.

"We'd love for everyone to come to Maggie's Irish Pub and Grill to celebrate Miss Mae's life," Ella said. "Thank you for coming."

One by one, mourners strode forward, and gave their respect to Jerry until only she and Jerry stood alone by the open grave. "Do you have to go back to work?"

"Nope. I'm here for you. We have to be at my house at six for dinner with my kids and my friend, Dr. Derek McGregor. So, let's do this."

"Stand here with me for a few more minutes." He wrapped his arm around her and turned, facing the place where Mae's body lay. "I'm scared. The boy in me. I feel so alone."

She nodded. "Greg, my husband, when he was sick, I didn't feel alone. Just his presence gave me something to hold onto." She swallowed down the emotions rising within. "After the funeral, I put my children to bed and had a friend stay at my house with them while I went to his grave."

She fought back the heartache ready to surface. "…I stood there for hours in the rain alone, staring down at the filled-in plot of land. I loved him more than I'd ever loved anyone else. He had a moment of clarity right before he passed away. He said." She inhaled and closed her eyes. "He said, 'Remember me like I was at the beach. Remember the love we shared. Remember true love doesn't die. You'll never be alone because my love is deep inside you like yours is within me.' My heart broke when he took his last breath. My heart is still broken, although it's healing. I feel alone most of the time, but sometimes…" *with Cade* "…I don't feel so alone, so broken hearted. You won't always feel like this."

He nodded and tucked her into his side. "Thanks."

She stood in silence, ready to stay for as long as he needed.

Chapter Twenty-Four

With dinner over and Jerry, Kyle, and Jason gone for the night, Ella walked around her bedroom naked debating whether to step out of her comfort zone and tryout the sex toy she'd kept hidden in her makeup drawer. She finger combed her damp hair and braided it. Derek wasn't due back from the hospital for hours, and he would probably sleep on the couch. In all the years she'd known him, he only ventured into her bedroom once when he helped hang the nude photos of her pregnant with the twins. *That was a disaster.* Greg's face had turned purple. He took the photos down and burned them. As comfortable as he was with her nudity, he did not like it displayed in picture form, not even for just him.

In an attempt at procrastination, she closed the white window shutters in the bedroom. Her bedroom faced the backyard and no one but the squirrels and chipmunks would see her, but Cade complained it wasn't safe. He requested she close her shutters every night. She did to please him.

She sashayed into the bathroom and took a deep breath in. *If I don't like it, I'll tell Garrett my butt is off-limits.* She giggled. *I'd never be able to tell him that. Derek, I could tell. He's easy to talk to, but Garrett?* She'd blush and stumble all over her words. *I'd make a fool of myself.*

She opened the middle drawer under the vanity. Heat blossomed in her cheeks. Butterflies fluttered in her belly. *I can't believe I'm doing this.* She picked up the pink plastic box filled with instructions and supplies and laid it on the golden granite countertop. Her pulse raced as she lifted the top off.

"Holy shit." She picked up the pink butt plug wrapped in plastic marked "Sterilized for Ella" in pink marker. She'd heard they were really small, and the one she held was, but it expanded out like a waffle ice cream cone. She gazed at it and then turned around. She bent over and looked at her ass in the mirror. "Garrett is certifiably crazy." She shook her head and held in a chuckle. "I'm nuts for trying this." She pivoted around and placed the toy down.

Taking her time, she used up a few tubes of lube before she decided her bottom could handle the experiment.

She lubricated the plug and walked to her bed. She'd gone over his instructions a dozen times. She'd used one of the individual tubes of gel and filled her dark passage with lubrication after her shower. She held the end of the plug and climbed onto her bed. She turned over, rested her forehead on her white pillow, and tucked her knees under her chest.

She exhaled and pushed the plug past the circle of muscle and into the passage. Her pussy quivered and moistened. Her ass burned as it stretched, but the muscles relaxed as she worked through a breathing cycle. She arched her back and lifted her ass as she exhaled. She pushed more of the rod in. The slight burn heated her passage, her belly, and her pussy.

She closed her eyes and imagined the plug as

Garrett's cock as she slid the widest part past the entrance. "Garrett," she whispered. *Derek would drop his camera and stand at the edge of the bed. Garrett would flip her over.*

She rolled onto her back and leveraged the handle of the plug against the mattress. She sat on her knees, arched her back, pressed her hands flat behind her, and pushed more of the plug inside her.

"Fuck me," she whispered.

She gained her balance and slid her right hand between her legs. She rubbed her clit, lifted her hips and gently dropped her hips and pushed the rest of the plug inside her passage. *Garrett, I love you. Fuck my ass. Derek, lick my pussy.*

"Yes." Her clit throbbed. "Derek, lick me." She circled her clit, dipped her fingers into her pussy. "Derek, fuck me."

The mattress dipped. A large hand cupped her throat, forcing her head back farther. She opened her eyes and met Derek's gaze. She gasped. "Derek."

He brushed her hand away from her pussy. "This is my pussy to play with, not yours."

Her heartbeat drummed out of control. "Uh."

"Proper response is 'Yes, sir.' Do you understand?"

"Yes, sir," she said.

"Hands and knees." He let go of her neck.

She dropped forward into position. *You're in charge.*

"What are you supposed to say?" Derek asked.

"Yes, sir," she said.

"Mmm."

Fabric rustled. The mattress dipped and rose. His

hands caressed her ass cheeks and pulled them apart. Thick fingers traced along the edge of the plug around the entrance. "My cum is going to be dripping from here very soon."

She moaned. *I want that. I want to you to fuck me like you love me.*

His fingers traced down the center to her pussy. "You have the most beautiful pussy I've ever seen. I've masturbated over the pictures I took of your pink pussy. But Garrett's cum clung to your folds, and his cum slipped from your pussy lips and onto your thighs in those photos. Tonight, my cum will be inside and on you."

"Yes, sir," she whispered. Her legs trembled.

"When you choose us, I'll be your husband as much as Garrett. You will be mine. I've loved you for years. I've always wanted a life with you and Garrett."

She bit her bottom lip to keep the tears at bay. "You have? I didn't think…"

His cock pushed into her pussy.

She gasped. Her ass contracted around the plug with a new desire. The fantasy of both cocks inside her was going to be reality.

He placed his hand on the middle of her spine and pushed down.

She lowered her arms and straightened them above her head.

He slapped her right cheek.

She sucked in a breath. The shock of the light swat dissipated, leaving a pleasant residual warmth.

"I love you," he said. "I've held back for Garrett, but he's ready to share you. He's ready for me to show you the kind of husband you're getting with me. After watching you push that plug into your ass and finger fuck yourself, I'm ready to get rid of this hard-on I've been sporting because of you since yesterday morning."

Thwack. Heat flooded her ass. Her passage squeezed tight, sending a new sensual sensation of desire into her girl parts.

"Yes, sir. Again." She arched her back and stuck her ass higher in the air for another swat.

"I'm in control, Ella. Me. Not you." Thwack. His hand gripped her burning bottom cheeks and jiggled.

"Yes, sir." Her pussy contracted as desire ran like wildfire through her veins. *Control me like Cade does.* Juices moistened her inner thighs.

He glided his hand over her ass and dipped his fingers into her pussy. "A bright-pink ass to match a glistening, pink pussy."

She moaned low and deep. *Again. Do it again.*

As if he'd heard her thoughts, his hand lifted and landed in three swift swats on each butt cheek.

Her legs shook as her center rippled with delight.

His cock pushed into her wet pussy. "You don't come until I tell you."

"Yes, sir." Her core buzzed with energy. The plug added extra fullness to her pussy.

He thrust and retreated with long, slow strokes. Mini contractions surged in waves with each thrust and command.

"I'm going to come." Her legs trembled. Her stomach tightened.

"Do not come until I tell you." He rocked back and delved into her. He leaned over her. His hand landed beside her head. His other hand slid between her legs. His fingers circled her swollen clit. His pelvis tapped at the handle of her plug with each powerful thrust.

She panted to keep from coming as all her nerve endings drove her toward bliss. *So much like Cade. So much power and confidence. So much control.*

She contracted her abs, squeezed her pussy around his cock, and held her breath.

"That's it," he said. His fingers pushed in around the edge of her clit, pinched and held it.

She held still as her clit stung with pain.

He thrust faster and deeper as he held her clit as tightly as a clamp.

In and out. In and out.

She squeezed her pussy tighter and tighter. She burned for completion. Her clit stopped aching. Perspiration dotted her flesh.

He pulled out and lifted his hips.

"Look at my cock."

"Yes, sir." She turned her head and looked back at him. Juices covered his hard cock. Beads of cum dripped from the head. She licked her lips. *I'm going to suck your cock. I'm going to drink your cum. Oh. Shit. I'm going to come.* She inhaled. The scent of sex seeped into her nostrils.

He lowered his cock to her pussy as she strained to watch. He pumped his hips and powered his cock into her. "Come, Ella."

With the order, she released her coiled muscles. She let go of the last morsel of control and surrendered to his wish. "Yes," she cried out in a sultry tone different than with anyone else.

Her pussy clenched and released around his beautiful cock. Cum spurted within her.

He groaned and shuddered. He flopped to his side

and pulled her along with him. "Your pussy is milking me dry."

"Mmm," she whispered. "Yes, sir." Her pussy walls continued to contract in delicious waves.

He rocked his hips. His cock glided a little out and then all the way in. He kept fucking her slowly, gently, and lovingly. "I love you. I wish we could have children."

"Me too," she whispered. "I always wanted a big family. But it's not in the cards."

"The platonic thing is not going to work with us," he said. "We have too much chemistry to stop from fucking every chance we get. I talked to Garrett and Cade and we're all comfortable with you fucking the three of us. We keep it monogamous in our group and never stray. No condoms. No STD's. No worries. Are you comfortable with sleeping with each of us? Sometimes all of us in the same day?"

With Derek, her voice worked. They'd always been honest with each other. He delivered all three of her children. He'd taken care of her as her doctor, counseled her when she needed it, and encouraged her over the years. He never judged her. "I feel like I shouldn't be okay with it, but I am. I love you and Garrett. I have for years. I need Cade too. I don't know what is going to happen or which lifestyle will be the best for me. So much is up in the air. But this feels right."

After the house is sold and the wedding is over, I can sit down and decide what to do about Cade and the dirty duo.

His hand slid to her breast and traced the outside of her nipple. "We have time to figure it all out. But now we can have sleepovers without anyone getting angry."

"So you were angry Cade slept over the other night?"

"Very." He pinched her nipple.

Her pussy contracted.

"Mmm," he mumbled. "You're so sensitive."

"You're not angry anymore?"

"How could I be? You introduced me to Jerry Wynn. Was bringing a T-shirt to sign over the top?" He rolled onto his back. His hard cock slid from her pussy. "Climb on top of me and put my cock in your pussy."

"He got a kick out of you bringing a shirt. It wasn't over the top." She turned around and crawled on top of him. "Want to see your cum between my legs?"

His cock jerked. "Stand up and show me."

She straddled his body, pulled her pussy lips apart, and watched his gaze drift between her legs. "This is your pussy tonight."

"My pussy all the time," he whispered. "My cock wants a taste of your cream, kitten."

She lowered to her knees and inched down onto his cock. She moaned as his cock moved the plug inside her.

He cupped the back of her head and pulled her to his chest. "Squeeze me. I want to hear your pussy slurp my cock."

She clenched her pussy hard.

"Sit up and fuck me," he ordered.

She pushed against his chest and sat up.

He grabbed her hips. "Fuck me, kitten. Fuck me hard. Make me come."

She humped his cock. Her breasts bounced up and down. Up and down. Faster and faster. She leaned forward and ground her clit against him. She pushed back and he thrust up.

He gripped her hips.

"I'm coming." Her soul shattered into a billion pieces as he put a claim on her heart next to Garrett and Cade. She collapsed on him.

"That's it, kitten." His fingers dug into her. "You're sucking my cum."

"Are you and Garrett really okay with me taking my time?" *I can't make a decision. I love all three of you.*

"Yes." He kissed the side of her forehead. "This is new for you. We may want to move immediately to marriage and forever, but you need time to get Cade out of your system. There is only one of him. Really, it's not a fair competition. One man can't compete against two, unless you're Jerry Wynn. I'm glad he's not interested in you. I don't know what I'd do."

She laughed. "Jerry is a friend—only a friend."

He rolled over and took her with him until he was on top of her. "May I stay the night?"

"I'd like you to stay. The boys are sleeping over with friends. I don't have to be at work until ten."

He waggled his brows. "Don't move. Keep your sexy legs right where they are, and your pussy where I can see it. I'll clean you up and show you how to care for your new butt toy."

She closed her eyes, avoiding the dark place she ran to the last time he attempted to pamper her. No tears. No sadness. Love filled her heart. Love and peace. Cade gave her the freedom to love again. Cade gifted her the peace to move on. Derek gave her the ability to accept her wilder side. Garrett healed the wounded heart from Greg's death.

Josie had been right. Greg would want her to love again, to have love, to be loved. Whether she made a commitment to one man or two was up to her.

Chapter Twenty-Five

She glided the cotton sheet up his smooth back as they both exhaled. Unlike his son Cade, Pappy Jackson didn't talk at all during the massage. He didn't moan or hum or fall asleep. He breathed slow and steady, following the pattern of her inhalation and exhalation as she worked.

She rested her hands on the back of his head and called on her inner Zen to end the session with the same soothing energy they'd had throughout it. "Take your time getting up. I'll be in the waiting room or my office. Okay?"

"Thanks, Ella," Pappy said. "I won't be long."

She lifted her hands off his head and raised her hands to her nose. A new mixture of ylang ylang and sandalwood essential oils she'd blended specially for him brought a smile to her lips. Flowers and woods for a sensitive and strong man and father.

On her way out of the room she rubbed in hand sanitizer, eliminating the calming scent she now associated with him.

With key closing procedures finished early, she looked over the wedding checklist on her laptop. The wedding dress was taken care of along with the flowers, catering, and cakes. Sammy's wedding ring had a small balance. Damn.

Jerry's referrals brought in a ton of business, but

she needed money now to pay for the ring and catching up on business expenses.

She checked her schedule and phone messages. Troy wanted her to call him. She dialed his number and prayed she'd get his answering machine.

"Ella, Ella, Ella," Troy answered. "How are you?"

"Busy. How are you?" *Get to the point. I'm ready to go home.*

"I'm in a bind," he said. "I need a favor, and I hope you can help me out."

"I'm beat. I can't do another massage tonight." She was done for the day. Cade was out of town on business. Garrett and Derek were working. She planned to soak in a hot bath and go to sleep early.

"No massages tonight. I want you to bring over four cases of the oils we talked about offering in your sensual product line. Derek told me you tested them on him. The thing is this…" He continued talking while imploring her to help him. He had everything she'd need along with a personal assistant to get her ready, but he needed her immediately.

She almost refused, but he mentioned the potential profit, and she looked at the amount she owed on Sammy's ring and the bill for her overdue lease payment. The taxes were coming due, and she hadn't gotten a contract on her house, an. *No bath or early bedtime tonight.* "Okay, Troy. Where do I go? What do I wear?"

He rattled off an address, and told her he had clothes, makeup, and a hair stylist on standby for her. "See you within the hour."

"I'll call you when I leave my house." She ended the call, grabbed her purse, and night deposit. She would clean up the room in the morning. She had to get the oils, and hustle to the address. If she sold everything she brought, she would have the most profitable day in the history of her career.

She strode into the waiting room.

Pappy stood at her soap and oil display with a bar of honeysuckle soap to his nose.

"How much is a bar?"

"You can have one for free. If you like it, you can buy one next time." *I'm going to make a bar of soap with ylang ylang and sandalwood as a "thank you" for all you've done for Colleen's wedding.*

"Thanks." He put the soap in the side of his brown cargo pants. "Can I walk you to your car?"

"Sure." She adjusted her black tote on her shoulder.

"How much do I owe you?" he asked.

"Nothing. Gosh, you and your wife have done so much already. A massage was the least I could do." She walked past him and turned off the lights in the massage room.

"Thanks. Can I help you clean up?"

"I'm going to do it in the morning." She closed the door and peeked into the second room *Perfect.* "I've got to run to a party where I'm selling some of my specialty oils." She walked to the entrance.

"You should bring some of your soaps too. If they want your oil, they'll want your soap." He opened the door and waited as she set the alarm and locked the door.

"That's a great idea. I'll bring some." She needed help getting the product into and out of the car. "I'm driving Cade's car. It's in the back."

"I'll drive you around the building."

She decided not to argue with the hulk of a man, so she climbed into his white truck.

"Do you mind if I cut to the chase?" Pappy asked.

She blew out an exhale.

My first real meeting with the man, and he decides to be bold. Great. Ugh.

"Say whatever you'd like." With the universal-love energy from the spa gone, she'd rather face his possible disdain for her head on than wonder every time she saw him. He didn't do the hugging test Cade and Jason warned her about via text. She could always get out of the car if it went really badly.

"You're a great massage therapist."

"Thanks." She exhaled, not having realized she had been holding her breath. Starting with a compliment was promising.

"Jason is a great kid. You know he doesn't need me to teach him anything, don't you?" He started the car, pulled around back, and parked in the space next to hers.

"I'm sure you're teaching him a lot. He doesn't know everything, even if he thinks he does." Time ticked away. She needed to move the conversation along. "Is there something you need me to talk to him about?"

"The boys told you about Mrs. Kellen, right?"

She clenched her jaw. *Mrs. I'm-going-to-flunk-your-boys Kellen.* "What about her?" *Maybe Garrett could talk to the superintendent about her.*

"They passed her class."

She raised her brow. "When did that happen?" *Her final is in three days.*

"Cade brought them. They took the final exam in front of the principal and a professor from the university. Cade demanded a review of their grades. Mrs. Kellen's position as head of the department is under review…" Pappy's mouth continued to move as she tried to process everything he said.

Grade changes. Straight A's. Dual Valedictorians. The boys hadn't said a word.

She clasped her hands in her lap. "Cade got the principal to watch them take the finals. They wouldn't do anything for me."

Pappy nodded. "Once Cade makes up his mind to do something, the earth moves to accommodate him." He tapped his fingers on the steering wheel three times like Cade had a habit of doing. "Why have you declined the dinner invitation at my house this Sunday?"

"I'm working Sunday. It's not on my schedule because they are high-profile clients visiting for an event. To be blunt, dinner with the Jackson family is a huge step. I'm not sure we're ready for it."

"Cade loves you. I am pretty sure you're in love with him. Are you scared to get to know us as a family? As potential in-laws? Am I close?"

She closed her eyes. *In-laws? Love?* Did Cade tell his father he loved her? Why would Pappy think she loved Cade? She did, but she hadn't told Cade she loved him yet.

"Don't be scared. We're pretty normal. We love your children. We love you." He smiled, showing off his perfectly straight, white teeth. He looked so much like Cade, she smiled back at him.

"I'm not scared. A dinner with our families seems like a promise. Maybe in another month…" If Cade still desired to be with her, and she'd made a decision on a relationship between the three men. She shrugged. "Right now, I really don't have time." *I can't afford to cancel work appointments.*

"If it is the money issue—"

"—What money issue?" *Has Cade told you about my financial mess?*

"I know you're struggling. You owe on your property taxes. You owe on your lease. You owe on credit cards, and you're trying to sell your house to get out from under all the bills. If money is stopping you, I can write a check and make it disappear. You don't need to work like you do. Cade will take care of you."

"My financial situation is none of yours or Cade's concern, and I would appreciate it if you butted out." Her face burned. She had to be as red as a lobster. "I'm sorry, but my business has kept me and my children clothed and fed. I plan to dig myself out of the hole I ended up in. If that is all, I've got aromatherapy massage oils to sell, and I don't want to be late."

He beamed with what looked like joy. The man made no sense. Why was he smiling?

"I'd like a massage every two weeks for the next four months. Email me with times and dates. I expect you at my house Sunday night at eight for dinner with the family. I've gotten acceptances by Matilda and Nathaniel Granger along with your daughter and her fiancé, and Jason and Kyle." He unlocked the car.

Matilda and Nathaniel? Ugh. "I—"

"I know you're not working until eight on Sunday. Kyle already told me you were free. You have no excuse for not coming."

"I can't get out there in time for dinner. I have a

few personal matters I can't reschedule." She wasn't up to meeting all of Cade's family on their turf.

"Anything can get rescheduled."

She unbuckled the seatbelt. *I actually do have appointments.* "Mr. Jackson, some things can't be changed. I'm sorry, but I've got to decline the offer. I won't make it in time."

"It's moved to Cade's house. You can be there by eight, right?" His left brow arched, and his head tilted to the side.

"Can't dinner wait until after Colleen's wedding?" She was resigned to having dinner with them. "I don't like being railroaded."

"I can't promise it won't happen again." He grinned from ear to ear. "If you'd tell me why you can't reschedule, I'd be more accommodating."

She opened the car door and got out. "I'm sorry, but I can't make it Sunday. I'll email you about massage dates if you still want them." *Please don't want any more massages. I love your son, but I'm not ready to give up Garrett and Derek. I may never be.*

"Eight-thirty at Cade's on Sunday. The massage appointments are business, so yes, I want them."

"I'm busy."

"Eight at Cade's on Sunday."

"My daughter is pregnant, and she'll have already eaten by then."

"She can eat again. Pregnancy either makes you hungry or sick. Eight at Cade's. No is not an option." His smile was infectious.

She grinned again. *Damn it.* "So Cade gets this from you? He pushes and pushes and pushes until he gets what he wants?"

He laughed. “Yes. It comes from my side of the family. You’d know that already if you would accept dinner invitations with us once in a while.”

The man was almost as charming as his son.

“Fine. Eight on Sunday.” She closed the car door and berated herself for giving in.

“Ella,” Pappy said out his window.

She opened the SUV’s door, and got in. She acted as if she hadn’t heard him calling her. Her cell phone rang as she closed the door. She ignored the phone and started the car. Her response would not be appropriate, if she talked to him. She overreacted, but she couldn’t get a handle on herself. *Must be PMS.*

She glanced over and hoped Pappy had driven off. He hadn’t. He sat watching her and smiling like a fool out the window. She could suck it up and have dinner with Cade’s parents and the Grangers for the greater good of the family.

She opened the window on the passenger side. “Is there something else, Mr. Jackson?”

“We’re not that bad, Ella.”

“I never thought you were. I’ve just got a lot going on and…” She sighed. “…not enough hours in the day to get it all done.”

His bright smile dulled. “I thought you were having dinner with Cade on Sunday.”

“No. I wasn’t. I’m working all day.” She closed her eyes briefly. “It’s fine. See you Sunday. Enjoy the rest of the week.”

“You too,” he said. “I’ll see you at Cade’s.”

She closed the window and backed out of her parking spot.

Suck it up. Get over to Troy’s and sell oil.

Chapter Twenty-Six

She stared into the black, leather-framed, full-length mirror in the draped off section of the ballroom of Troy's home. Her hair was teased and curled in long ringlets. Her makeup accentuated her eyes and lips, but not so much so she looked plastic. She appeared younger, less flawed.

The white, lacey bralette and miniskirt showed off her curves. She'd gained weight, not tons, but enough so she looked healthier than she had in years. Three weeks with her three men feeding her had made a difference.

"You look fabulous." The clothing stylist unhooked the bralette and refastened it tighter. "As you walk through the room to your booth, invite guests to follow. This is your first time, so you'll have a lot of followers. If anyone gets touchy, nod to one of the men in all black. They'll take care of it."

"Okay. Thanks."

"Lift your arms up over your head," Penny said.

Ella lifted her arms. "Like this?"

"Drop your arms to your sides."

Ella obeyed as the stylist walked around her three times. The woman stopped in front of her, ran her fingers over the top of the bralette, then over her chest, down her abs, and over her hips.

"Are you comfortable?"

"Yes. It's like wearing a bikini, kind of." *Parts are parts. No big deal.*

"If you're ever uncomfortable, raise your hand, and one of the men in black will come and check on you. Troy is a stickler for rules—Safe, sane, and consensual at all times."

"Got it." Derek and Garrett went over the same rules with her. "I read the disclosure, and I set down my hard and soft limits. I signed everything." *And called Derek on the way over to make sure I'd be safe by myself.*

"All right. Go get 'em, girl."

Ella squared her shoulders and strutted out of the curtained off area. She stopped on a dime.

Troy stood in front of her and offered his hand. "Take my hand."

She placed her hand in his. "Do you always escort newbie vendors to their booths?" She kept her gaze at his face, and not the tip of his cock peeking out of the waistband of his black lounge pants.

"Actually, I do." He strode forward into the sensually decorated room with her by his side. "We had an issue with a vendor tonight, so I'm showing everyone you're not judgmental. You're here to introduce your line and answer questions. Smile. I owe you."

She grinned and made eye contact with a brunette wearing sexy, hot-pink lingerie.

"Hey, I'm Ella. Follow me, and I'll show you my line of specialty oils and soaps. We'll have a little fun, try some samples, and talk about aftercare."

"Are you the one endorsed by Dr. McGregor?" the brunette asked.

"Yes," Troy answered. "Jackie, meet Ella O'Brien."

Ella shook the woman's hand. "Nice to meet you, Jackie."

Troy tugged her hand and forced her to walk, instead of stop and greet potential customers. At the very end of the open room stood a spectacular, glittery display of her products. A cashier wearing a matching outfit to hers held a computer tablet next to the display.

Troy picked up a bottle of honey and raspberry oil. "Have you tested this on anyone?"

"I've tested every product here. I have sample bottles, and you're welcome to test it anywhere you'd like," she said. "That particular oil is Dr. McGregor's favorite. I think the lemon cream would be great on you, Troy."

She sashayed over to the bottles and cups and distributed samples. Questions poured in. Time slipped away as she helped match the customers with scents. She brought three times as much as Troy requested, and it paid off.

Another group of customers left. She took the break to set out the final bars and bottles of her products before the last wave of potential clients wandered to her section.

Troy's hand gently touched the small of her back. "There's half an hour left, and the men coming this way are colleagues of mine. They are expecting a different vendor, not you. If you want to leave, you can. If you want to stay, and possibly sell more, I'm here to explain the change in product and vendor to them."

"I'd like to stay." She pivoted and faced him. "My goal is to sell everything I brought. I'm going to make sure anyone who enters my area buys."

He grinned. "You're a shark."

She blushed. "I'm motivated." *I'll have Sammy's ring and rent paid, if I sell the rest.*

"You're my kind of woman." His hand drifted over her ass. "Show a little of this."

She reached behind her and moved his hand up to the small of her back.

"Stick to my policies, Troy. No touching me."

"And no moaning on the table." He smirked. "I'll be a good boy, Ella. If you want to finish your night strong, show a little ass, and bend over with your legs straight as much as possible."

"My products sell themselves."

"Yes, but you could help them along, darling. Sell the illusion."

"I don't have to. My products are real." *Don't be a creep. You've done so well up 'til now.*

"I know. *You're* the real deal." His gaze rose over her head. He puffed out a chuckle. "I guess two out of your three men decided to come check on you."

She gasped. "Shit." *Derek came and brought Garrett.*

He dropped his hand from her back. "Hurry back to your display. Forget bending over. I don't need a pissed off Garrett Winthrop making a scene."

She rushed to the display and squared her shoulders. She fidgeted with the hem of the mini skirt barely covering her pussy as her gaze darted between Troy leading the scantily clad group of potential clients toward her and Garrett and Derek wearing jeans and boots and nothing else as they joined the back of the group.

"I'm sorry, but the vendor broke my rules. I'm all about pushing boundaries, but never crossing the line. Never. A person gives any type of no-go sign, and you stop. Period." Troy stepped right up next to her at the display table.

"Now this vendor, Ms. Ella O'Brien, handcrafts her soaps and oils, buying only the best ingredients…" Troy wrapped his arm around her, and placed his hand on her hip as he advocated for her products.

She listened and made eye contact with each of the men. Garrett sported a wicked smile and winked with pride. She stood a little taller with his approval.

"What about skin irritants? I can't have guys coming back to me with rashes on their dicks."

She didn't catch who asked, but she smiled and nodded to the group. "All the ingredients are listed on the bottle," she said. "I've been selling my products for three years and have not had any issues. If a client has a history of skin sensitivities, I have a soap for that." She picked up the soap she developed when Greg had suffered with skin lesions.

"What about taste?"

"Fucking fantastic," Troy said. "I've tested the honeysuckle and coconut cream pie on pussy. Oral sex has a new name, and it is Oils by Ella."

Ella gazed at Troy, seeing him in a new light. He was all about making a profit. Maybe he wasn't so creepy. Could Troy be a decent guy in disguise? He seemed to believe in her and her products. Derek's instincts were usually right, and he trusted Troy.

"Why did you develop your products?" a man wearing black trousers and black leather loafers asked.

She'd prepped for the question, but it still seemed

to make her heart bleed. “My husband had terminal cancer. Anything he washed with irritated his skin. The chemical smell from the medicines lingered. I’ve made my own soaps for years, but…” She inhaled. “Um, the products helped him. I got requests from friends and began selling them.”

She stared at the bar of soap in her hand. Greg had loved the sweet maple scent in the oatmeal soap.

“I’m sorry,” Troy whispered. “I didn’t know.” He squeezed her against his side.

She blinked away the memory and raised her head. “It’s okay. It was a long time ago.”

“I think these products, and the ones she has in development will fly off the shelves. Try them out, and call me for orders.” Troy side-hugged her again and stepped forward. “Don’t be shy. Try them.”

One by one, the bottles and bars disappeared as Troy escorted his colleagues to the checkout girl and out of the room.

Waiting patiently, Derek and Garrett leaned against the wall across from her display and talked quietly.

She took inventory of her boxes. She’d sold everything except two bottles of lemon cream oil and five bars of lavender soap. *Not too bad for a first time.*

“Guys, I could use some help,” she said.

They sauntered over and stood beside her, one on each side.

“I kept hoping you’d bend over, and give us a peek,” Garrett said. His hand slid under her skirt, and over the delicate lace panties Troy provided.

Derek’s hand glided under the skirt, lifting it up and tucking the edge into the waistband. “Panties need to go.”

"We're out in the open," she said.

"We're the only three in the room," Garrett said. "The place is empty, except for Troy, and he's busy with his buddies." He nudged her bare foot with his boot. "Wider."

She widened her stance. "What if someone walks in?"

"Are you scared?" Garrett gathered her panties and pulled them down her legs.

She lifted each foot, leaving the panties on the floor between her feet. "Troy is a client. I'm pretty sure a few of the people I met earlier are massage clients of mine." She gazed down at him. "I don't want anyone to see us."

"I smell neglected pussy," Garrett said, and gazed up at her. He firmly gripped her thighs as he pressed his mouth to her mons.

Derek's hands caressed her hips, opening her ass cheeks. "Troy knows what we do. He helped me pick out the nipple clamps I used on you last week."

"I don't want him to—"

Garrett lifted her right leg over his shoulder and kissed her clit. Her heartbeat hammered against her chest.

"Please, don't let him see me like this."

"I love you," Garrett whispered against her pussy.

"If he sees you," Derek whispered into her ear. "It's because I want him to see. It is my choice." His slick cock pressed against her dark passage.

"Yes, sir. Did you put something on?" She rolled her hips, opening her pussy for Garrett to lick her.

"Your oil." Derek pushed against the tight circle of muscle.

Tongue dipped into her center. She sighed and relaxed her posture.

Derek's cock entered her dark passage for the first time. "Prep is everything, Ella."

No burning, no heavy stretching, no pain, only fullness like he'd explained to her when she started wearing plugs regularly.

"Will I come like this?" She wasn't sure it was possible.

"You're going to come, babe." Garrett kissed along her slit to Derek's balls. She heard him sucking, but part of his lips brushed against the edge of her pussy.

Derek's cock retreated a few inches, then thrust forward.

"Stop sucking my balls. I want you inside our Ella, sliding your cock against mine."

Garrett's tongue slid along her slit, opening her pussy lips, and uncovered her clit. He circled the swollen bead over and over as Derek rocked in and out of her dark passage. Teeth grazed her clit and then tongue laved over it.

"Mmm," she moaned.

Derek's hands slid to her chest, pushed the bralette up, and revealed her breasts. His fingers and thumbs gently tugged at her sensitive nipples.

"Your pink nipples pressed beautifully against the white fabric," Derek whispered. "I wanted you to take off the bra, and offer your body to me for a demonstration. I wanted to lick the oil off your pretty breasts, spread your pussy lips, and fuck you."

Heat flowed to her breasts.

"Come for us," Derek commanded.

"Yes," she cried out. Her chest arched as she let go,

obeying him. Juices gushed from her sex. She dropped her head back against Derek's bare chest, giving in to the delicious pleasure he'd allowed her.

"We're not done," Derek said. In and out of her ass he thrust, building another, stronger climax.

Up and down, and side to side Garrett lapped at her pussy.

She raised her hands over her head. "Whatever you want. Wherever you want. However you want me."

Garrett licked over her mons to her belly. He brushed her clit against his bare skin as he stood up. His cock reached her pussy, and ever so slowly he inched inside her.

Her pussy walls spasmed as soon as his cockhead pushed inside.

"I'm going to come. I can't stop it." She hadn't meant to be loud, but everything seemed heightened.

"Let me hear you come." Derek pinched her nipples as tightly as the clamps they'd experimented with. He and Garrett thrust their cocks into her. Their rods slid against each other. *Two men. Two beautiful and gorgeous men inside me. Two men I love.*

Electricity charged from her breasts to her pussy to her ass. Her center contracted around their cocks. Derek twisted her nipples to the point of pain then let go. Her breasts throbbed as bliss thundered through her. She bounced up and down between them as they wildly thrust and retreated in tandem.

The friction. The delicious pounding of their cocks. The beauty of their hard bodies pressing and gliding against hers. Filling her. Taking her. Giving her their love, their desire.

The pleasure increased as they worked together to

keep her climax going. Her pussy pulsed, and ecstasy hit her again. She screamed words she hadn't expected to exit her mouth. "I love you, Garrett. I love you, Derek."

"Yes." Her men grunted as their cocked jerked inside her, hitting sweet spots, spurting their cum. She milked their cocks, wanting to keep this feeling and them in her life forever.

Garrett's head rested against Derek's shoulder. "I love you, Derek. I love you, Ella. I needed this so badly tonight."

She curled her arms around Garrett's waist. The truth fell from her lips. "I love being with you both. I want to stay the night at your place. I'm ready to take the next step and see how this might work long-term. Can we?"

"Yes," they answered.

"I need to be with you. I need both of you," she said.

Garrett kissed Derek's lips and stepped back. His cock slid from her wet pussy as Derek pulled his cock from her dark passage. They carefully placed her on her feet and took off the bralette from her chest.

Standing naked before her two men, confidence filled her. "I did pretty well tonight."

"You killed it." Garrett pulled up his jeans. "And you rocked that teeny dress thing."

"Our sticky cum on your thighs makes me want to fuck you again," Derek whispered.

"You were amazing," Troy said.

Her stomach tightened into knots. She stood butt naked. Troy probably saw them fucking.

"Um, thanks," she said.

"I hope you have a plan for mass production, because we just made Oils by Ella a million-dollar company." Troy sauntered into her view. He kept his gaze at her face and genuinely smiled.

She rolled her eyes. "Right." *He looks like he's telling the truth. Could my luck really be changing?*

Garrett stepped to her side and took her hand in his.

"I'm serious," Troy said. "We'll talk business in the morning. I'll bring breakfast to your spa at six-thirty. Go and celebrate."

Derek stepped behind her, his hand slid under her arm, and cupped her breast.

"Do you have a robe Ella could wear out?"

"Yes. There's one inside the private entrance. Take the robe." He shrugged. "Don't take the robe. No one will see her."

Garrett strode forward. She followed. Heat rose up her neck and covered her face as sticky fluids trickled down her legs.

"See you tomorrow, Ella," Troy said.

She lowered her gaze to the floor, and nodded. *Ugh. At least her business policy didn't include anything about accidental naked exposure.*

Chapter Twenty-Seven

Sitting at her office desk, Ella traced the signatures on the copy of the signed house contract. *Fifteen days. Fifteen days and it won't be mine anymore.*

The doorbell chimed.

Tired of waiting at the restaurant for me, Troy?

"I'll be right out," she shouted. She closed her laptop and shoved the document into her purse. A quick discussion about increasing production with Troy, and she'd be off to Cade's for the Jackson family dinner she'd avoided while Sammy and Garrett were out of town on a work assignment. Eight weeks of postponements—the family dinner Pappy insisted on having, the wedding Colleen cried daily about not having, the decision to choose between Garrett and Derek or Cade she hadn't made. *I love and need all of them.*

She walked to the door and pulled up the top of the pink bustier Cade bought her for the main family event. The thing kept slipping down. Her breasts had gotten bigger, her belly had gotten bigger, and her hips had expanded too. Eating revolved around everything her men did—sex, exercise, movies, cars. *Damn, they ate all the time, and I am eating bite for bite with them. I've got to slow down and lose some weight.*

She opened the door, ready to talk business.

"Troy, I…" *Shit.* "Felicity." Her cheeks twitched.

Her jaw clenched as she curled the corners of her lips into a tense smile. *Calm the crazy woman down.*

The woman's eyes darted from the untouched display to the office to the massage rooms to the laundry room. The two part-time massage therapists she'd hired were already gone for the day.

With her hands open and her purse tucked to her side, Ella walked forward. "Can I help you with something?"

Wearing a black, business pantsuit and running shoes, the pretty brunette in her late forties stood in place near the display closest to the massage room on the right.

"No." Felicity's fingers traced the side of the six-foot level Jason had used to add another shelf to the top of the display. But Jason put it in the closet after he finished.

"Okay." Ella inhaled. "Um. Let's walk out together."

Gazing through the glass front door she saw Troy's car in the parking lot at the restaurant across the street. A police car was parked next to Troy's convertible. If a problem erupted with her crazy ex-client, she'd ditch her heels and run to the restaurant.

"Where are you going?" Felicity tilted her head. She stepped forward away from the display. The woman held the level in her right hand and swung it like a walking cane as she leisurely strode toward Ella.

"Just meeting a business partner. He's expecting me." Ella hugged the wall on the opposite side of the room as she quickly hurried toward the door. The clicking of her heels on the tile echoed like thunder in the small space.

"Why are you running?" Felicity hissed.

She pushed the door open. "I'm late."

With one foot outside the door, Ella pushed off her back foot, ready to sprint. But Felicity grabbed her upper arm and yanked her back inside.

"Shit."

"You're fucking all your clients, aren't you?" Felicity asked.

"No. I don't do that." *You're out of your mind.* "What do you want?"

"You're fucking my husband. You took him from me."

"I'm not involved with anyone who is married. You've got the wrong massage therapist." Ella slammed her forearm down on Felicity's wrist. The woman's grip released. Ella ran out of the spa.

"I know it's you," Felicity screamed. "You've taken Cade from me. He loves me. He doesn't love you."

Ella stopped on a dime and glanced back at the woman. "You're married to Cade?" Cade wasn't married. She'd met his entire family. Garrett and Derek checked him out. Cade wasn't dating anyone besides her. "Cade Jackson?"

The woman looked down for an instant.

Cade has a stalker. Cade has a real life, dangerous stalker. And she's after me.

"He's mine, and you're not…"

Ella turned her head back to the lights of the restaurant across the street. She lifted her foot and…

Whack.

She opened her eyes. The ground seemed to spin under her. Her head pounded. Her face. Her arms.

Her…

Whack.

Whoosh. All the air left her lungs. She bounced on the concrete.

I've got to get out of here, away from her.

Pounding. Pounding. Her head. Feet.

I have to get out of here. She pushed up onto her hands and knees, and vomited.

"You are never touching my husband…"

"Holy shit," Troy shouted. "Get the fuck away from her."

Whack.

"No," Ella screamed. She fell to her side. Her head, her ribs, her leg.

Multiple moving sets of brown eyes stared into hers.

"I've got you." Troy whispered. "Fuck. Do not close your eyes again. Do not fall asleep."

She closed her eyes. "Cade."

"Open your eyes."

"I'm fine. Oh, God, I'm going to…" She retched.

"I'm taking her to the hospital. I'm not waiting for an ambulance," Troy said.

He lifted her up. The earth spun so fast it turned to gray.

Then black.

Chapter Twenty-Eight

Cade paced the hallway with his father, waiting to hear from the doctor. His Ella had been attacked. No one seemed to know details other than Troy found her at work. Jerry called him. Jerry Wynn was her emergency contact. *Jerry Wynn. Not me.*

"She's going to be okay," Pappy said.

He nodded. *I should have picked her up from work. I should have hired her a security guard. She wasn't supposed to be alone. The other evening therapist was supposed to be with her.*

"Nikki just texted. Your assistant got arrested tonight," Pappy said.

"Felicity? For what? DUI?"

"I don't know. Nikki's going down to the police station to find out. Felicity is in the probationary period, right?"

Cade stopped.

"Yeah. This morning I told her she wasn't a good fit, and needed to find another job. I gave her a month to find something else. Where is everyone?" He pulled out his phone. "I'll call again. Maybe they'll answer this time."

"You two want some coffee?" Troy asked from behind them.

Cade turned around. "Yeah. Have you seen Garrett or Derek?"

"Yeah, they—"

The door to Ella's room opened up.

Cade strode forward, leaving Troy and his father behind.

In a wheelchair, Ella sat so small, the pretty pink bustier and skirt he'd bought her for dinner with his family was torn and dirty. Her beautiful, brown hair, pulled to the side, and shaved…*Stitches*. Green-framed, dark sunglasses. *The ones Jerry always wore*. Her little nose and cheek. *Scraped up*. Her arm. *Road rash.*

His heart stopped beating. Gray swam around him. *My Ella.*

"We're heading to labor and delivery at Garrett's work hospital," Jerry said. He pushed the wheelchair toward the elevator. "Come on. I haven't told Garrett or Derek what happened, yet. Colleen is in trouble."

"Mr. Wynn," a nurse in green scrubs stopped him. "Here's her paperwork, and her prescription has been called in."

"Thanks for helping get her released so quickly," Jerry said "I'll make sure she follows the doctor's orders."

Cade's mind connected the dots about Colleen, and his feet started working again. Within three strides, he walked beside Ella. "Ella needs to rest."

"Yes, she does," Jerry said. "She should be on her way home, not to another hospital, but Colleen and the baby are in trouble. And I'm counting on Derek to do his own thorough examination of Ella after we check on Colleen."

"I'm fine." Ella's weak voice called to Cade's most basic needs to protect her. "Please, I need to see my daughter."

"You need to be here," Cade said. "Sweetheart, there are a lot of stitches on…"

Jerry's head started shaking from side to side, and his eyes widened. *"Stop talking. Don't get her angry," he mouthed.*

"After we make sure Colleen is okay, I'm taking you home with me, and—"

"—We're going to see what happens," Jerry interrupted. *"It's serious with Colleen," he mouthed to Cade. "You might need to stay."*

The elevator doors opened. He and Jerry walked in with Ella, turned around, and faced the main nurses' station.

With his phone to his ear, Pappy stood beside Troy.

"I'll meet you at the hospital," Pappy said.

"I'll handle her business with Kyle until she's better. I'm running down to the police station to make a statement," Troy said.

"Thanks, Troy," she whispered. "I'll be at work tomorrow."

"No," Jerry said. "No work, Ella. Kyle and Troy can handle it."

Her jaw clenched.

"We'll deal with it tomorrow," Cade said, and pressed the button to the first floor.

Thankfully, the elevator closed.

"How long will it take to get to Colleen?" she whispered.

"Car rides and concussions don't really mix," Jerry whispered. "Probably twenty minutes. At this time of night, it might be sooner, but not much."

"My dad has my car," Cade said. "I'll hold her while you drive."

The elevator doors opened, and they walked out. He picked her up in his arms, cradling her.

"I've got you, sweetie." *I'm never going to let you go.*

****

Inside a pastel green, labor and delivery room in the hospital wing of the high-security building housing Garrett's unnamed company, Cade held Ella's hand as Derek removed the needle from her arm. Derek's expression seemed normal, but the intensity in his hazel eyes as he systematically and delicately examined her was anything but normal. His hands moved quickly over her body, stopping to adjust her clothes and moving downward.

She whimpered here and there, but she spoke.

"Colleen is three rooms down on the right," Derek said. "You're not leaving until I give you a real exam."

"I'm fine," she said. She touched Jerry's dark sunglasses over her eyes. "Can you dial back the lights?"

Derek lowered his chin and gazed at Cade.

Cade nodded. "She's not leaving until you see her." He carried her out of the room and placed her on her feet outside Colleen's room.

Supporting her weight, Cade placed his hand on the flat handle. "Ready?"

"Are the stitches covered? I don't want anyone seeing them." She gently patted her head.

He moved a section of hair over the shaved area on her head. *You need to be in a hospital room. You're not okay. Not okay at all.* "They're covered, but Ella—"

"—I need to see my daughter."

He pushed the door open.

With strength he hadn't expected, Ella sprinted to Colleen's side. The bright personality of the young woman was gone leaving an ashen and scared little girl in her place. A baby-blue blanket covered up most of the pastel-pink gown she wore. Garrett stood behind Ella. His face drained of color as he made no effort to hide his visual exploration of her from head to foot.

Ella wobbled but grabbed onto the metal bed rail with one hand and stroked Colleen's long blonde hair with the other.

"Momma." Big, crocodile tears fell from Colleen's beautiful, blue eyes. "It's that bleeding thing you had."

"It is, but you and your sweet little baby will be just fine. Derek is very optimistic. Your baby boy has a strong heartbeat, and he's strong-willed like his mom and dad. You just need to stay in bed and rest." She kissed her daughter's head.

Cade's heart swelled with deeper love for Ella. Seeing her fight through pain and a concussion to be there for her child brought up all the reasons he'd waited for the right woman to have his children. The perfect woman stood—under a power only a mother or father would comprehend—supporting her daughter when most women or men would be in bed nursing their own wounds. *Why didn't I meet you six years ago? We could have had a family together.*

Colleen's hand slid over her belly. "Do you really believe he's going to be all right?"

"Yes, sweet pea. Your baby is very strong. He just needs to stay in there for a few more weeks."

"Where are the boys?" Cade asked. *They should be here.* "Sammy?"

"The boys left twenty minutes ago for Sammy's.

They're staying there for a few days to help out." Garrett's hand slid around Ella's waist.

She hissed.

Red crept up Garrett's neck to his chin and steadily rose to his forehead. "Sammy is outside talking on the phone with his parents. He'll be back soon."

The door opened, and Derek poked his head inside. "Colleen will be ready to go home soon. Sammy's team is getting the supplies, and they're scheduling shifts to monitor her."

"Really?" Colleen asked.

"Yep. Sammy is medically trained, and so is everyone on his team. You're in great hands," Derek said. "They know what to do. And you've got me checking on you too."

Colleen burst into tears. "But I'm scared." She turned to Ella. "Momma, I'm scared."

"Sweet pea," Ella wiped the tears from Colleen's eyes. "You're going to be just fine. Your little guy is going to keep growing and getting bigger and stronger. You have to keep the fear away. Think happy thoughts. Visualize him growing into a linebacker like your Sammy was in high school."

"Quarterback," Colleen said in a tiny voice. "He was the quarterback."

"That's right. Quarterback," Ella said. "Derek wouldn't let you leave, if he thought for an instant you needed to be here."

"Listen to your mother." Derek's gaze swept to Ella. "Ella, I need to see you once I get everything squared away with Colleen."

"I can't," Ella said.

"I'll make sure she doesn't sneak out of here,"

Cade said. *She couldn't make it down the hall before collapsing.*

"Mom?" Colleen said. "What happened to you? Why are you dirty? Why are you wearing sunglasses? Why is your face—"

"—I fell. I'm fine. I can't wait to see this little guy." Ella covered Colleen's hand with hers. "I remember when I was in labor with you. Your dad and Garrett were in the delivery room. Your dad went down first."

"Went down?" Colleen eyes widened, and a hint of amusement came to her lips.

"Your dad fainted straight out," Garrett said. "Your mom looked at me, and I started laughing. I couldn't stop until I went to help him and saw what he saw. I stumbled back into a table and cracked my head."

Cade couldn't help but grin. *Tough guy Garrett Winthrop can't handle seeing the reality of childbirth.* "I find that hard to believe." He walked forward and joined the three inside their private bubble instead of standing outside as an observer.

"Greg and I ended up with stitches while Ella labored to push you out. We semi-recovered. Then you came." Garrett placed his hand over Ella and Colleen's on Colleen's belly. "We both fainted at the same time. Ended up with more stitches. We did better with the twin's birth."

"They only got one set of stitches with the boys." Ella's lips trembled. "You, my lovely daughter, gave your father and uncle two set of stitches which is quite an accomplishment."

"How come I never heard that story before?" Colleen's blue eyes twinkled and a pink blush filled her cheeks.

"We swore Ella to secrecy," Garrett said. "Sammy won't faint. You're in good hands with him."

Two drops of tears ran down Ella's cheeks.

Cade wrapped his arm around her, above Garrett's supporting her. *I've got you.*

Garrett released her and plucked a tissue from the counter behind him. He handed it to Ella and replaced his arm, snuggled below Cade's. "Your mom was amazing."

Cade gazed down at Colleen. "You're going to be an amazing mom too." *You're maturing every day.*

"Thanks, Mr. Jackson, um, Cade."

I'm waiting for the day you call me Daddy Cade. Maybe it will be the baby first. I'll be Granddaddy Cade.

"Did I ever tell you when your dad and I took you to the beach without your mom for the first time?" Garrett asked.

Colleen shook her head.

Cade listened to story after story of Colleen's early years with Greg, Ella, and Garrett. The history between Garrett and Ella held so much emotion and depth, the kind he wanted with her, longed to have, hoped to have as they grew old together.

A soft knock on the door grabbed his attention.

A short-haired brunette wearing pink scrubs with rainbows and pots of gold printed on them rolled a wheelchair into the room and parked it next to Ella beside the bed. "Miss Winthrop, are you ready to go?"

"Yes, ma'am," Colleen said.

Sammy walked into the room smiling. "Baby, we're heading ho…" He paused and stared at Ella. "Uh.

We're ready to go home. Ella, are—"

"—Ella," Derek interrupted. "I'm ready for you."

"I'm fine," Ella insisted. She let go of Colleen's hand and wobbled a little as she stepped back, making room for Sammy.

"I've got Colleen," Sammy said. "Go with Derek, Ella. I'll text when we get home. I think we're going to get married at my house in our bedroom tomorrow evening. Just my team and y'all. We don't want to wait any longer."

"Okay. I love you, Colleen and Sammy." Ella lifted her foot. Her head tilted to the left. She reached forward.

Cade tucked her into an embrace, carefully cradling her head, avoiding her stitches. "I've got you, sweetheart."

"Get her out before Colleen sees the blood in her hair," Garrett whispered. "I'll be there in a couple minutes. I want to know what the hell happened."

"She was attacked at the spa. My company will handle security for her and the spa," Cade whispered. "The three of us will never be gone at the same time."

"Agreed. She gets no choice." Garrett slapped him firmly on the shoulder, and gripped it, holding on to him in solidarity exactly like Cade had seen him do with Derek in a farewell.

With Ella in his arms, Garrett by his side, and Derek waiting in the hall, the weight of all the problems Cade faced lessened. *They love her as much as I do. How can she choose between Garrett and Derek, and me? We each bring something different and valuable to her life.*

Garrett let go, shifted toward Sammy, and stood

like a soldier ready for battle.

"Colleen will…" The nurse discussed discharge instructions.

Cade walked Ella to the door.

Ella stumbled but Cade pulled her upright.

She gripped his hand at her hip. "I'll be over tomorrow after work, Colleen." She turned her head toward her daughter.

"Maybe you could tell me more stories about Dad and Uncle Garrett?" Colleen asked.

"I'd love to," Ella said. "I'd really love to."

Cade escorted Ella into the neutral hallway. With a wheelchair in front of him, Derek stood near the nurses' station a few yards away.

She inhaled deeply. "I'm not getting in that."

"Either you get in, or I'm carrying you," Cade whispered.

The door to Colleen's room behind them opened.

Garrett stepped into Cade's personal space. Fierce blue eyes called for a battle. "What the fuck happened?"

"I'm not—"

"—Nothing," Ella interrupted Cade. "Shut up, Garrett. You're giving me a headache."

Garrett grabbed the sunglasses from her face and sucked in a gasp. His eyes widened to epic proportions, gazing at Cade. His hands trembled as he rubbed them against his stomach "Who?"

"I don't know yet. But we'll find out," Cade whispered. "Whoever did this will be punished." *I will make sure of it.*

She stepped forward and grabbed the glasses from Garrett. Her eyes fluttered. Her hand holding Cade's lost its strength.

Cade moved on instinct and dove forward as she fell. He slid on his knees, caught her, and cushioned her head before she hit the ground. He pulled her against his chest. *You used up all your strength for your daughter.*

She blinked bloodshot eyes at him, the bruising under her makeup darkened, making the injuries she sustained more apparent than before. “Cade, the lights are too much. I need Jerry’s glasses.”

He picked up the glasses from the gray-speckled linoleum and placed them on her. “I’m taking you to Derek. You aren’t thinking clearly. You need a doctor.”

“I need sleep.”

“Derek is examining you.” Garrett’s voice softened. The normal orders he barked came out more like begging, pleading. The hard, outer shell of the man seemed to crack as the need for her permission to be examined and her stubbornness blocked his efforts. He couldn’t force her, not with witnesses present. “It’s free.” He gripped Cade’s arm.

With Garrett’s help, Cade stood up and shielded Ella from the harsh florescent lights with his palm.

“Garrett, I’ve already been examined. I’m—”

“There is my argumentative patient,” Derek said, lightening the tense mood. “I’ve got your records from the hospital. Jerry is coming back in a few minutes with clothes for you.”

“I don’t need this,” she said.

“Humor us,” Cade whispered. “Please, you were in and out so quickly—”

“—She refused anything but stitches,” Derek said. “I’m going to finish examining her. It’s free, Ella.

So…" He paused and gazed down at her.

A couple nurses in pink and blue scrubs with multicolored teddy bears printed on them strolled down the hallway from the nurses' station and stopped a few feet behind Derek.

"Need any help, Dr. McGregor?" the taller nurse asked.

"Do I, Ella?" Derek asked.

"No, sir," she whispered.

The nurses turned on a dime and strode back to their station.

Cade carried the love of his life down the sparkling-clean hallway and into the sky-blue labor and delivery suite closest to the nurse's station. *It took all three of us working together to get you to agree to let Derek examine you.* He placed her carefully on the bed.

The strong, independent woman whose presence seemed to occupy every inch of space in a room, lay dwarfed in the birthing bed. So fragile. Helpless.

"Guys, I need you to leave," Derek said. "Go hold babies in the nursery or something."

She pushed more upright on the bed. Her head slightly bobbed from side to side. She fought against injury and exhaustion to sit up straighter and gain a few more inches of bed space.

Cade placed his hand over hers. *You're so determined to keep control when all you need to do is give it to me. I'll carry your burdens. All of them.*

"This is ridiculous. I'm going home." She swung her legs over the edge of the bed and stood up. "See, I'm fine." She took a step. Her knees shook. She dipped. Cade stepped in and caught her again.

"Thanks," she whispered. "I'm not sure what

happened."

"You're not leaving until Derek says you can," Cade said. *Stop fighting. I've got you.*

Garrett stood unusually quiet next to him.

A knot formed in Cade's stomach. Her dilated and red eyes tore at his heart. Her limp body in his arms broke a piece of his soul. Her resolve to go home without being examined made no sense. *Are you worried, sweetheart? Did the doctor at the hospital tell you something? Are you hiding something from me? Did you tell Jerry a secret, but not me?*

He gently placed her on the bed again as a gray-haired nurse walked in holding a tray of medical supplies and a bag of clear fluids.

"Mr. Winthrop and Mr. Jackson, it's time to go," the grandma-like nurse said.

Cade's feet seemed like they were stuck in concrete, immoveable.

The nurse set down the tray on the counter, pulled the rolling IV machine over, and quickly connected Ella to it. She picked up four empty vials and placed them on the bed next to Ella's hip.

"You already took blood," Cade said.

"These are for extra tests. I'm running everything possible," Derek said.

The nurse finished taking the blood samples and walked to the light panel beside the door. She dimmed the lights and took out supplies from the cabinets near the sink on the opposite side of the room.

"I'll keep an eye on her," the nurse said.

Derek nodded. He slung his arm around Cade's shoulders like they were best friends. Maybe they were in a way. *Weird.*

"Come on, big guy," Derek said.

Cade's feet released from the stuck position, and he walked with Derek's guidance toward the door. They stopped outside the entrance to her room.

"She's dehydrated," Derek said. "She's injured. It's going to take a little while to get all the tests done, but she's got heavy bruising on her back near her kidneys, and on her leg. Her head… Shit. She refused treatment, but Jerry talked her into stitches. All in all, she's going to be fine. She's in shock."

Garrett's face seemed to close off any emotion. His blue eyes seemed vacant. "She knows she's hurt or she would be fighting tooth and nail to get out of here. That nurse would have gotten an earful, and possibly a fistful by now, but she's as quiet as a mouse."

"I'll tell Garrett what I know while you're in there with her," Cade said. *I don't know shit, but I'm going to find out. Jerry, what the fuck is taking you so long?*

Chapter Twenty-Nine

Derek smiled as he sat on a stool between her legs examining her. “Almost done.”

Yeah, you better be. He’d touched and probed every inch of Ella’s body.

“When was your last period?” His fingers slide from inside her, and he stood up.

“I don’t know. Maybe ten days before Garrett came home? I can’t remember.” She covered her eyes with her forearm and tried to concentrate. “That can’t be right. I can’t think.”

“Almost three months ago?” Derek walked to the side of the bed. “Huh. I’m going to help you to the bathroom, and you’re going to pee in a cup for me.”

“Ugh. Fine.” She uncovered her eyes and squinted. *The lights are obnoxious.*

He slid his hands under her legs and back and lifted her up.

“That’s not helping me. It’s taking me,” she said. *Thank you. I’m not up for walking.*

He shrugged. “I love you, and I’m your doctor. You have to follow my orders."

“Do you think I have an infection?”

“Maybe. You have a lot of injuries, but thankfully, they’re mostly superficial. There is a spot over your kidneys I’m concerned with.”

He placed her down. She peed, noticing some

blood in the cup. He placed the cup in the stainless-steel window cabinet, carried her back to bed, and tucked her in.

"I'm going to grab a nurse and check the test results. I'll be right back." He kissed her on the lips. "Don't worry. I'm going a little overboard because I love you."

"I love you too. I'll try not to worry." *Please don't let me have internal bleeding or cancer. I want to be here for Colleen. I want to marry Cade and have Garrett and Derek as my lovers, my husbands too. How the hell will that work? Cade will never go for it. Damn, my head is killing me.*

She closed her eyes and prayed fate wouldn't be cruel.

The soft click of the door opening startled her. *Felicity?* She braced for…

"How's our patient?" the voice of the grandma nurse asked.

Ella opened her eyes and then closed them tightly at the blinding light. *Not Felicity. I'm with Derek. The hospital.* Slowly, she eased her lids open enough to see without the ache in her head becoming unbearable.

In his blue scrubs with pink frogs on them, Derek helped the nurse set up a portable ultrasound machine next to her bed.

"Do I really need that?" she asked.

The seasoned nurse beamed as she handed Derek the ultrasound wand. Her smile grew as she walked around the bed to Ella's opposite side.

The door opened, and Garrett and Cade strode into the room toward her.

The lovely nurse picked up her hand. "You're

pregnant."

"No," Cade gasped. His hand dropped. His cup of water fell and splattered on the floor.

"What?" Garrett said.

"I can't be. It's a mistake," Ella said. *None of them can have children. It's a tumor. I have a uterine tumor. I have uterine cancer. I'm dying.*

"There is no mistake," the nurse said. "You are definitely pregnant."

I've been moody, sensitive, crying at the drop of a hat. I've had an upset stomach, felt queasy. I can't be... It's impossible. "I'm under stress, not pregnant."

"You bastard," Cade grumbled. He grabbed Garrett's t-shirt, and drew back his arm.

"No, Cade. No," she shouted. "Oh God." She covered her ears as a nightmare became reality.

Garrett dodged the punch heading for his face. His shirt ripped from Cade's grip.

"What the fuck?" Garrett placed the bottle of milk in his hand on the closest counter.

"Congratulations, asshole. You've won. She's officially yours," Cade shouted. His entire body shook. His face reddened to a deep crimson. He glared at Ella. "You knew. You knew you were pregnant all along. You called Jerry instead of me. My God, Ella." He whipped around. "You've been playing me all this time?"

The door swung open, and he vanished in an instant.

The healthy glow in Garrett's face faded to a ghostly white. "It can't be mine. I don't want..." He turned around and walked out the door, leaving Ella with Derek, and a nurse with a nervous and seemingly sad smile.

"They're in shock." Derek adjusted her on her side. "I want to check your kidneys first. Then we'll see how far along you are."

He lifted her gown up over her bottom and back and gently pressed a wet wand on her back over her spine.

"How can I be pregnant?"

"I'm not sure," Derek said. "But you are. When did you have your tubal ligation? It's not in your chart."

"I never had one. You and Garrett had vasectomies forever ago. Cade had one. Don't you get tested once a year?"

The wand slipped. "Wait. What? You never had one? Greg told me and Garrett you had one."

"I didn't. Could I have cancer?" She curled her knees to her chest and held the blanket tightly. *Tumor on my ovaries? Am I going to die?*

"None of us had vasectomies. Cade had his pipe cleaned, but I think he might actually believe he can't have kids." He turned her onto her back. "You have a nasty bruise. No working for two weeks."

"What?" *No. No. No. This can't be happening.*

He cleared his throat as he gazed into her eyes. "Let's take a look, and…" he paused, a smile formed on his lips. "Garrett has a really low sperm count. Really low. He's probably not the father."

She covered her eyes with her hands, trying to cut out more of the light. *I don't have a pregnancy rider for my insurance. I can't afford a baby. Shit. Shit. Shit. I can't take off work.* "I have to work tomorrow. I can't take off. I can't be pregnant."

Derek guided her legs apart. The hard plastic wand

slid inside her.

The nurse's soft hand squeezed Ella's. "Oh, look, Mrs. Winthrop."

She opened her eyes, seeing on the monitor the life growing inside her. "I'm thirty-seven. My grandchild is going to be older than…"

"Garrett will be back. Cade will too. We'll get DNA testing done," Derek said.

"They don't want kids. Cade doesn't want children. He wants to travel and have couple fun. Garrett has never wanted them. He likes giving them back at the end of the day." She gazed up at him. *I can't ask if you can be the father in front of her.*

There was a soft knock at the door.

"See," the nurse said. "Garrett is back."

"Come in," Derek said. His fingers clicked on the keyboard. He moved the wand inside her and sucked in a big lungful of air. "Oh. My. Goodness."

"Twins," the nurse said. "What a miracle. Twins."

"Fraternal twins." Derek said.

The short-haired brunette who'd discharged Colleen peeked her head into the room. "Dr. McGregor, Jerry Wynn is here to see Mrs. Winthrop,"

"I don't want to see anyone," she whispered. *There can't be two. There can't be.*

"Ella?" Jerry said. His head appeared above the nurses. "Can I come in?"

She bit her bottom lip to stop from crying.

Derek waved him in.

"Where are Cade and Garrett?" Jerry sauntered into the room.

The nurse gazed at Jerry and then at Ella. "Could he be?"

"No," Ella whispered. *What the nurse must think of me.*

"Too bad," the nurse mumbled. "He's gorgeous. You'd make beautiful babies with him."

"Babies?" Jerry stepped to Ella's side. His gaze darting to the monitor and back to her. "Cade got you pregnant, and he's not here? Not possible. The man has 'Dad' tattooed on his forehead."

"They're probably Cade's, but they might not be," Derek said.

"Does she need to stay the night?" Jerry asked. "Can I take her home?"

"She's fourteen weeks. I can't believe I didn't recognize the symptoms," Derek said. "Nurse Long, could you give me a few minutes with Mr. Wynn and Mrs. Winthrop."

The nurse let go of Ella's hand. "This really is a miracle. You're already past the first trimester. The babies look great. I'll be back in a few minutes." She exited the room.

"I love you." Derek pressed a kiss to her lips. "I'm going to support you no matter who is the father. I'll talk some sense into Garrett and Cade. I'll swing by your place later." He kissed her again. "I gave up my dream of children as soon as I fell in love with you. I hope I'm their father. I could be. I actually could be."

His hand glided over her breasts and belly to her mons. "I'm going to pamper you like you've never been pampered in your life. I love you so much. So. Fucking. Much. If I'm not the father, I want one with you. I want to have my baby growing inside you."

"Slow down, Daddy," Jerry said. "Shit. Twins. Well, Ellie, are you the most fertile woman on the planet, or what?"

"One more pregnancy after this one," Derek said. "I've always wanted three kids. At least three, maybe four, or five or six."

"Oh, my God. Are you crazy?" she said. "Garrett and Cade just walked out, and you're talking more babies?"

The room filled with Jerry's laughter. "Ellie, I can't wait to tell everyone. We're going to give you the biggest, most outrageous party ever. We'll make everyone wonder if I could be the father. That will get Cade and Garrett scrambling back and begging for your forgiveness." He sat down next to her and held out his phone.

She winced at the movement.

"Sorry," Jerry said. "Smile, Ella." He tenderly kissed her cheek. The phone's light flashed in her eyes, blinding her, and sending her head spinning.

"Don't do that," she grumbled.

"Sorry. Had to be done. Derek, come on. I'll get a pic of all of us, since you're gonna at least be an honorary uncle, if not my bestie's baby-daddy."

Derek climbed in next to her.

Jerry took picture after picture without the flash. He whispered words of support and encouragement over and over as he kissed her cheek and slid his arm under her neck as she started to weep.

"Smile, Ellie," Jerry said. "This is for the twins. They'll never know this wasn't the happiest day of your life because we'll tell them how much they were wanted from the minute we found out.

Her lips quivered. "Give me a second," she said. Ignoring the aches, pangs, and throbbing misery from her body, heart, and head, she wiped the tears from her face. She ran her fingers through her hair and pulled it forward over her neck. She opened her eyes as wide as possible, and smiled as big as she could.

"That's my Ellie," Jerry said. He took several more pictures. "You know Wynn is a great name for a girl or a boy."

"She's ready to go," Derek said. "Stay with her until I get there."

"She's going to have a really hard time getting rid of me," Jerry said. "I love babies. I can already see two pairs of matching boxing gloves in their future." He lifted her up and carried her to the door.

Derek slid his hand behind her neck. He kissed her. His tongue slid between her teeth and stroked her tongue. His hand glided over her breast. His lips lifted from hers. "I love you. I'll see you in a couple hours."

Jerry carried her out of the room and down the hall. "Derek is excited. He's going to help, and you've got me too. Garrett and Cade will come around."

I doubt Cade or Garrett will have anything to do with me. "How long until my head stops hurting?"

"A week. You're staying home from work if I have to stand over you all day long, every day." He opened the passenger side of the minivan.

"I finally sold my house. Cash buyer. I have to be out in two weeks."

He exhaled. "You're not going to be in any shape to do that. We'll figure it out. Don't worry about it now. You have to heal."

Yeah. I can't do anything but worry. I have to be at work. I can't lose a day of profits.

Chapter Thirty

Staring at the police reports, Cade's face boiled while his heart slowly died. His assistant admitted to trying to kill Ella. *My Ella... I miss you so much.*

His phone rang. He exhaled. *Derek.*

"Hey, Derek."

"I've got an appointment available Friday," Derek said. "I need a DNA and sperm sample. Ella is having some tests run in a few weeks and paternity tests are on the list. Garrett has the least probability of being the father. Statistically, we've got the best chance of being dads."

"I had a vasectomy. It was a private pay. I got tested. I'm shooting blanks." *How many times do I have to tell you the same fucking thing? I'd give anything to be the dad. To have my children growing in her belly.*

His cock rose to attention. *Down buddy. She's not ours anymore.*

"Get me a DNA sample. Pick up a kit on your own, or get the one I have for you at my house." Derek hung up.

He dialed his father.

"How you doing son?"

He tapped his fingers on the report. "Terrible. How long before everyone knows Felicity attacked Ella because of me?"

"What happened was not your fault. No one blames

you. The boys are pissed you broke up with their mom."

"It is my fault. Ella wouldn't have ended up in the hospital if Felicity—"

"Cade, stop doing this to yourself. You've taken steps to keep her and her spa safe. Jimmy is guarding her house. The team of security you now have in place at her spa will keep the entire neighborhood safe. Please, stop blaming yourself. Not one person saw Felicity as a threat."

"I should have seen the signs." She asked about the soap he used. She changed appointments in his calendar to when he blocked time off to be with Ella. Made speaking engagements he asked to send his regrets to. *I should have seen she wasn't stupid. She was. No. She is a stalker.*

"There weren't any," Pappy said. "She covered her tracks like a pro. It's over. Ella is safe. She'll recover. Now, it's your turn to step in and apologize. Go tell her you love her. Quit finding excuses to back out of the…different relationship." He cleared his throat. "For whatever reason, you, Garrett, Derek, and Ella love one another." Pappy inhaled and exhaled, then lowered his voice. "I've never seen you happier. She glows when she is with Garrett and Derek. She sparkles with you. When the four of you are together, y'all shine brighter than the sun. I don't begin to understand how something like that works, but it does. Don't throw it away because you want to be the father of her children. Compromise, Cade. Maybe you open up your house to Garrett and Derek, and share Ella long-term? Be a stepdad to the babies. Momma and I support you. We all do."

"She's having someone else's babies. I can't watch her go through that, grow closer to them. I can't do it." *I blamed her for the pregnancy. She had no idea. I yelled at her. I can't face her.*

"Well, the alternative seems a hell of a lot worse. At least talk to her. You walked out on her without even discussing options. I didn't raise you like that."

"I shouldn't have called you." *You don't understand.*

"I love you, son. Man up and call her. I'll see you at the wedding ceremony tonight at Sammy's."

"I'm not going. I'll call when I figure out what I'm going to do." He ended the call.

He crumpled up the police report. He had to do something. He couldn't sit at his desk anymore. He had to take the tests Derek wanted and get away. Far. Away.

Chapter Thirty-One

Sitting on a white leather chair at Garrett and Derek's kitchen bar, Cade lifted the cup of coffee to his lips and took a swig.

"I can't believe she's pregnant," Garrett said, holding a bottle of water. "They're not mine. Shit. I haven't had a high enough sperm count to get a girl pregnant in my entire life. My guys work hard, but twins? Not fucking possible."

"I had a vasectomy."

"No, man. Derek said your file showed a pipe cleaning, not a damn scoop and trash," Garrett unscrewed the cap of his bottle.

I know the damn doctor performed a vasectomy five years ago. I got tested afterward. "You or Derek are going to have twins."

"Derek is a fertility specialist. He says you could be the father."

"I don't know what he saw, but it wasn't my file. How many times do I have to tell Derek I'm shooting blanks? I shouldn't be here. Giving you a sample is a waste of time." He put the cup down. *I'd give anything to be the father. Anything.*

"Hey, I did it," Garrett said. He placed his water bottle down on the black and gray granite counter. "And I'm telling you, I'm a hundred percent sure I'm not the father."

"You have sperm. I don't." *My assistant tried to kill Ella. I accused the woman I love of lying to me. I walked out on her when she needed me the most. I've never walked out on anyone in my life. I fucked up beyond fucked up. She'll never forgive me. I can't forgive myself.*

"Let's get this over with." Garrett walked around the side of the counter. "Follow me."

Cade slid off the chair and strode behind the man he'd become friends with. Garrett was built like a fucking brick house. A good-looking man. A trustworthy man. An honest man, worthy of his Ella. Garrett and Derek could take care of her, but they worked as much as he did. The three of them took care of her best. Without him, who would hold her when she needed to cry? Who would take care of her when Garrett and Derek were working? Who would be her steady man, available to drop anything and go to her? Who would love and accept all of her?

"In here," Garrett said, and walked into a bedroom with a giant bed, sized for at least three, maybe four people.

"Your bedroom?" Cade arched his brow as he gazed at Garrett.

"Yeah. You scared or something?" Garrett glared at him.

"No."

"Good." Garrett walked past him to the bed. "I've got some photos of Ella's pussy. Might get you in the mood."

Cade strode to Garrett's side next to the edge of the intricately handcrafted wooden bed. The detailed sex scenes between gods, demi-gods, and humans carved into the headboard blew his mind.

"Did you carve those?" *I bet you did.*

Garrett picked up a large flat packet on the duvet. "Yes, sir. I designed and made it for me and Ella a long time ago." He pulled photos from the manila packet. "I'll grab the kit while you look at the photos."

"In front of you?" His dick jerked to attention. *Down buddy. Damn. What is going on? Do I want him to watch? I bet Derek watches you all the time.*

"Yes." Garrett's brows scrunched together. "Derek's orders." His hand drifted over his bulge and adjusted it. He cleared his throat. "I'll be right back."

"I'm not into guys," Cade said. "I mean. I like you and all, but this is kind of weird."

"It's weird for me too. Derek and I have been together for years. You're a good-looking guy, and I'm not ashamed to say I love ya, man. You're a good man to Ella and the kids. You're supportive of me and Derek. We're friends and you're in our inner circle. But, watching you jerk off is going to be strange." Garrett walked into the bathroom.

Cade exhaled. *Shit. My dad thinks I love you. He probably thinks we're fucking. I do love you for all the reasons you love me too. But not love like sex love. It's a respect kind of love.*

He turned to the photos on the bed and quietly moaned. Ella's lean, athletic legs splayed open. Her shaved pussy glistened with juices. Cum shot from Garrett's cock toward her.

He placed the photo to the side and the scene came to life with the next picture he uncovered. Cum nailed her clit. Her pussy seemed to squeeze in an orgasm in the still photo.

He unzipped his jeans. *My cock. My cum. On you.* He fisted his cock and uncovered the next photo. Cum flew from two cocks onto her pussy. *I want my cum with theirs on you. I want my cock in that photo with theirs.*

"Nice form," Garrett whispered. "I nearly come in my pants every time I see those photos."

Cade's hand pumped up and down his cock. "Show me the next one."

"You're like Derek with your sex orders." Garrett quickly arranged the photos in succession and spread them on the duvet. "Here's Ella sucking me off."

I should want to punch him. I should...

Garrett stepped back and behind him, revealing the incredible pictures he placed in sequential order within his direct view.

"Holy shit," Cade said. His gaze moved swiftly from one to the next, making the photos run like a short film. He thrust into his palm.

I need you. I need your hands on mine, Ella. Your lips covering my cockhead. Your mouth sucking me down your throat. His chest rose and fell as his balls clenched tightly against his shaft.

A firm grip covered his and guided him into a stronger, steady fucking rhythm.

"Ella," Cade whispered.

"Her wet lips feel so good gliding down to the base of my shaft," Garrett whispered. His solid body supported Cade's back His hand guided Cade's over the top of his cock and dragged the precum down his shaft, lubricating his flesh like her wet mouth had done so many times.

"Yes." Cade grunted. "Ella."

Garrett's other hand wrapped around his waist. His lips pressed to Cade's ear. "Fuck her. Fuck that mouth."

"Uhn." Cade grunted and thrust his pelvis forward. "Take my cum down your throat."

"Give it to her," Garrett whispered. "Fuck her harder. She wants it, Cade. She wants…" His hot breath panted against Cade's ear. Garrett thrust with Cade. Garrett's hard cock ground against his ass. "She wants your cum."

Cade grunted as he thrust into Garrett's hand then pushed back against Garrett's hard cock. He widened his stance and together they thrust and countered. *My cum in her mouth. My cum with yours. My cum down her throat, over her chin, dripping down her chest.* "She's so beautiful."

"Yes, she is. She loves to swallow our cum. Give it to her."

"I need her breasts rubbing against my leg. Her hands massaging my balls. Her mouth sliding up and down my cock," Cade mumbled. "Need you, Ella. Need you."

His hand slid to his balls as the grip around his cock tightened and pumped faster and faster. *So wet. So fucking good.*

"Come, Cade. Come."

"Fuck. I'm coming. I'm coming." He arched his back, dropped his head back, and thrust his cock into the tight fist. His legs shook as cum flowed like a river out of his cock. "So good. So. Good."

His grip loosened, and his hand slipped down to his side. Garrett took over, gliding up and down his shaft, milking the rest of the cum into the cup he'd not realized was there. His heart beat wildly as he let

Garrett pull every drop from within.

“There,” Garrett whispered. “I got it all.” His hand slid down along his shaft to his balls, and caressed him.

Up and down, Cade allowed Garrett’s gentle, yet firm touch. Leaning on Garrett for support, Cade’s cock hardened, ready for another round. Fingers massaged under his balls to his ass.

Can I share my bed, my Ella, with two other men for the rest of my life? I’m not into men, but I’m not punching Garrett. I’m letting him touch me. Why am I letting him touch me?

Garrett’s lips pressed against his ear. “We’re going to get through this. It’s going to be okay.”

“It’s not.” Cade adjusted his stance, taking over control. He covered Garrett’s hand, stopping the exploration. “I can’t watch her have a baby with another man. I want her to have my child. And she’s having Derek’s…twins.”

“Don’t think about it. Take it one day at a time. I’ll get the cheek swab.”

Cade nodded, but held Garrett’s hand on his cock. He leaned back against him, again, needing Garrett’s strength and support. He needed comfort, the comfort Ella always gave him.

“My dad thinks we should all live together, but I can’t handle the thought of Ella’s body growing with another man’s chi—” He choke up. “—children. I love her.”

“Hey, we’ll figure all this out. Give it some time. We’ve had a big shock. Ella is…shit. She’s going to have to tell Colleen and the boys. Those are going to be tough conversations. They know about all of us, but damn.”

"God, how did this happen?" Cade mumbled. *Accepting Derek and Garrett as her permanent lovers is one thing, but having them grow the family I want with her. I can't.*

"Derek and I believed my brother when he told us Ella got fixed. Ella believed him when he told her we did. None of us need to make any decisions right now." He slid his hand up Cade's cock. "Stay here. I'm getting the swab."

Standing with his jeans at his knees, he found balance again with Garrett's help. He stared at the photos scattered on the bed. *My beautiful, loving Ella. I love you, but I can't face you. I can't.*

"Open," Garrett said softly.

With his gaze on the photos, Cade parted his lips. The swab brushed against the inside of his cheek several times and slid from his mouth. He moved aside the photo on top of the small stack he hadn't seen, yet. He stared into Ella's carefree gaze. Garrett smiled, holding her in a low dip. Derek stood behind her laughing. The three of them nude and happy in the bedroom.

"Cade, I'm going to tell you something. Don't freak out."

I'm past the losing it stage. I let you jack me off, and I fucking liked it. What the fuck does that mean? I should be beating the hell out of you. Why do I want you to hug me instead?

Cade huffed and shifted his gaze to him. "Yeah. Throw it at me."

"Derek thinks you have a shot at being the dad. He wants you with us in this. I want you with us. Ella needs all of us. I can't believe I'm saying this, but I like you in a way I'm not fully comfortable talking about."

His jaw tightened. "Ella says she tells you fucking everything like you're a damn psychologist. Now, I'm doing the same damn thing. I don't like guys, except Derek, and I'm not sure where my feelings changed, but I don't hate you. Far from it. The four of us can handle this bump on the road as long as we're together."

Cade pulled up his jeans and zipped them. *This cannot be happening.*

"What the fuck are you telling me?" Cade glanced toward the entrance to the hallway and back at Garrett. "I want to marry Ella." He shook his head. "I used to." *I want her in my bed, pregnant with my children, with my last name, safe and happy. But I want you and Derek with us too.*

"Ella needs three men. Me, Derek, and you. You bring something to our unit we don't have. I'm attracted to you like I am to Derek."

Cade's balls tightened in his pants. "Holy shit. I've got to get out of here." He strode into the hallway and stopped. He glanced over his shoulder. A weird ache filled his chest. Garrett stood like a soldier, but the same sadness he saw in Ella's eyes when she talked about Greg seemed to fill Garrett's.

"Your personality is like Greg's, only you want the best for Ella," Garrett said. "Greg always wanted the best for himself. Ella's needs always came second. Not with you. Her needs come before yours. You love her like I do. Don't throw us away. Believe me, you'll regret it."

Cade closed his eyes. "I can't do this right now." *I don't know where I fit. She's going to marry Derek, not me. She's going to look to him like my mother looks to my father. And I don't know how to deal with you. I liked you touching me. I loved those pictures. I wanted...hell, I want to be in them with you.*

"Call me. We need to talk this through," Garrett said.

He opened his eyes and gazed back into the hallway. "I'll call. Tell Ella, I'm sorry."

"Tell her yourself, Cade. None of this is your fault."

Cade strode forward. With each step, his heart sank closer to his stomach. *So much of this is my fault.* He unlocked the front door.

"Cade, come with me to talk to Ella," Garrett said. "She needs you."

"No." Cade turned the silver doorknob. "She needs Derek." He opened the door and walked to his car. He climbed in and drove out of the driveway onto the street.

Maybe I can get the vasectomy reversed. Maybe Ella will want my child too

He dialed Josie.

"Hey, Cade," Josie answered.

"Hey. I'm going out of town for a while. I don't know when I'll be back."

"You and Ella eloping?"

"No. I'm going to France."

"Why? Business? Did Ella do something?"

"My assistant tried to kill Ella yesterday. Ella's… I can't talk about it. I've got to go."

"Cade, stop. Don't go. Come over here. I know what happened to Ella. She doesn't blame you. She's got the best head on her shoulders of anyone besides you I know. She knows it isn't your fault. Felicity is crazy."

"I didn't put it together, and I should have. But, there's more. I'll let you know when I get there. I've got to go." He ended the call before she could say anything else.

Guilt and confusion dug into his soul. *Am I gay? But I'm not into guys. But I liked his hands on me. I wanted Ella. I didn't protect her. I thought she was safe. How can I protect her from women who stalk me? She could have lost the babies because of me. She's pregnant with another man's child. The woman I love will love Derek more than she loves me. They're having children. Twins.*

He'd never run from anything in his life. Until now.

Chapter Thirty-Two

Derek's heart burst with love as he gazed at Ella sleeping in his bed. *I'm going to have a family. Babies. I'm going to be a father. Ella wants more children. She wants my children.* He ached to fuck her, but she needed to heal. He'd brought her home early from Colleen's to rest.

"Cade is on his way here," Garrett whispered from behind him. "He got stuck in the same traffic your parents did on the interstate and missed the wedding ceremony. He swung by the reception and talked with Colleen and Sammy, but missed you and Ella."

Derek turned around and motioned for Garrett to follow him. "So, he's come to his senses?"

"He's all over the place." Garrett walked into the hall beside Derek. "I didn't help matters by telling him how I feel."

"Did you tell him what his father said to me?" Derek slipped his hand into Garrett's and led him into the guest bedroom next to their bedroom where Ella slept.

"I didn't get to. He mentioned his father thought we should all move in to Cade's place. Together. Me. You. Ella. Cade. Under the same roof."

Derek closed the door and walked to the bed. "Ella's hell-bent on buying land and building a house and warehouse. We'd have to convince her." *Cade would demand she marry him. She would lose the Winthrop name.*

“She wouldn’t need much convincing. He’s the one who is stuck in yesterday’s trauma.” Garrett let go of Derek’s hand and sat at the edge of the bed. “I can’t believe I gave him a hand job. Shit. I know he’s freaking out. Remember when you did that to me the first time?”

“Do I ever.” Derek stepped between Garrett’s legs and embraced him. “I was so worried you’d beat the shit out of me, but hoped you’d accept me.” He rubbed his hand down the powerful muscles of Garrett’s back. “I saw a future with you and the woman of our dreams back then. We have it now, but we need Cade. Our Ella needs three men. If we were in the same house, we could be a true family. My parents could move in here.”

Garrett’s hands slid under Derek’s jeans. “I loved you back then. I didn’t want to hurt you. I wanted to kiss you, but it scared me. Cade is scared. We have to convince him that it’s okay to love a guy. That he hasn’t changed. That the three of us can keep Ella safe. That we’re all better when he’s with us.”

“We’ll convince him,” Derek said. *Ella is safe when we work together. We’re all safer as a unit.* He patted Garrett’s back. “Let me talk to him.”

“I need him,” Garrett whispered. “I don’t want to live without him.”

“We all need him. He manages all our lives outside work, even mine. I don’t know how he keeps up with my schedule at the hospital, but he does. He sends a box of snacks to the hospital for me once a week. He adds reminder notes to pick up Ella for sleepovers at our house, not his.”

Garrett laughed. "He sends me dinner at the office most nights."

"He wants to be with us. I bet he's going to sit down with us and hash out a plan for the future." *I'm going to need Cade with a houseful of kids. I'll have at least three. Cade could have a couple with Ella too. We can plan our family together.*

Garrett slapped him on the ass. "I'm going to take a shower. You go and see if he used his key or is standing at the door waiting for us."

"I'm going to try to talk to him either way," Derek said. He pivoted and walked out of the bedroom and down the hall. He peeked in on Ella.

The covers were crumpled in the middle of the bed beside Cade. Ella's head tucked under Cade's chin, and her nude body sprawled over his bare chest. His shirt, tie, and jacket were laid on the chair in the corner.

Derek walked into the room and over to the bed. "I'm glad you came in and made yourself at home."

Cade whispered. "I took my shoes off in the foyer. I saw the note."

So you do follow rules? "Can we talk?" Derek whispered.

"I don't want to wake her." Cade closed his eyes. "This is killing me."

"We can work this all out. Ella loves all of us. We're in good financial shape and comfortable with our sexuality. It would be unorthodox, but we can live together. Your parents and mine both support our relationships." *You're here, so at least a part of you wants to make our situation permanent.*

"I don't see how," Cade mumbled. Tears fell from the corners of his eyes. "She wants children, and I can't give them to her. I'm not staying. I'm going on a business trip overseas in the morning."

"You can't leave. Not now. You *can* have children. The twins could be yours." *Why don't you believe me? I've never lied to you.*

"I can't have kids. I called. I double checked. I'm flying up there to get my medical records and have a consultation with two other doctors to see if the procedure can be reversed."

I don't know who you're talking to, but they are total fucking idiots. I have showed you the results of the tests I ran. They aren't fucking mistakes. "Have them send me the records and put me on conference call with them during your consultation. Do not let anyone do anything without me being there."

He nodded. "Okay."

"We need to talk about you and Garrett," Derek said. "What happened between the two of you—"

"—was a mistake, and one that will never happen again."

Ella moaned and shifted. She rolled her hips and lined her pussy up with his bulge.

Cade gently rubbed her ass. "I love you."

She sighed.

Garrett is right. You, Cade, are one hundred percent freaked out over the hand job. You're making sure your desire for her is the same. It is. I promise. You're into her more than you've ever been into anyone, but you love Garrett. Maybe you've never married because you need a man in your life too? Garrett is the same. I am too.

"Don't fuck her. She's healing," Derek said.

Cade inhaled and opened his eyes. "I'm not going

to. I love her. I don't want to hurt her."

"Leaving will hurt her. You'll break her. Please, don't go." Derek shoved his hands in his pockets. *You can't get on a plane tomorrow. I have to stop you.*

"She's safer without me. Please, let me have some time alone with her before I have to go. I promise I will call you and Garrett every day."

"Do not leave the house without telling me," Derek said.

Cade turned his head to the side and closed his eyes. "I'll talk to you later."

A miserable pit formed in Derek's stomach. He wanted to throw up. *Ella will never get over you. Garrett won't either. They don't fall often, but when they do, it's with their whole heart. Don't throw their love away.* "This is not goodbye." He walked out of the room and closed the door.

Garrett stood nude at the door to the guest bedroom. "I think we've lost him."

Derek's heart sank to his stomach. "Me too."

Chapter Thirty-Three

Sitting in the black leather chair in the back of Maddie's salon, Ella looked around the crowded salon, recognizing several faces from her vendor parties with Troy. Privacy was one of Troy's rules, and she'd found that everyone adhered to that particular one as if it was a religion.

The front door swung open and the little bells jingled. Ella turned away. *Shit.* Cheerleader Josie found her.

She gazed into the mirror. Maddie gently brushed her hair over the section in the back where the stitches came out earlier that morning.

"You'd look good with short hair," Maddie said. She lifted the portion of hair she'd been playing with for ten minutes and let it drop.

"I'm going to wait until it's shoulder length," Ella said. *Ugh. Here she comes.*

"Ella Winthrop." Josie's beautiful, forest-green, A-line dress swayed with each purposeful step. She stopped beside Ella and glared at her in the mirror. She flattened the edgy, geometric designed, gold necklace against her chest and readjusted it between her breasts.

"Yes, Josie?" Ella clenched her jaw and pursed her lips, ready for whatever assault of words came out of the woman's mouth. *I don't need this right now.*

"What did you do to make Cade go on an extended

vacation to France? He isn't saying anything. You're not talking. I don't see Garrett's ring on your finger. And what the hell is going on with you and Derek?" Josie crossed her arms over her chest and tapped her foot.

"I really don't need this right now."

"I don't care if you don't need this. I do. I need to know. My God, Ella…" Josie looked her up and down. "I might have missed the wedding because of that damn jam on the interstate, but not seeing you for a few weeks shouldn't have turned you fat."

"Shut up, Josie," Maddie said as the women nearby stared at them.

"I will not. Ella, why did you dump Cade? What did you say that sent him running across the damn ocean to get away from you?" Josie tapped her foot.

"Cade dumped me."

"He did not." Josie stepped in front of the full-length mirror, put her hands on the arm rests, and leaned forward. Her nose almost touched Ella's. "He loves you. He is sorry about what his assistant did to you. He's destroyed over it. Get your ass on a fucking plane and go get him."

Maddie grabbed Josie's wrist. "You. Me. Ella. In the back." She tugged Josie into the supply room.

I should sneak out. I should just grab my purse from the rolling tray and leave.

"Ella, Get in here. Now," Maddie ordered.

Ugh. "I'm coming."

She stood up and pulled down the black maternity dress Derek's parents bought her. The outfit highlighted her belly. She had two more trimesters to go, but her twins weren't hiding anymore.

Josie's eyes bugged out of their sockets. "Oh. My. God."

Ella stuck her hands on her hips. "Yeah. I'm knocked up. Cade walked out. He doesn't want kids. I'm about to have another set of twins, and I don't know who the father is yet. So, tell me why Cade flying somewhere on vacation is my business?" *He's taking a vacation while my heart aches for him. While I'm here worrying about who might be the father of my babies. They're probably Derek's, but they could be his or Garrett's. Damn it.*

The pretty blonde blinked, inhaled, and dropped her hands to her side. "I'm going to kick his ass. He is moaning and groaning about how much he loves and misses you, and *he* walked out."

"It's complicated," Maddie said.

"You should have married Cade a long time ago," Josie said. "You should have married him that weekend I set you up with him. You really don't know if the father is Garrett or Cade?"

"Or Derek," Maddie added.

"Derek?" Josie's mouth dropped open as her gaze narrowed on Ella. "No wonder he left. I'd leave. My God. How could you do that to him?"

"You think I got pregnant on purpose? You think I decided…" Ella threw up her hands in the air. "…I've got three hot men to play baby Russian roulette with me. Oh, how fun. Let's see which one of the men—who were all supposed to be sterile—I can rope into fatherhood. Yeah. That's a great idea. Only, the man I wanted to marry doesn't want anything to do with me."

She turned around to leave, but Maddie grabbed her and pulled her back.

"You can love three men. It's okay. You can be happy about the babies, Ella. I know how much you wanted more children. I know you would have a dozen more, if Greg hadn't gotten sick. Maybe this is a sign. Maybe…" Maddie hugged her. "Maybe Cade will come back, and you'll have more children. Maybe Derek will want more children. Maybe Garrett will."

Closing her eyes, Ella embraced her best friend. Maddie had been there through all the miscarriages, and the last one when she tumbled down the staircase from the last fight between Greg and Garrett. That loss, the last chance at having another beautiful baby with Greg, hurt the worst.

"I'd have more children," she confided. "I do love Cade. But I love Garrett and Derek too. I love them all. But Cade is gone, and I don't know how to live without him. I feel like a part of me has died. I miss him so much."

Another set of arms curled around Ella. "I'm pregnant too. Six weeks. We planned it," Josie whispered.

Maddie laughed. "Oops. I'm pregnant too. Eight weeks. Found out this morning."

Josie giggled. "Congratulations."

"Congratulations." Ella couldn't bring herself to laugh and share their joy the way she would have done a week ago. She didn't want to marry Derek or Garrett, but she did want to live with them, love them, and be with them forever. She wanted to marry, have his last name, and maybe have a baby with him, if he could have children like Derek had told her. But Cade would have to come back to her first and then accept Garrett and Derek as part of her package.

"Thanks," Josie and Maddie said.

"It's going to work out, Ella," Josie said. "I'll whip Cade into shape. When will you find out which one is the father?"

"I'll know something in about two weeks."

"Cade loves you, Ella," Josie said. "He's head over heels in love with you. He'll be back whether he is the father or not."

"He doesn't love me anymore. My life is too complicated." *I told him to walk away because I wasn't strong enough. He listened.*

The arms holding her squeezed her tighter.

"He'll be back," Josie whispered, but her tone didn't sound terribly confident. "He's a fighter. He doesn't give up. He doesn't stop until he has what he wants. He wants you."

"Yeah," Ella whispered. *He feels guilty. The food. The gifts. The 'I love you' notes don't mean anything when he doesn't answer my calls.*

"It's the three of us," Maddie said. "Friends forever. Through thick and thin. Good times and bad."

"Friends forever," Ella and Josie said. They smiled at each other. "Through thick and thin. Good times and bad."

"And once Cade gets his head screwed on straight again, and he's back," Maddie said. "Then, Ella, you're going to give us all the juicy details of your sex life. We're going to live vicariously through you. Got it?"

Laughter bubbled up from Ella's belly and out of her mouth. "Got it."

"Cade knew about Garrett and Derek?" Josie asked.

"Hell, yes, he knew," Maddie said.

"Then, I want to hear…" Josie whispered. "…every detail of how a woman handles three, demanding men, and still goes to work in the morning."

"She gets knocked up with twins," Maddie said. "That's how."

Chapter Thirty-Four

Pumping sanitizer into her hand, she stared down at her belly bump.

She rubbed her hands together and then glided them over the babies. *I love you. And I love your father, whichever of the three it is.*

She opened the door to the waiting room. “I’ll be in my office, Troy. Take your time.”

She walked through the spa into her office, and powered off her computer for the day.

“Ella?” Troy called for her.

“Be right there.” She walked into the waiting area carrying her purse and night deposit.

“Hi, partner.” He hugged her and took the deposit from her hand. “You’re looking sexier than ever.”

She rolled her eyes. “Whatever. You’re going to the bank for me tonight?”

“Yes, ma’am.” He placed his hand gently on the small of her back. “Still nothing from Cade?”

She shook her head. *Breakfast, lunch, dinner, fresh flowers, and new clothes arrive daily from him, but no calls or any word he is coming home.*

“I was supposed to be your only client today. I’m going to tell Derek you were in the room with two women before me.”

“You’re full of crap. Those were my new hires, Evangeline Zanipolo and Rory Quince. Rory is going to be your massage therapist until I get better. I'm taking a break for a while." *Probably until after the babies are born.*

"Good. I'm helping Kyle design your manufacturing warehouse. The new place is promising." He guided her toward the exit. "Derek said you were working on some new product?"

"I have a new oil for our line. As soon as Derek gets here I'll give you the samples I made for you. They're in his car."

"Mmm." He waggled his brows. "Can't wait. Derek sent me the promotional photos for our line. They're fantastic. More risqué than I expected."

"You said genitals would be appropriate for the private marketing. They're all classy."

"Are they of you?" He pulled her closer. Her belly pressed against his front.

She winked and whispered, "Wouldn't you like to know?"

Since he saved her life, and they'd officially partnered after the sale of her house, she'd gotten to know him enough to tease him a little. He was a good man and turned out to be the best kind of partner. Without him, she wouldn't be comfortable taking a break from massage therapy and focusing on her oils, soaps, and shampoos.

"I would," he whispered.

"They are of me, Derek, and Garrett, but don't tell anyone."

"I won't tell a soul. So, how are the renovations on the house?" He let go of her and guided her to the door.

She spotted Derek pulling up to the space in front of the spa in his new minivan.

“Renovations are good. Derek and Garrett are supposed to be moving in today.”

“So is Derek the proud daddy?”

“We find out today.” She gazed down and rubbed her belly. *You two are getting so big.*

“How is Colleen?”

“She’s good. Took the news about my pregnancy better than I ever expected.” She grinned. “She’s hoping for sisters.”

He chuckled. “She’s a good kid.

She walked forward with him. “I think you should take over for me at the party tonight. I’m getting pretty big.” *And I’m tired.*

“I need you, and the vendor next to you is providing you with some sexy maternity clothing. No worries. Just show up.”

“Okay.” She stepped outside into the cool night air and breathed in deeply. *I wish Cade were here.*

Troy set the alarm system and locked the door. He walked her to the passenger side of Derek’s van and opened the door. “Where are the samples?”

“In the back seat,” Derek answered. “The photos on them are to show clients the different body parts they should be tested on. The ones for sale will have the standard Oils or Soaps by Ella label printed on them, no photos.”

“Did you set up everything for the event tonight?” Troy asked.

“Got it covered. All Ella has to do is show up,” Derek said.

The backseat door slid open. She reached in and handed him the bag. She lifted one of the samples up. “This one is Raspberry Crème.”

Troy looked at it. "Holy shit. Is that you and Derek?"

She blushed. "Maybe we won't use that photo for promotions."

He took out one sample bottle at a time, examining each closely. "No. No one will know, but me. God, you're the best damn business partner I've ever had." He kissed her cheek. "Don't let those two keep you up all night."

She rolled her eyes. "I'll see what I can do." She climbed in the front and buckled her seatbelt.

Troy closed the minivan doors and walked to his car loaded with samples.

Derek backed up and drove out of the parking lot. "I talked to Cade today."

Her heart skipped a beat. "Really?" She gazed up into his hazel eyes.

He nodded. "Yeah. He's a mess. Been a mess. But you know that."

Do I? Pappy and Josie says he's miserable, but is he?

"Why will he call you and Garrett but not me?"

"He's back in town. He wants to see you."

"I don't want to see him." *He's going to take one look at me and leave again. I can't go through him walking out, ignoring me, or yelling at me.*

"If he's the father to the babies, you're not dropping us for him, right?"

"No. I love you," She reached over and touched his thigh. "Cade is done with me regardless, and I'm done with worrying."

His hand covered hers. "I love you, but Cade isn't done with you. The gifts he sends shows you that."

"Well, I'm done with him. I'm tired of his guilt gifts. He needs to stop. Felicity is in a mental health facility. She's the one who should feel guilty, not Cade. He had nothing to do with it."

Derek made the man noise he typically did when he was frustrated with her.

"Can you please try and be positive?" Derek said.

"No. I'm done being positive. I'm being realistic. Fuck all this shit. If he ends up being the father, then he will have to fight me for custody. He'll have to—"

"—Stop it. You will do no such thing. You and Cade are going to talk. Really talk. So, you're going to stop your nonsense and get your ass up and meet him, if I have to drag you somewhere, or tie you up and force you to stay in the same fucking room with him," he shouted.

She shut her mouth and folded her hands on her lap. Derek never yelled. In all the years she'd known him that was the first time he'd ever raised his voice in her presence.

He breathed. "Ella, you're going to speak with him today."

She gazed out the side window as they drove past the street she would drive down to get to Cade's house. *I'm not speaking to him ever again. He said he'd never leave me. He said he'd love me forever. He lied.*

Chapter Thirty-Five

On her hands and knees and tied to Garrett’s Greek gods inspired bed, Ella closed her lips around the head of Garrett’s cock.

Underneath her, Garrett thrust up into her mouth as she bobbed her head and sucked him down, swallowed, and tasted the salty musk of the first spurts of cum. His tongue tapped her clit, and Derek’s cock shuttled in and out of her pussy.

She’d already climaxed three times, and her body still held the aftershock orgasms pulsing around Derek’s girth.

Derek’s cock jerked and shot hot liquid deep within her. He shuddered.

“Mmm,” she moaned around Garrett’s softening cock. She slowly sucked up to the head and swallowed every last drop of his cum.

Derek held her hips as Garrett held her belly and they all shifted to their side. Garrett faced her, his mouth at her pussy and his dick enveloped by her lips. Derek behind her, his cock buried in her pussy and his mouth pressed to her neck.

“So, two more pregnancies?” Derek whispered.

She swallowed once more and released Garrett’s cock. She kissed the top and stretched her arms and legs, and freed the tension on her wrists and ankles from the silk ties.

"One more. Maybe two. We'll see."

Derek's limp cock slid from her center. "I'm going for another set of twins, then."

"We'll have to get Jason and Kyle to add an addition to the house." She had moved in with Garrett and Derek while her boys worked on renovating the fixer upper and building the warehouse on the land she bought on the outskirts of town. Kyle and Jason had moved in with Jerry Wynn who lived next door to her new place. "The house we're supposed to be moving into today. What happened to the movers?"

The mattress dipped and Derek's warmth left her back. Derek untied her wrists while Garrett untied her ankles.

"They didn't show. The dates got messed up," Derek said.

Garrett sat up and flopped over to his other side and kissed her mouth. "Sorry about the detour from the results. I saw you and my dick took control."

I'm not ready to see the results. Not yet. Maybe after the event tonight. She slid her leg over his thigh. "I love making love to both of you. But you're going to make me late for the event at Troy's."

Derek pressed a kiss to her shoulder. "I love you. I'll be back in a minute to clean you up."

Garrett lifted his head. "Love you, Derek."

Derek leaned over and kissed his mouth. "Love you too."

She sighed. *Honest. Faithful. My rocks.*

Garrett snuggled in closer and held her. Relief seemed to cover him. "I love you so much. I hope you and Derek have a bunch of kids."

You looked at the results. Derek is the father.

You're too happy for the babies to be yours. You'd be sick as a dog if you found out they were yours. It would have been easier to explain if you were the father. So much easier.

Warm, wet towels slid between her legs.

"Kitten, lift your leg over Garrett's waist so I can clean your pussy," Derek ordered.

Her pussy contracted as the cloth slid over her clitoris. "I'm a little sensitive." *And my hormones are out of control. I could have sex all the time.*

"You are insatiable," Derek whispered.

"We haven't had sex in a month. I've been ready for more than a week," she said. She bit her lower lip as the cloth glided back over her slit and ass. She glanced over her shoulder at Derek. His hungry gaze heated her pussy and juices wet her folds. *I could go for another round. That look does all the right things to me.*

Garrett kissed her forehead. "Go get dressed. No more sex tonight. You're not up for more, even though your pussy is trying to convince us you are."

She crawled off the bed and sashayed to her closet. She slipped into a white maternity dress and no panties. *I'm going to be bold tonight. Show a little pussy like the other female vendors. Tease Garrett and Derek. Demonstrate to Derek how happy I am he's the father of my children, and let him undress me if he wants. I'll even let him fuck me. Mmm. Maybe they'll rethink their "no more sex tonight" edict.*

She strode out of the closet. Her gaze drifted to the unopened, white envelope on the nightstand beside the bed. She stopped next to it and plucked the envelope from the top. *I'll read it after I sell everything tonight. I'll cry over Cade and then move forward.*

“Cade, Garrett, and I had a conference call earlier today and opened our letters,” Derek said. “We’re all happy about the results.”

“Great. I’ll read it later. I need to focus on selling my product.” She smiled as big as she could. *I can’t think about this right now. I’ve got a solid business with Troy, and I can’t fuck it up.*

“You need to read it now,” Derek said. “You’re not going anywhere without reading the results.”

She cocked her head to the side. “Excuse me?”

“You heard me. You’re not avoiding Cade. You’re not avoiding the results. We agreed we’d read them as soon as they came. We did. Now you have to.”

“I don’t have to do squat. I know Garrett isn’t the father. He’s too damn happy. You said everyone was happy about the results, so Cade isn’t the father. He’s got to be fucking ecstatic. Zero ties to me, now. He can stop with the gifts and the guilt and move on to—”

“—I gave Cade a hand job the day he left,” Garrett blurted out. “He’s calling me and Derek because he has never felt anything toward a guy. He doesn’t know how a situation like this would work. He’s been in France waiting for a damn appointment with the guy who did the vasectomy on him. It’s been one major clusterfuck. And I just broke a promise to him by saying anything.”

“Um. What?” Her blood boiled. She turned around and met Garrett’s gaze. “You did what? With *my Cade*?”

“O-kay.” Garrett backed up as she advanced on him. “Not the reaction I expected.”

She poked his chest. “You kept this from me all this time? What the hell is wrong with you?”

“You’re having boy-girl twins,” Derek shouted.

"Garrett is the father and—"

"—I'm going to kill—" She started yelling.

"—Cade is too," Garrett said. He held up his hands in surrender. "The girl is mine. The boy is his."

"Don't even…" *Cade is in love with Garrett, not me? Oh my God. Oh. My. God.* Instead of bursting into tears, she walked out of the bedroom and grabbed her purse from the entry table. She strode out of the house and to her car—the car Cade gave her. She climbed in and drove.

They lied. They hid it. What the hell have I done?

Chapter Thirty-Six

In the sectioned-off area of Troy's party, Ella dressed in the white-silk gown left for her by the vendor who would be in the booth next to her. The virgin theme didn't really fit in with her pregnancy, but she liked the fabric of the dress and the lack of undergarments. She boiled with all the hormones raging through her system, and she stewed over the secrets Derek and Garrett kept from her.

She opened the curtain and walked out barefoot into the open…and *empty room*? She turned around and peeked back into the dressing room. Troy walked in and smiled. "Hey, partner." He kissed her cheek. "You look extremely fuckable."

She rolled her eyes. "You're pushing into the creepy zone."

He chuckled. "When those yahoos get on your nerves, come on over. My door is always open to you." He placed his hand on her bare back above her ass where the dress draped in a low U showing the tip of her butt crack. "Everyone is waiting on you."

"Where are the other vendors?"

"This is a private party," He guided her forward toward her regular white booth in the corner.

She gathered the white silk curtains to where her display was supposed to be and opened them. She stepped forward, seeing Garrett and Derek in gorgeous black suits with baby-blue shirts and ties. Then she stopped as her gaze took in the room.

Three rows of chairs covered in white linens, gathered and tied with big, white-satin bows in the back filled the space between her, Garrett and Derek, Cade's and Derek's parents dressed for cocktail hour, and Cade wearing a black tux at the very back of the room facing her.

Oh my God. Cade and Garrett are getting married. They're getting married. They're going to be a couple. Her heart stopped beating. "This can't be happening."

"It is happening," Garrett said.

Pappy stepped forward toward her, wearing a black suit and tie. "Welcome to your first official McGregor-Winthrop-Jackson Family Intervention. It's Cade's turn to host, but because he's a part of this, I get the privilege of hosting tonight."

He took her hand and led her forward past family dressed in evening wear to the front where the man she loved and lost stood. His face seemed stricken with sadness, dark circles surrounded the most handsome brown eyes she'd ever seen. Her big, powerful man had lost weight, leaving him still broad and strong, but not nearly as brawny and confident as he'd been.

"Ella, please listen to Cade. He needs to talk to you. Be honest with him. Then, we can move on to the next phase of the intervention." Pappy took one step back and stopped.

The brown eyes she'd longed to see locked on her.

Her body trembled. *I can't handle you marrying Garrett. I can't handle that. I want you to love me. I want you to marry me.* She held her belly, unable to speak.

"I'm so sorry. Please forgive me for not knowing about Felicity. Please. I…I'm sorry I left. I didn't believe Derek. I didn't believe it when I asked my doctor about it. I've assumed positive all these years meant there were no sperm swimming in the cup. But I was wrong. I even went to France and talked to the doctor. It was one big fuck up. But I'm so happy to be having a son with you."

"There's nothing to forgive," she whispered. *Your heart loves who your heart loves.* "Felicity wasn't your fault. I never blamed you."

The misery in his eyes seemed to lift a little. "I love you, Ella. I don't want to spend another day without you. I've missed you. I can't live without you."

But you have been by your own choice. She swallowed hard. "What about Garrett?"

He bent down on one knee. "Will you…" he shook his head "…Wait. What about him?" He glanced over at Garrett. She glanced over at Garrett.

Garrett shrugged. "What about me?"

"You love him more." She burst out crying. "You called him. You never called me back. You never called. You didn't even text."

"I told you," Kyle shouted. He stood up and crossed his arms over his chest. "I told you to call and give her notes. Not just the notes. I know what I'm talking about."

Pappy walked forward. "That was my fault. I told him words don't mean much. It's all about actions."

"Are you kidding me?" Mamma Louise said. "Pappy, I told you she needed gifts and love notes, but you should have told him a call means the world to a woman when they can't see each other."

Cade pulled Ella onto his knee and hugged her. "I love you. Marry me, Ella. I've messed up, but I love you."

"But you love him too," she whispered.

"I love him. I do. It's weird. But, it's you I want to marry. I want you in my bed every night," Cade's voice soothed her fears, eased her anger, and calmed her nerves. "Tell me you'll marry me right now."

"I love Garrett and Derek too," she said.

"We've worked it out. The three of you will live with me. You will spend your nights with me, but you can join them whenever I'm out of town or… I'm okay with your relationship with them."

She gazed at her men over her shoulder. They nodded and grinned.

She turned back and found Cade's honest gaze. "I'm not ready to get married." *I love you, but are you going to leave me again when I have Derek's child growing inside me one day?*

He held up a black velvet box and opened it.

She closed her eyes. *He's really proposing.* She opened her eyes and stared at the beautiful engagement ring.

He took her hand. "Ella, you're ready. I'm ready."

"But I'm not done having children, Cade. Derek and I want more children. Maybe three more children.

"Definitely three," Derek said.

"I know. I want more too." He slid the ring onto her finger. "But I want you to have my last name. Derek and Garrett are already moved in to my house. Everything except the bedroom, but they've got a temporary bed until Garrett has time to take his down and move it. We've worked it out. I've asked Jason,

Kyle, and Colleen for your hand in marriage. All I need is you, Ella."

"You have us too," Pappy said. "Everyone in our family is supportive of the four of you."

"And you know you have us," Derek's mom said. "We have grown to love Cade and his family as much as we do you and Garrett."

"Marry him," Garrett whispered from behind her. "He loves you. He likes having us around. Don't make us have to move again. Derek is a nester, and I'm tired of moving. I've done it too much in my life."

"Are you going to leave me when things get hard, Cade? Marriage is hard work," she said.

"I'm never leaving you again for as long as I live."

"Pappy, get the judge," Derek said. "Ella needs to sign the papers, and we can have the ceremony."

"Ella O'Brien Winthrop," a man said nearby. "Do you take Cade Daniel Jackson as your husband?"

"I do," she answered. *I'm really getting married.*

Cade slid a wedding band on her finger as he held her.

"Cade Daniel Jackson, do you take Ella O'Brien Winthrop as your wife?"

"I do," he answered. He handed her a band, and she slid it onto his finger.

"By the power vested in me…" The judge continued talking as Ella found herself lost in Cade's handsome face.

"…Pronounce you Mr. and Mrs. Cade Daniel Jackson. You may kiss your bride, Mr. Jackson."

He kissed her lips. Electricity crackled and rushed through her system, making her shiver.

"Cade," she whispered breathlessly. "Is this real?"

"That is what I call a successful intervention," Pappy said. "Welcome to the family. You're hosting the next one. Take your wife home."

Momma Louise pushed a clipboard into Ella's hand. "Sign."

Ella stood up. She took the pen from the clip, inhaled deeply, and signed the legal document binding her life to Cade's.

"Now, go celebrate," Momma Louise said.

Cade swept her up off her feet. "Let's go." He strode forward and stopped. "Come on, Garrett and Derek. Let's show my wife her new home."

Garrett led the way out of Troy's house, and they all climbed into the back of Garrett's black limo.

Sitting on her husband's lap, she relaxed against him. "So, how is this going to work?"

"There are two adjoining doors to our rooms. One goes to their room, the other to the nursery," Cade explained. "You sleep with me unless you're sleeping the night with them. I promise you, I'm okay with your relationship with them, and they are comfortable with mine with you. They're welcome to come and get you from my room or bed, and I can do the same. We've been working on logistics while I've been in France. Before I found out you were carrying my child, I was planning a way to make this work."

"With some help from me," Garrett said.

"Really?"

"Really," Cade said.

Garrett placed his hand on her knee and slid it up under her dress between her legs.

She opened her legs for more of his touch.

Cade lifted the hem of her skirt up over her belly

and watched Garrett dip a finger into her pussy.

She rubbed her lips together and let her bent knees fall open. She leaned back against Cade's arm. "You're okay sharing me?"

"I'll get you to myself tonight," he whispered. "Yes, I'm okay sharing you with them. But make no mistake, Ella Jackson, you are mine."

"I am," she whispered. "I love you, Cade Daniel Jackson."

"What about me?" Garrett asked.

"Me?" Derek asked.

"I love you guys too," she said. *Life is almost perfect.* "What about us all sleeping in the same bed?"

Cade laughed. "Me and you in my bed."

"We should all celebrate tonight," Garrett whispered. "We all do need to sleep."

"Maybe," Cade mumbled. He placed his hand on Garrett's thigh. "We'll have to see."

"Once the twins are born," Derek said. His hand covered Cade's under her dress. "Believe me, we'll all fall in bed together at some point."

Ella pushed down the top of her dress and uncovered her breasts. She placed Derek's hand on one and Cade's on the other while Garrett's fingers played with her pussy.

"I'm married to Cade, but all of you are my husbands. All of you have my heart, my soul, and my body. Equally. Forever."

Epilogue

Butterflies fluttered in Ella's stomach as she traced the engraved names of her three men on the bottom of the silver frame. *I hope they're ready to take this next step.*

The large nude portrait of her guys standing side-by-side as she knelt at their feet inside the specially made frame would be the focal point in the bedroom they would all sleep in for the rest of their lives. She lifted the frame onto the hangers above the bed Garrett and Cade designed and built together for the four of them. The specialty mattress arrived that morning, and she'd spent the rest of the day moving Garrett and Derek's things into Cade's renovated bedroom.

She stepped back on the firm bed and gazed at the wall of photos she'd hung. The color photos on canvas popped against the light gray walls. The suggestion she made of them posing for nudes as a family turned into a reality that changed everything.

Her gaze shot back to the portrait she just hung. Cade's lopsided grin. His hungry eyes. Garrett and Derek's matching full grins on either side of him. The arch in her back. The angle of her ass lifted to see a glimpse of her pussy.

Her center clenched and juices moistened her nether lips. *I want that again. I want them to follow-*

through with those looks.

She slid her hand over her bare breast and up to her lips as she gazed to the right. The photo she'd hung of Cade kissing Garrett and then beside it of Cade and Derek's first kiss. *Will he like them? Is it too much?*

Cade hadn't done more than kiss either one of them, but he embraced them in longer hugs and talked more openly when they were all together. The close relationships between all her men grew from that one magical day.

She climbed off the bed and turned down the covers. Her men were due home any minute from dropping off the twins Mason and Faith at Cade's parents' house.

The princess pink mat Derek preferred her kneel on at his arrival waited for her by the bedroom entrance. She walked over and glanced at the clock.

"Ella," Cade shouted. "Did the mattress arrive?"

"Yes, sir." She knelt on the mat and rested her butt on her heels. Her chest constricted as she glanced around the room at all the photos. She closed her eyes. *Have faith in his decision. He planned the room. He wouldn't go this far if he wasn't positive it would work.* She took a deep breath of confidence and opened her eyes. "I'm in the bedroom."

The familiar sound of her three men's bare feet on the tile floor warned her to move into position.

Her heart pounded with anticipation. *Please love the portrait. Please let this really be what you all want too.* She dropped to her knees and lowered her chin to her chest. She stared between her legs.

"Wow," Cade whispered. "You've been busy."

"We look fucking amazing," Garrett said.

"You weren't supposed to do all this yourself," Derek huffed. "But you did a great job… Oh, yeah. Look at that one."

She looked up.

Derek pointed to the photo of Derek and Garrett sucking her breasts and Cade licking between her legs. She held her breath and dug her fingers into her thighs to keep from touching her wet pussy. *I want the real thing, not the pose.*

All her men stood naked in a straight line showing her their gorgeous side view as they held their hard cocks and gazed at the photos.

"I'm partial to the one of Ella tied to the bench." Cade put his arm around Garrett's shoulders. "Smell that?"

Garrett nodded. "Our Ella."

"Her pussy is so wet right now," Cade whispered. "I'm ready for a taste. What about you?"

Garrett nodded. "Derek?"

The men turned around and gazed down at her. Pearls of cum beaded at the top of their cocks.

Ella spread her legs farther apart. *I'm ready for anything as long as it includes the three of you.*

Derek angled his head to the side. "You've been a good girl for us, haven't you?"

"Yes, sir," she whispered.

"No fucking a fake cock?" Derek asked.

"No, sir." *I wanted to. God, I wanted to.*

Cade chuckled. "Do you ask her that every day?"

"I have to," Derek said. "I caught her using the dildo of my cock a couple months ago when I surprised her with lunch at the office. She tried to hide it by not moving. But the warehouse office smelled like pussy.

I've had to make special rules just for her."

Cade squatted. "Sweetheart, we know you've been hormonal, but you have three men to pleasure you. The toys are for when one or two of us are away on business. Got it?"

"Yes, sir."

"Ella, stand," Derek ordered. "Nighttime is changing for us."

She rose to her feet.

Cade walked over and climbed on the bed. He lied down with his head on the middle pillow. Garrett strode to the other side of the bed and stood facing her

"If there is a time you need some space, you tell us," Derek said. "We'll do the same. Otherwise, Cade sleeps in the middle, and we surround him in any order we choose." He leaned over and whispered. "Cade wanted to be in the middle. He knows you need us and he now knows he needs us too…" He shrugged. "…Not in the same way as Garrett and I need each other, but close."

"Thank you for telling me," she whispered.

Derek kissed her lips. "We all took the weekend off. I told them you're ovulating."

Her body buzzed with electricity. *I told yours and Cade's parents too. They are excited to have more grandbabies.*

"Did you hit the switch for the cameras?" Garrett asked.

Her breathing accelerated. *You want this filmed?* She and Derek were the exhibitionists of the family, not Garrett. Definitely not Cade.

"The first thing I do when I come home is turn on the bedroom cameras," Derek said. His hands caressed down her back. He whispered. "I want to film us making a baby or three."

Her belly warmed up to her heart. "Your pleasure is mine."

He kissed her cheek.

"Would you carry me to bed like you always do when I'm with you and Garrett?" She asked. "I love the tradition and want to keep it."

He swept her up into his strong arms. "Always, kitten."

She curled her arms around his neck and relaxed. *Confident. Unwavering faith in their love for each other. Loyal beyond words.*

He carried her to bed and took out the blindfold she kept in the nightstand drawer. He held her as he climbed onto the bed and sat next to Cade. "Put on the blindfold and straddle Cade's face. Suck the cock at your lips."

She gazed at Cade. *You look happy. Are you happy? Is this what you want?*

He licked his lips. His brown eyes seemed to twinkle in the soft light of the room. "Follow Derek's orders."

She straddled Cade's face and slipped on the black satin blindfold. "I won't be able to reach him."

"Who is in charge?" Derek said.

"You, sir." She closed her mouth and waited. *You and Cade are always the ones in charge.*

The mattress barely shifted as the two men beside Cade moved around her.

Derek's cock pressed against her lips.

She opened her mouth and fell into the submissive role she loved. His long cock slid against her slick tongue.

Derek's hands cradled her head. "That's my good kitten. I missed you today. I love you."

He retreated from her mouth.

"I missed you too," she answered like she did every night. "I love you more than you will ever know." Her lips remained parted, and Garrett's thick cock glided over her tongue. The salty taste of man ran down her throat.

"I love you, babe. I missed you. Let's make another baby together," Garrett said.

Her heart soared. He hadn't wanted another baby of his own, but she did. She wanted at least one more with each of her men. She smiled as his cock retreated her tongue to the tip.

"Happy?" he asked. His cock jerked, and he pulled out.

"Thrilled. I love you so much, Garrett." Each man brought a layer of love she needed to thrive. The support and encouragement they gave her to fulfill her wildest dreams made this moment of acceptance of their alternative life better than she imagined it could be.

Cade's tongue dipped into her pussy entrance. "Sweetie, I love you." He lifted her hips and held her up off the bed. "Up and down and around her thighs…"

Wide straps wrapped around her thighs and belly, under her breasts, over the top of her breasts and around her upper arms.

"Garrett, attach them to…" Derek laughed. "You made it, and I'm telling you how it works."

"This is going to be fun," Garrett said.

Without any warning, hands pushed her away. She

swung out and dropped forward, suspended by whatever contraption Garrett and Derek thought up.

"What the hell?" *How'd they hide this?*

Derek's hands grabbed her hips and his cock met her pussy. "It's a type of sex swing Cade helped me build." He pulled her toward him and onto his hard cock. "Only better."

He pushed her away and the spin of wheels on a track sounded above her.

She flew forward and spun in a circle. "What are you doing? *Fuck me to orgasm, please. No more teasing.*

Garrett's hands gripped her shoulders as Cade's found her hips.

Garrett kissed her ear. "Testing out the possibilities."

She fell forward and her belly flew up like she raced downward on a rollercoaster. Her belly dropped and she gasped. Adrenaline rushed through her and to her surprise her pussy rippled with delight.

The large hands of the man she worried most about curled around her thighs. Cade's hot cock tunneled into her pussy. "Guys, I'm gonna come hard."

"We've got you," Garrett whispered. "Stick with the plan."

He withdrew and thrust as her pussy rippled in waves of pure begging bliss for him to keep fucking her.

Her top half lowered and she swung forward and back onto his cock. Back and forth. In and out. His desire. His need burned inside her. His cock seemed to grow as her pussy clamped down like a vise to keep him. But she swung forward and back. Faster. Slower.

No steady pattern. His decisions dominated the movement as she continued to surrender to the men she loved.

More. More. More.

"That's it, Sweetie," Cade groaned.

"Cade, I can't stop from…" *I'm coming. So good. So perfect.* Control over her orgasms shattered as she fell into subspace. Under their control the world turned into a perfect place. One hard cock after another pulled her in and gave her everything she ever wanted. The three men's sperm inside her body fighting for the chance at fertilization of her eggs waiting for them opened her spirit to believe love conquered all obstacles.

Six hands untied her. She lay on Cade's chest. Her legs straddled him.

The blindfold slid from her face.

Derek's hazel eyes appeared in the low light. "Our sexy woman is finally happy."

Cade laughed. "We're all finally happy."

One bed. One family. One wonderful life.

About the Author

Anna started writing romance as a by-product of insomnia. After a year of late night reading, she borrowed her son's laptop after he went to bed and set about breathing life to her very own characters. After a month of writing, she was surprised with a new laptop of her own to pursue her dreams. With a B.A. in English Literature and a desire to fill her world with wonderful stories, she and her close friends could not just talk about, but gush over, she shed the job as mom of three in the midnight hours and assumed her alter ego of dirty girl.

~*~

Visit Anna at
http://www.annaloresauthor.com

~*~

To chat with Anna Lores and other Wild Rose Press authors of erotic romance, join us at www.groups.yahoo.com/group/thewilderroses.

Also Available

Theirs to Protect

By Melissa Klein

http://amzn.com/B01MCYB8DW

College student Claire Matthews has panty-melting fantasies about her roommates but can't imagine choosing just one. Then her rapist is released from prison, and she knows it's time to disappear. First, she needs a memory of the delicious duo to take with her.

Firefighter Sean Dalton is mind-blown when Claire suggests a threesome. Watching her kiss his friend under the mistletoe is a turn-on. Being asked to share is like adding gasoline to a fire. He's shared a woman before, but he's been crushing on his sweet and sexy roomie since she moved in. He's not about to say no.

Chicago police officer Max Devon isn't new to the ménage scene, but he knows Sean has a thing for Claire and he won't be the third wheel again. Been there, done that, has the scars to prove it. Still, he's not immune to Claire's charms. He'll play her game, but only if he's in charge. Then he'll know when it's time to withdraw from the relationship.

A night of blazing passion leads to more than one discovery. Sean is caught off guard by his feelings for Max, Max struggles to keep his distance from both his roommates, and Claire must make a choice—flee or stay. Trusting these two strong men with her heart and her life means endangering them and giving in to the belief she is theirs to protect.

Also Read

Luke's Redemption

A King Security Novel

By Anni Fife

http://amzn.com/B01M4ITMS7

Red-hot sex. Searing betrayal. A passionate and elusive love..

Chased by her criminal kingpin father, Katya Dalca runs to New Orleans and straight into the arms of Luke Hunter. Sucked into the carnal world of the French Quarter, she succumbs to Luke's potent sexuality. He not only steals her breath, he steals her heart and the only leverage she has against her father. She is left with no choice except to pick up the pieces and rebuild her life alone.

Undercover DEA agent Luke Hunter thought his newest assignment—recover a stolen flash drive to gain the trust of the Russian mob—was like any other. But his target brings him to his knees, and after one taste of her intoxicating beauty, he's in too deep. Doing his job means walking away, leaving his heart behind with nothing but a promise to reunite. It's a promise he can't keep.

When Katya's past reaches out and her world unravels, her only hope is the one man she is most vulnerable to—Luke.

Thank you for purchasing this
publication of The Wild Rose Press, Inc.
If you enjoyed the story, we would appreciate
your letting others know by leaving a review.
For other wonderful stories, please visit our
on-line bookstore at www.wilderroses.com.

For questions or more
information contact us at
info@thewildrosepress.com.

The Wild Rose Press, Inc.
www.thewilderroses.com

Stay current with The Wild Rose Press, Inc.
Like us on Facebook
https://www.facebook.com/TheWildRosePress
And Follow us on Twitter
https://twitter.com/WildRosePress

www.ingramcontent.com/pod-product-compliance
Lightning Source LLC
Chambersburg PA
CBHW070804030726
47504CB00003B/688
* 9 7 8 1 5 0 9 2 1 3 3 0 6 *